D1121574

Blood for Wine

Books by Warren C. Easley

The Cal Claxton Oregon Mysteries
Matters of Doubt
Dead Float
Never Look Down
Not Dead Enough
Blood for Wine

Blood For Wine

A Cal Claxton Oregon Mystery

Warren C. Easley

Poisoned Pen Press

First Edition 2017

10 9 8 7 6 5 4 3 2 1

Library of Congress Catalog Card Number: 2016961971

ISBN: 9781464208386   Hardcover
       9781464208409   Trade Paperback

Poisoned Pen Press
4014 N. Goldwater Boulevard, #201
Scottsdale, Arizona 85251
www.poisonedpenpress.com
info@poisonedpenpress.com

Printed in the United States of America

For Anita, Dave, Gary, Guida, Judy, Kenny, Kent,
Larry, Linda, Stuart, and Terry.

"We few, we happy few, we band of brothers" (and sisters)
                                                    —*W. Shakespeare*

In vino veritas
In wine, truth

—*Pliny the Elder (AD 29-AD 79)*

Acknowledgments

I couldn't have written this book without the support, encouragement, and insight of my "in house" editor, Marge Easley, and my sounding board for authenticity and all things millennial, Kate Easley. Once again, I was aided by my intrepid critique mates LeeAnn McLennan, Lisa Alber, Janice Maxon, Debby Dodds, and Alison Jakel. Their honest, perceptive input went a long way toward improving the manuscript. Thanks, guys!

I owe a huge debt of gratitude to an old Navy fighter pilot named John, who also happens to be a lawyer and a good friend. Without his sage advice, I'm afraid Cal might have lost his license to practice law during the course of this book. In a similar vein, I'm also indebted to Mike Hallock, owner of Carabella Vineyard and maker of fine Oregon pinot noir wines, who tutored me in the art and science of winemaking. The vineyard described in this book is loosely modeled after Mike's superb family operation. Thanks to Jerry Siebert and Rosann Jurestovsky, who read an early draft of this story and provided exceedingly valuable input. Thanks also to Tom McCauley, who provided insight into the workings of Big Pharma.

Even with all this support, it still fell to my editor, Barbara Peters, to find and help me correct the remaining weak points in the story. Thanks, Barbara, and the whole amazing crew at Poisoned Pen Press.

Prologue

She sat reading a thick paperback, the smoke of her cigarette rising languidly from an ashtray at her elbow. The man sat across the room engrossed in his cell phone. He sat outside the circle of light cast by her reading lamp, so only the small screen illuminated his face. She laid the book down, looked over at him, and sighed. He looked calm, his face almost tranquil, she thought. She liked that about him, the hidden power of a coiled spring. He looked up at her and gave what passed for a smile. "You're right. It's time to go," he said.

She took a deep drag on her cigarette, ground the butt into the ashtray, and exhaled a plume of gray smoke as she got up.

He stood and studied her for a moment. "You look nervous."

"I'm fine." She smiled. She could always produce an unforced smile, even in the most stressful situations. "I'm anxious to get on with this."

"Get the keys. You're driving."

They didn't talk much on the drive to the overlook. She was focused on getting them there without incident while he just sat there with that placid look, a duffel bag resting between his feet. The man knew the way since he drove the last time they visited the spot. "Slow down, the turn's coming up on the right," and as she wheeled off the highway, he added, "Watch the potholes."

The headlights bored a shaft into the darkness, illuminating an ascending dirt road cut into the hillside. They hadn't gone far when the man said, "Okay, cut the lights. The farmhouse is coming up on the right." A smear of yellow light through the trees marked the structure at the end of a long drive. They drifted by the driveway, rounded a curve, then pulled off the road and parked at a break in the trees. She shut off the car, and they sat for a while with only the ticking of the cooling engine to break the silence. A lopsided, pale yellow moon had just cleared the horizon, and lights glittered on the valley floor like a reflection of the stars. She felt a stab of guilt when memories threatened to avalanche, but she held herself in check. *Stick to the plan*, she told herself.

He unzipped the duffel bag and handed her a prepaid cell phone. "Call him. Make it good, and remind him that this is your little secret."

Her eyes had adjusted, and even in the low light she caught something different in his face, a kind of blankness, like he was wearing a mask with nothing behind it. She pushed the unsettling feeling down. *What do you expect? He's got a job to do.*

When she finished the call, she handed him the phone. He smiled. "That was good. Very convincing."

She nodded, lit up a cigarette, and blew a stream of smoke out a gap in the window. "He bought it, and no way he's telling anybody. He's on his way."

The man glanced at his watch. "It'll take him around fifteen minutes to get here." They stared out at the valley lights without speaking. A thin band of clouds now shrouded the moon like a dirty rag. Eight minutes later the man retrieved a pair of thin leather gloves and put them on slowly and deliberately. When he reached back into the bag, a twinge of excitement stirred in her. She expected him to pull out the handgun he'd shown her, but instead he withdrew a sixteen-inch steel shaft.

"What's that fo—?"

The first blow hit her on the bridge of nose, stunning her. The second blow killed her.

Chapter One

I didn't throw a dart at a map, but it was something damn close that had led me to this spot in Oregon. I came up from L.A. for a weekend just to look around, knowing only that I needed to move somewhere but not having a clue where. Back in happier times, my wife, daughter, and I had passed through the Northwest on vacation and were taken by the natural beauty of the place and the friendly, laid-back attitude of the Oregonians we met along the way. So, I thought, why not Oregon? I found a real estate agent online and flew into Portland without any idea of what I was looking for. The agent looked crestfallen when I announced I could only spare a Saturday for house-hunting. Sunday, I told her, was reserved for a trip to the wine country. I'd heard Oregon was producing some pretty good wines, and I wanted to taste some.

Between my not knowing what I wanted and the real estate agent's insistence on showing me suburban bungalows with manicured lawns, the Saturday hunt was a bust. That Sunday I found myself lost somewhere in the hills above the little town of Dundee, a small burg in the heart of the Oregon wine country. I was searching for the turnoff to one of the wineries on my target list when I spotted a for-sale sign at the top of a narrow, unpaved lane named Eagle Nest. Instinctively, I followed the rutted lane and found the advertised property—five acres that sloped gently southward to a fence line below. The acreage was dotted with old growth Douglas firs and featured a vacant farmhouse that stood like a fortress near the southern boundary. I parked at the gate and walked the drive leading down to the house, a turn-of-the-last-century four-over-four with a gabled roof and a high brick chimney. It was roofed in old growth cedar shingles and clad in what looked like the original shiplap siding, painted white with dark green trim, the paint job chipped and faded. Through the windows I spied scuffed oak floors, high, crown-molded ceilings, and a rough-hewn stone fireplace.

The farmhouse had good bones, but it was the view that sold me. In the foreground, I saw a panorama of rolling hills dressed with orderly rows of grapevines interspersed with stands of conifer and deciduous trees. The valley beyond the Pacific Highway was bounded by the Cascade Mountains and the Coast Range and seemed to stretch all the way to California. It was a study in muted colors, like a Paul Klee painting, and in the distance, lit by the morning sun, the Willamette River wove through the tapestry like a silver thread.

As I stood there, something welled up in me, a sense of belonging that had no basis in rationality. It came up from the cedar planks I stood on, into the soles of my feet, through my gut, and into my heart. I had found my new home. My daughter suggested I call the place The Aerie, and the name stuck.

That was nearly a decade ago.

On the early-October night this story began, I was sitting out on the side porch with my dog, Archie, who lay next to my chair gnawing a bone cradled in his big, white paws. Arch is an Australian shepherd tricolor, large for his breed, but gentle and smarter than any whip. The moon hung low to the east that night, screened by come-and-go cloud cover, and the lights in the valley twinkled in the crystalline air. As a lawyer in a one-man practice, I'd spent the day in court in McMinnville, which bled my energy but not my appetite. I settled for a quick stir-fry made from leftover chicken to which I added some sliced carrots, fresh ginger, garlic, and green onions. I was finishing a bottle of Mirror Pond Pale Ale, and wishing dogs could be trained to do dishes, when my cell phone chirped. I'd had enough of people for one day, but when I saw it was Jim Kavanaugh, a neighbor and good friend, I decided to answer. "Jim, what's up?"

"Cal, oh, God, it's Lori. She's dead."

"*What?* What happened?" Lori was Jim's estranged wife.

"I don't know. It looks like, oh, Jesus, like someone hit her with something. She's covered in blood."

"Jim, Are you sure she's dead?"

"She's unresponsive, and I can't feel a pulse. I called 911, and the cops and an ambulance just arrived."

"Good. Where are you?"

"I'm up on Parrett Mountain, at an overlook. Uh, do you think you could come? I, uh—"

"Do you need a lawyer?"

He paused. "I don't know. Just come, okay?"

"Sure. I'll be there as fast as I can."

He gave me directions and I left immediately, leaving a disappointed Archie on the front porch. As I worked my way down to the Pacific Highway, my heart ached for Lori Kavanaugh, an ex-neighbor and friend. She and Jim had been married, what, three years? It was Jim's first marriage and her third. I can't say that I'd gotten to know her all that well. She was an attractive woman, tall and lithe with flowing dark hair and a face that turned heads. The owner of an up-and-coming winery, Jim worshipped her, but Lori seemed to struggle with being the wife of a vintner. Jim was serious about the wine business, and she seemed unable to cope with his absolute commitment to his craft. In any case, she walked out of the marriage about a year ago and moved to Portland.

As I turned onto Newberg-Wilsonville Road, my thoughts turned to Jim, who was devastated by the breakup and held on doggedly to the hope of reconciliation, as the spurned often do. A fourth-generation Oregonian, Jim had converted the entire family farm—some one hundred and fifty acres of southwest-facing land in the Dundee Hills—into a vineyard with the express purpose of growing grapes and making wine.

After suffering insect infestations, frost, mildew attacks, and ill-timed rain, the gamble was starting to pay off. His wines, especially his pinot noirs, were gaining a devoted following, and the entire region was attracting international attention. On the other hand, Jim always seemed to be stressed about money for reasons he never shared with me, another reason Lori may have seen fit to jump ship.

As instructed, I climbed into the hills loosely referred to as Parrett Mountain. What the hell was going on? What brought them together at this sparsely populated area? Had Jim asked me to come as a friend for support, or did he need a lawyer and was just unwilling to admit it?

I hoped it was the former, but my gut told me otherwise.

Chapter Two

"This is a crime scene, sir," the uniformed deputy standing watch at the turnout informed me. "If you have no official business here, please go back the way you came in." The deputy stood next to a line of two squad cars, an unmarked sedan, and an ambulance. Flashing their red and blue strobe lights, the squad cars were parked on the street facing the turnout with their engines running and their headlights on. The scene was bathed in a garish light, stark, like a black-and-white movie.

"I'm Cal Claxton," I told the deputy. "I got a call from my neighbor, Jim Kavanaugh. He said he found his wife here. He was upset, asked me to come over." I decided not to use the L-word.

"You can wait here on the street, I guess, but it's going to be a long night. Your friend's being interviewed right now."

"Thanks." I stepped aside and surveyed the scene. The overlook, an unpaved, semi-circular area, provided a commanding view of the valley and was bordered by a low guardrail that spanned the edge of a sharp drop-off. Two cars sat side by side, facing the view. The car on the right was Jim's Grand Cherokee. The car on the left looked like the Camry I remembered Lori driving. I could see what looked like a head leaning to one side in the driver's seat of the Camry, probably Lori's body. Jim was standing next to his Jeep, flanked on either side by two Yamhill County detectives whom I recognized as members of a major crimes response team. I had some history with their boss, the sheriff, but I knew these two as competent investigators. Jim's shoulders were slumped and his head slightly bowed as he responded to their questions, gesturing with both hands.

A panel truck arrived next, disgorging three crime-scene techs in white coveralls and the medical examiner, a tall, balding man named Merv Preston. He looked like he just got out of bed. The processing of crime scenes, particularly murder scenes, always moves at glacial speed, and this one was no exception. I stood there watching the action for over an hour, wishing I'd brought a warmer coat or, better yet, a thermos of coffee. Lori's body had been examined by the ME but was still in place, the techs hadn't finished with the cars and surrounding area, and Jim was still being questioned. Finally, one of the detectives, a heavyset man with receding hair named Hal Ballard, began escorting Jim away. I caught up with them just as Ballard was guiding Jim into the back of an unmarked sedan. I nodded to Jim and said to Ballard, "Hello, Hal, I'm a friend of Mr. Kavanaugh. He called me after calling 911. I drove over to see if there's anything I can do."

Ballard straightened up and looked me over. "As his lawyer?"

"No, no. I'm just a friend trying to help out."

"Well, I'm taking him in for processing. He's got blood on his sweater and hands. His Cherokee's got blood in it, too, so it'll be impounded. He'll probably need a ride home later tonight." He shut the back door of the squad car and added softly, "If we don't book him."

"Aw, come on, Hal. He called this in, for Christ's sake."

Ballard shrugged and opened the car door. I called in to Jim, "I'll pick you up in McMinnville."

I knew Jim's bloody clothing would be impounded, so I swung by my place and grabbed a pair of sweatpants, a sweatshirt, and a pair of old slippers so he wouldn't be forced to wear a county-issue jumpsuit home. Jim emerged in those clothes two and a half hours later. He was a big Irishman with large, calloused hands, broad shoulders, and a full beard that looked rust-colored, almost orange, under the fluorescent lights. His eyes, normally a couple of blue lasers, were dull, red-rimmed, and swollen. He crunched my hand in his massive paw. "Thanks for the sweats, Cal, and thanks for waiting. Jesus Christ, what a night. Let's get the hell out of here."

I was relieved to see he had no noticeable scratches on his face, hands, or arms. Anything resembling defensive wounds would have been an even bigger problem than I figured he already had.

I did my best to comfort my friend as we headed back to Dundee, but he was inconsolable. Having lost my wife to suicide a decade earlier, I knew the razor-blade-swallowing pain Jim was feeling. When I couldn't think of much else to say, we rode in silence, the Pacific Highway like a ghost road in the early morning hours. My headlights finally shone on the small, understated sign marking the turn into his winery, Le Petit Truc, which Jim once explained to me meant "the little thing" in French. We drove through shadowy rows of grapevines, past a series of outbuildings, and parked in front of his house, a meticulously restored Craftsman built in the teens of the previous century.

He turned to me, his face almost pleading. "I know you're tired, but why don't you come in. I've got a bottle of Kilbeggan, and I need a drink."

He needn't have worried. I needed a drink, too.

Jim withdrew the whiskey and two glasses from a built-in cabinet in the dining room. Nodding at the bottle, he said, "This stuff goes way back. Kilbeggan was a monastery built in the sixth century by one of the Twelve Apostles of Ireland, St. Becan." He dropped his gaze, shaking his head. "Lori gave me this."

After handing me the drink, Jim excused himself, his face grim. "Gotta make some calls. Lori's got a mother and stepbrother in Portland. The cops offered, but I told them I'd do it. I'm regretting that now."

He came back looking even more shattered, sat down across from me at the dining room table, and ran a hand through his hair. "Oh, God, I just broke her mother's heart. She's sick, too. Cancer." He exhaled a long sigh. "This is like a nightmare. I don't get it. I mean, what the hell happened out there? Someone try to rob her or what?"

"Why were you meeting at such a secluded spot?"

"She called me. Said she wanted me to meet her there, that she'd been doing some thinking about us." He shook his head again, and a wisp of a smile came and went. "She said it was a favorite place of hers. I'd never been there. She went to high school in Newberg, so she knew about it, I guess." He leveled his gaze at me. "I couldn't believe it, Cal. It was like old times. She told me to bring a bottle of wine, too."

I nodded. "She just called you unexpectedly?"

"No. Actually, we've been talking off and on for the past month or so. Had lunch with her once. Things were getting back on track, but we were going slow and not saying anything about it to anyone. She insisted on that." He looked away and drained his glass as his eyes filled. "I was ecstatic," he added, his voice suddenly husky.

"What happened when you got to the overlook?"

He studied the nicked surface of the table between us for several moments. "I parked next to her. As I swung in, my lights shone on her for an instant. Her head was kind of off to one side, but I didn't think anything of it. I was so damn glad that she was actually there, you know? It seemed too good to be true."

I nodded again.

He got up, poured himself another drink and topped me up. His hand, ink-smudged from having given a set of fingerprints, trembled slightly. "Anyway, I could just make her out in the car. She didn't move. I remember thinking maybe she fell asleep. I knocked on the passenger side window, then opened the door." He dropped his head. "The dome light came on and there she was, drenched in blood." He looked up at me. "It's a fucking blur after that. I screamed, I think, and shook her. Her head fell toward me, and I got blood all over my hands, my sweater. I fumbled around trying to get a pulse, but I couldn't feel anything. She was limp. Like a rag doll. My phone was in my car, so I went back and called 911."

"Did you see her purse? Was there any sign of a robbery?"

He nodded. "I remember it sitting on the passenger side seat. I think I might've pushed it onto the floor. I don't think it was open or anything, but I'm not sure."

"You, uh, mentioned blood. Did you see any wounds?"

Jim blew a breath through his lips and closed his eyes for a moment. "Oh, God. The side of her head, her hair, all matted with blood. Someone hit her with something. Hard."

"Did you see a weapon?"

"No. I don't think so. I would have noticed it, I'm sure. But I didn't search around or anything."

"Uh, what about the blood? Did it look dark or seem sticky?"

He looked queasy for a few moments, and I thought he might throw up. "No. It was fresh, still oozing from the wounds."

"What did you do until the police arrived?"

"I just sat there, holding her hand and crying like a fucking idiot." He brought his eyes up and met mine. The blue lasers were pumping now. "I want to find the son of a bitch who did this, Cal."

"Me, too."

Jim had another Killbeggan, and we talked some more. When he finally put his head down on the dining room table, I coaxed him over to a couch in the living room and got him to stretch out. After covering him with an afghan, I left him there and went down to the outbuildings and waited for his field boss and general handyman, Juan Cruz, who rolled in at six forty-five.

A proud man with short cropped hair and a neatly trimmed mustache, Juan crossed himself when I explained what happened. "I left Jim sleeping on the couch," I added. "You might want to look in on him in the next hour or so. I'll check back this afternoon."

Like a dull yellow coin, the sun lurked behind a band of gauzy clouds that morning as I drove through the vineyards toward The Aerie. The shock of Lori's death had muted somewhat. Her death was an absolute, and now something less certain but perhaps more disquieting took up residence in my head. I didn't think for a moment that my friend killed his wife, but with blood on his hands, in his car, and a history of estrangement, I knew the investigative detectives would have a much different take.

There was more to come.

Chapter Three

There's nothing like missing a night's sleep to dull one's enthusiasm for work the next day. I had a nine o'clock appointment, so I needed to get my butt down to the office, which I did after feeding Archie and downing a bowl of granola and a double cappuccino. A stand-alone with a flat roof and a six by six front window, my law office sat on the east end of Dundee on the Willamette River side of the highway. It had been a barbershop—the only one in town—for forty-odd years before the barber died. The building sat idle for a decade before I came along and gave it a bit of a makeover and hung my shingle out.

The morning air had a nice fall snap to it, so I put a pressed log in the woodstove after straightening up a little. I was the head janitor as well as the only lawyer in this operation. My nine o'clock arrived at 9:13, a woman named Audrey Steele who was trying to make a break with an abusive husband. She was thin with slightly stooped shoulders, wispy blond hair, and doe eyes that told a sad tale.

"Are you clear on what we're going to do in court on Friday?" I asked her after she got through fawning over Archie, who lapped up the attention shamelessly.

"Yeah, I think so. We're gonna ask the judge for a restraining order."

"That's right." I took her through the questions I planned to ask her at the hearing and some of the photos to be introduced into evidence. The photos showed a battered but defiant woman with a bruised forehead, a split lip, and a chipped front tooth. I got angry all over again just looking at those shots. When we finished up, her lips began to quiver and her eyes brimmed with tears. I came around the desk, handed her my handkerchief, and patted her gently on the shoulder.

"We're going to win this on Friday," I told her. "You wait, things are going to turn around for you." Me, the eternal optimist.

After she left, I busied myself sorting out my client billing for the previous month, a job I always put off until the last minute. I rarely got my going rate because it had gotten around that I was willing to accept barter and string out payments. A soft touch, that was me. This behavior was frowned on by my accountant, Gertrude Johnson, who was also my neighbor to the north. September had been slow, raising the possibility of a cash crunch, a specter that moved in and out of my life like the winter fog in the valley.

I was nearly done when my cell went off. "Hey, Cal, it's Winona." Nine years ago, Winona Cloud asked me to help her find out why her grandfather disappeared, a task that nearly got us both killed and resulted in her being charged with killing the man who murdered him. We uncovered the truth about her grandfather, and after two hung juries, the murder charges against her were dropped. The violent ordeal we shared forged a strong emotional bond that blossomed from friendship into something more than that. But neither of us was ready for a committed relationship. As a strong Native American woman, she felt the alienation of a people whose culture had been systematically destroyed. This gave her a fierce sense of independence. I, on the other hand, felt the alienation of having my world ripped apart in a single afternoon. This made me leery of attachments. A matched pair.

"What's up?" I asked.

"I'm in Idaho, on the Snake River, near Mackay Bar. We're doing that species survey on steelhead and Chinooks I told you about." A PhD biologist and expert in habitat restoration,

Winona was a consultant who did a lot of work for the Inter-Tribal Fish Commission. "It's gorgeous up here, Cal. Look, this is short notice, but I've got a couple of slack days. Why don't you come up for some steelhead fishing?"

I groaned. Spending time with Winona and steelhead fishing were at the top of my drop-everything-to-do list. "I'd love to, but something's come up." I went on to explain what happened to Lori Kavanaugh.

When I finished, Winona said, "Oh, that's terrible. I remember them. An interesting couple. He's the winemaker, big, outgoing guy with a red beard. She was the tall, sultry one. Right?"

"Yeah. He's pretty broken up, and I'm worried that the cops are going to come at him hard."

"God, Cal, he didn't do it, did he?"

"I can't imagine it."

"You sure?"

"I knew *you* were innocent, didn't I?"

She laughed at that and rang off after promising to call me when she got back to Portland. It was good to hear her voice.

I went back to work, calling Jim a couple of times but without reaching him. Sometime after noon, I took Archie out for a break and then we crossed the Pacific Highway—known less colorfully as 99W—to get a coffee and something to eat at the local bakery. The highway sliced Dundee in half, and that two mile commercial strip constituted a notorious bottleneck, particularly on summer weekends when Portlanders flocked to the beach, or in the fall when they swarmed to the wineries up in the hills for a day of tasting. After years of wrangling, a plan to route a bypass around the town was settled on and construction was underway. Agreement on the bypass finally gelled when Dundee realized it had become a *destination* rather than a wide spot in the road, and that a bypass would not be a train wreck for its burgeoning economy.

Run by a young couple who recently moved from Arizona, the Bake My Day was billed as an "artisanal" bakery. Their coffee was excellent, and they made *pain au chocolat* that was irresistible, especially if you had it right out of the oven in the morning. I was famished, so after tethering Arch outside I ordered a grilled cheese sandwich, a bowl of French onion soup, and a double cap.

"So, Cal," Jamie, the female half of the team asked after I finished ordering, "did you hear about the murder last night?"

I nodded but was taken aback that word of Lori Kavanaugh's death had gotten out so fast. Before I could respond she made a face and added, "One of our customers was out jogging this morning and found the body, a young Hispanic man, facedown in Chehalem Creek. Probably a drug deal gone bad, the cops told him."

"Huh," I said and went on to tell her about Lori's murder. Both Jamie and her husband, Todd, knew Jim and to a lesser extent Lori. Dundee was a small town, and Jim was the unofficial mayor. They were horrified at the news. We talked for a while and when Archie followed me out, Jamie said, half jokingly, "Stay safe, Cal."

As we waited for a break in the traffic, I wondered if the death of that Hispanic man was somehow tied to Lori's murder. After all, what was it, maybe seven or eight miles from Chehalem Creek to where her body was found? Then again, the Pacific Highway was a known drug corridor between Portland, a couple of gambling casinos, and the coastal towns. People got popped every now and then, and leaving a body in a creek would make a statement worth paying attention to.

The traffic cleared momentarily, and my dog and I dashed across the highway. Just as I sat back down at my desk, my phone rang. "Cal, it's Jim. My friends from last night have reappeared along with reinforcements. They've got a search warrant, too. I'm feeling a little threatened here."

"Okay. Don't answer any questions until I get there. I'm leaving right now."

I got up, glanced at my watch, and said to Arch, "What took them so long?"

Chapter Four

I locked up my office, loaded Archie into the backseat of my old BMW, and started into the Dundee Hills, also called, more properly, the Red Hills of Dundee due to the reddish cast of the soil. Formed by a violent history of colliding continents and relentless lava flows, the hills were rich in iron and other minerals, which made them ideal for growing grapes—one of the many oddities of viticulture I'd picked up from Jim Kavanaugh. "It's all about the dirt, Cal," he must have told me a dozen times. "You can't make good pinot noir without good dirt, and these hills have it."

I thought back to the day I met Jim, not long after I arrived from L.A. I'd passed his turnoff several times before noticing a sign one Saturday announcing the opening of a tasting room. I drove in and parked next to an old wooden barn with an arbor attached to one side, shaded with wisteria in full, purple bloom. Jim stood in the dappled sunlight behind a small bar lined with wine bottles. I was his only customer that day, and soon we were sitting at a small round table with a bottle of Le Petit Truc between us, his first pinot noir vintage. He was rough around the edges, but with a self-deprecating sense of humor and a laugh that could shake a room. But there was an intensity about him, too. I sensed it immediately. The man was an artist and, as I was to learn, his medium was the pinot noir grape.

I'll never forget that first glass of pinot he poured me. I loved wine but was more of a cabernet sauvignon type in those days, the prevailing wine grape down in California. I liked the deep color and big, back-slapping flavor of a good cab. Jim's offering was a distinct departure. The color was less intense, but jewel-like when held to the light. The flavor was subtler and more complex, coming in lean and then blooming on my palate. I was an immediate convert. Jim's face lit up at my enthusiastic reaction, saying, "It's young and exuberant right now," as if speaking about a child of his. "It'll smooth out and get a lot better."

He was right, and I was a delighted witness to his growing prowess over the years as a maker of fine pinot noir wine.

Le Petit Truc lay southwest of my place a couple of miles, off Worden Hill Rd. As I pulled into Jim's long drive, I could just see the tip of a serrated line of Douglas firs that marked the west side of my property further up in the hills. The vineyards on either side of the drive were alive with men and women picking grapes, and I had to brake to let a forklift stacked with bins of just-picked, dark purple fruit cross the drive. I parked behind a line of official cars and left Arch with the windows rolled down. I found Jim inside the warehouse next to a moving conveyer belt laden with grapes. He was talking to a uniformed deputy. He looked shrunken and haggard, his face drawn and lacking color. I knew firsthand what a night of grief could do to a man, but I was still shocked.

When I approached, he said, "Hey, Cal, thanks for coming. They've already taken my laptop from the house and a computer I keep in the tasting room for recordkeeping. They're in the barn now, looking for God knows what. I mean, what the hell is this?"

He handed me a copy of the warrant. It looked fairly standard except for one item. "They're looking for the lug wrench for your Grand Cherokee?"

Jim shrugged. "Yeah, I don't get it. They've got my damn Jeep. As far as I know, the wrench is under the backseat where the jack's stored."

"Okay," I said, trying to look unconcerned. I didn't like the sound of that but saw no need to alarm him. Sometimes the purpose of a search warrant is to prove something is *not* there.

While we waited, Juan Cruz came in a couple of times to confer with Jim. I caught enough of their conversation to learn that the pressure was on to finish the harvest because of impending bad weather. Meanwhile, I watched as four women at the conveyer belt sorted the good clusters of grapes from the occasional bad, or broke off a stem containing bad fruit, all done with blinding quickness. The search crew emerged forty minutes later, empty-handed but apparently unvexed. Hal Ballard, one of the detectives at the scene the night before, approached us, nodded to me, and said to Jim, "Mr. Kavanaugh, we'd like you to come down to the office in McMinnville. We have some more questions to ask you."

Jim's eyebrows dipped and two vertical creases appeared between them like little geysers. I knew that look. He was pissed. "Are you kidding me?" He swept an arm toward the vineyards. "We're trying to finish up the harvest here. I can't leave right now."

Ballard held a neutral expression, but he stood up a little straighter. "I'm afraid that's not possible, Mr. Kavanaugh." He glanced at me, then looked back at Jim. "Time's critical right now. We want to find out who killed your wife." True enough, I thought, although I was pretty sure they thought they had their man.

Jim dropped his head, massaged his temples for a moment, and said, "Bloody hell," under his breath. "I can't believe this is happening."

I said, "Come on, Jim. I'll drive you."

He looked up at me and then at Ballard. "Okay, but give me some time to talk to my field boss. We've got a lot going on today."

The Yamhill Sheriff's Office was located in the county seat, McMinnville, a bustling Willamette Valley town twelve miles south of Dundee. Once underway I said, "Look, Jim, you need a lawyer at this juncture. I'll represent you today until we sort this thing out. If I tell you not to answer something, don't. Even if you know the answer, okay? Going back over what you saw last night and all is fine, but anything beyond that, let me make the call."

He nodded, exhaled a long breath, and slid down in his seat. "They don't think I did it, do they? Hell, you think I'd kill anyone during the harvest? No fucking way."

I had to laugh. Anyone who knew Jim well knew that was an absolutely true statement. The grape harvest was the biggest and most important event of his life, and he would never allow anything to compromise that.

"I know that, but Ballard and his partner don't. You're the husband, suspect number one as far as they're concerned. Maybe all this is just to clear you so they can move on. Let's hope so." The lug wrench bothered me, and so did the seized computers. People say a lot of stupid things in the digital space for reasons I've never understood. "Anything on your computers that I should know about? You know, any correspondence with Lori, or mentioning her to someone else? Something that might prove embarrassing?"

He puffed another breath. "Ah, fuck. Back when we were splitting up, I suppose I wrote some angry stuff. Will they go back that far?"

I laughed my answer. "How about recently? You said you guys were getting back together."

He shifted in his seat, and his look turned decidedly sheepish. "I swear, I'm my own worst enemy."

I waited for him to continue.

"Uh, that lunch with Lori I mentioned. It didn't go so well. She seemed really glad to see me, so I asked her to move back to Truc. You know, dumb me, I just sort of blurted it out halfway through the meal. Well, she started hemming and hawing, and I just lost it."

"What did you do?"

"I got up, and the damn table fell over."

"You knocked the table over?"

"Yeah, but not on purpose. Anyway, I walked out and didn't look back. When I got to my car, I realized I screwed up. By that time, Lori was already pulling out of the parking lot. I went back to the restaurant, helped them clean up, and left a fifty dollar tip. I sent her an email apology, and I didn't hear anything back until she called last night." He let out a long sigh, formed a quarter-inch gap between his thumb and forefinger, and glared at it. "We were *that* close to working things out." Then he put a hand to his face and choked off a couple of sobs. "Now she's gone."

We rode in silence for a while. That kind of public display of anger could be very damaging, and I hoped the episode would go undiscovered. I wanted to ask about the sought-after lug wrench—like could it double as a murder weapon?—but thought better of it. If it was an issue, we'd learn soon enough. Archie, who figured out long ago how to use the button to roll the back window down, had his head out the window breathing in the crisp fall air without a care in the world. I envied my dog at that moment, something I found myself doing on a fairly regular basis.

A post-war, two-story building with a brick façade, the Sheriff's Office sat in the middle of downtown McMinnville. The interview room was so brightly lit I wished I'd worn my shades, and the body odor of previous occupants still lingered in the stale air. The other detective at the scene the night before, a woman named Sonia Rodriquez, accompanied Ballard, who did most of the talking. Rodriquez was younger and looked fresh as a daisy. Ballard, on the other hand, sported a dark stubble, and his eyes had a couple of half-moons under them shaded to gray.

He began the interview by taking Jim back over his account of the night before in excruciating detail. Yes, he received a phone call from Lori around nine thirty inviting him to meet her at the overlook. Yes, the purpose of their meeting was to talk about reconciliation. No, he had never been to the overlook before. It was her idea to meet there. No, he did not see any cars coming out as he was coming in, and no, he didn't see anything in or around the car that could've been used to kill his wife.

If Ballard and Roqriquez were looking for inconsistencies in Jim's story, I didn't sense they found any. I breathed a little easier. At this point, Ballard veered into new territory. "Mr. Kavanaugh, you told us you've been separated from your wife for the past year, but neither party filed for divorce, is that right?"

"Yes, but we were talking about getting back together."

Ballard nodded. "How would you characterize your relationship with your wife?" I didn't like the question but let it go. Jim's sometimes stormy relationship with Lori was certainly no secret around Dundee and easily discoverable.

Jim squirmed a bit in his seat and opened his hands for emphasis. "Like I told you, we were exploring the possibility of getting back together. That's why she wanted to meet in that romantic spot. You'll find a five-year-old bottle of my pinot in the Jeep and two crystal glasses. We were going to drink it last night." Good answer, I thought.

Ballard nodded and leaned in a little. "So, your relationship was all good, huh? No arguing or anything? I mean, you *were* separated, right?"

Ballard glanced at Rodriquez, who smiled and said, "No arguing? Wish my marriage was that good."

Jim said, "Well, you know, we had our ups and downs."

I was prepared to cut off that line of questioning right there. Ballard must have sensed that because he changed direction again. "So, you told us that your wife called you around nine thirty last night. Did you recognize the call when it came in?"

Jim pulled absently on his beard for a couple of beats. "Come to think of it, I don't think her name came up on my phone. I remember being surprised when it turned out to be her."

Ballard nodded. "So, your wife normally called you using her personal cell phone?"

"Well, yeah, but she hadn't in quite a while. We were mostly e-mailing this time around."

Ballard nodded. "She never called before using a phone you didn't recognize?"

Jim knotted his brow and shook his head. "No, I don't think so."

That tack puzzled me, but I let it go as well. Apparently the call Jim got didn't come from Lori's cell phone. That seemed odd. At this point, Ballard nodded to Rodriquez, who extracted a photograph from a file folder in front of her and slid it to Jim. It was a high resolution photo of a black tool, made of thick steel, with a handle that flared into a wider section from which a four inch hexagonal socket extended at a right angle, the business end of a lug wrench. It looked more like a battle ax than a tool for changing tires. It was hard to tell for certain, but it appeared to have some dark stains on it.

Ballard said, "Do you recognize this?"

Jim looked down at the photograph and started to speak, but I interrupted. "Don't answer that," I told him. Then in an aside, I said in his ear. "Does that look like the lug wrench from your Jeep?"

He nodded.

"Okay, but we're not going to make things any easier for them." I looked up. "Next question?"

Ballard said to Jim, "Do you know where the lug wrench belonging to your Jeep is?"

Jim looked at me, and I nodded. "Under the backseat, where the jack is, far as I know."

Ballard glanced at Rodriquez, then shook his head. "We didn't find it there. Could you have mislaid it somewhere?"

Jim started to answer, but I cut him off. "Thank you, detectives. We want to cooperate, but this is going too far afield. I'm afraid we're going to have to call it quits here."

A couple of pros, Ballard and Rodriquez looked at each other, then at me. Ballard smiled but without mirth. "So much for cooperation, eh, counselor? Have it your way. Make sure your client stays close by. We'll be in touch."

When we got outside, Jim said, "Fuck, I didn't like that at all. What's the deal with that lug wrench, anyway?"

"My guess is they think it was the murder weapon. You sure your lug wrench was in your Jeep?"

"I thought it was. We used it a couple of months ago to change a tire on a tractor out in the vineyards. The lug nuts on the tractor are the same size as on my Jeep. But I think it got put back. Is that what they think? That I walked up to Lori's car and killed her with the wrench from my Jeep?"

"That was no random line of questioning. You're definitely a suspect. There's a good chance they've already found the murder weapon and that this interview was about trying to get you to say that wrench was yours."

"Oh, that's fucking great. What the hell? Am I being set up?"

"Let's not jump to conclusions," I told my friend. But it sure looked that way. His presence there, her blood on him, and now his lug wrench as the murder weapon? No, that didn't look good at all.

Chapter Five

Jim fell silent on the way back to Le Petit Truc. When I pulled into the customer lot next to his barn, I said, "You okay?"

He grimaced. "I've got to arrange the funeral. Her mom's ill, so she's leaving it all up to me. What do you think of my asking Sean McKnight? I mean, at least I know the guy. Lori went to his church a couple of times, even dragged me there once."

McKnight owned Stone Gate Farm, prime acreage that abutted Jim's vineyard, and he also did double duty as the pastor of a small church in Newberg—a church with hip music, an upbeat message, and a packed house of believers every Sunday. "Sure. Makes sense. I hear he's a decent guy."

Jim nodded. "Her mom and stepbrother came in this morning. I put them up at the Vineyard Inn until the funeral. They went to McMinnville to see the body and talk to Ballard and Rodriquez." He rolled his eyes. "Hope she doesn't trash me."

"Trash you? Who, Lori's mother?"

"Yeah. I know Lori did a lot of complaining to her mother about my legendary temper. Every time I made her cry, she'd call her momma and tell her what a tyrant I was."

Oh, great, I thought. Just what we need. "Well, maybe Lori told her about some of your good points, too."

"Oh, right. That would have been a short conversation." He waved a hand in disgust. "Meanwhile, I'm slammed here. We're only halfway through the harvest." He turned to me. "These are the best damn grapes I've ever seen, Cal. Sugar levels, color, taste, everything came together this year. I could smell it. There's a certain scent out in the vineyard when it's right, when it's the perfect time to pick." His face clouded over again. "I was hoping Lori would be here to see this, you know, like maybe she'd finally get it about me."

I nodded. "What got between you two, anyway?"

He exhaled a long breath. "She thought she married a rich gentleman winemaker. I turned out to be more of an in debt farmer, you know, a guy who takes a shower *after* work." He smiled ruefully and shook his head. "At least that's the way she saw me. She was uptight about money, too. At one point she suggested we sell Truc and move to Portland, where I could quote, unquote, get a real job. She didn't realize that was like asking me to cut off an arm and a leg. But, shit, I still loved her, even afterwards, when I was scared she was going to force me to sell Truc as part of the divorce."

"Anything else between you?"

He chuckled, opened his hands, and leaned back. "Look at me. I'm no prize, and she was so damn beautiful. I never really understood what she saw in me." He cast his eyes down. "Maybe she got a little restless. I don't blame her if she did." Before I could ask more about that, he patted Archie on the head and swung his big frame out of the car. "Gotta get busy, Cal. Thanks again. I'll be in touch."

• • ● • •

Arch and I were back in my law office bright and early the next morning. I had a scheduled meeting with a prospective client, a man who owned a tony wine and cheese shop in Carlton. I suffered through the all-too-familiar story of another failed marriage and agreed to handle his divorce. I hated divorce cases, but I had a mortgage to pay and a dog to feed.

Dundee sat between the larger towns of Newberg and McMinnville, and its news, such as it was, got reported in either

the *McMinnville News Register* or the online *Newberg Graphic,*
or both. When my new client left, I checked them both for
coverage of Lori Kavanaugh's murder, as well as the murder of
the Hispanic man I heard about the morning before. Both papers
covered Kavanaugh's murder, but only the *Graphic* reported on
the latter. It was a brief item.

Man Found Murdered in Dundee

The body of a man was found in Chehalem
Creek early Tuesday morning by a jogger.
He had been shot to death, and no iden-
tification was found on the body, according to police. The man was five-feet-nine
inches tall, 145 pounds, with a goatee
and mustache, and appeared to be Hispanic
in his early to mid-thirties. Anyone with
information regarding his identity should
contact the Dundee-Newberg Municipal Police
immediately.

I sat at my desk absently clicking the top of my ballpoint
pen. I wondered if the victim was just passing through or a
local. I'd know soon enough. Dundee, and for that matter the
whole valley, was tight-knit and word got around fast. I looked
up at Archie. "Coincidences do happen occasionally, right, Big
Boy?" He cocked his head and blinked at me a couple of times,
a clear signal that he was reserving judgment on that question.

The following day, I got another call from Jim. Ballard had
just arrived with a second search warrant. I was tied up with a
client, and by the time I made it to Le Petit Truc the search team
was gone. "All they took this time," Jim explained, "was a can
of Chem Arrow and a nearly empty tube of Dexter Lithoplex."
He wrinkled his brow. "Go figure."

"What are those used for?"

"The Dexter's to lubricate the automatic door in the barn,
and the Arrow's for packing wheel bearings on the tractor."

"Huh," was all I could think to say. What the hell could they
be looking for?"

Chapter Six

Lori Kavanaugh's memorial was held that Saturday at the Joyous Word Christian Center in Newberg. Lit with an abundance of natural light and lined with enough unfinished cedar paneling to smell like a forest, the chapel was filled to capacity that day with her friends and acquaintances and also just about every wine luminary in the valley. The latter showed up, not because they knew Lori all that well—most of them didn't—but as a show of support for Jim, a respected and admired member of their circle.

Pastor McKnight laid out a message of hope. They should rejoice, he told the throng, because Lori had gone to a better place, and Jim would someday be reunited with her. I envied those who listened and were comforted by his words. For me, a funeral was a funeral, the ultimate separation.

Jim had invited me to sit with the family, and I wound up next to his niece, Sylvia, and her husband, Eddie, a couple I'd met a few times at Le Petit Truc. The Mannings, I recalled, lived in Lake Oswego, an upscale suburb south of Portland, where they owned and ran a private investment firm. Eddie was the CEO, and I couldn't remember what Sylvia did. Lori's stepbrother, introduced to me as Aaron Abernathy, sat next to them wearing a plaid coat over a cowboy shirt, skinny jeans, and gauges in his ear lobes the size of silver dollars. Hipster funeral attire, I concluded. The mother was next to him. She was tall like her daughter, but deathly pale and bent now, as if the weight of her daughter's casket rested on her shoulders.

The procession to the cemetery snarled traffic on the Pacific Highway. It began to spit rain, and by the time the last cars had parked and people made their way to the gravesite, emotions were raw. Jim, a couple of Lori's friends, and her mother were sobbing. Abernathy seemed agitated, his face contorted by what looked like something more than grief. McKnight said some final words, and the casket was lowered into a neatly punched hole in the grass and showered with flowers thrown by the mourners.

As we walked away, Abernathy sidled up to Jim and said in a loud voice, "You've got a lot of nerve coming here."

Jim stopped, faced him, and opened his hands with a look of utter disbelief. "What are you talking about? She was my wife." They stood glaring at each other, and everyone within earshot froze, some in mid-stride. "Look at *you* in that silly costume," Jim went on. "What, you find my wife's death *ironic?*"

"It's who I am, man," Abernathy snarled. He turned to walk away and then made a kind of guttural, animal sound, whirled around, and took a swing at Jim. Jim ducked, and Abernathy careened past him, lost his balance, and wound up sprawled on the muddy grass. "You son of a bitch," he said, pushing himself back up.

Eddie Manning jumped between the two men. "Hey, cut it out! Both of you!" Abernathy stepped forward and threw another punch. This one didn't miss. Eddie staggered back and put a hand over his eye. "Jesus, what the hell's the matter with you?"

I jumped in next and spread my arms like a boxing referee. "That's enough. Show some respect for Lori, all of you."

Abernathy pointed a quivering finger at Jim. "You killed her, you bastard. You're gonna go down for this." Then he stomped away with the mother struggling to catch up. The rest of the mourners stood in stunned silence for a couple of moments before dispersing in what was now a downpour.

Eddie, Sylvia, Jim, and I stood there, oblivious to the rain, as people made their way to their cars and drove away. Sylvia and I took a look at Eddie's eye, which was more grazed than smacked. Jim said, "Took one for the team, huh, Eddie? Thanks."

"You owe me," Eddie said, showing the thinnest of smiles. A handsome man by any standard, he had dark hair, deep set, russet colored eyes, and a habit of tugging absently at the small diamond stud in his ear. "What was he thinking, anyway?"

"You heard him," Jim said, rainwater dripping off his nose. "He thinks I killed Lori."

Sylvia hugged Jim's arm, her eyes swelling with indignation. "That's ridiculous. He's just looking for someone to blame, Jim."

"That's right," I said. "People lash out when they're upset. He'll probably regret this when he has time to think about it."

"Yeah, well, Lori's mother and her hipster stepson both hate my guts," Jim said. "I shudder to think of what got said at that interview with the cops."

Jim had a point. The mother may have reinforced what Ballard and Rodriquez were already uncovering, that Jim and Lori's marriage hadn't exactly been a model of harmony. The interview could have quickly focused on Jim and his outbursts of temper. Ballard and Rodriquez wouldn't have outright accused him of anything, but the inference would have been there, which might explain Abernathy's violent reaction.

All they need now, I thought to myself, is to tie a murder weapon back to Jim. That would give them motive, opportunity, and means, and make an arrest a near certainty. But Jim, always the winemaker, had more pressing things on his mind. He swiped rainwater off his forehead, cursed, and said, "I've got to get back to Truc, folks. This rain's sucking the sugar right out of my grapes."

I watched him hurry off with Eddie and Sylvia and for a moment found myself envying my friend for having a passion so great it dwarfed everything else in his life, even the death of his beloved wife and the threat of being accused of her murder.

Chapter Seven

The temperature dropped and the gray, sodden clouds kept dripping rain. As I drove back to The Aerie, I thought again about the murder weapon. If they were able to tie it to Jim, would that force me to doubt his innocence? As an ex-prosecutor, my cynicism ran deep, but the thought of Jim being guilty hadn't even crossed my mind. Had he snapped and done something unthinkable? Hell, I'd prosecuted plenty of men who killed their wives in a fit of passion. It wasn't an uncommon crime. But I just couldn't imagine it in Jim's case. Sure, my mercurial friend had a temper, but he wasn't a violent man, and he worshipped the ground Lori walked on. And sure, he had just hurried back to work on the day of her funeral. But that was Jim.

I thought of his call to me after he found Lori's body, his voice like a wounded animal's, and the depth of his sorrow as we talked that first night. And today at the cemetery—I'd never seen such a grief-shattered face except in the mirror.

No. With Jim, what you saw is what you got. More evidence might come, but my faith in Jim Kavanaugh's innocence was unshakable.

The rain gave way to a brisk wind that blew off the valley, shredding the cloud cover. I strained against it to open the gate at the entrance to my property. Archie greeted me with a muddy tennis ball in his jaws, and I gave him some needed exercise by tossing it as hard as I could. He normally caught it on one bounce, but if I threw the ball high enough, he fielded it like Willie Mays. My arm gave out before his energy did, and by the time we got to the house, I could see more rain in the distance, a diffuse gray mass being towed below a new band of galloping clouds.

We stood silently on the side porch and watched the new front come in, which announced itself with a sound like distant applause in the swaying firs. I breathed in the smells the rain engendered—musty whiffs of wet earth mixed with the scent of saturated fir bark and needles. Northwest forest smells.

I didn't realize I was a pluviophile—a lover of rain—until I moved up here. Clearly, I was cut out to be an Oregonian.

I fed Arch, started a fire with some kindling and a couple of oak logs, and poured myself a glass of Moulin des Vrilleres, which I sipped while I cooked. I liked the pinot gris from the Dundee Hills well enough, but my favorite white was the flinty, bone dry sauvignon blanc made around the hill town of Sancerre in the Loire Valley. I sipped while I cut up some small red potatoes, slathered them with olive oil and sea salt and popped them in a hot oven until they were crisp on the outside and soft and steaming in the middle. I served them with a slab of broiled rockfish and some steamed green beans. Simple but satisfying.

The events of the day had hammered me, but after dinner I felt restless and knew sleep wasn't going to come easily. Still curious about the murdered Hispanic man, I checked the *Newberg Graphic* for any additional information. There was none, so I tapped out a text to a contact there, a young reporter who'd done a profile piece on me a while back, covering the pro bono work I did in Portland. It was a Saturday night, so I didn't expect an answer until the next day at best, but twenty minutes later this text pinged in: The man's name is Luis Delgado. He's undocumented, from Oaxaca. This came in from an anonymous source, so not official. Police are trying to find next of kin.

At least I had a name, and I wasn't surprised that no one had come forward, in view of Delgado's undocumented status. The local police don't go out of their way to hassle folks on that issue, but trust was next to zero in the Hispanic community, which supplied nearly all the field hands and many of the field bosses working the Dundee Hills vineyards. I immediately thought of Jim's field boss, Juan Cruz. He knew nearly everyone who worked the vineyards and most of their families. I would talk to Juan, although my interest in Delgado was nothing more than a nagging hunch.

• • ● • •

Between clients on Monday, Jim called and invited me to a feast that Thursday to celebrate the end of harvest. "I couldn't call it off," he explained. "I owe my crew for a great job this year. It won't be easy, but I'll get through it." He gave me Juan Cruz's cell number, and I caught Juan out in the vineyards. He thought the name Luis Delgado sounded familiar and promised to see if he could find a contact. Before we rang off he said, "This idea that Jim had anything to do with Ms. Kavanaugh's death is crazy. Jim has the roar of a lion but the bite of a flea. I have a hard time getting him to buy gopher traps."

Jim called me on Thursday morning and told me to come to Le Petit Truc early, if possible. He had some wine he wanted me to taste. Not one to pass up a barrel tasting offer, I got there around two and found him in his largest outbuilding, the warehouse where he aged his wine in sixty-gallon French oak barrels and carried out his fermenting and bottling operations. The air was heavy with the smell of wine, but it was a decidedly sharper and earthier odor compared to what comes from a bottle. Holding a bent glass tube with a large squeeze bulb in one hand and a wineglass in the other, he stood in a narrow aisle with oak wine barrels stacked four high in steel racks on either side of him. "Cal," he said when he saw me, "wait until you taste this." I was relieved to see he looked rested, more like himself. He held the tube up. "This is not a turkey baster. It's called a wine thief."

I smiled. "Okay. What are we going to steal?"

"Some of our reserve from last year. The fruit's from our Pommard clone. I used a proprietary yeast and whole cluster fermentation."

"Whole cluster? What does that mean?"

"Stems and all. If the stems are nice and ripe they can add structure and complexity to the wine."

"How do you judge that?"

"I taste the stems. Last year they were right for it. This year— even more so." He removed the stained wooden bung from a barrel, extracted some of the wine, squeezed it into the glass, and handed it to me. He nodded, his eyes expectant. "It's not ready to bottle yet, but it's getting there."

I tipped the wineglass at a forty-five and held it up to the light. It glowed like polished ruby. I righted the glass and gave the wine several swirls before closing my eyes and putting my nose to it. The aroma opened up like a blooming flower. "Hell, I could just smell this stuff."

"It's got a great nose, doesn't it?"

I nodded and swirled it again, took a sip, and held it for a few moments before letting it flow off my tongue to the floor of my mouth. It was slightly astringent coming in, but full and rich with a finish that lasted longer than the last note on the *Sergeant Pepper* album. "Damn, this is outstanding, Jim," I told him. "Wait until the *Wine Spectator* reviews this. You've outdone yourself."

Jim allowed himself one of the few smiles I'd seen since Lori's death. Nothing pleased him more than to have someone like his wine. "I knew it was going to be a good vintage, but I had no idea. And the best is yet to come, my friend."

We sampled from a few more barrels, and then I followed him around to the terrace of his wine tasting room, where preparations were underway for the feast. Long tables draped with white tablecloths were being set, and platters of filets, pork tenderloins, and salmon steaks sat next to a barbecue fashioned from a fifty gallon steel drum that had been cut in half and welded end to end. Wearing a chef's hat, Juan Cruz was busy stoking the charcoal and preparing to lay in a stack of foil-wrapped baking potatoes. The weather was clear, and radiant heaters were in place to keep the chill off.

"No music this year," Jim said, his face clouding so fast I thought he might break into tears.

Candice Roberts, who doubled as Jim's sales manager and hostess of his wine tasting room, came out carrying a huge bowl of mushroom risotto. She was tall with a shock of bouncy blond hair, slate blue eyes, and a take-charge attitude. She managed Jim's financial matters like a field marshal, bringing a semblance of discipline to the monetary side of Le Petit Truc. Jim often referred to her as his "secret weapon" and warned me not to make the mistake of calling her Candy.

"Hey, Cal," she greeted me. "There's a big platter inside with the fixings for fish tacos. Would you bring it out, please? And there's another bowl of risotto that needs to come out, too."

I got busy helping out and pretty soon people began arriving—field hands and their families, friends and neighbors of Jim's, and a handful of customers, big spenders at the tasting room who wanted to be part of an authentic harvest feast. Soon the terrace was buzzing with conversation, although the mood was somber in view of the tragic event. When Candice finally announced it was time to eat, it took her two tries before people started filling their plates and finding a seat.

Jim got up with a glass of pinot in his hand. "As you all know, I suck at speeches." He paused to a titter of laughter. "I'd just like to thank each and every one of you for all the support this year." He turned to the tables where most of the pickers and their families were seated. "And thank God we beat most of the rain." More laughter and a bit of subdued cheering. "It was a great harvest, the best we've had here by any measure, and now all those beautiful grapes have been crushed and are safe and sound in the fermenters." His looked turned solemn. "Some of you suggested I postpone or cancel this feast, but I know Lori would have wanted us to carry on the tradition." He raised his glass. "Join me in a toast. To Lori." His voice cracked as he added, "Wish you were here with us."

I found a seat between Eddie and a man named Richard Amis, a psychiatrist practicing out of McMinnville, I learned. Amis had a broad forehead, pale, heavy-lidded eyes, and a faintly patrician bearing. He hadn't gotten the casual dress memo. "So, Cal," he said, "I suppose you're here like me, because you love Jim's wines."

"Right. Jim and I go back quite a few years. I live not too far from here."

His smile broadened. "My wife and I just opened one of his pinot reserves we laid down four years ago." He rolled his eyes. "Oh, my God, what a magnificent quaff. Lush, you know, but silky, with layers of crushed plum, black cherries, and just a hint of cassis. And the finish"—he closed his heavy lids for a moment—"like velvet."

Crushed plum? Cassis? What, no pencil lead or essence of leather? Where do people come up with this stuff? I forced a smile. "Sounds great. Was that the 2012?"

"Yes. Do you have some?" When I nodded, he eyed me expectantly and added, "Have you tasted it yet?"

"Yeah. It's good." I paused for a moment. "I'm, uh, better at drinking wines than describing them."

Eddie flashed a boyish smile. "Cal practices law down in Dundee, and he also does pro bono work in Portland."

Amis made a face. "Oh, my God, Portland has gone downhill, hasn't it? I mean, the last time we went to the Schnitzer, we got asked for money four or five times between the parking garage and the theater. It really upset Veronica, and she said never again."

Sean McKnight, the pastor at Lori's funeral, was sitting across from us. He was tall with square shoulders and a mane of long, silver hair. He said, "You know, we're told the economic crisis is over, but there's still an awful lot of people out there who are really hurting."

"Well," Amis responded, "if Portland didn't coddle these people there wouldn't be such a problem. The city's a magnet for every lowlife in the country."

I started to respond, but Eddie cut me off. The man was a peacemaker, apparently. "So, Sean, you still growing hazelnuts and kiwis at Stone Gate?"

McKnight smiled and nodded. "Yep, we're still plugging away. We're planning to put in a new variety of kiwi that we've been experimenting with. No fuzz on the skin, and it ripens on the vine. Looks promising."

Amis drank some wine and regarded the pastor over the rim of his glass. "No fuzz and ripens on the vine? Sounds like grapes to me." He laughed, but nobody joined him. "Seriously, wouldn't you be better off growing grapes? With your elevation and orientation, the wineries that don't have enough acreage would beat a path to your door."

McKnight smiled as if he'd heard that tune before. "Don't choose to grow grapes. Wouldn't know the first thing about it."

Amis drank some more wine and shook his head. "Nuts and kiwis. What a pity. The Dundee Hills may be the best place in the world outside of Burgundy—hell, maybe the best place, period—to grow pinot noir grapes."

An uncomfortable silence followed Amis' comments. I got up to build a salmon taco and ran into Jim at the food table. He'd been sitting with Juan and the field hands. He shot me a relaxed smile and said under his breath, "Be nice to that guy, Amis, sitting next to you. He's a *very* good retail customer."

"That's asking a lot. He's a wine sno—"

"Oh, shit," Jim interrupted, looking past me. "We've got company."

I turned around and saw a white Yamhill County Sheriff's patrol car coming down the drive, followed by an unmarked sedan. "Stay cool. I'll go see what they want."

Ballard and Rodriquez got out of the unmarked. By the time I reached them the laughter and conversation at the feast went silent, and I could feel the gaze of fifty people on my back. I smiled as cordially as I could manage. "Evening, detectives, can I help you?"

Rodriquez shuffled her feet and Ballard stepped forward, his face tense. "Is your client here, counselor?"

"Of course, it's his harvest feast."

Ballard nodded. "Maybe you could go get him. That might be the easiest way to do this."

"Do what?"

"We've got a warrant for his arrest for the murder of Lori Kavanaugh."

I blew a breath and shook my head. "You're not serious."

Ballard shrugged. "We are. We think he killed his wife, and now the D.A. does, too."

I waved for Jim to come join us. My heart sank as he approached. His face held an annoyed, what-the-hell-now? look. Annoyed was one thing, but having your life turned upside down was quite another, and that was exactly what was about to happen to my friend.

Chapter Eight

Jim was escorted to the patrol car. He turned back to me. "Tell Candice to carry on, Cal. There's plenty of wine and food left."

I nodded. "I'll be at the county jail just as soon as I can. And listen, Jim—don't talk to them. Name, rank, and serial number. Nothing else." A murmur went up from the guests like the buzz of a beehive as he was cuffed and loaded into the cruiser. Everyone remained seated except Candice, Eddie, and Sylvia, who rushed up to me. Sylvia's eyes were wide with confusion and fear. "What just happened, Cal?"

There was no sugarcoating it. They all saw the handcuffs. "Uh, Jim's been arrested. I've got to go to McMinnville to see what this is all about."

"Sylvia and I are going with you," Eddie said.

I turned to Candice. "Tell everyone this is just a misunderstanding, that they should continue with the feast."

Candice made a brave face. "I'll do my best."

Sylvia and Eddie rode with me to the Sheriff's Office in McMinnville, where Jim was being processed prior to incarceration in the county jail. As we got underway, Eddie said, "I don't get it. Jim told us he wasn't a suspect."

"Yes," Silvia added, dabbing at her eyes with a tissue. "He said all they had against him was the fact that he and Lori had a rocky relationship."

"That's about all I know, too," I said. "They might claim that gave him a motive, and the fact that he found her very near the time of her death proves he had the opportunity."

"Oh, sure," Eddie shot back. "He killed her, then called the police. That makes a lot of sense."

I shrugged. "They might argue that he either lost his temper and killed her in a moment of passion, or he planned it all along. Either way, they'll say he wanted the police to believe he discovered the body."

"What about a murder weapon?" Sylvia asked. "I mean, how was she killed?"

She and Eddie didn't need to know about the lug wrench. "I'm not sure, but they must have found something that led to the arrest."

Eddie said, "I never blamed Jim a bit for losing his cool with Lori. She was such a selfish bit—"

Sylvia said, "Don't, Eddie. What would Jim say if he heard you running down Lori, for God's sake?"

"Well, you know it's true, Syl," Eddie shot back. "She thought she was going to be crowned the wine queen of Oregon when she married Jim. Boy, was she surprised."

When we arrived at the county jail, I asked to see Jim and was told he was still being processed. We waited an hour and a half in a cold, echoing hallway until a uniformed woman showed up and escorted me to a secure conference room. Wearing a bright orange pullover and pants, a pair of white canvas slip-ons, and stainless steel handcuffs, Jim was led to a chair across from me. The guard uncuffed him, nodded to me, and left the room.

Jim puffed a breath and shook his head. "You'd think I was Hannibal Lecter."

"Did Ballard and Rodriquez try to interview you?"

"Yeah. I told them I wouldn't talk without you present. What did Eddie and Sylvia say?"

"They were incensed. They came with me."

He blinked rapidly a couple of times and looked down, avoiding tears. "My sister's gone. They're the only family I've got.

But they shouldn't have come." He exhaled and shook his head. "This is humiliating. First the goddamn fight in the cemetery, now this. Did you talk to Candice?"

"Yeah. Don't worry, she's handling the situation back at Truc."

He ran a hand through his hair. His beard suddenly looked unkempt, as if being arrested caused it to go wild. "I wanted that dinner to go well, you know?" He looked at me, his eyes shiny in the garish fluorescent lights.

"I know. Look, Jim. I need you to focus. We have important issues to deal with here."

He put his hands up. "Okay, okay. What happens next?"

"You'll be arraigned on Monday morning. They'll outline the charges against you, and you'll be given an opportunity to enter a plea."

He nodded. "Not fucking guilty, that's my plea. You're going to be my lawyer, right?"

"For this phase, then we'll see."

He was incredulous. "See about *what?*"

"This is an important decision for you. You may want to shop around."

He waved a hand dismissively. "When can you get me out of here?"

"I'll ask for a bail hearing at the arraignment. The judge will set a date. But, getting you out on bail is problematic."

"What's that mean?"

"There's no bail for murder in Oregon unless we can show that the prosecutor's evidence is lacking, and that's a very high bar."

"What if I don't get bail? How long before we get this thing cleared up?"

I knew this question was coming and dreaded it. "Uh, it could be twelve months or more before your case comes to trial."

"*What?* Are you kidding me? I'd be sitting in jail all that time?" That can't happen, Cal. I've got wine to make. If I can't work I'll lose Truc, and I'll go fucking crazy, too."

I put a hand up. "Whoa. We'll argue hard for bail. Don't get ahead of yourself."

"Alright. Suppose I do get bail, what'll it cost me?"

"It varies with the judge, but murder comes in high, two hundred fifty, maybe three hundred, possibly more."

"Thousand?"

I nodded. You don't need a bond in Oregon, but you'll need to post a ten percent deposit. When you show up for trial, you'll get it back less the fifteen percent the court keeps."

"So, I need thirty-five thousand in cash up front? He slid down in his seat. "Oh, shit, I don't have that kind of cash lying around right now."

"You don't?"

"Nope. I run close to the bone. Our grapes came in way above what I forecasted this year. That required a big crew, and I just paid them all. That depleted my cash drawer."

"Can't you borrow against your property?"

He puffed a breath and shook his head. "Already been to that well. I'll, uh, have to sell some Remonds, maybe discount some bulk wine for a fire sale."

"Remonds?"

"French oak barrels, best on the market. Got a pretty high inventory right now. Maybe I can sell twenty-five or thirty to someone on the hill. Candice can take care of that and see about moving some wine in a hurry."

We agreed that I'd talk to her about setting this up and tell her not to pull the trigger until we knew how the bail hearing came out. At this point it was clear Jim couldn't afford one of the bigger law firms in Portland for his defense, which is what I was going to advise him to consider. After all, I was a one-man show, and a murder trial sucks up the resources like an industrial vacuum cleaner. But he couldn't afford the retainer for those firms, let alone the fees.

There was another issue that crossed my mind—if I took the case I needed to be damn careful it didn't break me as well.

Jim seemed to sense my concern. He opened his big hands and leaned forward. "Look, Cal, I want you to represent me. And don't worry, I'll pay your fee, I promise you."

"I know you will, but I can't take my entire fee in wine." We both laughed, and then I met his eyes. "I want you to know that I believe in your innocence."

"I didn't think you lawyers were supposed to worry about that."

I smiled. "You're right. It's not supposed to be about guilt or innocence but whether or not the prosecution can prove its case. There are plenty of lawyers out there who'll gladly take any case that comes along, but I figure life's too short to spend it trying to get people off."

He held my gaze. "Thanks, Cal. I'm glad you're in my corner."

It was settled. I would defend my friend against a charge of murder brought by the District Attorney of Yamhill County on behalf of its citizens. I pulled out a small spiral notebook and a pen I'd found in my glove compartment and took Jim through the few questions I could think to ask at that point. I learned that he never kept his Jeep locked and that it was used frequently by Juan and some of the field hands to take trailer loads to a compost heap they kept on the east end of the property. There had been no break-ins or suspected ones, either, at Le Petit Truc.

"You mentioned using the lug wrench on your tractor," I went on. "Who was involved in that work?"

"Juan and one of the field hands, Xavier Duran, I think. We were repacking the wheel bearings." He snapped his fingers. "Maybe that's why the cops took that can of Arrow. That's the grease we use."

I nodded. "I think they're going to claim a lug wrench like yours was used as the murder weapon. Maybe they think the grease can help them tie it to you."

Jim smirked. "Sounds like they're reaching."

"We'll see what they have. Now, what about Lori? Do you know of anyone who would want to harm her?"

He flinched at the sound of her name. "Like I told the detectives, no one."

"What about friends, people she would confide in?"

He massaged his forehead for a moment. "She didn't have a lot of girlfriends, you know? Candice was one, and Sylvia. Some others I can't think of right now. The woman who cut her hair, I think."

"Candice's last name is Roberts, right?"

"Yeah. They were pretty tight."

"What about you? Any enemies I don't know about?"

He managed a smile. "Just my competitors. But it's always been friendly competition, with the exception of Blake Daniels, I suppose."

Daniels owned Rolling Hills, a big winery whose acreage was separated from Jim's by Sean McKnight's farm. I knew he was divorced and had a reputation as a player. "What's the problem between you and Daniels?"

He shrugged. "Philosophy, mainly. He's nouveau, you know. It's all about technology with him. He's got a master's in enology from UC Davis. I'm old school, self-taught."

"What's the difference?"

"I'm all about the Burgundian method. I mean, who can argue with centuries of success? We're after quality not yield. We use a slow fermentation with native yeasts, age in French oak instead of stainless steel, and we don't rush a damn thing except the grape harvest. No pesticides, either. For Daniels, profits are front and center. He can't seem to get it in his head that a ton and gun operation like he runs is not going to produce a truly fine wine. We used to be, you know, cordial, but as Truc started to build a name, he's become a real asshole."

"Competition alone made you two enemies?"

Jim's eyes narrowed, and I thought I saw his jaw flex beneath his beard. "I didn't like the way he looked at Lori, either. The man thinks he's a fucking gift to women." He shifted in his seat and looked past me. "We were out drinking one night after a vintner's social. I went to take a leak, and when I came back, Daniels has his head in close, talking to Lori at the bar. It wasn't the first time he'd been sniffing around her. I spun him around, and we would have gotten into it right there if Eddie hadn't stepped in."

"Looks like Eddie makes a habit of intervening on your behalf."

"Yeah, you could say that. He's a good kid. Crazy about my niece, too."

"What about Lori's stepbrother, Abernathy? I wouldn't say he's any fan of yours."

"Aaron? Yeah, he and I clashed from day one. I can't abide that hipster bullshit." He laughed dismissively. "He wanted me to loan him the money to start a retail marijuana business in Portland. Thought I was loaded, I guess."

"What did you tell him?"

"To pack sand, that's what. He would have smoked up all the profits."

"Did Lori pressure you any?"

"Nah. She wasn't about sharing our money with anyone."

"How did he get along with Lori?"

"They weren't blood, and they weren't close. He probably thought she should have done more to twist my arm about the head shop, but I can't say for sure. The Old Man, Aaron's dad, thought the world of Lori, so maybe some jealousy mixed in, too."

We talked some more, but that was all I got that was potentially useful. Jim borrowed my notebook and wrote out a couple of pages of instructions for Juan and another couple for Candice and gave them to me. I waited while the guard came in and led him out. "I'll check in with you tomorrow," I told him. "Keep the faith."

Keep the faith. I said that as much to myself as to Jim. I didn't like the way this was lining up. Clearly, the murder charge, whether we eventually beat it or not, was a shot below Jim's waterline, a shot that was premeditated and well executed. And win or lose, the cost of conducting a full-blown murder trial was prohibitive, to say the least. Of course, there was one way to short circuit this—not by developing an alternate theory of the crime, but by finding out who really killed Lori Kavanaugh.

That was a tall order, but sometimes the best defense is a good offense.

Chapter Nine

"Let me know when the arraignment is, Cal. I want to be there," Eddie said, after I briefed him and Sylvia on the way back to Le Petit Truc.

"It'll be short but not sweet," I warned. "They'll charge him, we'll plead innocent, and we'll ask for a bail hearing."

"I don't care how short it is, I'll be there if I can."

The crowd had cleared back at Le Petit Truc, and Juan and Candice were both busy on the terrace with the cleanup. They looked up in unison when we approached. "Jim's okay," I said. "He was concerned that his arrest would spoil the feast."

Candice furrowed her forehead. "People left early, but they managed to finish off most of the food and wine. I told them it was a mistake, like you suggested, but some people knew about the incident at the cemetery and left shaking their heads." She drew her mouth into a firm line and looked me in the eye. "No way Jim would harm a hair on Lori's head. Are you going to defend him, Cal?"

I nodded. "Looks that way."

"Good."

I gave Jim's note to Juan, and after reading it he said, "No problem. We'll make sure the fermentation goes well. Jim shouldn't worry about this." He folded the note, placed it in his shirt pocket, and shifted his feet. "I checked on the man you asked me about, Luis Delgado. He was a *coyote de drogas*, a drug smuggler, but small time, you know? He also worked in the fields and vineyards, some, in between trips to Mexico."

"Did he have family here or friends he hung out with?"

"I'm still working on that. I'll let you know."

"That would be helpful. Another thing"—I took the notebook out and paged through it—"Jim mentioned a man named Xavier, Xavier Duran. He said he helped with some work on the tractor a couple of months ago. What do you know about him?"

"He's new to the hills. A good mechanic."

"Did he handle the lug wrench from Jim's Jeep?"

Juan paused for a couple of beats. "I guess so. All three of us did."

"Did the wrench get put back in the Jeep?"

"I think so, yes."

"Who put it back?"

He paused again. "I'm not sure. Probably Jim."

"Any way I could talk to Duran?"

Juan nodded. "He has some English. I'll set it up."

Before I left, I explained the bail situation to Candice and gave her Jim's note. I also told her I wanted to talk to her, and we exchanged cell phone numbers.

It was early days, but I left Le Petit Truc that night feeling like I wasn't in this fight completely alone.

• • ● • •

That Friday, I coupled a court date in McMinnville—the restraining order hearing for Audrey Steele—with a short visit to Jim in the county jail. His beard was even more disheveled, and his eyes had taken on an almost feral quality. "I don't know what's worse, Cal," he told me by way of a greeting, "thinking about my wine going to shit or about my wife lying in a cold grave."

He broke down, and I held my friend while he sobbed. "Give it some time," was all I could think to say.

After regaining his composure, he sat down. "Did you give Juan my note?" I assured him I had and that the fermentation was proceeding apace. "What about Candice? She think she can raise the cash?"

"She said don't worry about the money. She'll get it."

That seemed to calm him down somewhat, and after going through the arraignment procedure, he wrote out another set of notes for Juan and Candice. I left feeling uneasy. Some people are psychologically ill-equipped to deal with incarceration, and Jim was obviously one of those people. I hated to think what a year of waiting for a trial would do to him, or, God forbid, losing the case. A fist formed in my gut and twisted a half turn.

• • ● • •

Archie lobbied hard for a jog that Saturday morning, but the temperature dropped overnight and a cold rain had swept in off the valley. I stood at the kitchen sink sipping a cappuccino as drops of viscous rain sloshed against the windows and my resolve weakened. Arch lay in front of the kitchen door, his chin resting between his white-booted paws and his big chestnut-colored eyes watching me expectantly. "It's not going to happen, Big Boy," I told him as I carried my coffee into my study and logged in.

My heart swelled a little when I saw an e-mail from my daughter, Claire. With a newly acquired Ph.D. in environmental science, she was doing research on climate change at Harvard now. Complaining about starvation wages, she asked if I could spring for a plane ticket so she could come home for Christmas. I told her I could and that I would try to arrange some decent snow on Mt Hood for skiing, too.

I was lost in thought about Claire when Juan called with two pieces of information. First, he gave me the cell number of Xavier Duran, who, he explained, would be expecting a call from me. Second, he told me Luis Delgado used to hang out at a little bar in Dundee called the San Blas with a guy whose street name was El Burro because of all the crack and heroin he carried up from Mexico.

"Will he talk to me?"

"I don't know, Cal. He works for cartel scum." He paused for a moment. "Is this about Jim?"

"I'm not sure yet, but I want to talk to this guy. Today, if possible. Tell him I'm not a cop or a narc."

Another pause. "I'll try to set it up. He likes the happy hour at the San Blas. I'm told he's in town, so tonight's good. If he's there and agrees I'll bring him out to your car, say, around five thirty. He won't want to be seen talking to a gringo."

That afternoon, Xavier Duran met me for a coffee. A cheerful man with an open demeanor, his account of the work on the tractor was similar to Juan's. They all used the lug wrench, and if anyone put it back in the Grand Cherokee it was probably Jim. "How easy would it have been for someone to take the lug wrench out of the Jeep after Jim put it back?" I asked.

"Oh, no problem. It's never locked, and everyone knows that."

At five twenty that evening I sat at the far end of the San Blas parking lot in my old 3-series Beemer, which was idling with the heater on. Juan arrived shortly after me, went into the bar, and several minutes later came out with a beefy, slope-shouldered guy with an intricate crosshatch of neck tattoos. I rolled the window down, Juan introduced El Burro, nodded to me, and left.

"I'm sorry that your friend, Luis Delgado, was killed," I began after he seated himself and closed the door. He nodded, his eyes shadowed in the low light. "I'm a lawyer here in Dundee, and I'm not involved in the case in any way." Another nod. "A friend of mine was killed the same night Delgado was. You may have read about it, a woman named Lori Kavanaugh." He shrugged. Complete indifference. "People are saying that Delgado was killed because of his business dealings in Mexico." I paused, and El Burro's face remained impassive. "I'm wondering if you have an opinion about this."

He smiled without showing his teeth. "Luis was not killed because of his business. This I can tell you."

"What happened then?"

He shrugged. "I don't know. He told me he had a driving

job. Very easy and good money. Next thing I know, he's shot through the head."

My pulse went up a notch. "Driving job? What kind?"

"All he told me was it was easy money."

"Who was he driving for?"

"He didn't say." El Burro shot me an annoyed look. "He didn't tell me everything about his life, man."

I nodded. "Sure. Uh, would anyone else know what the job was or who he was driving for?"

He turned to face me, and the dome light revealed his eyes, a couple of hard, black beads. "Juan Cruz told me I could trust you to keep my name out of this."

"You can. This is just between you and me."

He paused and stroked his chin, his yellowish nails standing out against his dark beard. "Luis met a woman not too long ago. Her name is Isabel. She might know something."

"Last name?"

He shrugged again. "Take Tenth, toward the river. Her house is on the right, just before the tee. I dropped him there once." He closed his eyes for a moment. "A small house set far back. This is all I remember." He glanced at his watch, snapped the car door open, then paused before getting out. "You can tell the police this, if you want. Maybe it will help them catch the *cabrón* who killed my friend." He wagged a finger at me and scowled. "But remember, no El Burro."

Ice was beginning to stick to my windshield, but I wasn't that far from Tenth and, as it turned out, there was only one house near the tee that was set back from the street. I pulled into the long gravel drive and parked in front of a squat house with faux cedar siding, zero landscape shrubbery, and an empty carport. A dim porch light shone and an even dimmer interior light gave off an eerie reddish glow, providing some hope Isabel might be home. A name—Isabel Rufino—was scrawled on a piece of tape stuck to the mailbox confirming I had the right place. I rapped on the front door, and to my surprise it swung open. The air in the house was warm and stale and carried a faint, acrid odor. The reddish glow seemed to come from a room off a short hallway—the kitchen, I guessed.

Was something smoldering? A fire? I called out again, and when no one answered, entered cautiously to have a look.

The interior light *was* coming from the kitchen, where an electric burner on the stove glowed a bright cherry red like a big, angry eye. The surrounding walls were hot to the touch, and the paint near the stove had yellowed. A small teapot with water in it sat at the ready on the sink next to the stove.

I turned off the burner, and the kitchen became as dark as the rest of the house. I had no business being there, but what the hell, I was already inside. I switched on the flashlight feature on my phone. There were a couple of dirty dishes and a glass in the sink, a few canned goods in the cupboard, and a lightly stocked refrigerator.

The walls were bare in the living room, the furniture undisturbed, and I saw no personal photographs or books. The medicine cabinet in the bathroom was bare except for a canister of dental floss and a squeezed-flat tube of toothpaste. The closet in the bedroom was cleared out except for a couple of tattered dresses drooping from hangars in the corner, a pair of high heels with one heel broken off, and a worn pair of sneakers. I almost missed two small photographs lying facedown in the top drawer of a nightstand next to the unmade bed, the type of photos used for applications. A young woman stared back at me. She was pretty, her gaze direct, and her smile laced with innocence.

The only other thing of interest I noticed was a menu lying on the top of a battered, mostly empty chest of drawers in the bedroom. It was from a small restaurant in Newberg called Picante's. Next to the menu I noticed a set of finger marks in the fine layer of dust on the chest. The marks looked fresh. Too fresh to have been made by Isabel? I couldn't tell, but the thought set the back of my neck tingling. Maybe I wasn't the first person to look the place over.

I assumed the woman in the photos was Isabel and pocketed one of them. A menu in the bedroom was a little unusual, and there was no mention of take-out on it. She might be a waitress at Picante's and had used the menu to memorize the dishes, I decided.

After scraping a skin of ice off my windshield, I sat in my idling car in front of her place and mulled things over. Chances were Isabel's hasty departure was related to Delgado's murder. It could have just been a panicked reaction, or she might've run because he told her something she knew might get her killed. If El Burro was right, that Delgado was not the victim of a drug squabble, then his murder could certainly be tied to Lori Kavanaugh's.

How far did Isabel run, I wondered, and what were the chances of finding her? I didn't have a clue, but I did have a distinct feeling of being drawn into something, and that little voice in my head—the one I hardly ever listen to—said watch yourself.

Chapter Ten

I awoke on Sunday when the furnace clunked on at six-thirty a.m. and set the radiators clattering. Archie took my movement as a signal the day was beginning, and after stretching from his pad in the corner, came over and gave me his customary greeting—a couple of slobbery kisses. I got up, dressed, and followed him down the back staircase. He looked at me expectantly, so I fed him, then made a cappuccino and stood sipping it while looking out the window over the kitchen sink. Tendrils of ground fog hung at every low spot like deflated clouds. But a couple of shafts of sunlight penetrated the cloud cover, and I took that as a good omen.

I called the Dundee-Newberg police and told them I had information about the Luis Delgado murder. The sergeant on duty told me the case was assigned to the Yamhill County Major Crimes Response Team and gave me a number to call. Next thing I knew I was talking to Detective Hal Ballard again. Yamhill County, after all, wasn't that big a place. I told Ballard what I'd learned, leaving El Burro out of it. When I finished, he said, "Let me see if I've got this. An anonymous source tells you that Luis Delgado's murder was not a drug hit, told you where to find his girlfriend, and when you went to talk to her, she had apparently left her place in a big hurry."

"That's right. The woman's name is Isabel Rufino. I think she left because she feared for her life. Maybe she knows something about Delgado's murder." I hesitated for a moment. "He was killed a short time after Lori Kavanaugh. I think the two crimes may be related."

Ballard chuckled. "I knew that was coming. Look, Delgado was a known mule, and he was killed in the time-honored fashion of professional drug hits north of the border—a small caliber round to the head. The girlfriend probably figured she was next. Don't blame her for running."

"Well, it wouldn't hurt to find her. I think she might be working at a restaurant in Newberg called Picante's."

"Sure, and it wouldn't hurt if I knew the name of your source, too."

We ended the conversation on that happy note. I knew Ballard wouldn't warm to the idea I suggested, and I figured not much energy would be expended to find Isabel. I decided to do that myself, so that night I drove over to Picante's, a small taqueria claiming "authentic Mexican cuisine and local, craft beers." I sat at the bar, and when the bartender brought me a Mirror Pond I asked, "Does Isabel Rufino work here?"

He paused and studied me for a moment. "You're not ICE, are you?"

"No." I fished a card from my shirt pocket and handed it to him. "I'm an attorney from Dundee. She might have information that could help a client of mine. I'd just like to talk to her, that's all."

"She *was* working here. I guess it was four days ago, now, she didn't show up for work. Haven't seen or heard from her since. Is she in some kind of trouble?"

"No, nothing like that. If she comes back in to pick up a check or something, have her call me at the number on the card."

I left Picante's disappointed. Even if Isabel came back in, I knew she wouldn't call me. Why, I asked myself, would she get mixed up with a scumbag like Delgado? Sure, I was reading a lot into that smile of hers. A memory of one of my daughter's first boyfriends flashed back to me, a scruffy kid who'd dropped out of school to perfect his video gaming and get closer to his marijuana habit. It took me a while to figure out that he was Claire's "project," that she firmly believed her love could save him. Maybe that's how Isabel saw Delgado. Maybe she had that nurturing instinct like Claire. Or, maybe she wasn't all that innocent.

In any case, she was on the run from someone. I hoped I would find her first.

• • ● • •

Jim's arraignment was first on the docket on Monday morning at the Yamhill County Circuit Court, which adjoined the Sheriff's Department and the County Jail. Judge Clarence Whitcomb presided, a good judge whose opinions were seldom overturned. More importantly, I was pretty sure he knew Jim Kavanaugh by reputation. This would be important for the bail hearing I was going to request. Jim was charged with criminal homicide by Yamhill County's top prosecutor, Helen Berkowitz. She was small, almost frail-looking, but possessed a steel-trap mind, a rapier wit, and a pair of dark eyes that could flash lightning bolts. I knew attorneys who had turned cases down when they learned Berkowitz would be at the other table.

Jim pleaded innocent, of course, and we learned that Berkowitz intended to seek a grand jury indictment, which got scheduled for the following Tuesday. I asked Whitcomb for a bail hearing as soon as possible, citing the criticality of Jim's work, something that the judge would understand. If that fell before the grand jury proceedings, that was okay, I figured, as long as I got Ballard's and Rodriquez's notes, and any witness statements and lab reports in time to prepare for the hearing. Whitcomb put us on the docket for the following Thursday.

After the hearing, Eddie pumped my hand and thanked me. "So, this grand jury hearing—how big a deal is it?"

I shook my head. "It's a done deal. He'll be indicted for sure. Grand juries are supposed to be a check on the government's prosecutorial powers, but in this county, and hell, in this whole state for that matter, indictments are almost a certainty, a rubber stamp for the prosecution."

Eddie's face fell like a landslide. "Won't you be arguing the case?"

"No. I won't be involved and neither will Jim. The prosecutor and the investigating detectives simply lay out their evidence to the jurors, and they decide whether to indict or not."

"Will an indictment hurt his chances at trial?"

"No. All an indictment means is that five out of seven jurors agree that there's enough evidence to take Jim to trial. Guilt or innocence doesn't really enter into it. Trouble is, people don't really understand that. They hear someone's indicted and they think the person was convicted or will be as soon as the case goes to trial."

Eddie swallowed and shook his head. "Could that tank the business? I mean, who's going to buy wine made by a man indicted for killing his wife?"

"Well, not everyone's misinformed, but it'll test Le Petit Truc's brand loyalty, for sure." That's the best spin I could put on it. The situation was dire, and now Eddie knew it. He left looking like I just stacked a couple of feed sacks on his back.

I met with Jim an hour later at the jail. "So, what's the game plan for the bail hearing?" he asked when they brought him in.

"I just filed a discovery request for copies of the police report and supporting documents. After I look over what they've got, I'll make a determination as to whether we can go on Thursday or whether we need more time to prepare."

"*More time?* Come on, Cal, Thursday already puts me behind the curve. Fermentation's *not* just about dumping some yeast in and taking alcohol and sugar readings, you know. And the beginning's crucial. I have to be there to see it and smell it and touch it. It's an art."

I put a hand up, which was becoming a familiar gesture when it came to Jim. "I know. I'll work as fast as I can, but I won't go into court half-cocked, either."

He lowered his eyes, resignation flooding his face. "So what happens at the hearing?"

"Two things. First we're going to show that you're a pillar of the community, that you don't represent a flight risk or a threat to anyone. Second, and this is the tough part, we need to convince the judge that their proof is not evident, that the prosecution's presumption is weak."

"It's like a trial?"

"Sort of, but more informal. We'll want to call some witnesses to vouch for your character and then raise some questions about their case. I'll have more to say about that after I see exactly what they've got." I hesitated for a moment. "Look, Jim. No promises. Most people charged with murder don't get bail in this state. It's a rarity."

He nodded and put his hands up. "Yeah, yeah, I got the fucking message."

I left that day with another set of notes for Juan and Candice, as well as the names of four community leaders Jim felt might be willing to attest to his character at the hearing, including the head of the local food bank and the chairwoman of a court-appointed, special advocacy program for kids. I didn't know Jim was involved in either program, but that didn't surprise me. He wasn't one to call attention to himself. What did surprise me was his choice of special advocacy, a demanding volunteer job. "Where do you find the time for that?" I asked him.

He smiled with modesty. "I make the time."

When we finished up, he locked onto me with his blue lasers. "Thanks, Cal. I'm counting on you, buddy."

I nodded and gave him what I hoped passed for a confident smile. But I didn't feel confident at all. What I really felt was a ton of pressure not to let this good man down.

Chapter Eleven

I received a copy of the police report by special courier the next morning. It took me two and a half hours to read through the complete file. Lori Kavanaugh had been killed by blunt force trauma, two blows to the head, one of which was fatal. A lug wrench of the type used in Jim's Grand Cherokee was found one hundred seventy-two feet below the turnout on a steep embankment, suggesting the assailant tossed it there after the murder. It was found the next day after conveniently coming to rest against a small tree in plain view. The wrench had blood, tissue, and hair on it belonging to Lori, as confirmed by DNA analysis, and the geometry of her head and facial wounds was consistent with the wrench being the murder weapon. A search of the Jeep and the barn where it was normally parked was negative for a lug wrench.

A core temperature taken at the scene and a liver temperature at the autopsy set the time of death between nine and ten, which put Jim's arrival, by his own admission, squarely within that interval. Of course, we knew this since Lori's blood hadn't coagulated by the time Jim discovered the body.

Her purse and wallet were found intact on the floor of the car. The wallet contained several credit cards and forty-three dollars and twenty-eight cents, ruling out robbery.

It was noted that the suspect said he received a phone call from the victim at around nine thirty on the night of the murder, but Lori's cell phone showed no record of such a call. An incoming call was noted on Jim's phone at 9:32, but it was from an untraceable mobile phone.

The wrench recovered at the scene was also smeared with traces of a lubricant and had several fibers stuck to it. Microscopic analysis showed the black fibers were trilobal nylon, consistent with the fibers from the floor mats in Jim's Jeep. The lubricant was identified by atomic spectroscopy as Chem Arrow 2000. This matched the chemical signature of the material in the can taken from his barn.

I felt some relief that no fingerprints were found on the murder weapon. If prints could have been traced back to Jim or any of his employees, it would have proved beyond any doubt that it was the wrench from his Jeep. The fact that no prints were found was interesting. The killer obviously wore gloves, so it could have been that his handling of the weapon obscured any usable prints. A lucky break, if that were the case.

The transcript of Lori's mother's statement was pretty much what Jim had feared. She described the relationship between her daughter and Jim as "stormy" as evidenced by the numerous times Lori had called home in tears to complain about Jim's behavior. Many of Lori's complaints were centered around Jim's obsession with his work and his lack of business sense, which made her feel financially insecure. Several e-mails culled from Jim's computer painted essentially the same picture. As with the lack of fingerprints, I was relieved that there was no mention of the lunch date where Jim had put his bad temper on public display.

In sum, it was damaging testimony, but couples fight all the time, and there was no indication that Jim had ever physically abused his wife.

I had to force myself to examine a series of eight-and-a-half by eleven, high definition photographs of the crime scene. Lori's head was pitched to her left, resting against the driver's side window. Blood spatter could be seen on the headliner, the windshield, and even in the backseat. The coroner's notes indicated the first blow was to the bridge of her nose, and the second to the right side of her head. The blows were delivered by a right-handed person sitting next to her. It was noted that Jim was right-handed.

Jim wore a light-colored wool sweater and jeans to the crime scene. The pictures of him, both close-ups and full-body shots, showed dark stains on his sweater, jeans, hands, and even his face. The stains were identified as Lori's blood. It was clear from the patterns on his chest and thighs that he had wiped his bloody hands on his sweater and on his jeans. I sat looking at the pictures for a long time. Then I slammed a fist down and fetched a magnifying glass from a bottom drawer in my desk. Archie got up from his mat in the corner with his ears down and gave me a worried look.

After studying the pictures carefully, I pushed myself away from the desk, put the magnifying glass down, and looked over at my dog. "I'll be damned, Arch. Maybe we've got something here."

I spent the rest of the afternoon rounding up Jim's character witnesses and speaking to several Northwest Jeep Dealers and a helpful young man in customer service at the company that manufactured the Chem Arrow 2000 lubricant. I left the office that evening feeling better than I expected. Proving Jim didn't kill his wife loomed on the horizon like a mountain to be climbed, but meanwhile it looked like we just might have a shot at bail, a long one, but a shot.

Chapter Twelve

"How's life treatin' you, Calvin?" It was Bettie James, the first friend I'd made in the wine country. She stood behind the bar at the Brasserie Dundee at a little past noon the next day. The first of several restaurants with serious menus to pop up in town, the Brasserie was owned by Bettie, who did all the cooking.

"Busy. You?"

"Oh, I'm gettin' by." She cocked her head and eyed me. "You involved in that mess with Jim Kavanaugh?"

I nodded. "I'm defending him."

"Figured you might." She slid two wineglasses into an overhead rack, folded her arms across her ample chest, and clamped her eyes on mine. You didn't dare even blink when she did that. "He didn't do it, did he." It wasn't a question.

"No. He didn't."

She smiled, a flash of white teeth against dark skin. "He's a big bear, but no way he hurts anybody, 'specially that wife of his. I've known some bad dudes in my day, and none of them were generous." She racked two more glasses. "Jim extended me a line of credit for some of his pinot when I was getting started. No questions asked."

Candice Roberts arrived just as Bettie was called into the kitchen. She wore jeans, calf-length boots, and a loose-fitting cable knit sweater. An ex-tennis pro and at least six feet tall, her thick, honey-blond hair framed an oval face that looked back at the world with a frank, open countenance.

"Thanks for meeting with me," I said as she slid into the booth.

"No problem. How's Jim? God, I can't imagine that man confined to a jail cell. And to think, he's in there having to cope with Lori's death, too. He really loved that woman."

"Yeah, it's rough on him. I just came from McMinnville. He's worried about the bail deposit."

She rolled her eyes. "Jeeze. Tell him not to fret. We'll be okay. Just tell me when to make it happen." She leaned forward, her eyes brimming with concern. "How do things look?"

"Too early to tell. Right now, I'm focusing on the bail hearing and getting some background information." I didn't mention my search for Isabel. Candice didn't need to know that. We both ordered glasses of Le Petit Truc pinot and the *plat du jour*— spiced apple and butternut squash soup and a salad with arugula, sliced pears, and hazelnuts. "I was a little surprised that pulling thirty thousand dollars out of the business would be so difficult," I said. "Why is that?"

She curled one end of her mouth up and shook her head. "Jim's a great winemaker but a shitty businessman. We're digging out of a deep hole. When he decided to grow grapes and make wine on the property, he didn't just ease into it. He borrowed heavily, you know, to pay contractors to remove the orchards, build the warehouse, and expand the barn. He had to buy winemaking equipment. Of course, he had to have all top-of-the line stuff, French oak barrels, stainless transfer tanks, the best destemmer and bottle lines, forklifts, fencing, the list goes on. The fencing alone cost a fortune. The whole property had to have an eight foot fence around it to keep the deer out. Oh, and then there's the propane cannons to scare the birds." She rolled her eyes again. "Sales were slow in the beginning, of course, and he almost went belly up."

"How did he survive?"

"That was before my time. I think he found an investor who bailed him out. But he's never shared that side of the business with me. Sort of a silent partner, I guess you could say. Someone smart, whoever it is. Jim's got maybe the best acreage in the Dundee Hills for pinot—soil content, elevation, orientation, drainage, the whole package—the *terroir*, as the French say. And Jim's the consummate winemaker, a true artist. That's a great combination."

Our food arrived, and she continued. "Matter of fact, that whole south-facing section Jim's on is primo."

"That would be Sean McKnight's land and Jim's?"

She took a sip of soup and nodded. "And Blake Daniels' acreage, too. Those three parcels make up a huge swath of land most pinot noir growers could only dream about."

"And Sean McKnight wants to grow kiwis at Stone Gate."

She nodded. "Right. Jim went to Sean to see if he would grow grapes for Le Petit Truc. Offered him a good deal, but he turned us down. Sean's pretty set in his ways. I don't think he wants on the wine bandwagon. And Blake Daniels has been all over Sean to buy his farm outright."

I nodded, drank some wine, and regarded her over the rim of my glass. There was nothing delicate about Candice. She ate the way she did everything else, with a kind of gusto, commenting on the flavors and closing her eyes now and then to savor a bite. I said, "What got you into the wine business?"

She laughed. "I was out wine tasting with a friend. It was just after I quit the tennis tour. We wound up at Le Petit Truc, and I went wild over the pinots. Jim and I got to talking, and the next thing I know, he tells me he's looking for a marketing manager. Well, I said—and by this time I was feeling no pain—I have a marketing degree from Arizona State, and I'm unemployed." She laughed again. "He hired me on the spot."

"Says a lot about Jim. Smart man."

"Says a lot about me, too. I hadn't even thought about what I was going to do after tennis, and suddenly I had a real job. Anyway, I fell in love with the business, and Jim, of course. He's the best boss anyone could have."

"He tells me you and Lori were friends. Do you know of anyone who wished her ill or might want to hurt her?"

Candice didn't hesitate. "No. No one."

"What can you tell me about her?"

Her smile faded, and she chewed her lower lip for a moment. "Lori. Still can't believe she's gone. She wanted nice things, she wanted status, and money, of course. I think it had a lot to do with her childhood. Her dad left when she was young, and her mom struggled to make ends meet the whole time Lori was growing up." She dropped her eyes. "I don't want to speak ill of the dead—and for God's sake, don't let this get back to Jim—but I always felt like she had a dark side."

"How so?"

She raised her eyes and looked flustered. "Oh, I don't know… that she wanted a lot more than she had, maybe."

I nodded. "Married twice before Jim, right?"

"Yeah. Lowlifes like her dad, I think. You know how that goes. Then she finally wised up and married a decent guy."

"But she wasn't that happy, right?"

Candice sighed. "No, not really. Lori just didn't understand Jim." She rolled her eyes to the ceiling. "God knows I tried to get her to give him some space and be patient. Jim's playing a long game, I told her, but she just didn't get it. I heard she was seeing a shrink, too, but that didn't seem to help."

"Who told you that?"

"Oh, a woman I know in McMinnville. She's a gossip, but she usually gets it right. The shrink's name is Richard Amis. He has an office in McMinnville."

I nodded. "Wasn't he at the feast the other night?"

"Right. He's a great customer of ours. Kind of a wine groupie, if you know what I mean. Can't get enough of the lifestyle thing. Knows his wines, though. I think his wife has Napa Valley connections in California." She sipped some wine and eyed me over the glass. "He's Willamette Valley's Dr. Feelgood."

"You mean he writes a lot of drug prescriptions?"

She nodded. "Exactly. Well-to-do people in the valley go to him for depression, anxiety, that sort of thing. He's very liberal with the Xanax and Valium, I hear." She held her wineglass up and smiled. "This stuff works a lot better, and it's all natural."

"Did you know that Jim and Lori were talking about reconciling?"

"No. That surprises me. I had coffee with Lori several weeks back. She didn't mention anything about that. As a matter of fact, I got the distinct impression she was seeing someone."

I lowered my spoon and leaned forward. "What gave you that idea?"

Candice gave me a conspiratorial wink. "Women know these things. She looked as gorgeous as I've ever seen her, and that's saying something. Her hair was done, makeup just right, a new outfit, even perfume. I knew she hadn't dressed up that way for me, and when I mentioned how great she looked, she smiled for just an instant and then said something vague, like, 'Oh, I have an appointment after this,' and never elaborated."

I thought of Jim's comment about Lori possibly being restless during the marriage. "Did she ever cheat on Jim?"

Candice took a sip of wine and paused for several seconds. "I had my suspicions, you know, just picking up on some of her remarks."

"Do you know who she might've been seeing?"

"Nope. I never reacted to her hints. I didn't want to know, to tell you the truth." Candice looked past me for a moment and chewed her lip again. "A part of me wanted to tell Jim, but, of course, I wasn't sure, and it was none of my business, anyway."

"Could it have been Blake Daniels?"

Her eyes flared for just an instant and she smiled. "Oh, he's a player, all right, but what gave you that idea?"

I shrugged. "Just a wild guess from something Jim mentioned. Would she have told anyone else? Sylvia, for example?"

"Oh, I doubt it. Sure, Sylvia was sympathetic to some of Lori's complaints about Jim, but Lori would figure something like that would get back to Jim in a heartbeat. Sylvia loves her Uncle Jim."

"What's she like?"

"Oh, you know, she's the devoted wife type, a little uptight for my taste. She and Eddie are all about their investment business. Eddie's supposedly this financial genius. Sylvia handles the office, I think." She made a face. "She dotes on Eddie."

"What about Lori and Eddie? How did they get along?"

"Eddie's supportive of Jim. I think he resented Lori always bitching about Jim and the wine business. But, you know, he's pretty focused on becoming the world's next billionaire."

"Do you know of anyone who would want to harm Jim?"

She lowered her wineglass and leaned in a little, her eyes growing large. "You're thinking Jim's being set up? I wondered about that."

I shrugged again. "Can you think of anyone who would go to that extreme?"

She studied the tablecloth for a few moments. "No. No one around here. Maybe some wanna-be from California or some crazy Frenchman who lusts after Jim's vineyard. I don't really know why, but the wine business stirs strong passions. Sure, it's an ancient art and there's money to be made, but there's something deeper at work, you know?

No, I didn't know, but I was beginning to see her point. Winemaking was a hell of a lot more than fermenting grape juice, and the Dundee Hills seemed to occupy a special niche in that world. That was pretty much all I got from Candice, aside from a confirmation that she had neither seen Jim nor heard of him acting violently toward Lori. We split the bill at her insistence and both slid out of the booth at the same time. She reached to shake my hand, took it in both of hers and looked at me. Her eyes were the color of a river in low light. "I'm glad you're in our corner, Cal. Thanks." She squeezed my hand and then turned and left, her walk demonstrating that she'd lost none of her athletic tone.

I popped my head into the kitchen on the way out and thanked Bettie.

"How'd it go?" she asked.

"Not bad." After all, learning that Jim had a silent partner, something he'd failed to mention, and that Lori might've had a secret lover, was a pretty good hour's work. And there was a chance Richard Amis—aka Doctor Feelgood—might know who the lover was.

Chapter Thirteen

The first thing to catch your eye in the McMinnville Circuit Court was the large Oregon State Seal above the judge's bench. The oxen and covered wagon on the seal were reminders of Oregon's pioneer roots, and the large video flat screen hanging nearby spoke to the state's arrival in the digital age. The courtroom was wrapped in blond birch paneling and furnished with matching benches, tables, and chairs. Wall-to-wall carpeting helped soften the acoustics.

We all rose for Judge Clarence Whitcomb, who came in from a side door, took his seat behind the bench, and gaveled James Kavanaugh's bail hearing into session. The charge was read—criminal homicide—and Jim's innocent plea noted. I had Juan Cruz and two other character witnesses waiting outside. Whitcomb decided to hear the flight risk arguments first so that the two character witnesses, at least, could be on their way.

Completely undeterred by the fact that Jim was accused of murdering his wife, Marcy Duncan, chairwoman of the CASA—court appointed special advocacy—program for the county, sang Jim's praises. "Over the past eleven years, Mr. Kavanaugh has been one of our most reliable volunteers," she told the court. "He's changed the lives of a number of kids who needed support while going through the court system, usually as the result of the disintegration of their family from some catastrophic event." She produced a stack of thank you letters and read a couple of poignant passages that praised Jim.

"Is he involved in a case at the moment?" I asked.

Duncan looked uncomfortable. "Well, his, ah, situation here might change things, but yes, he's been involved—a nine-year-old who's now in foster care. She lost both parents in that horrific car crash on the Pacific Highway several months ago."

The head of the Dundee Food Bank, Clyde Winkler, was clearly intimidated by the gravity of the proceedings but managed to give a decent account of Jim's work on the board of that organization, noting that he donated, not just his time, but dozens of cases of wine for their annual fundraisers over the past five years.

Berkowitz was silent through this testimony, and by the expression on her face, unconcerned that I was showing Jim had strong ties to the community. She would focus on demonstrating that her case against Jim was solid. If she did this, Whitcomb would have no choice but to deny bail, even if the Judge were convinced Jim did not represent a flight risk. The Oregon Constitution made that crystal clear.

I put Jim on the stand next. It was a calculated risk, because it provided Helen Berkowitz a chance to cross-examine him. But I wanted him to tell his story and felt that, as long as he didn't get angry, he would hold his own and project an air of honesty and even righteous indignation.

"Tell us what happened the night of October twelfth," I began. Jim went through his version of the story convincingly and with palpable emotion. When he finished, I said, "Describe for us what you do for a living, Mr. Kavanaugh." He talked briefly about his winemaking business, and when he finished, I said, "Would you consider fleeing the state or country at any point in time during the winemaking process?"

"No. I would not." He looked over at Whitcomb. "Your honor, I'm the one and only winemaker in my operation. My wine won't get made without me, at least not properly. I wouldn't think of leaving."

I swear I saw a faint crease of a smile on Whitcomb's face, but when I blinked it was gone. People in Oregon understand the devotion to one's craft.

Wearing a dark pants suit with flared legs and standing an inch below five feet, Yamhill County Prosecutor Helen Berkowitz was up next. She opened with a cross examination of Jim that went nowhere. I breathed a sigh of relief. My gamble had paid off.

Sensing a loss of momentum, Berkowitz excused Jim and launched into a graphic description of the murder, which included showing Whitcomb several photographs of Lori Kavanaugh's bludgeoned body. Then she briskly summarized the county's theory of the case—that Jim had gone to meet Lori at the turnout, had brutally slain her, and then tried to make it look like he discovered her dead body. She showed Whitcomb photos of the murder weapon, including one showing where it was discovered. "So, you see your honor, we were fortunate that when Mr. Kavanaugh tossed the wrench after this senseless murder, it came to rest against this tree. Otherwise, we might never have found it." Berkowitz peered up at the judge at this point and squared her narrow shoulders. "And we'll show that the wrench belonged to Mr. Kavanaugh, that it came from the very Jeep Grand Cherokee he drove to the scene with."

Berkowitz put Detective Harold Ballard on the stand, and the veteran cop walked the court through the evidence they had, starting with Jim and Lori's strife-torn relationship. He read from Lori's mother's statement, some of the more damaging e-mails, and then in a surprise move, read an account of the infamous lunch, where Jim upset the table and stormed out. Apparently, they traced the restaurant through Jim's e-mail apology to Lori and, being good detectives, followed up with an interview.

From there, Ballard covered the physical evidence linking the murder weapon to Jim's Jeep, the fact that the lug wrench in said Jeep was missing, and that Jim was covered in the victim's blood when the Detective and his partner arrived at the scene.

I didn't find much to question or object to. It was what it was.

When Ballard finished, I cross-examined him carefully to dig for any information that hadn't shown in their report but didn't find anything of note.

I called Juan Cruz to the stand next and had him explain that Jim's Jeep was always left unlocked, and virtually all the workers at Le Petit Truc had ready access to the lug wrench in question. "So, your honor," I concluded, "someone planning to kill Mrs. Kavanaugh and blame it on my client could have easily taken the wrench from the Jeep in question. Furthermore, the evidence presented does not prove the recovered wrench even belongs to Mr. Kavanaugh."

That brought Berkowitz out of her seat. "Which is it, Mr. Claxton? Was the murder weapon from your client's Jeep or are you suggesting some kind of bizarre coincidence here?"

I turned to my diminutive adversary. "This isn't a trial, counselor. I don't have to choose at this juncture." I turned back to Cruz. "Do tools go missing at the winery?"

"Quite often. We have a lot of acreage and high turnover. Things get lost or stolen. That wrench was used a lot." He shrugged. "It might be somewhere on the property, or someone walked off with it. Hard to say."

Berkowitz was back on her feet. "Your honor, Detective Ballard covered the fact that the wrench was searched for and not found."

"The search warrant only covered the barn and immediate area," I countered. My client's winery extends over one hundred and fifty acres."

After Cruz stepped down, I produced a letter from the regional Jeep sales and service manager stating that there were an estimated forty-five hundred Grand Cherokees in the greater Portland area with the exact same lug wrench and black nylon floor mats. In addition, I showed the court a copy of an e-mail from the maker of Arrow 2000 lubricant stating that they sold an estimated fifteen hundred cans of that particular grease in Oregon and Washington over the last five years.

Berkowitz was on her feet again. "Your honor, these statistics are silly. Mr. Kavanaugh's lug wrench is missing, the one we found at the scene contains materials similar to those traced back to his SUV, and his barn—"

"Similar being the operative word here, your honor," I cut in. "This entire case is circumstantial."

Berkowitz shot me a glance that said *Really?* and then summoned a look of impatience for the judge. "Your honor, we all know that if it walks like a duck and quacks like a duck then it's most certainly a duck."

Of course, Berkowitz was right. My defense was flimsy at best.

Hal Ballard gave me a surprised look when I called him back to the stand. I handed him a photo showing Lori Kavanaugh's body and the interior of her car. I said, "Kudos on these crime scene photos, Detective. These high definition shots are impressive."

Ballard nodded, eyeing me warily. He knew compliments from a defense attorney were not to be trusted.

"Your report states that the assailant was sitting next to the victim, in the passenger's seat, when the attack occurred. Is that correct?"

"Yes. And the medical examiner noted the assailant was right-handed, like Mr. Kavanaugh." He shot me a look of righteous indignation.

"Of course, we're not disputing the favored hand of the assailant." I took the photo from Ballard and gave it to Whitcomb. Then to Ballard, I said, "So, when he struck the victim with the wrench, it created blood spatter. Is that correct?"

Ballard shifted in his seat and shot a quick look in Berkowitz's direction. "That's right."

"Let me make sure I'm being precise here. By blood spatter I mean the small, high velocity droplets that were created when the victim was struck first in the face, and then on the head. These droplets have a unique, tear-drop shape or signature. Is that correct, Detective?"

"Yes."

I handed him two more photos. "These shots show that the spatter went in all directions, is that correct?"

Ballard put on a pair of reading glasses, leaned in for a closer look at the photos, and looked up. "Yes."

I handed both photos to Whitcomb, then turned and faced Ballard, who was now avoiding eye contact. "So, tell me, Detective, did you find any traces of blood spatter on my client?"

Ballard shifted again but didn't look at Berkowitz. "Well, we found lots of blood on him. He wiped his hands and that smeared the spatter marks on his sweater."

"What about his face, the backs of his hands, his hair, his watch face, his shoes? Did you find *any* blood spatter at all on Mr. Kavanaugh?"

Berkowitz came out of her chair like she was propelled by a spring. "Your honor, Mr. Claxton has dragged us down into the weeds. We haven't completed all our forensic analyses. This is premature and ridiculous."

Whitcomb swung his gaze from Ballard to Berkowitz, then back to Ballard. "Answer the question, Detective."

"No. We did not find any blood spatter on Mr. Kavanaugh."

"Let me clarify," I said. "You did look for blood spatter on Mr. Kavanaugh, but you did not find any. Is that correct, Detective?"

"Uh, yes it is."

"How do you explain this?"

Berkowitz popped back up. "Your honor, these are details best left for—"

Whitcomb put a hand up. "I'd like to hear the answer. Detective?"

Ballard shifted in his seat again and said in a voice that had clearly lost some steam. "We assumed Mr. Kavanaugh wore some kind of protective clothing during the assault or somehow washed up afterwards."

"Protective clothing? Washed up?" I shot back. "Did you find any evidence of that at the crime scene? Any evidence at all?"

"Uh, no we did not. But, the—"

"Thank you, Detective Ballard. That's all the questions I have."

The room went silent. Whitcomb looked at me, then Berkowitz. "Do either of you have anything else to present?"

I said no, but Berkowitz stood there for a while trying to look unflustered. I could almost hear the wheels spinning in her head.

"No, your honor," she finally said, "just my closing remarks."

"I don't need any closing remarks," Whitcomb said. "I've heard enough. You've both given me a lot to think about. We'll reconvene at one o'clock this afternoon for my decision. We're adjourned."

Juan was waiting out in the hallway and was disappointed we didn't have a decision. I told him I'd call and sent him back to Le Petit Truc. The last thing he said was, "I think the judge's on our side, Cal."

I checked my calls—two from Eddie Manning and one from Candice Roberts. I called Candice first and told her we were waiting for a decision. "Okay," she said, "I've got everything arranged. Just say the word and I'll bring you a certified check. I'm feeling good about this, Cal."

Eddie apologized for not being there and pressed me for a prediction I was unwilling to give. "What's your gut say?" he finally asked in frustration.

"The odds are against us."

Whitcomb was back on his perch at one sixteen. They brought Jim in and we stood together at our table. Grim-faced, the judge eyed us both, then drew a bead on Helen Berkowitz and got right to the point. "Your case may be strong enough to secure an indictment against Mr. Kavanaugh at the grand jury hearing, Ms. Berkowitz. However, I did not find your proof sufficiently evident for the question at hand. In particular, I found the blood spatter evidence, or lack thereof, significant. In addition, I am convinced that Mr. Kavanaugh does not represent a flight risk and that he does not pose a danger to the community. Therefore, I'm granting bail of three-hundred-fifty thousand dollars with the following conditions—Mr. Kavanaugh is not to leave the state without permission. He is to surrender his passport, if he has one, and he is to wear an ankle monitor until the charges against him are adjudicated." With that, Whitcomb gaveled the hearing closed and left the courtroom.

Jim let out an emphatic "Yes" and gave me a bear hug that damn near cracked a rib. "Thank you, Cal. I knew you could do it." Then, holding my shoulders at arm's length, he added, "You'll let Candice know, and she'll bring the money to spring me, right?"

"Yes. We'll have you out of here in no time."

As the bailiff approached to take him back to his jail cell, Jim said, "Tell me one thing. How the hell were you so certain that I didn't have any of that spatter on me? I mean, when you asked that question, I just puckered up and held my breath. The night of the murder, they looked me over with a magnifying glass."

I had to chuckle. "They teach you in law school to never ask a question in court you don't know the answer to. The answer to that question was so obvious I damn near missed it. I realized it *had* to be true. If you didn't kill Lori, then there was no way you could have had any blood spatter on you. It was as simple as that."

Jim was led back to his cell a happy man. I was more subdued, knowing that this was just a skirmish, that the real battle was yet to be joined. Helen Berkowitz and her team would have plenty of time to figure a way around the blood spatter problem I threw at them, and getting a jury to buy a frame-up was always a tough job in any case.

Better to fight the next battle outside the courtroom? I wondered.

Chapter Fourteen

Candice brought the money and passport and then hurried back to Le Petit Truc to meet some wholesale customers. I paid Jim's bail deposit, surrendered his passport, and then waited while he was fitted with an ankle bracelet containing a GPS chip. When Jim emerged, he pulled a pant leg up to display the bracelet, a steel wire reinforced band with a transmitter the size of a small lemon attached. "The price of freedom," he quipped.

A lone reporter and photographer from the *McMinnville News Register* awaited us. I let Jim proclaim his innocence in one sentence and then gave them a terse statement. I was relieved at the minimal coverage, particularly at the absence of anyone from *The Oregonian* or *The Statesman Journal* out of Salem. Not surprising. Like all major newspapers, they had both undergone draconian cuts in their staffs over the last couple of years.

On the way back to Dundee we rehashed the hearing, and then I brought up my interest in Luis Delgado and my search for Isabel Rufino. When I finished, Jim said, "So, you think Delgado might've helped the killer get away and then took one between the eyes for his trouble?

"Could be," I told him. "The cops think it was a drug hit. Anyway, I'm trying to find Rufino."

"Before the killer does."

"Right. I think she knows something." Then I switched to another subject. "I had lunch with Candice the other day. She mentioned that you have a silent partner."

"Oh, she did, did she?"

"Yeah. I'm wondering who it is?"

"It's Eddie and Sylvia."

"Nice of them. What kind of deal did you cut?"

"He and Sylvia have a private investment firm in Lake O. They're printing money. Anyway, they loaned me enough to keep me from going under. I'm paying them back with interest. Winemaking's a capital-intensive business, man, and it takes a long time before you see a payback."

"What if you can't repay him?"

"They get Truc. I signed a note."

I tried to hold a neutral look. "They insisted on your land as collateral?"

Jim shifted in his seat. "No. They wanted to give me the money outright, no conditions. They're the salt of the earth, those two. It was me—I insisted on doing it right."

"Why are you so touchy about this?"

"Jesus, Cal, think about it. I had to borrow money from my sister's kid to save my business. It's fucking embarrassing. I didn't tell anyone about this, not even Lori."

"That reminds me. Candice mentioned Lori was a patient of Richard Amis. Is that right?"

"Yeah. She was, ah, having some depression issues. We thought Amis might be able to help."

"Why didn't you mention this?"

He shrugged his big shoulders. "I don't know. Lori didn't want anyone to know. I guess I was in the habit of not saying anything."

The sky had cleared, and by the time we reached Le Petit Truc the vineyards were bathed in the soft gold light of the dying sun. I glanced up into the hills toward my place and hoped Archie wouldn't be too upset with me if his dinner was late. The first thing Jim did was march into the warehouse to find Juan. I tagged along out of curiosity. The air in the building was even heavier now, a dank, forest-floor kind of odor signifying sugar being converted to alcohol in a chemical process as old as civilization. Jim had Juan take him to each fermentation bin where he pored over the logs, discussing temperatures, acidity, alcohol, and sugar content, and when next to punch down.

When I asked what the latter term meant, Jim said, "The pulp, skins, and stems get pushed up to the surface by the CO_2 that's evolving." He picked up what looked like an oversized plunger attached to a broom handle leaning against a fermenter bin and handed it to me. "We use this tool to punch the crud—called pommace in polite company—down to keep everything well mixed. Go ahead, give it a try."

I mounted a stepladder next to the bin and set to work. Juan laughed at my awkward strokes, and Jim even managed a thin smile. "This is hard work," I told them, and then on my final thrust, splashed fermenting grape juice in my face.

Juan stepped in and steadied the ladder. "Don't quit your day job, Cal."

Afterwards, we found Candice bent over a computer in the tasting room. She looked up and said to Jim, "How's the crush look?"

Jim nodded and clapped Juan on the back. "Not bad. Not bad at all. Maybe I shouldn't have worried so much. I've got you two, after all." He tried to smile, but it failed to launch. I read his look—he was out on bail, his grapes were safe, but the love of his life was still dead.

Juan smiled modestly, and Candice said, "Does that mean we both get big raises?"

"Of course not," Jim said, trying to look stern. "An appreciative boss is payment enough."

At this point, Eddie and Sylvia arrived and after hugs, high fives, and a reprise of the hearing, we sat down at a table on which Candice had set a couple of bottles of his 2012 reserve and a big, crystal tulip glass for each of us. She opened the first bottle and poured a little into my glass. "Do us the honors, Cal."

I swirled it, breathed it in, and then tasted it. "Umm. This will do nicely." I took another sip, closed my eyes, and put a hand up. "Wait, wait, I'm getting something else here…silky layers of fig sauce, and some crushed plum with a hint of cassis, and, oh my God, some pencil lead, 2H, to be exact."

The table erupted in a chorus of groans. Jim actually smiled. "God save us all from wine speak. Just drink it and shut the fuck up." It was good to see my friend relax a little.

Eddie said, "Cal, you sound like that shrink, Amis, the biggest wine snob in the valley, and that's saying a lot."

Candice stopped giggling long enough to say, "Don't take Amis' name in vain. He's a great customer. Which reminds me, his wine bash is this Friday night. Everybody in the wine world's coming."

"Does my invitation still stand?" Jim said.

Candice swiveled in her chair. "Of course, Amis called and made a point of telling me he wanted you to come, unless, quote, unquote, your schedule doesn't allow it."

"How diplomatic of him." Jim swung his eyes to me and raised his brows.

I nodded. "Absolutely. You should go."

"Okay, I will, but I'm inviting my lawyer, too." Jim looked at me again and managed another smile. "When Amis opens his wine cellar, you don't want to miss it. Bring your Portland friend, Winona," he added. "I know she loves wine, and Amis always welcomes attractive women at his parties."

Sylvia said, "We've got another engagement, but it was nice of Richard to include us." Then to me she added, "What happens next on the legal front?"

"The grand jury hearing's scheduled for Tuesday. As I've told most of you, the prosecution will probably get an indictment. They almost always do."

"Even with the lack of blood spatter?" Eddie asked with an incredulous look.

Jim scoffed a laugh. "They're going to say I cleaned up somehow or wore a raincoat or some damn thing."

Juan laughed. "That's stupid."

"Cal's already got a lead on the killer," Jim went on. "He's trying to find—"

I cut Jim off with a laugh and shot him a quick warning look. "Jim's exaggerating. We're just getting started. The only thing I'm sure of at this juncture is that someone's trying to set him up." I didn't want anyone to know about Isabel Rufino or the person pursuing her, even Jim's inner circle.

• • ● • •

Archie greeted me at The Aerie that evening like I'd been gone for thirty years. It was dark, but that didn't stop him from trying to talk me into a game of slobber ball. I made him leave his ball on the porch and took him in and fed him. I was pleased that I had the foresight to thaw a chunk of steelhead in the refrigerator. After putting Leonard Cohen on the sound system, I snipped off some rosemary sprigs from a potted bush on the porch, chopped them together with a clove of garlic and made a paste of it with olive oil and lemon zest. I slathered the paste on the fish, broiled it up, and served it with steamed broccoli, leftover white rice, and a glass of chilled Sancerre.

Archie lay watching me cook, alert for anything edible that might get dropped. When I finally sat down to eat, I raised my glass to him and said, "Here's to a better than average day, Big Boy," and right on cue, Cohen began singing "Anthem." It was my deceased wife's favorite song. My heart squeezed a little in my chest, but I was stronger now, and the song brought more joy than pain. But Cohen was right. There was a crack in everything, but I wasn't sure much light got in.

I just finished cleaning up the kitchen when Archie broke into a chorus of sharp barks, letting me know we had a visitor. He led me to the front door, I switched on the porch light, and we both stepped out on the porch. A truck had pulled past a big rhododendron that blocked my view. I heard a door shut and then a figure emerged out of the darkness and stopped at the foot of the steps.

"Hello, Cal. It's Sean McKnight. Remember me?"

After telling Arch to hush, I said, "Of course, Sean. What can I do for you?"

He clutched a thick, legal size envelope in both hands and squinted up at me. "I realize it's late, and I apologize for barging in on you like this, but I'm wondering if I could, ah, discuss something confidential with you."

"Now?"

"Yes, if you can spare the time."

Chapter Fifteen

I think it was Bettie James who quipped once that the biggest draw at the Joyous Word Christian Center, Sean McKnight's church, wasn't Jesus but the Reverend himself. He was an inch or two taller than me, trim and athletic looking, with long hair that had silvered prematurely and was pulled into a tight ponytail. He had a squared-off, resolute chin but soft brown eyes that rested below a set of dark, yet-to-gray eyebrows. I led him into the front room, switched on a light, and offered him a seat. I sat down across from him and Archie lay down next to me, his eyes on the stranger.

McKnight was still clutching the envelope with both hands when he spoke. "I, ah, stopped by your office this afternoon but you weren't in, and I felt like this couldn't wait another day. I hope you don't mind."

"Not at all. I was in court. What's on your mind?"

His eyes were cast down on the Oriental rug between us and when he looked up I saw anguish and something else, possibly shame, on his face. "You have a reputation for helping people out. I've, ah, I've made a terrible mistake. I need some advice."

Welcome to the human race, I thought. "Why don't you tell me about it?"

He opened the envelope, withdrew a single sheet of paper, and handed it to me. "I received this package at my church office yesterday with this note in it."

Without knowing what it was but out of habit, I pinched the sheet between my thumb and forefinger in one corner and held it in front of me like a piece of evidence. By the looks of it, the note had been written by a right-handed person using his or her left hand.

> These photos are set to be e-mailed to all members of the Joyous Word Christian Center and plastered across social media. If you wish to buy them back, the price is $300,000 cash. We will contact you for your answer in three days. We'll know if you go to the cops. Don't even think about it.

I nodded at the envelope, which he still clutched in his lap. "The photos must be very embarrassing."

He swallowed hard, withdrew three color prints, and handed them to me. They were stills taken off a video clip with date and time stamps on them. The first photo showed a couple locked in a deep kiss inside a car parked in a lot. The low profile of a motel loomed behind the car. The next shot showed the couple getting out of the car. McKnight was in profile, and the woman was looking dead-on at the camera. She was tall and shapely with long, auburn hair and a rivetingly beautiful face. I studied her expression for a moment and thought I saw sadness there, like she knew what she was doing to this man. The third shot showed them going into one of the motel rooms.

I said, "Are there shots of you two inside the motel?"

McKnight nodded.

"In bed together?"

He nodded again. "They're, ah, very explicit. There must have been a camera in the room."

I handed the photos back to him. "I advise you to go to the police. They know how to handle extortion."

He leaned forward, a look of sheer panic on his face. "I can't do that. I want those pictures back, but I don't have that kind of money. I thought maybe you could negotiate with them, I don't know, get the price down somehow."

I shook my head. "I don't think there's anything I can do, Sean."

He locked his eyes on me. They burned with equal amounts of urgency and earnestness. "Look, Cal. I'm not asking this because I want to duck the responsibility. I've never done anything like this before. It was a terrible mistake, and I've fully owned up to God for it. I'm going to do the same to my wife and family and the church." He exhaled a long, plaintive sigh and leaned back. "I don't expect to be forgiven, don't want to be, but if those photos get out, it's my family that'll be hurt, and the church will be destroyed. I can't let that happen."

Of course I should have said no. I had every reason to. My plate was full, and, come on, a man of the cloth, a married man, screwing around? What hypocrisy, right? Deserves what he gets. But there was something about Sean McKnight I liked, and who was I to judge this man, anyway? And nobody deserved to be hung out to dry by some bottom-feeding blackmailer in any case.

As for the full plate, well, like Warren Zevon said, I'll sleep when I'm dead.

"Okay," I said, "we'll need time. When they contact you, stall them as long as you can."

"What reason do I give?"

"You said you didn't have that kind of money, so what would you do if push came to shove?"

He grimaced like I'd shot him in the gut. "I'd, ah, have to sell Stone Gate, I guess. I—"

"That's perfect," I cut in. "Tell them you'll have to put your farm on the market. That'll take time."

Pure anguish washed across his face, and he cast his eyes down. "My God, what have I done?" he said.

"It won't come to that," I said, sounding more positive than I felt. "It's the best way to buy us some time. They might threaten you and demand a shorter time, but hold firm. Meanwhile, I know a PI in Portland who's good at finding people. If we can find this woman, maybe we can apply some back-pressure. I have a feeling she was a pawn in this thing, too."

"You won't hurt her." It wasn't a question.

I looked at him, shocked. "Of course not. But I might threaten her with hard jail time. The PI won't be cheap. I'll need a three-thousand-dollar retainer to get started."

McKnight readily agreed and wrote me a check on the spot. I went to my study and brought back a notebook and pen and had him take me over the whole, sordid tale. The woman's name was Amanda Burke, which probably wasn't her real name. She started attending Joyous Word about ten weeks earlier. McKnight had an open door policy, he explained, and she started dropping in for spiritual counseling. "She told me she was looking for a fresh start with God and with life," he said. "She seemed stiff and nervous at first, but after a while she began to open up." He hesitated and I thought he was going to tear up. "She was so sincere, almost child-like. We had these long, intimate conversations, and I found myself opening up as much to her as she was to me." He shrugged. "Anyway, I turned my back on everything I knew was right just to be with her. But I never felt seduced. It just happened."

I nodded. The truth was, I'd gotten involved with a married woman after my wife died, but I didn't think sharing that would help the good Reverend. When I pressed him on where Burke lived he said, "She was vague about that, said she lived out in the valley, but I figured she lived in Portland."

"Why is that?"

His look turned wistful. "Oh, we met there a couple of times, and she seemed to know too much about the city, the names of the bridges, that kind of thing." A smile creased his lips. "She wasn't a very good liar. She told me she worked as a receptionist in a medical office, but I didn't believe that either."

"Why not?"

"She seemed way too sharp to be a receptionist. It just didn't fit."

I shook my head. "So, all we've got are photographs of her and the fact that she might live and probably work in Portland. My

PI's good but not that good. What else did she tell you during these long conversations? Did she mention friends, relatives, places she frequented, her dentist, *anything?*"

McKnight started shaking his head, then stopped. "Well, there is one thing," he said, looking, of all things, embarrassed. "She has some tattoos—a Chinese dragon about the size of my hand on the small of her back and a matching fu dog on either shoulder blade. They're very intricate. Beautiful pieces of art, actually. She told me they were recent."

I nodded. "Good. That might help."

We finished up, and as McKnight was descending the front steps, he turned back to me. "One thing I don't get about this. Amanda brought up finances a couple of times, you know, very cleverly, by talking about her situation first. I remember telling her the only thing I had was my property. So, they must know I don't have the kind of cash they're asking for."

"Yeah, well, maybe it's not cash they're after." The comment registered, but he didn't respond. "Let's wait to see what happens next," I added. "Let me know the minute they contact you. Better do it in person, not by phone. They're probably watching you, so make sure you're not being followed."

He looked at me, shame and bewilderment vying for dominance on his face. "How could I have sunk this low?" he said more to himself than me.

I had no answer to that.

I took Arch out for a walk after Sean McKnight left. A mist of rain seemed to hang in the air as if there were no gravity, and every now and then the moon would light up between gaps in the fast-moving cloud cover. We were nearly down to the mailbox when a recent arrival in the neighborhood—a great horned owl—announced himself with a *hoot-hoot, hoot, hoot* territorial call from high in a Douglas fir. Arch replied with two soft barks without looking up.

I worried that Sean McKnight left with more hope than was warranted and wondered if the PI I used would have the time and resources to put this on the front burner on short notice.

We turned around at the mailbox just as the moon broke free and cast our shadows on the drive. McKnight had gotten himself into a hell of a mess, but what struck me most was that this blackmail threat could potentially put into play another large tract of land in the Red Hills.

Coincidence? I didn't think so. That triggered another thought—was I now representing two clients whose cases were interrelated? If that turned out to be true, and if their interests began to conflict, I would be confronted with an ethical dilemma. I'd cross that bridge if and when I came to it, I decided.

There was something else, too. The Reverend still seemed to have feelings for the woman who had swung a wrecking ball into the center of his life. I said to Archie in a voice loud enough for the owl to hear, "The workings of the human heart. A mystery I'll never understand."

Neither my dog nor the owl cared to comment.

Chapter Sixteen

"So, you want me to find two young women. One could live here in Portland. The other could be anywhere." It was the next day, and I was having lunch with my friend and private investigator, Hernando Mendoza. I'd spent the morning doing pro bono work at my Portland office and had arranged this lunch at our favorite Cuban restaurant, Pambiche.

"That's right," I said. "Isabel Rufino's on my dime for the murder case I'm working. I, uh, don't want to run up a big bill because I haven't even gotten a retainer yet. Just run her through your databases and see if anything comes up. She's probably undocumented." I gave him a copy of her photograph with her last address in Dundee written on the back.

Nando popped a shrimp in his mouth, licked some orange and garlic mojo sauce off his thumb, and chewed for a moment. "This winemaker friend, he is good for your fee?"

I nodded. "Yeah, but it might be a little slow in coming. He makes world-class pinot noir, but his cash flow's a little anemic."

Nando chewed some more and gave me that skeptical look that always annoyed me. "Time is money, Calvin." My friend had rowed himself from Castro's communist island in a homemade boat and was now an avowed, free-market capitalist who shared his philosophy of economics freely.

Not wishing to hear the lecture that was going to be repeated by my accountant, I said, "The other woman's for another client." I explained the extortion plot against Sean McKnight, gave him the photographs of Amanda Burke, and described the tattoos on her back. "Maybe you could have one of your guys cover the tat parlors in town," I suggested. "McKnight said she told him she had the tattoos done fairly recently. The artist might remember her. As you can see, she's very attractive."

Nando glanced down at the photos of Burke. "Yes, I would remember her. She has great beauty." He shook his head. "A woman like that puts ink on her body to what, make herself *more* beautiful? It is craziness." He swung his gaze back to me. "There are many such tattoo shops in Portland. Such a job will be expensive."

"The tats are supposedly high art, so start at the high-end parlors. I need results yesterday." Nando frowned but took the job. I wrote him a check for two thousand.

We finished lunch, and Nando had me follow him out to where his new car was parked, a metallic silver Lexus GS. "Wow," I said, "this must've set you back."

He shrugged his thick shoulders and smiled broadly. "My real estate business is thriving, Calvin. Everyone wants to live in Portland these days, particularly those moving up from California. Refugees of the global heating."

"It looks that way. I spent the morning counseling folks who are being forced out of their apartments by landlords anxious to jack up the rents." I smiled to lighten the moment. "Don't evict anybody without cause, or you might see me in court one of these days."

He shrugged again. "I took the risk by investing my money. Should I not reap the reward?"

"You're a Portlander, Nando. Do you want your city to become another L.A. or San Francisco? Rents are skyrocketing here."

He gave me a blank look. "Are these not prosperous cities?"

My friend didn't get it, and I didn't feel like arguing the point, at least not at this juncture. He had a heart as big as his island homeland, but when it came to money, not so much. "Stay in touch," I told him. "I'm on a tight time line."

I went back to my Portland office, which still had a faded sign above the door that read Caffeine Central, the name of the coffee shop that used to rent the first floor space. The shop closed shortly after a large Starbucks opened a few blocks further down on Couch Street. The landlord, by the way, was Nando Mendoza. He allowed me to set up a practice there at greatly reduced rent, and now Caffeine Central was a go-to place for pro bono legal advice in the city.

After seeing several clients, I locked up at four and swung over to the Pearl District to pick up Winona Cloud. I'd taken Jim at his word, that she would be welcomed at Richard Amis' party that night. Winona lived on the second floor of a trendy, converted warehouse that used to store bourbon, a smell that still lingered faintly in the walls. She buzzed me in, opened the door, and hugged me. Her raven hair was pulled back tightly, accentuating big, hazel verging to green eyes resting above perfectly sculpted cheeks. When she smiled, dimples drilled her cheeks like tiny whirlpools. Damn, what a beautiful woman. Wearing a turquoise silk blouse, a dark skirt, and black boots, she gestured at the striking squash blossom necklace adorning her chest. "Since I'm going into the white-man's territory, I decided to make my ancestry clear."

"Good idea. Maybe you can dance for them or sing some tribal songs in Sahaptin."

She cocked her head and smiled with sarcasm, but that didn't stop the dimples from forming. "Very funny, white man."

We crept our way south on the I-5, the dense, rush hour traffic another reminder of the southern invasion. It was as if one car too many had arrived, putting Portland's nineteen-fifties infrastructure on overload. I filled her in on Jim Kavanaugh's situation and the plight of the good Reverend Sean McKnight. When I finished, she said, "So you're thinking these two situations are related?"

"The thought crossed my mind. Candice Roberts told me the broad swath of land encompassing Le Petit Truc and McKnight's farm is ideal for growing pinot noir grapes. Both parcels are potentially up for grabs, and the combined land would be exceedingly valuable. Makes you wonder."

She nodded. "The niece and her husband, what do you know about them?"

"Not much. Nice folks. Well off. Very supportive of Jim. They're both into their investment business. If Jim's business falters, they'd have a decision to make."

Winona sighed and leaned back in her seat. I glanced over at her, her eyes shading to green in the afternoon light. Her face darkened, and a muscle flexed on the line of her jaw. "Whoever the killer is, he's a cold blooded bastard who's probably killed two people already, and you're out there asking questions and poking around. Whoever it is won't like that." Winona sighed again, and I could feel the heat of her gaze on the side of my face. "I don't have a good feeling about this, Cal."

I felt an involuntary ripple of discomfort. I'd learned to pay attention to Winona's intuition, which bordered on the psychic. But what I'd uncovered so far didn't amount to much, and besides, we were on our way to drink some good wine.

"Hey," I said, "lighten up. The wine's free tonight."

Chapter Seventeen

"Holy shit, looks like the mother ship," Winona said as we crested a rise in the long drive leading to Richard Amis' house. We came from The Aerie, where I fed Archie and let him out with a warning not to get skunked. I'd changed into my newest pair of jeans, a button-down shirt, and a lightweight leather jacket. With the exception of court appearances, weddings, and funerals, this was about as dressed up as I ever got.

Located southwest of Dundee, off the Lafayette Highway, the house dominated a low hillock that had been meticulously stripped of all native vegetation to maximize the visual impact. The house was circular in design, one story stacked on another with wide eaves, a wrap-around second floor balcony, and spacious bay windows. Lit up from within and silhouetted against the fading light, it looked like it was about to lift off.

I whistled softly. "Jim said the house was avant-garde, and he wasn't kidding."

Winona laughed. "I'll bet the architect had an aversion to blocks growing up."

The front door was open, and we followed the sounds of laughter and conversation down a narrow hall that opened through a wide arch into a room jammed with people. We worked our way through the crowd, me making introductions and Winona turning heads. Candice was right. Just about every mover and shaker in the Willamette Valley wine scene was on hand. I spotted Jim in a corner, standing alone and gazing out a bay window with a glass of wine in his hand. Not a good sign. Framed by the window, he looked even bigger than he was, like a trapped bear.

"Okay," I said as we stepped up beside him, "The party starts now."

He turned and flashed a smile of relief, then pumped my hand and hugged Winona. "Some house, huh? "Come on, let's get you some wine."

He steered us to one of the two wine serving stations in the room, hosted by an attractive young woman in a crisp, white coat. "I suggest you start with a white," he said to Winona, "and since you hang out with Cal, I'm guessing he's brainwashed you about Sancerres."

Winona and I both laughed, and she said, "Guilty as charged. My favorite white by far."

"Okay, I recommend you both try the J. Christopher Sauvignon Blanc that this young lady's pouring. Made from the same grape as your French Sancerre. A little more fruit-forward than that Loire Valley stuff you're so fond of, but pretty decent."

After we secured our wine, Jim drew in closer, glanced around, and said in a low voice, "I'm glad you're here, both of you. I'm feeling about as welcome as a turd in a punchbowl. People seem a little uncomfortable drinking with an accused wife murderer. Can you imagine that?"

"Nonsense," I said. "You haven't been convicted of anything."

Winona leaned in. "I've been there, Jim. Stay centered in your innocence. People will sense it. If they don't, it's their problem."

"Thanks, Winona," Jim said. "Cal told me about your ordeal." Then he managed a smile. "Hey, enough of this pity party bullshit. Come on, let's go meet the host."

Richard Amis stood with his wife in a group of people near a set of French doors that opened onto a large flagstone patio. Outside, I saw a knot of men huddled beneath a radiant heater next to a large swimming pool covered with a blue tarp. I recognized a couple of Dundee Hills vintners in the group.

Talking shop, no doubt. Across the crowded room, a clutch of women were circled in animated conversation. I thought of what Candice said about Amis' practice, and wondered how many in the group were patients of Dr. Feelgood.

Amis saw us approaching and smiled expansively. He was tall and thin, and his attire—a blue blazer, gray slacks, and Gucci loafers—was set off with a crimson bow tie. I guessed he was going for the conservative commentator look, but I thought of Pee Wee Herman instead. His wife, Eleanor, wore an elegant electric blue dress, diamond earrings, and a plastic smile. She struck up a side conversation with Winona and soon after they drifted off together, along with the others. There seemed to be unwritten rules for the circulation of people at cocktail parties, but I had no clue what they were.

After some awkward chitchat, Amis turned his half-shrouded eyes to me. "The arrest was a real shocker. Were you expecting it?"

I sipped some wine, and Jim shuffled his feet. "Well," I said, "I knew the cops didn't have much, but it's almost a knee jerk reaction to charge the spouse in a case like this."

Amis nodded, looked at Jim, and produced what passed for a smile. "Glad to see you out and about." Then he swung his eyes back to me. "Congratulations on the bail hearing."

I nodded and sipped some more wine. I wasn't about to discuss the case.

To both of us he said, "Well, I'm sure you're anxious to clear this up. I'd hate to see your business damaged by this craziness."

Jim shuffled his feet again. I said, "We're pushing for an early trial date. Meanwhile, I think most people still subscribe to the notion of innocent until proven guilty."

Amis nodded and replicated the thin smile. "Well, most of the people in this room certainly do, myself included." He let the comment hang there for a moment, suggesting the rest of the world might view it differently. Then to me, he said, "You've got quite a challenge ahead of you for a one-man law firm. I've been an expert witness in some murder trials, and I know how demanding they can be." He swung his eyes through Jim and back to me. "Do you plan to liaise with one of the large firms in Portland?"

"I hadn't—"

Jim cut me off. "Fuck no, Richard. We don't need any help from Portland." He gestured in my direction. "Cal went to law school at Berkeley and was a big time prosecutor in L.A. We're going to prove my innocence." Jim, my biggest supporter, just added a couple more bricks to my load. He saw it as a one-man show, and I had yet to disabuse him of that notion. The truth was that if this went to trial I would almost certainly have to add another attorney to the payroll.

Amis smiled. "Well, let's hope so."

Two other couples joined our circle, and I excused myself to get some of Jim's pinot, only to find out the server had just run out. I turned around and there was Amis. I must have looked disappointed, because he said, "Don't worry, Cal, I have some more of that in the cellar. Come on, give me a hand. I need to bring more wine up."

I followed him through the archway and down a long hall to a door he unlocked with a key from his pocket. "I keep my cellar locked out of habit," he said as he switched on a light and began descending the cellar steps. "Some of my most treasured possessions are down here."

The steps led to a large room with a stone floor and wine racks everywhere. The racks were fashioned from unstained teak, and one wall featured a rectangular alcove with a huge painting of a vineyard. Fully leafed-out and bearing clumps of purple fruit, the vines in the painting faded into a blood-red and gold setting sun. In the corner, a full sized, white marble statue of a young man, bearing a strong resemblance to Michelangelo's David, stood resting an arm on a stout grapevine dripping with fruit. I felt like I'd walked into a shrine instead of a wine cellar.

"Beautiful painting," I said. "Looks like the Dundee Hills."

"As a matter of fact, that's a westerly view of Jim's lower acreage. Eleanor snapped a photo one evening, and I liked it so much I commissioned the painting. Came out rather nice, I think." I nodded my approval and glanced at the statue. "That's Dionysus," he went on, "the Greek god of the grape harvest, a second century version. The Romans called him Bacchus, of course."

Of course. I nodded again and surveyed the scene—bottles precisely arranged, the shelves labeled and numbered like a library, a stepladder on rollers to reach the top shelves. "Impressive, Richard. How many bottles do you have down here?"

He allowed himself a modest smile. "Oh, last time I looked I was north of five thousand." My God, I thought, he'll never drink that much wine in three lifetimes. When does a collector become a hoarder? He motioned toward the left wall. "Mostly Bordeaux, Burgundy, Loire Valley, Rioja, and Mosel on that side." He swung his arm the other way. "Oregon and California wines over there, with a bit of Argentinean and Chilean thrown in. The front's stocked with wines that are ready to drink, all Oregon tonight." He extracted four six-bottle carriers from beneath the stairs, handed two to me, and nodded toward the front. The Le Petit Truc's up there." Grab six if you wouldn't mind, and three of the Domaine Drouhin and three Carabellas. I'll get the rest."

When we were both loaded up, I said, "Ever think of owning your own vineyard?"

His eyes became full for an instant. "Oh, you know, I'm too busy with my practice."

I nodded and decided to seize the moment. "Lori Kavanaugh was a patient of yours, right?"

He looked at me, his eyes half shrouded again. "You know full well that I can't respond to that, Cal."

"I'm wondering if you know the name of the man she was seeing before she was killed?"

His eyes flared again, stronger this time. He tried to cover it with a look of absolute incredulity. "If I knew the answer to that, which I don't, I couldn't divulge it." With that, he turned and started up the stairs.

"Of course," I called after him, "but a man's life's on the line here. All I need's a name, and no one needs to know how I found out. Think about it, Richard." He kept walking and didn't look back.

I knew he'd turn me down but hoped I'd learn something by blindsiding him with the request. I did.

I dropped the wine off and was threading my way through the crown when I ran into Candice Roberts. She wore a killer little black dress and a loose, boozy grin. She grasped my arm and swayed just a little. "What's up, handsome? Did you bring your significant other?"

"Yeah." I pointed to her across the room. "Winona. The woman next to the hostess."

She giggled then made a face. "She's gorgeous. Crap, and I thought I had a chance tonight."

I laughed. "I'm flattered. Look, Candice, I only know a couple of those vintners out there on the patio. Why don't you introduce me around?"

She squeezed my arm. "Okay, but you're no fun."

Candice made short work of the introductions, and we all watched as she swayed back through the French doors and disappeared into the crowd, which was becoming thoroughly lubricated by free-flowing wine.

"Smartest thing Kavanaugh ever did, hiring her," one of the vintners said.

Blake Daniels, owner of the Rolling Hills Winery, laughed. "He better put her full time on damage control." Daniels was shorter than me and powerfully built with hawk-like eyes, and short-cropped black hair that was just a shade too black to be natural. He regarded me and smirked. "How's it look for your boy, counselor?"

I leveled my eyes at him and smiled without much friendliness. "Last time I checked I wasn't representing any boys."

He held my gaze for a couple of beats. "I'm talking about Jim Kavanaugh. You going to get him off?"

"He never should have been arrested. He'll be vindicated in court, if it isn't thrown out first."

An uncomfortable silence ensued as Daniels and I glared at each other. The owner of Carabella Winery, a former client of mine, stepped in. "Hey, Blake. Cool it. I'm sure Cal didn't come here tonight to talk about this."

"I don't blame him." Daniels shot back. "Looks open and shut to me." With that, he turned abruptly and walked back into the party. Two other vintners followed him.

The Carabella owner broke the second silence by launching into a description of his work with native fescues and wild flowers. "We're planting them to enhance the soil and keep down invasive species without chemicals," he explained. This kicked off a lively discussion of the pros and cons of organic viticulture.

At a lull in the conversation, I said, "I've heard a rumor that outside interests are very keen on acquiring land in the Dundee Hills. Have you guys heard anything?"

They all laughed, almost in unison. The winemaker at Beaux Freres said, "We've all been approached by real estate firms. They want to buy our land at top dollar. But that has quieted down, I think. They didn't find any takers."

"Any idea who the buyers are?" I asked.

He shrugged and looked around at the group. "I never heard, and they weren't saying. Probably California types. The drought down there's hitting them pretty hard."

Another vintner chimed in, "Or the French. They've got their eyes on Oregon as well."

The Carabella owner said, "Well, it doesn't take a rocket scientist to know that things are heating up in California, and pinot noir grapes aren't fond of heat. Lying north of them gives us a huge advantage. We're at roughly the same latitude as the Burgundy region, and the French are always looking for more prime acreage." He laughed. "But I don't think any of us are interested in selling our land. We're a stubborn bunch."

When the talk shifted back to winemaking, I excused myself to find Winona. The place was buzzing with conversation and laughter by this time, the wine having done its work. I spotted her in a circle of women that included Eleanor Amis. As I approached, Winona shot me a rescue-me look. I took the cue and pulled her out, explaining to the group I had someone I wanted her to meet. In truth, I wanted her to taste some of the other great wines being poured that night like the Beaux Freres, Carabellas, and Domaine Drouhins. When we finished the 2013 Beaux Freres, I said, "That got ninety-six points on the Wine Spectator scale."

She nodded. "It was nice, like a basket of Oregon berries, but the Le Petit Truc I tasted had more depth and lingered on the tongue a lot longer. Why didn't *The Wine Spectator* rate Jim's pinot? He would have crushed it." She giggled. "No pun intended."

I laughed. "I guess he wasn't on their radar back then."

After we finished our circuit, I glanced at my watch and exhaled a sigh. "This is about as much cocktail party as I can take." We waved our goodbyes to Jim, who had joined the vintners out on the patio. Jim looked a little more relaxed, and I even saw him smile. Amis had joined the circle of women, who seemed to hang on every word of a story he was telling. "They won't miss us," I said, then added, "Where's Candice?"

Winona laughed. "Probably working on her makeup." She didn't elaborate until we were outside. "I, uh, went down the hall a while ago to find the lady's room and opened the wrong door. Candice was in there with that good-looking guy with the dark hair. They were, uh, not discussing the wine business."

"Which dark-haired guy?"

"He was out there with that group on the patio when we got here. He came back in right after you joined the group."

"Blake Daniels?" I said. "What the hell's Candice doing with that jerk?"

As we drove back toward The Aerie, I explained the bad blood between him and Jim that resulted from Daniels' apparent interest in Lori Kavanaugh. Winona said, "Maybe Candice didn't know about that. She was pretty drunk."

"Maybe so, but damn…"

At The Aerie I got out and opened the gate, expecting to see Archie come charging up the driveway. But he was nowhere to be seen. "Archie?" I called out. "Where are you, Big Boy?" Still no sign of him. "That's weird," I said when I got back in the car. I should have known something was wrong.

Chapter Eighteen

I coasted into the garage, switched off the ignition, and handed the keys to Winona. "It's cold out here. Why don't you just let yourself in. I'm going to find Arch. He's probably gone through one of the holes under the fence on the east side where all the skunks hang out." Using my smart phone as a flashlight, I made my way around the garage and picked my way through the fallen apples I'd yet to rake up. I was almost to the fence line when I heard a scream.

Winona!

I spun around, sprinted for the house and nearly went sprawling when I hit the squishy apples. She screamed again, my name this time. It sounded like it came from the west side of the house. I took the low stone fence bordering the drive like a hurdler, bounded up the front steps, careened around the corner of the covered porch, and nearly tripped over her in the darkness. She was groaning and trying to get up on her hands and knees. "Someone was in your house," she said. "He hit me with something."

I dropped to one knee, adrenaline flushing through me like a tsunami. "Are you okay?"

"Yeah, I think so."

"Where'd he go?"

"Into the backyard, I think."

I peered into the darkness enveloping the back of the house and then started to get up. Winona grasped my arm. "No, Cal.

He hit me with something hard, maybe a gun. Don't go back there."

"Okay. Quick. In the house." I helped her inside, sat her down, and looked at her wound, a burgeoning lump above her right eye with a vertical split oozing blood. I handed her my handkerchief. "Do you need an ambulance?"

"No. I'm okay," she answered through gritted teeth as she pressed the cloth in place. "I heard a noise on the side of the house. Thought it was Arch. Where is he?"

My chest constricted. "I don't know. If you're okay, I'm going to check out the house and then go look for him."

"Go. I'll call 911."

I checked both floors after retrieving and loading the Glock 19 I kept in a shoebox in my closet. The gun was loaned to me by Nando Mendoza, who always rebuffed my attempts to return it. "You live in a lonely spot and have made some enemies over the years, my friend," he told me. "You need a means of defending yourself." I wasn't a big fan of guns, but at that moment the heavy chunk of murderous steel felt damn good in my hand.

Winona's eyes flared when she saw the weapon. "Be careful, Cal. He could still be out there."

"I will. Whoever it was is probably long gone. Keep the doors locked."

Outside, a thick cloud cover blocked light from the waning moon, and the only noise was the faint yip, yip, yip of a band of coyotes down in the quarry. I picked my way back through the fallen apples and went up and down the east fence line calling Archie's name, the Glock resting in my right hand. Nothing.

I started along the south fence line next, working my way through dead blackberry canes and clumps of Oregon grape. Halfway across I found him. He lay next to a gap that had been freshly cut in the chain-link fence. A guttural sound issued from my chest as I dropped down next to him. His eyes were closed, he wasn't moving, and there was a greasy wad of what looked like vomit on the ground next to his head. I put a hand on his ribs. Was he breathing? I couldn't tell.

I scooped up all seventy-five pounds of him, rushed to the garage, and laid him on the backseat of the car. After backing out, I called Winona on my cell. "Come on out. Arch's been poisoned. We're going to the vet." Then I thought of the vomit and nearly ran into Winona as she was coming out the front door. "Wait for me in the car. I'll be right there." I dashed into the kitchen, grabbed a plastic bag, and went out the side door to collect a sample of the upchucked material.

Winona was cradling Arch in the backseat when I returned. "I think he's breathing, Cal. *Hurry.*" She still had the handkerchief held to her head, and she'd lost some color. The handkerchief was soaked with blood.

"You sure you're okay?"

"I'm more worried than hurt, and angry. What about the cops?"

"Shit. I forgot about them." I handed her my cell phone. "Call them back. Explain the situation. Tell them we'll contact them as soon as we can." I took the next curve too fast and nearly spun off the narrow road. "Then call Hiram Pritchard. He's in my contacts. Ask him to meet us at the Animal Care Center." Hiram was a great veterinarian, a good friend, and aside from me and possibly Winona, Archie's favorite human.

Hiram met us at the back door of the center, which was on the south end of Dundee. I was carrying Archie, and Winona followed, holding the bloodstained handkerchief against her forehead. Hiram looked at me, Archie, and then Winona. "Oh, my, we have two casualties."

"I'm okay," Winona said. "Deal with Archie first."

Hiram spun around. "Follow me. I'm all set up to pump his stomach." I lugged Arch down the corridor and into a treatment room. "He's breathing," Hiram confirmed , "but just barely." When I gave him the bag of vomit, he smelled it and shrugged. Nothing caustic or acidic. He pulled back Archie's eyelids. "Pin pricks. He's heavily sedated." He had me hold Arch's mouth open while he worked a clear plastic tube down his throat and into his stomach. The tube had a hand-powered vacuum pump attached at the other end. After several pumps, a chunky, yellowish liquid began to drain out of Archie's stomach and into the sink. When the flow subsided Hiram gently removed the tube. "Now we wait." He placed his hand on Archie's side. "His breathing has evened out some. Let's hope not too much of what he was given was absorbed into his bloodstream."

I felt a surge of hope. "He's going to make it?"

"I don't know, Cal. But he's a fighter, and he has a lot to live for."

Winona clutched my arm, tears streaking her cheeks. I said, "What do you think he ingested?"

"Impossible to say. Whatever it was, I'm pretty sure it was wrapped in ground beef by the looks and smell of the effluent."

"The son of a bitch," I said under my breath.

Hiram looked at the bag of vomit. "Vomiting probably saved him. I've got to report this, and the police can have it analyzed." Turning to Winona, he said, "Now, let's have a look at that lump on your head."

After ruling out a concussion with a quick eye examination and cleansing Winona's wound with disinfectant, Hiram said, "I can close that gash with a butterfly bandage, or you can go to the ER and have them stitch it if you're worried about a scar."

"Can you stitch it?" she said. "I know you've patched up Cal more than once."

Hiram smiled, crinkling the skin at the corners of his soft gray eyes. "Don't tell me you share his irrational fear of hospitals?"

"No. But I'm not going anywhere until Archie comes to."

Hiram proceeded to sew up the wound expertly while Winona sat there stoically, without the aid of anesthetic. She didn't flinch. I wasn't the least bit surprised. She's a warrior.

We settled into the treatment room, huddled around my dog. His breathing was still ragged as far as I was concerned, and with each hesitant breath my heart stopped until the next one came. The time dragged, and it must have been near midnight when he whimpered, a weak, barely audible hm, hm, hm. I got up and stroked his head. "Come on, Archie. Time to wake up, big fella." He opened his big, copper-colored eyes and tried, but failed, to lift his head off the table. "It's okay, Arch," I told him.

"Take your time." Winona stood next to me stroking the thick fur along his side. He tried to move again, this time lifting his head and neck off the table, whimpering more strongly.

Hiram said, "Lift him off the table. He wants to stand up."

I was so elated that he seemed light as a puppy when I picked him up. Holding him around his chest and stomach, I lowered him down onto his extended legs and slowly released him. He stood for a moment before taking a couple of wobbly steps and wagging his stump of a tail. I looked at Winona and beamed, my heart swelling so much I could hardly breathe. Then I hugged my friend, all six foot three of him. "Thanks, Hiram. I'm in your debt. Again."

After walking Arch up and down the hall for several minutes, we called the Sheriff's Department back and were told they had dispatched a patrol car to The Aerie to investigate. As we were leaving I said to Hiram, "Any way you could find out what was in that hamburger? You know, on a fast track? The Sheriff's Department will take eons to have it analyzed, if they ever bother in the first place."

Hiram nodded. "Will do. I want to catch the person who did this as much as you do."

When we returned to The Aerie, a Yamhill Sheriff's cruiser with two deputies waited in front of the house along with an unmarked county car with a single crime scene technician. We gave our statements, which didn't amount to much. I saw nothing, and the only thing Winona knew was that her attacker was a male, because she heard him grunt when he hit her.

I showed them my study, which had obviously been searched but not upended. My laptop was on the floor, suggesting the intruder might have dropped it in his haste to get out. The back cover had been removed, but the hard drive was still in place, and it was still operable. I also showed them the point of entry—a window in the laundry room I'd left unlocked—and the hole cut in the fence. The technician dusted for fingerprints inside and out and photographed a couple of footprints in the damp soil near the fence line, the latter made by jogging shoes by the look of the waffle pattern. The imprint was about my shoe size, maybe a little smaller.

• • ● • •

"It wasn't a random burglary, was it?" Winona said. We sat at the scarred oak table in my kitchen. Archie lay next to Winona, whose bare feet were partially tucked under his chest for warmth. His head was upright and his eyes alert. He apparently had had enough sleeping for one night. The deputies had left forty minutes earlier, and we had just finished straightening up my study.

"Nah. Run of the mill burglars don't bother with places that have big dogs patrolling the perimeter. Whoever did this was looking for something and had thoroughly cased the place."

"Why didn't you tell the deputies that?"

I shrugged. "I was tired and didn't want to prolong their stay. I'll call Hal Ballard in the morning and tell him. He's the lead detective on Lori's case." I shook my head. "Not that it'll do any good. The last thing they're interested in is an alternate theory for Lori's murder."

"We left the party at what, eight forty-five? That was early. I think we surprised him."

I nodded. "I agree. And that suggests he knew where we were." I shuddered perceptibly at the next thought. "If we hadn't come home early, Archie would probably be dead now."

Winona slid a foot from beneath him and used it to gently stroke his flanks. The coyotes yipped a couple of times, and Arch made a grumbling little sound in response. "What do you think's going on?"

"Someone's worried I might know too much." The irony made me smile. "Turns out, I don't have anything but a belief Jim's being set up and some hunches, like maybe the guy who hit you is the same guy looking for Isabel Rufino—"

"The killer."

"Right, of Lori and Delgado. Then there's Lori's lover."

"You think he could be the killer."

"I think she knew the killer, so, yeah, that's a possibility. I think they drove out there together, and then Lori called Jim on a phone that couldn't be traced."

Winona looked puzzled. "Why?"

"I can only think of one reason why she didn't use her cell phone—she thought they were luring Jim out there to kill *him.*"

Winona gasped. "Oh, my God. Then the killer turned on her. Oh, that's cold blooded."

I nodded. "Lori was a patient of Richard Amis, and I think he might know who the lover is."

"Really?"

"I caught him alone tonight and asked him flat out. He denied it, but for a psychiatrist he's not a very good liar. He flunked the eye test."

The coyotes yipped some more but from further away. Archie ignored them this time. Winona snuggled her foot back under him. "Why the elaborate frame?"

"Greed, maybe. Jim gets convicted, or, hell, just indicted, and his winery's up for grabs."

She smiled grimly. "Eddie and Sylvia grab it?"

I shrugged. "Maybe, or maybe it's someone else trying to force the land on the market, someone who doesn't know that they are Jim's silent partners. Jim told me nobody knows about their arrangement."

She nodded. "Or maybe it's not greed at all. Maybe it's simple. Someone hates Jim's guts. After all, he lost his wife and could lose his winery, the two most important things in the world to him."

We sat in silence for a while. Winona wrapped her arms around herself, shuddered, and looked at me, her face darkening. "You need to be careful, Cal. We have a name for a guy like this in Sahaptin. He's a *Kw'alali,* a monster."

I nodded and focused on the discolored, stitched up lump on her forehead for a moment, then looked down at Arch and nodded. "Yeah, it was already war with this *Kw'alali,* but now it's personal."

Chapter Nineteen

That night, Winona slept nestled against my back with an arm resting on my hip and her knees crooked into mine. The warmth of her body next to me was a comfort, but I lay awake long after her breathing became rhythmical. Words, images, and fragments of thoughts tumbled in my head like clothes in a dryer, and, every so often, they seemed to coalesce to remind me of what a close call it had been. They're safe, both of them, I kept telling myself in response. The last thing I heard before I finally drifted into sleep was the *hoot-hoot, hoot, hoot* of my new neighbor, the great horned owl. He was out there, high up in a fir tree with big, luminous eyes that cut through the darkness. What had he seen?

The next morning I fortified us with an omelet made with Gruyere cheese, green onions, and smoked Chinook. Then I called Detective Ballard. "I'm glad your dog's okay," he responded after I finished describing the break-in. "We'll check in with the team that investigated the burglary."

"Look, Hal. It was a hunt for information. Whoever he was just wanted to creep the place. Nothing was really disturbed." We went back and forth for a while, a sparring match in which I didn't land any punches. With the scalp of a cleared murder case on his teepee, Ballard didn't want to hear that he could have gotten it wrong. And it wasn't just him. Prosecutor Helen Berkowitz was busy preparing to win an indictment against my client. The heavy wheels of justice were turning, and I knew it was nearly impossible to slow them down.

Archie and I dropped Winona at her place in the Pearl District and then headed the few blocks to Old Town and my office. Since the situation with Jim broke I'd fallen woefully behind there and welcomed a chance to catch up. It was past noon and I was still grinding away on a mountain of paperwork when my cell phone chirped. It was Lori's stepbrother, Aaron Abernathy. Using a number Jim gave me, I had called him earlier that morning and left a message, hoping I could meet with him while I was in Portland.

"Go ahead, I'm listening," he responded after I explained the reason for my call.

"This won't take long, but I'd rather not do it over the phone."

"I've already given a statement to the police, man."

"I know that. I've read it along with your mother's. This is just routine follow-up. It won't take much time."

After a long pause he blew a breath. "I take my break at two. Meet me in front of The Smiling Leaf on Southeast Division, near Thirty-fifth."

Once a typical, tight-knit Portland neighborhood of modest homes and quirky businesses, Division Street now sported upscale restaurants, multi-story condominiums, and trendy shops to meet the needs of a hip, wealthier clientele that was streaming into Portland like a millennial tidal wave. I finally found a parking space three blocks off Division and left Arch in the car with the windows cracked.

The Smiling Leaf was set back from the street in a converted Craftsman, which, according to the signage, was now a medical and recreational marijuana store. Abernathy stood on the sidewalk wearing sunglasses and a bulky coat. His hair was waved up in front and buzz cut on the sides, which lent emphasis to the big silver rings wedged into his sagging earlobes. "There's a coffee shop across the street," he said as I walked up. "They're not busy, and I need caffeine. We can talk in there."

After we sat with our coffees, I said, "How's the cannabis business?"

He smiled despite himself. "Booming."

"What do you do at the Smiling Leaf?"

"I'm in line for assistant manager."

"Nice. Yeah, I read the other day that sales are running way ahead of projections, which is good for the state coffers, right?"

He smirked. "The taxes are highway robbery, man."

I smiled in sympathy. "I heard you want your own store. Can't blame you."

He sat up a little straighter, trying not to look surprised. "Who told you that?"

"Jim Kavanaugh. He said you asked him for a loan, but he couldn't swing it."

He took a sip of coffee. "Yeah, well, that's the way it goes. Some people are just cheap."

"Oh, so not getting the loan upset you?"

His jaw muscles flexed a couple of times like he was biting down on something hard. He licked his lips and forced a smile. "I got over it."

I drank some coffee and looked at him, wishing he'd take the damn shades off. My best reads came from people's eyes. "What was your relationship with Lori like?"

"Fine. We didn't see each other much, but it was fine."

"Had you seen her lately, like the last several weeks?"

"Once or twice, I suppose, when she looked in on her mom."

"Do you know the names of any of her friends, anyone she was seeing after the breakup?"

He squirmed in his seat a little and nudged his glasses up the bridge of his nose with a finger. "No, not really. She didn't share shit like that with me."

"How about her boyfriend? Did she mention his name to you or your stepmom?"

His jaw flexed again, and the faint trace of a blue vein appeared on his neck. "You hard of hearing or what?"

I opened my hands and put some cordiality into my smile. "Sorry. Just trying to do my job. Would your stepmom know anything about Lori's personal life after the separation?"

He set his coffee down, got up abruptly, and jabbed a finger at me. "She just went into hospice care and doesn't have much time. She lost her only child, and now she's dying."

I lost the smile in a hurry. "I'm sorry to hear that, Aaron." He spun around and started for the door. I said, "Oh, I forgot one thing." He hesitated, his hand on the door knob. "Where were you the night Lori was killed?" I knew what he'd told the police, but I wanted to see his reaction.

He turned around. "I was with my stepmom." I could feel his glare behind the dark lenses as he added, "Let me ask *you* something—You're getting paid to get a killer off. How can you look yourself in the mirror?"

I didn't respond to his question, and he walked out without looking back.

• • ● • •

I took the Ross Island Bridge across the river, and then, after getting off at the I-5 Wilsonville exit, headed west on Wilsonville-Newberg Road. Maybe not the fastest way back to Dundee, but I liked the winding drive along the Willamette River. When I turned off Pacific Highway onto Worden Hill Road, Archie whimpered a couple of times in the backseat. "One more stop and then we'll go home, Big Boy," I told him.

When we arrived at Le Petit Truc, Arch jumped out and followed me into the warehouse, but after sniffing the air a couple of times, he backed out and parked himself at the entrance. I found Jim in the small laboratory located in the far corner of the structure. "How's the fermentation going?"

Wearing a white lab coat spattered with purple stains, he looked up from a thick logbook and smiled. He always seemed happier in his element. "We're close. PH and total acidity are coming into range, and the sugar's nearly there on most of the fermenters."

"What's next?"

"In another five or six days we'll be ready to barrel. We use an old Burgundian trick called *sur lie* aging." I raised my brows and he continued. "We rack off the junk but leave the fine dead yeast cells—called lees—in the wine when we barrel it. Gives us a secondary fermentation that adds richness and complexity to the flavor."

Jim would have gone on all afternoon, but after a few more exchanges, I changed the subject. "So, what did you think of Amis' bash?"

His face clouded over. "Well, I got through it. It was nice of him to invite me."

"Oh, you're his hero, I think. Have you seen his wine cellar? There's a painting taken from a photo of one of your fields down there along with a zillion bottles of good wine, including a lot of your own."

He laughed. "Didn't know about the painting, but his cellar's legendary. Like any creative endeavor, wine has its devotees as well as its artists."

"You see yourself as an artist?"

The question seemed to ignite something behind his deep blue eyes, and he combed his beard with his fingers before answering. "Is that so surprising? I mean, I start with grapes and work them into something beautiful and complex, something people value for aesthetic as well as gastronomic reasons. And they're willing to pay serious money for it. So, yeah, I suppose you could call me an artist, although I really see myself more as a craftsman in the long tradition of winemaking. Did you know archeologists found a wine press in a cave in Armenia that was dated to 4100 BC?"

"BC?"

"Yep. Hell, the Romans were Johnny-come-latelies, but you can thank them for the great wine producing regions in Europe." He opened his big hands, his eyes blazing with intensity. "For me, here at Truc, I didn't want to just grow something like hazelnuts or Christmas trees. I wanted to create something, and the first time I had a glass of really good wine, I knew exactly what it was."

I nodded and smiled, feeling that sense of envy again at Jim's ability to look at life through a single lens. "Well, the Dundee Hills are lucky to have you," I told him, and then watched as he busied himself with some log entries. When he looked up, I said, "Did you run into Blake Daniels last night?"

He dropped his eyes back to the logbook. "Just in passing. He and I avoided each other, as usual."

"Uh, Winona told me she took a wrong turn at the party and opened a door on him and Candice. They were playing tongue hockey."

His eyes sprang up to mine. "You're shitting me."

"Afraid not. How do you feel about that?"

He focused on something past me for a long time, then waved a hand dismissively. "Ah, she was drinking last night. She's a grown woman. She can screw whoever she wants."

"She knows an awful lot about your operation."

He locked onto my eyes, the blue lasers pumping. "I trust her, Cal."

"Okay. Did you happen to notice when Daniels left the party?"

"No, I didn't. Why?"

I unpacked what had happened at The Aerie. When I finished, Jim almost teared up. "I'm sorry, Cal. I didn't mean for this thing to spill into your life." I told him it came with the territory, and after he regained his composure he said, "What's this have to do with Blake Daniels?"

"Probably nothing. But I didn't see him at the party around the time we left."

Jim's eyes got big. "What, you think he was the guy at your place?"

I shrugged. "Just wondering. You told me he showed an interest in Lori, and Candice mentioned that she thought Lori might have been seeing someone before the murder."

He shook his head and squinted in disbelief. "You think Lori was seeing someone, and he was the one who killed her? And you think it could've been Blake Daniels? Jesus." His eyes narrowed to slits. "I'm going to kill the son of a bitch."

I put both hands up. "Whoa, big fella. This is pure speculation at this point. Don't breathe a word of it to anyone, especially Candice. Let me talk to her, okay?"

Jim agreed, but I left him in a highly agitated state, which worried the hell out of me. The last thing I needed was to have this get back to Blake, or worse yet, that Jim did something crazy. That wasn't my only worry. I was unsure how to play it with Candice, and I was still trying to digest my interview with anger-management poster boy, Aaron Abernathy

The expression *May you live in interesting times* popped into my head. The story goes it was a curse the ancient Chinese wished upon their enemies. It seemed to fit my current situation, even though I wasn't sure who my enemies were.

Chapter Twenty

There aren't too many things better than that first cup of coffee in the morning. I'd finished mine, a cappuccino as usual, and it was so good I made another and stood at the sink taking in the view. Although there was a dark band on the horizon, the clouds that brought rain through the night had cleared to the north. Two hawks circled slowly above the valley floor, which pulsed with fall colors—mostly greens, ambers, and golds interspersed with the occasional shell-burst of vermillion. It was as fresh and beautiful as the first time I laid eyes on it, and I knew I'd never tire of that view.

An hour after breakfast, I gathered up my jogging shoes and put them on. I'd seriously thought about having a set of earplugs handy for this ritual, which brought Archie to his feet and sent him spinning in circles and barking at such an ear-splitting pitch that I had to put him outside. When I finally emerged and we started down the drive, he burst ahead, only to stop and look back to make sure I was coming. Working dogs need jobs, and one of his was taking me for a run. He performed his job with the utmost seriousness, but at the same time it filled him with an almost delirious joy.

I walked to the gate, did some stretches, and then began jogging on Eagle Nest, the unpaved lane that led out to the road. It was clear and cold, and it felt good to stride out. But when I reached the junction, a banana yellow Fiat coming from the direction of Dundee pulled up next to us. A tinted window retracted, and Candice Roberts said, "Good morning, Cal. Out for a jog?"

"Oh, hi, Candice. Yeah, my dog's been nagging me all morning. I finally succumbed."

"Um, could we talk for a minute?"

I looked at Arch, who was down the road giving me the stink eye. "Sure, park your rig and walk with me. Otherwise, Archie will have a temper tantrum."

She turned onto Eagle Nest, parked, and joined me, wearing jeans, a sweatshirt, and a worried look. I started walking at a fast pace, which she had no problem matching. She said, "I went in to Truc this morning to catch up. You know, this last week's been crazy. Jim was out in the warehouse fussing over the fermenters. I go in to say hi, and he starts acting all weird. When I ask him what's wrong, he says I need to talk to you." She paused. "I think I know what it is, but, anyway, here I am."

"What do you think he's upset about?"

She shook her head. "I think your friend, Winona, saw me with Blake Daniels."

"I did mention that to Jim." I paused to give her a chance to reply.

She shrugged and opened her hands. "Hey, I was a little drunk. The guy's sexy. What's the big deal, anyway?"

"Blake Daniels is a competitor of Jim's, and you know Truc's business inside out."

She blinked at me a couple of times in disbelief. "You mean Jim's worried I'll betray him to Blake?"

"No. He has absolute confidence in you. It was me who raised the question."

She leveled her gaze at me, her eyes narrowed down. "What the hell, Cal? I'm a single woman, and it's my own business what I do. I would never tell Blake anything about our operation."

I shrugged. "It's my job to wonder about things, Candice." I hesitated, because the next question would tip her about my suspicion of Blake Daniels. She stood there, her hands on her hips, her slate-blue eyes locked on me. They were like open windows, but at the same time they held a hard edge. I decided to chance it. "Where did Daniels go after you two finished making out? I didn't see him later in the party and neither did Winona or Jim."

Her look turned puzzled. "He left early. Didn't tell me where he was going." She rolled her eyes. "Probably had another date."

"What time did he leave?"

"Some time before eight. Why?"

"My place was broken into the night of the party between eight thirty and nine," I said, and began describing what happened at The Aerie.

By the time I finished, her eyes were wide with astonishment. "Oh, my God, you think Blake was Lori's lover, don't you? You think he killed her."

Just like Jim, I had to slow her down. I could see why they got on so well. "No, but I'd like to eliminate him as a suspect."

Her eyebrows dropped for a moment, and then an ah-ha smile spread across her face. "I can go undercover, Cal. He's into me. I could encourage it, see what I can find out."

"Absolutely not," I shot back. "If he is involved—and I have no evidence of that—it could be dangerous."

Her eyes narrowed down again, and she set her jaw. "I can take care of myself. Wouldn't you like to know if he was seeing Lori, or where he was the night she was killed?"

"Sure, but—"

"Then it's settled."

"It's not settled, damn it. It isn't worth the risk."

She raised her chin and pushed her lower lip out, a look I bet carried over from her childhood. "I'm going to do it so you might as well get on board, Cal. I owe it to Jim."

I heaved a sigh. "So how do you propose to go about this?"

She shrugged. "First off, I'll make sure he knows I'm interested. Then I'll just play it by ear, ask lots of questions, see what develops." A smile lit her face. "It's a lot like going to the net in a tennis match—once you commit you have to rely on your instincts."

I nodded faintly and said, "Okay, keep me in the loop, when you plan to see him, what you're going to do, that sort of thing. Agreed? And this is just between you and me."

She laughed and started back toward her car. "You're cute when you worry, did you know that?" she said over her shoulder.

To Archie's eternal relief I started jogging, and it wasn't until I stood breathing hard in the middle of a field of weathered tombstones that I finally gave substance to the partially-formed thought nagging at me—Candice was a clever girl and quick on her feet, but who was it she planned to fool—Blake Daniels... or was it me?

I ran hard the two and a half miles back to The Aerie, with Archie prancing out in front, yelping now and then, an expression of pure ecstasy. After a shower I logged on to my computer to scan *The Oregonian* and the *New York Times*. Halfway through the *Times* I went into the kitchen and came back with a plate full of sliced apples, some walnuts, and a couple of squares of dark chocolate for desert.

After reading and eating, I sat back and propped my feet on the desk, my old roller chair groaning in the process. My thoughts turned to Jim's silent partners, Eddie and Sylvia Manning, the note they held against Jim's property. I Googled Eddie Manning and wound up on the website of his and Sylvia's company, Tilikum Capital Management. The company had an advisory board consisting of Portland business and political heavy hitters and boasted "a proven track record of beating the S&P 500 index through smart, aggressive, and data-driven investments." I learned that Eddie founded the company twelve years earlier using a small inheritance and grew it into a business with a multimillion dollar investment portfolio. In 2013, the Oregon Business Council awarded Eddie its top Leadership Award for his efforts.

I knew *Tilikum* was a Chinook word for people, tribe, or family, so I chafed at the expropriation of the Native word for an investment firm. Among the financial reports I read through—all of them glowing—was a brief item stating that a deal with a for-profit entity called Cornerstone University had been cancelled three months earlier. Tilikum must have been buying up the loans and collecting on them, since the article mentioned that Tilikum bought and collected debt in higher education, health care, consumer credit, and sub-prime loans. I knew how it worked—buy the delinquent debt at pennies on the dollar and hound people for the full amount. I sat back in my seat and shook my head. Apparently, this is what was meant by "smart, aggressive, data-driven investments."

I wondered just how solid Tilikum's balance sheet was, and just how well-off Eddie and Sylvia were. After calling Jim to get his number, I caught Eddie at home and made a date to visit Tilikum Capital Management the following afternoon.

There was one other thing on my mind—today was the day Sean McKnight was supposed to be contacted by his blackmailers. Would they squeeze him or give him more time? I hoped to hear, and that reminded me to check in with Nando on the search for Amanda Burke. I reached his voicemail and left him a message to call me.

I sighed and looked over at Arch, who lay watching me in his favorite corner. "So many balls in the air and nothing to show for it, eh, Big Boy," I said. He wrinkled his coppery brows and whimpered a couple of times. I took it as an expression of sympathy, but he probably just wanted to go outside.

The day stayed dry, so I decided to tackle some outdoor chores I'd been putting off. After changing into an old pair of jeans, boots, and a sweatshirt, I went out behind the garage where a large pile of oak rounds awaited me. Seasoned for two years, they were ripe for splitting, a task I began a few weeks earlier. I pulled off the tarp that covered them and set to work with my ax. I could have bought split firewood and probably should have to save time, but I liked the workout and the satisfying *thunk* when my ax hit its mark and the obstinate wood split, exposing the clean, pale-yellow interior and releasing the faint but distinct odor of the wood.

I was on my third or fourth round when Archie started to bark. I set my ax down and walked around the garage just as Sean McKnight's truck pulled to a stop. I hushed Arch and waited for the Reverend to climb out. Like Candice, he looked worried and clutched another envelope.

"Hello, Sean," I said. "I've been expecting you."

Chapter Twenty-one

"I asked for time to put the farm up for sale, like you said, and he told me if that was the case, he wanted fifty thousand up front. Earnest money, he called it." McKnight grimaced. "Earnest money? He's got a lot of nerve, calling it that." We were sitting in the kitchen, me with a beer and him with a glass of apple juice. His silver hair was down along his shoulders, a three-day growth bristled on his drawn face, and his eyes had retreated into their sockets from lack of sleep.

"What did you tell him?"

"I said I'd have to borrow that at the bank. I've got that much, but I'm not going to part with it unless I have to. I figured that would buy us even more time."

"How did he react?

"He yelled at me, said he wanted it as soon as possible. I told him he couldn't get blood from a stone."

"Good. How did he contact you?"

"By phone this time. A male voice, but garbled. I could hardly understand it."

"Did he say anything else?"

"Just that he'd be in touch, and warned me again about the cops." He handed me the envelope he carried into the house. "This came in the mail yesterday."

I extracted a letter from the envelope and read it. From a real estate firm called Hanson Properties, located in Salem, it stated that they represented a client interested in buying the McKnight property and requested an opportunity to discuss it with Jim.

I looked at him and raised my eyebrows. "Interesting timing."

McKnight nodded. "I've gotten several solicitations like this over the last couple of years, but, yeah, the timing of this one's suspicious. I called the number at Hanson. They told me the buyer's name is confidential and that the party's anxious to close a deal. Any way to find out who it is?"

"Maybe, but if this is connected to the blackmail, you can bet it won't be easy. Where did you leave it with Hanson?"

"I told them I'd get back to them."

"Good. Delay three or four days before you do, then put any meeting off another week. When you get another call from your boy, tell him you're waiting on the loan approval and working on a deal with Hanson to sell."

He nodded again, his eyes filled with anxious concern. "Have you found Amanda?" It seemed like more concern for her than his situation.

"Not yet, but if she's in Portland, we will."

He dropped his eyes, sighed, and said in a barely audible voice, "My wife, Emma, left Friday to go stay with her parents in Ashland."

"I'm sorry, Sean."

He looked up and forced a thin smile. "That's alright. It wasn't much of a marriage, anyway." He sighed again, and his eyes filled with tears that didn't flow. "I told my daughter what I'd done, and I don't think she'll forgive me. I'm going to resign from the church this week."

"We have a shot at getting those pictures back," I responded. "Maybe you should hold off."

His face grew taut, and he stared into the middle distance between us. "No. This is the way it has to be."

Arch and I showed Reverend McKnight out, and he left without saying another word. I went back to the woodpile, glad that I still had plenty of oak left to split. Witnessing the destruction of a man's life was not a pleasant thing, and every splintering crack of the ax made me feel a little better. My home here in the Dundee Hills was my sanctuary, and now it seemed that greed and murder were loose on this beautiful land. I raised the ax and brought it down harder. The round cleaved cleanly, and the two halves spun off in opposite directions like a couple of gymnasts doing backflips.

• • ● • •

I was at Bake My Day the next morning having a *pain au chocolat* and a coffee when Nando finally returned my call. "Good morning, Calvin."

"You're a hard man to get a hold of these days."

He chuckled, his deep voice a rumble. "You know what they say, 'grow hay while the sun is shining.' I am looking at a property over on SE 16th, a big corner lot with a teardown on it. I think I can get four units on the lot."

"Just four?"

Missing my sarcasm, he said, "Well, maybe five, depending on the parking the city forces on me."

"Affordable rents, I hope."

He paused for a moment. "Well, for some, yes. They will be small units but very high end. That is where the money is."

I sighed my response, wondering where the evicted tenants of the "teardown" would go in this insane market, but eschewed any further comment on my friend's business dealings. "Any progress on finding the tattooed lady or Isabel?"

"I have a good man looking for Amanda Burke. Most tattoo artists post their images on the Internet. The first thing my investigator did was look for who is doing tattoos with a Chinese theme."

"The Internet, of course. I didn't think of that."

"Yes. Everything is on the Internet in America. He found over a dozen shops with artists who do Chinese dragons of one form or another. No fu dogs. He will visit them next with the photo of the young woman. Let us hope that she paid with a credit card."

"Excellent, Nando. Time's critical on this."

"I know, my friend. We also have a lead on Isabel Rufino. She is definitely undocumented, but the landlord she rented from told us a pastor at a church in Dundee gave her a reference."

"What's the church?"

"Iglesia Discipulos de Christo. The pastor's name is Gerardo Holquin."

"Good. I'll follow up on that."

"My thought, exactly."

After meeting with a client, who'd been arrested for her second DUI, and then taking Archie out for a stretch, I called the church and Pastor Holquin himself picked up. He said he was leaving for the day but agreed to meet with me the next afternoon, which worked out well since I could continue on from there to meet with the Mannings at Tilikum Capital Management.

At a little past one that afternoon, I called Jim to brief him on the lead to Luis Delgado's girlfriend, and then I reminded him that the grand jury would convene the next day to hear Berkowitz's case against him.

"So, if I'm indicted the press will pick it up, right?"

"For sure. They covered your arrest and bail hearing, and this will be an even bigger deal. It probably won't be good news, so brace yourself."

"I've got it. I'll change the name of my wine to Jim's Killer Wine. What do you think?"

It was a play on Dave's Killer Bread, a popular bread made in Portland by Dave Dahl, an ex-felon. I laughed, glad to hear the gallows humor. "By the way," I said. "Have you received anything from a real estate outfit called Hanson?"

"Yeah. A couple of days ago I got a letter saying they had a client who wanted to buy Truc."

"What did you do with it?"

He laughed. "I chucked it. I get offers like that all the time."

"Can you find it?"

"Doubt it. The trash has been picked up."

"Okay. Do you know if others in the Hills got letters like that recently?

"No, haven't heard anything, but I'll keep my ear to the ground."

"Do that. Look, Jim, if the press calls for a statement don't say one word more than 'I'm innocent' and refer them to me. Nothing else, no matter what they ask you."

I left the office that afternoon wondering about the Hanson letter, which was similar to the one McKnight had gotten. Was the person behind the McKnight blackmail making a play for Jim's property as well? After all, one way for Jim to pay his legal bills would be to sell Le Petit Truc. Or, had the blackmailer blanketed the Hills with requests to cover the one to McKnight? There was a third, less likely possibility—it was a coincidence and the buyer was legit.

As we climbed into the Hills, my thoughts turned back to Jim. Despite my optimistic words to him, my gut was in a knot. I still didn't like our chances. He was short on cash, and I was racking up a lot of hours. The trial date wasn't set yet, but added expenses loomed on the horizon—legal research, PI work, a blood spatter expert witness, and other experts I hadn't even thought of yet. To top it off, my hope of solving rather than trying the case seemed to be blowing in the wind.

That night I dreamed I squeezed through the gap the intruder had cut in the fence, which I had yet to repair. It was dark, but I blundered ahead, only to find myself pitching off a cliff and into the cold, putrid lake that lay at the bottom of the quarry. That plunge into the lake was a recurring dream that mirrored what actually happened to me eight years earlier. I sank like a stone and then clawed my way back to the surface and awoke gasping for air.

I swung my feet out of bed and calmed my breathing. Archie dutifully came over to comfort me, laying his head on my lap. I scratched the fur on his broad forehead and exhaled a long breath. "Damn, Arch, we need a break in this case."

Chapter Twenty-two

The next morning I was treated to a visit from an irate mother and her clearly unrepentant teenage daughter, who'd been arrested for trying to steal a two-hundred dollar pair of designer jeans in McMinnville. I needed more business like a hole in the head, but, on the other hand, I feared that Jim's case might drive me into a deficit position. I took the job. Judging from the spoiled, defiant demeanor of the daughter, I had nothing but pity for the mother. She was heading into choppy water with that kid.

I spent the rest of the morning searching for an expert witness on blood spatter. My first choice was a guy named Anthony Garrett in L.A. I'd gone up against him a couple of times in court down there and knew he was damn good. I left a message for him to call and continued searching. He called back an hour and a half later. He could squeeze me in. His fee was $750 an hour plus travel expenses if I had to fly him in to testify. I swallowed hard and hired him. The case hinged on this science. I needed the best.

I was heading off to meet with Holquin that afternoon when my cell went off in my pocket. It was Hiram Pritchard, my veterinarian. After we exchanged greetings and I updated him on Arch and Winona, he said, "I got the tox screen back from Archie's vomit. That hamburger he ingested was laced with Xanax, a lot of it. Someone ground up the pills, maybe a bottleful and mixed it into the meat. I'm glad you found him when you did. He would have never woken up."

A hot bubble of anger boiled up in my chest as the whole series of events replayed in my head. "I left that party early. If I hadn't…"

"Thank God for that. Xanax is a common anti-anxiety drug that's being used and abused by millions in this country, so I don't suppose this is very useful information."

I thanked Hiram and asked him to pass the information along to the Sheriff. I wasn't so sure the information was useless.

As I walked to my car, I could smell rain in the air and hear the traffic out on the highway. The sun sulked somewhere behind a cover of mottled clouds, and the wind gusted in from the south. With Arch sitting upright in the backseat, we joined the conga line of cars and trucks that had slowed to a crawl because of the work on the new 99W bypass at the south end of town. I didn't complain. The bypass promised to alleviate some of the congestion. It couldn't come soon enough.

The Inglesia Discipulos de Cristo, an old, steep-roofed, single story structure with a three story belfry, had obviously been recently painted because it seemed to glow white in the low afternoon light. The rain had started, so I cracked the windows just a little for Arch, who was lobbying with his eyes to go with me. "I'll be right back," I told him, and he gave me that sure-you-will look.

A woman arranging flowers in the vestibule directed me to Pastor Holquin's office, which was located behind the pulpit. A musty smell suggested the roof leaked, the floors were rough-hewn fir, and the high, narrow windows on either side of the sanctuary were covered with colored plastic to simulate stained glass. A barrel-chested man with dark, liquid eyes and heavy brows, Holquin greeted me with a smile somewhere between cordial and wary. I introduced myself and handed him a business card and a photograph. "I'm trying to locate one of your members, the young woman in the photo. Her name's Isabel Rufino. I think she might be able to help me resolve a legal matter I'm involved in."

He maintained the smile, but his face stiffened. "Legal matter?"

I told him about Lori Kavanaugh's murder and concluded by saying, "I believe Isabel has information that could help my client, James Kavanaugh, prove his innocence. More importantly, I believe she's in danger."

The smile faded, and his eyebrows dropped, kicking up a triplet of vertical creases in his smooth forehead. "Why is she in danger?"

"I think she may know something about the murderer, and I think he knows this and is looking for her, too."

Holguin eyed me over steepled fingers for a few moments. "I know this young woman. She is not a formal member, and we haven't seen her for a while. Her faith has, ah, strayed from the love and protection of Christ." He sighed deeply, and his eyes grew sad. "Drugs are such an evil influence. The devil incarnate."

I nodded. "If I can talk to her I might be able to lead the police to this man before he catches up with her."

"How do I know you have her best interests at heart, Mr. Claxton? She is very vulnerable, you know, and does not wish to go back to Mexico."

I met his eyes and held them. "I have a daughter about her age, Pastor. I give you my word, I will do everything I can to protect her."

He dropped his eyes to my card and flicked it with a fingertip a couple of times before looking back at me. "I believe that you would, Mr. Claxton. The problem is we lost touch with Isabel when she began seeing this man, Delgado. But I will make some inquiries."

• • ● • •

My next stop, Tilikum Capital Management, was headquartered in a four-story brick and mirrored glass building with an imposing arched and pillared portico. Located south of Portland in Lake Oswego, the building sat in the center of an exquisitely landscaped and water-featured corporate campus off Kruse Way.

I parked down from the building, and when I let Arch out he made a dash for the nearest strip of grass and left a pile next to a lovely koi pond. A man exiting the building in a blue suit and red power tie was in too big a rush to notice my dog's breach of etiquette. As he hurried to his car and drove off, I imagined him being sent out to buy up more student debt to fatten the portfolios of Tilikum's wealthy investors.

His uptight demeanor reminded me of my days down in L.A. when I used to suit up every morning, worrying about the tie going with the shirt, and rush off to work in an expensive car, puffed up with self-importance. That ego dance and all that came with it ended abruptly the afternoon I found my wife next to an empty bottle of pills. I was that person then, but not anymore.

The lobby of the building was as imposing as the landscaping— an enclosed space that vaulted up four stories, an elegant reception desk in the middle, huge glass doors to the first floor offices on either side, and a glass-fronted elevator behind the desk. A young blonde, Barbie's sister, only thinner, sat behind the desk. I introduced myself and was sent immediately to the fourth floor where, I was informed, Mr. Manning awaited me.

Eddie greeted me with eye contact, a broad smile, and a firm handshake. He wore a finely tailored suit and understated paisley tie with highlights matching his lavender shirt. The diamond stud in his ear had been replaced with a smaller, more conservative silver disc. In harmony with the building, his office was richly appointed in leather, chrome, and stained hardwoods, with an array of the obligatory photos attesting to a man with important connections. I caught a glimpse of him and Jim posing in a vineyard at Le Petit Truc and a shot of him with Governor Kate Brown. Just a guess on my part, but I figured a blank spot on the wall had been a photo of Eddie with our previous Governor, who resigned in disgrace midway through his fourth term.

"Impressive operation," I said, and that prompted Eddie to give me a flyover of Tilikum Capital Management, a deft summary done with disarming modesty. "People trust us with their life savings, Cal," he told me. "It's a sacred obligation we take very seriously." He didn't mention that a good part of their income derived from buying and collecting debt. Seeing all this financial firepower aimed at vulnerable people was unsettling, but I let it slide.

"We missed you at Amis' gig," I said when he finished. "Good wine was had by all."

He smiled, but his look turned serious. "How did Jim hold up?"

"He showed, and that took courage. His reception was mixed."

Eddie's face clouded over, and he shook his head. "This thing could be fatal to his business."

That was the opening I was looking for. "I can understand your concern. Jim tells me you own a piece of the action."

His eyes registered momentary surprise. "Oh, that. I'd almost forgotten. I'm more concerned about Jim. Le Petit Truc's his whole life, that and Lori, and she's gone now."

I locked on to his eyes. "What happens if he can't pay your note?"

He flashed his boyish smile without breaking eye contact. "No worries. I'll carry him until he gets back on his feet."

"That's admirable," I replied and then changed the subject. "Jim told me Aaron Abernathy approached you about a loan for a cannabis shop. How did that go?"

He laughed. "How do you think? You've seen him in action. He had zero-shit for a business plan. I told him it wasn't the type of investment we were interested in, and that was that."

I got in a few more questions before his cell buzzed. He looked at the screen, then back at me. "I've got to take this, Cal. Sylvia's down the hall to your left. She's expecting you. Thanks, Buddy, and keep me in the loop."

Sylvia's chestnut hair was pulled back and wrapped into a tight bun that accentuated her facial features, inquisitive gray eyes, a thin, slightly asymmetric nose, and a smile that never registered much wattage. But the smile was pleasant enough on that day and radiated a confidence I hadn't seen before. Sylvia was in her element.

"This is some building," I said after we exchanged greetings, and I was seated next to her on a burgundy leather sofa in an office that revealed little of her personality save a propensity for modesty and understatement. Her desk and backbar were loaded with stacks of paper in contrast to Eddie's pin-neat digs. A study in opposites, those two.

"In this business, appearances are everything. I miss our original office in downtown Lake O. It was a smaller building and a lot cheaper."

"You missed a good party Friday night."

She laughed. "I'm sure the wine flowed generously. Actually, we wound up doing nothing that night. We had another invitation, but we were both so bushed we stayed home. Don't let the fancy surroundings fool you. This is a tough business, Cal." She laughed again and rolled her eyes. "Investors are a needy, demanding bunch."

I asked a series of questions about Lori, honing in on her activities during the year she was separated from Jim. Yes, Sylvia saw her off and on during that time, and no, other than the fact that she was adjusting to single life, nothing seemed out of the ordinary, and no, Lori didn't mention that she was seeing anyone or even that she was trying to reconcile with Jim.

"You mentioned her adjusting," I probed. "Did she mention any therapy or drugs she might have been taking?"

Sylvia shook her head. "No, nothing at all. She didn't talk about things like that with me."

I nodded and took another tack. "Eddie mentioned that if Jim's business gets in trouble you would relax the demands of your note. How would you feel—"

"Of course we would," she cut in, her face registering no surprise at my question. "Jim's family."

At the end of my questions I said, "I'm sure Lori's murder came as quite a shock. Did Jim call you the night it happened?"

She met my eyes and smiled, her face revealing a shrewdness I hadn't seen before. "Are you asking if we have an alibi, Cal?"

I smiled back a little sheepishly. "Nothing personal. It's something I'm asking everyone."

"Eddie and I were at a Chopin concert at the Schnitzer with two other couples that night. You missed a great performance."

After she gave me the name of one of the couples, I thanked her for her time and, as I was leaving, turned at the door. "Uh, your company looks pretty interesting. I've got some cash moldering in an IRA. I'm wondering if I should roll it over into something more aggressive."

Her face brightened. "We've got a new fund in the medical field that's just opened up. Pays six and a half percent. You can let your returns accrue or take quarterly interest payments."

"That's a great return. Do you have a prospectus?"

"I'll call down and have Regina give you one on your way out."

"Would my money be safe?"

She smiled. It was laced with confidence. "We've never missed a payment in twelve years. It's a sacred trust with us, Cal. I'll have Regina throw in the last two independent audits, too. Look them over and if you have any questions, call me." She smiled again. "Why let your money molder?"

Why indeed, when I could make a handsome return off the backs of people saddled with medical debt, I thought but didn't say. But I quickly reined in my self-righteousness. After all, I didn't know exactly what was in my meager investment portfolio—oil companies, weapons manufacturers, frackers? Probably all of the above, for all I knew.

I picked up the prospectus and audit reports and read them over while the car idled with the heater on to take the chill off. It didn't take an accountant to see that Tilikum Capital Management had a solid balance sheet, certified by Hicks, Davies, and Todd, a local independent auditor.

Viewing your clients' interests as a "sacred trust" was admirable, I supposed, although that cut only one way—for the benefit of the investor. No, I didn't like the way Eddie and

Sylvia's company made its money. But if I was looking for a financial motive to kill Lori and snatch Jim's property through a frame-up, I sure as hell didn't find it.

To be honest, I was relieved.

Chapter Twenty-three

On Thursday of that week an article appeared in the *McMinnville News Register* that was subsequently picked up by the major newspapers in the Northwest.

Prominent Winemaker Indicted for Wife's Slaying

A Yamhill County grand jury has indicted James F. Kavanaugh, owner of the Le Petit Truc winery in the Dundee Hills, for the murder of his wife, Lori Feldman Kavanaugh. According to Yamhill Sheriff Detectives, Mr. Kavanaugh claimed to have discovered his wife's lifeless body at around 9:30 p.m. on October 3 at a turnout near Parrett Mountain Road in Newberg. She had been bludgeoned to death. The couple, who had been separated for a year, planned to meet at the remote spot to discuss their marital difficulties, according to statements made by Mr. Kavanaugh.

Lead Prosecutor, Helen Berkowitz, told *The News Register* that the investigation had uncovered forensic evidence linking Mr. Kavanaugh to a tire iron used as the murder weapon. In addition, Berkowitz stated that the Kavanaugh's marriage had been strife-ridden and that Mr. Kavanaugh had displayed public outbursts of anger toward his wife in the period leading up to the murder. "When shown the evidence," Ms. Berkowitz said, "the grand jury made the right call in indicting this man for the cold-blooded murder of his wife. The District Attorney's office looks forward to a speedy trial and conviction of Mr. Kavanaugh."

Mr. Kavanaugh could not be reached for comment, but his attorney, Calvin Claxton of Dundee, said, "James Kavanaugh is completely innocent of these charges, and we look forward to proving that conclusively in a court of law." A trial date has not been set.

Chapter Twenty-four

On the afternoon that news of Jim's indictment broke, I knocked off early and drove over to Le Petit Truc to check in on my client. The vineyards that had teamed with workers during the harvest were now deserted, the orderly rows falling away to the south and west like columns of marching soldiers. The work had shifted from the harvest and culling of the grapes to their fermentation, an ancient alchemy that promised to enhance the value of the bounty many times over.

Arch took up his spot at the entrance to the warehouse, and when I entered Juan waved as he drove past me on a forklift carrying a pair of sixty gallon oak barrels. Jim waited for him halfway down a long aisle stacked with barrels on either side. I watched as Juan moved down the aisle and skillfully maneuvered one of the barrels into place high atop three others in a steel rack. Jim saw me and waved. "Getting ready to barrel," he said as I approached. As I hoped, he was staying busy. Work was the best solace for my friend.

"I'm glad you have barrels left."

"Candice didn't sell them all. We've got just enough left to take care of this year's harvest."

"You told me once you don't use mechanical pumps, so how do you go from the fermenters to the barrels?"

He pointed to the forklift. "We pick up the fermenters with that buggy, raise them above the barrels, and then let gravity do the work. Mechanical pumps are bad news. Introduces oxygen."

"Then once it's barreled you sit back and let the magic happen, right?"

Juan laughed out loud. Jim said, "In this business you never get to sit back. Once it's in the barrel we start worrying about the next vintage. But, yeah, the next eighteen months or so is when the true character of the wine develops."

Juan gave me a thumbs-up. "This vintage will be the best ever. You should pre-order your cases now before the word gets out."

"I don't know, Juan. If the wine gets any better I won't be able to afford it."

Jim allowed himself a laugh. "Only if you win in court, Cal. Otherwise, we'll be giving the stuff away."

I watched them work for a while and then followed Jim over to the wine tasting room in the barn, where, he told me, Candice was working on the books. Archie was right behind us, and after being hugged by Candice, found a comfortable spot in the corner from which to observe the humans.

Jim looked at me. "We're short on cash, as you know. I told Candice to pay you out of cash flow, so you need to bill us each month until we get this cleared up. Does that work for you?"

"Yeah." I would have liked a twenty-five thousand dollar retainer, but what was I going to do?

Jim looked at Candice, who sat behind the wine bar with her laptop opened in front of her. "How do we look?"

She winced. "Well, Struthers and Bidwell both called after your arrest and cancelled big fall orders without any explanation. We lost several smaller distributors, too. I've got calls in, but people aren't calling back. It's not a good trend."

"Jesus, Candice, when were you going to tell me this?"

She shrugged. "I figured you had enough on your mind."

Jim tugged at his beard, then ran a hand through his hair. "Well, if customers don't like me being arrested, they're going to hate me being indicted." He looked at me. "But don't worry, Cal, we'll cover you no matter what."

I waved the comment off. Candice looked at me, her eyes hopeful. "Did anything useful come out of the hearing?"

I shrugged. "I don't really know. In Oregon, grand jury proceedings are not recorded. The only thing I'm entitled to see are the jurors' notes, which are never very useful. So, to understand their case against Jim, I'm forced to rely on the police reports almost exclusively."

Jim shook his head, and Candice looked indignant. "That's stupid. Doesn't that give the prosecution an advantage?" she said.

"Among many, yes."

An uncomfortable silence ensued, and I kicked myself for going negative. Jim said, "What's next?"

"There'll be a second arraignment, and we'll enter another not guilty plea. It'll be pro forma like the last one. Once that's out of the way, we'll get a trial date."

"What's the time frame for that?" Jim asked.

I shrugged. "I'll push for an early date, but like I told you, it's a slow process. Summer at the earliest."

Jim shook his head. "Jesus, that long?"

I nodded sympathetically, but there was no way to sugarcoat it. "Maybe longer. The court dockets are perpetually jammed."

Another silence ensued, which was broken by Candice, who turned to me with a mischievous look in her eye. "I told Jim about Blake Daniels."

I rolled my eyes. "Why am I not surprised?"

Candice looked at Jim but spoke to me, her tone earnest. "I wanted him to understand, to trust me, Cal."

I looked at both of them in turn. "Look, this is serious business, and it has to stay among the three of us. Agreed?" They both nodded. I turned to Candice. "Any plans to see him?"

A sly smile spread across her face. "Tomorrow night. His place for dinner. Stay tuned."

I glanced at Jim. He was clearly upset but held his tongue. He was right to trust her, I decided. And it was clear he cared about her.

Changing the subject, I said, "Did Lori use any medications, you know, something prescribed by Richard Amis?"

Jim scratched his chin through his beard. "Yeah, she was taking something for her nerves."

"What was it?"

"Xanax. I didn't like it. I think she was becoming dependent on the drug."

I swallowed my reaction to that news, nodded and went on, "I talked to Aaron Abernathy, by the way. He told me Lori's mom had gone into hospice care."

Jim winced. "Damn. Sorry to hear that. She's probably given up after losing Lori."

"You were right about Abernathy—he's caught up in the cannabis craze. He works at a shop on Division—"

Jim barked a laugh. "They better watch the cash box."

"The man has a temper, and he's still angry that you and Eddie denied him a loan. He probably feels like he missed the brass ring."

Jim's eyes narrowed as he got my drift. "Where was he the night Lori died?"

"He told me he was with his stepmom."

Jim's eyes went flat and cold. "Well, that's shit for an alibi."

I left Le Petit Truc that afternoon feeling relieved that Jim was holding up but also feeling queasy about the financial situation. There's nothing like working without a net. Candice's date with Blake Daniels was a concern, too. I worried about her being too confident. After all, the stakes for the game she was about to play were a lot higher than any tennis match she'd ever competed in. "Call me when you're out of there," I told her, "and don't try to do too much."

News that Lori had been using Xanax was huge. If she was still using it after she and Jim separated, then it followed her lover could have had access to it, and so, too, her prescriber, Dr. Feelgood himself. Okay, maybe the country was awash in Xanax like Hiram pointed out, but the fit was pretty damn good.

Chapter Twenty-five

I'd just pulled in and shut the gate at The Aerie when my cell phone chirped. It was Pastor Holquin calling to give me a cell phone number. "This might work for contacting Isabel," he said. "I didn't call the number. I was afraid I might frighten her off. She has probably heard enough from me and the church. God go with you, Mr. Claxton. I will pray for you both."

I went inside the house, fed Archie, poured myself a glass of pinot, and called the number. What Holquin failed to mention was that Isabel's English was just slightly better than my Spanish, which wasn't saying anything at all. We fumbled around trying to understand each other, so I tried to keep it simple. By the time we finished, I wasn't even sure she understood who I was or what I wanted, but she was surprisingly decisive when I suggested we meet.

"Okay, Meester," she said. "You come tonight. Southeast 158th and Martins Street. You can come at nine thirty. We will talk."

I agreed to meet her there, pleased that we had somehow communicated. Since I was due at Caffeine Central the next day, I decided to stay the night in the small apartment above my Portland office. I called Winona to see if she wanted to have a drink after my meeting. She agreed. Next, I called Nando to ask him to come with me for the meeting with Isabel to help translate. He didn't pick up so I left him a message.

I looked up the meeting place on a map of Portland. Ten miles east of downtown, the intersection of SE 158th and Martins lay between Johnson Creek and the Springwater Corridor Trail, the latter a segment of a forty-mile bike and hiking trail encircling greater Portland that meandered through neighborhoods, industrial districts, parks, and wetlands. The corridor had become populated—some would say overrun—with homeless campers who preferred some semblance of open space to a slab of concrete under a city bridge. She's probably camping nearby, I told myself. The Springwater Corridor would be a good place to hide.

In any case, it had come together rather nicely, I told myself. But there was a little voice in the back of my head that said, *too nicely?*

While Arch watched with his chin resting on his paws in the study, I slipped my laptop and a couple of files I'd need the next day into my backpack, which also contained a change of clothes. When I put the pack on, my dog scrambled to his feet and beat me to the front door, whimpering and wagging his entire backside. He was always up for a road trip.

We pulled out onto the main road around 8:50 as a light rain began falling from a low cloud cover that blotted out what was left of the waning moon. I took the 5 to the 205, exited at Foster Road, and followed it to SE 158th. I tried Nando twice more on the way in but without success. I began to worry about my ability to communicate with Isabel, but our date was set.

I parked along 158th, a half-block before it intersected Martins Road. A single street light provided scant visibility on the deserted street. I sat in the car for a while, just checking the scene out, and then tried Nando again. No luck. I got out after telling Arch to chill and walked across Martins Road in the direction of the Springwater Corridor. I figured she'd be coming from that direction, and, sure enough, I saw the shadowy figure of a woman emerge from a path through the trees. "Isabel Rufino?" I called out.

"*Si*," she said as she drew up close enough for me to see that it was, indeed, the young woman in the photograph. Spiraling mist sparkled in the street light above her, and the only sound was the crunch of gravel under her feet. She stopped, crossed her arms, and looked at me through lashes heavy with mascara. Her face was drawn and had a kind of hardness not evident in the photograph. Innocence lost.

I gave her the friendliest smile I could summon. "Thank you for meeting me," I began. "I want to—"

Her eyes widened, and I heard rapid footsteps behind me before being staggered by a blow to the head. I dropped to one knee and raised my left arm just in time to deflect a second blow. An attacker from the opposite side kicked me hard in the thigh. I toppled over and covered my head as blows rained down on me from both sides. Archie began barking and snarling furiously, and over the din one of the attackers said, "Tell Roberto that we're keeping the fucking tar, man. There's no deal. Tell him to stay off our turf."

"You've got the wrong—"

Both men began kicking me, and I could hear Arch lunging against the car window in an absolute fury. "There's no deal, motherfucker. Got that?" a second voice said.

"Stop it!" I screamed. "I'm an attorney from Dundee. You've got the wrong guy. I don't know anyone named Roberto. I came to talk about Luis Delgado's murder."

My assailants were having too much fun to listen to me. More kicks rained in and one caught me square on the temple. Before I blacked out I heard Isabel's voice, "*Basta! Basta!* Don't keel him."

When I came to a few moments later, Isabel and her friends were gone. As I rose up on my hands and knees blood dripped from my nose, and pain ripped through my body like a serrated edge. Archie's barking turned to a high-pitched whine as he watched me try to stand. I finally made it up and staggered to the car, pinching my nose to staunch the bleeding.

I got in the car, locked the doors and started it up. If they came back to finish the job, I wanted to be able to get out of there fast or maybe run the bastards down. Archie had jumped into the front seat and was busy licking the side of my face and making little whimpering sounds to calm me.

I took stock—I had a lump above my left ear the size of an egg from the first blow, a gash on my right temple from that well-placed kick, and a left arm that felt broken above the elbow. My nose throbbed but seemed to have stopped bleeding. Those were the sites that stood out on a body in more or less screaming pain.

With a clenched jaw, I worked my way over to the Pearl District using the Burnside Bridge to cross the Willamette and found a parking space a block and a half from Winona's loft. She buzzed me in, and I hobbled up to the second floor with Archie at my side.

When she opened the door, she sucked a breath and her eyes grew enormous. "Oh, my God, Cal!" she gasped. "What happened?"

I tried to smile through a thick lip to reassure her. "I met up with Isabel Rufino. It didn't go well."

Chapter Twenty-six

Winona led me through her apartment—an open plan with scarred oak floors and twenty-foot ceilings lined with exposed beams, ducts, and conduits—to the bathroom, which was the only other actual room in the place. She ran a pan of warm water and as Archie looked on began gently dabbing at my wounds and then applying antiseptic, bandages, and words of sympathy. "That's a nasty lump above your ear," she said after she finished cleaning it. "You could have a concussion, you know."

I looked in the mirror. "Doubt it. Both pupils are the same size, and I'm not dizzy or nauseous. I only saw stars with that one." Pointing to my temple, I added, "But this one caused a supernova."

"Ew," she said as she began to clean it. "That's an ugly gash. Where's Hiram Pritchard when you need him?"

As she nursed my wounds I began recounting what happened. When I finished she looked at me and shook her head. "Why did you meet her alone like that? Why didn't you wait for Nando?"

I shrugged and winced from the pain the effort caused. "I tried, but Nando was incommunicado, and I had no reason to expect trouble. I figured I had one chance to see if she knew anything. No way I was going to miss it."

"So you think you stepped in the middle of some kind of drug squabble?" The statement caused her to smile. She held up a hand and looked apologetic. "Sorry, but it was such a colossal misunderstanding."

"I know. I've got to improve my Spanish." That made us both laugh. A bit of comic relief was apparently needed at this juncture. "The squabble was over black tar heroin," I went on. "Maybe Delgado was the victim of a drug hit after all."

Winona considered this for a moment. "I don't think so. If he was, they would have killed you in revenge. Instead, they just beat you up to send a message to Roberto, whoever he is."

I shook my head in absolute despair. "You might be right, but we'll probably never know. I have her cell phone number, but I doubt she'll talk to me now."

"Maybe Nando can talk some sense into her. In Spanish."

"Yeah, that's worth a shot. I'm going to see him tomorrow if I can."

After Winona finished cleaning up and bandaging my head she said, "Okay, let's get your shirt off and have a look at that arm." We both gasped when we saw it was already swollen and turning several shades of purple. I felt a sense of déjà vu and then remembered why. I was in similar shape after a beating from a Russian cage fighter a few years back. A doctor named Anna Eriksen patched me up. I chuckled and shook my head.

"What?"

"I'm getting too old for this."

"Well, yeah. They could've killed you, Cal."

I pointed at the swollen mass. "I traded that for a cracked skull. I'll give it a few days." Winona frowned but knew my aversion to hospitals and didn't bother to argue. As we got up to leave we caught a glimpse of ourselves in the mirror and stopped. My nose was swollen and bruised, and the gauze bandage on my temple was already streaked with blood. Winona's wound, just a week old now, was no longer discolored, but the stitches were still in place.

Winona said, "Behold, the walking wounded," which set us both off again. I never realized a good beating could give you the giggles, but there it was.

That night we slept in her bed, which was three steps up on a landing, like a stage. I lay on my back and groaned for a while.

Winona snuggled in next to me and began gently kissing my eyebrows, my cheeks, and finally, ever so softly, my lips. I said, "I'm feeling better already." My body may have been pummeled but my spirit was willing, and together we found a way.

Afterwards, as she drifted into sleep, a squall blew through and pelted her windows with wind-driven rain. I lay there listening and thinking. Not really thinking so much as trying to cope with the stinging disappointment. My best lead had blown up in my face, and I wasn't sure where to turn next. A good man's freedom, reputation, and livelihood depended on my ability to solve this case. And now, for the first time, I glimpsed the possibility of failure.

It wasn't a pretty sight.

Chapter Twenty-seven

Winona wasn't domestic at all, but she did have a decent drip coffeemaker, and I had a couple of cups and a piece of toast before I felt good enough to climb into the shower. "Call me later," she said as I finally labored my way down her front steps with Archie in the lead. "And remember, if you get a headache or feel sick, go to the hospital."

I waved a hand in response without turning my head, because my neck was too stiff. Winona's grandfather had been a decorated war hero and an activist against the dams built on the Columbia River in the 1950s. She inherited many of his warrior traits and hated injustice as much as I did. But at the same time she was nurturing and compassionate, traits that softened her hard edges. I was damn lucky to have found her.

Nando called just as I pulled into one of the two parking spaces next to Caffeine Central. "I am sorry I missed you last night, Calvin. "I was with a lady friend and didn't realize the battery on my cell phone was dead."

"That seems to happen a lot when you're with a lady friend."

"I refuse to be a slave to my cellular phone. A nasty little ring from it can kill the buzz. How did the meeting with the Rufino woman go?" I filled him in, and when I finished a long pause ensued. "Oh, I am sorry, my friend. These people who attacked you need to be taught a lesson."

I gave him the phone number Pastor Holquin had given me. "Maybe you can contact Isabel and get the story straight.

There's still a chance she may know something about Delgado's driving job."

"Oh, I will do that for sure, Calvin. And if she does not answer or refuses to cooperate, I will go to the Springwater Corridor and hunt her down. After she has told me what she knows, I will also find her two friends and give them a good lesson in Cuban manners."

His voice had acquired a menacing edge. "They didn't kill me, Nando. I've got enough clients right now, so don't do anything crazy."

He saved the good news for last. "I think we have found the woman with the tattoos, Amanda Burke."

A door closes and another opens, I thought. "What do you have?"

"An artist at a parlor on Hawthorne thinks he may have done a dragon for her, but he claims he couldn't possibly violate confidentiality."

"How much of the two thousand I gave you is left?"

"Half."

"Start at two hundred."

After we finished talking, I locked the car and let us into the back of Caffeine Central, took my dog up to the apartment, and fed him some kibbles from a bag I kept for just that purpose. A queue of five or six prospective clients had already formed out on the sidewalk, and when I opened up and invited them in, I said, "We don't do take-a-number here, so remember the order you were in outside."

Portland's a clean, well-run city populated with friendly, inclusive, and compassionate people, but, like any big city in the post great-recession era, it had major problems. Topping the list was a homeless crisis that spawned tent cities of desperate people under every bridge and a gentrification wave that was changing the character of entire neighborhoods and forcing longtime residents out.

I spent the morning tending to the casualties of these problems—a couple of evictions without cause, including a single mother of three who received an eviction notice even though she had nearly a year left on her lease, a young couple from Alaska who had been cited for camping but claimed they were just sitting on their backpacks in Overton Park, and a young man so stoned I couldn't figure out what his problem was. I told him to go to De Paul over on Washington Street to detox, but I doubted he would.

"Why do you do this work in Portland for nothing, Calvin?" Nando had asked me once not long after I'd set up shot at Caffeine Central.

Spurred by the plight of a young, homeless artist with the street name of Picasso, I'd gotten involved almost inadvertently, so I had to think about my answer. "I spent a career down in L.A. prosecuting people," I told him. "In this country, if you're charged with a crime or a civil offense and can afford a good defense attorney, you have a shot at coming out unscathed. If not—if you can't afford an attorney—the system treats you harshly. I was part of that system. I guess I'm trying to give back, you know, tilt the playing field in the other direction a little."

He nodded. "It is better, I think, to be rich and guilty than poor and innocent." Nando accepted the system for what it was, so his statement was less irony and more a reason to pursue wealth. But when the chips were down, my friend had a strong moral compass. It wasn't long after that exchange that he offered me the use of Caffeine Central at a greatly reduced rent.

• • ● • •

On the way out of town that afternoon, I took the Hawthorne Bridge over the river, dropped down to Division Street and parked a half block from the Smiling Leaf cannabis shop. Aaron Abernathy was waiting on a well-dressed, middle-aged couple so I browsed the edibles isle, wondering which would taste better, the Hashey's Chocolate Almond Bars or the Infused Mountain High Orange Zest Mints? He finally noticed me and shot a dagger look my way. I smiled back, and when he finished up he came over to me, his distorted earlobes swaying like fleshy earrings, his face pinched with irritation.

"Looks like the other guy won, Claxton."

I forced a good-natured smile. "Accident."

"What is it now?"

I looked around. "Just curious to see how this retail pot business works."

He nodded at the couple leaving the store. "That was a three-hundred-dollar order. Those folks are going to party down. That's how it works." Then his eyes narrowed. "Get to the point, I'm on the clock."

"How's your stepmother?"

He dropped his eyes, and I saw his jaw clench. "What do think? She's dying." He was taking it hard, no question.

"I'm sorry to hear that. I, uh, do you think it would be possible to have a couple of minutes with her?"

He brought his eyes up. They'd gone hard as steel. "Let her die in peace, Claxton."

I nodded respectfully. "Look, Aaron, I'm just trying to tie up some loose ends."

He held my gaze, his jaw flexed again, and he licked his lips. "Yeah, well, I'd like to tie up your loose ends, believe me, but I've got customers waiting."

I could see his point. From what I knew about pancreatic cancer, it was swift and painful. The last thing Irene Halstead needed was some lawyer barging in on her. On the other hand, my client's life was on the line, and I was on the line to defend him. Maybe I shouldn't have asked permission.

Chapter Twenty-eight

It was pitch black and spitting rain by the time we pulled into The Aerie. When I entered the front door, a blast of cold air followed me, triggering the thermostat above the massive iron radiator in the hall. It came to life with a shuddering CLUNK, reminding me that my antiquated heating system was on its last legs.

I built a fire to take the chill off, and after feeding Archie I suddenly realized I was starving. I pounded some peppercorns and rubbed the course granules into both sides of a small filet, seared it in a hot, cast iron skillet, and put it in the oven to finish it. Meanwhile I added fresh chopped ginger, garlic, and red pepper flakes to hot oil in a wok and then dumped in a bag of fresh spinach and cooked it down while a couple of small potatoes nuked in the microwave. I served it all up—the *steak au poivre* medium rare—with a glass of Le Petit Truc pinot noir.

I think it was Jim who said to me once, 'A glass of good wine can turn an ordinary meal into a delight.' He was so right.

I was tired, and my left arm ached, so after dinner I retreated to a leather chair next to the fire, propped the still-swollen limb on a pillow, and began reading Woodrell's *Winter's Bone*. I must have been dozing when my cell pinged with a text, because I lurched forward, sending the book to the floor and Arch to his feet.

The text was from Candice Roberts: At his house. He's in the bathroom. What an arrogant asshole!

I sent this text in response: Get off your phone and watch yourself. This is not a game!

She shot back: No worries!

I liked her chutzpah, but it confirmed my worry that Candice wouldn't take her undercover work with Blake Daniels seriously enough, that she'd be overconfident in her ability to fool him and extract information. If Daniels fooled Lori Kavanaugh and was possibly behind Sean McKnight's blackmail plot, then he was a dangerous man, indeed. It was a chilling thought, and that night I drifted off to sleep full of worry about Jim's right-hand woman.

• • ● • •

"What in the name of hell happened to you, Cal?" Gertrude Johnson, my neighbor and my accountant asked me. It was Saturday morning, and we'd met up to chat at the fence line separating our properties, a habit we developed over the years. I gave her a brief description of the attack, blaming it on a miscommunication but without giving her many details. She made it clear she was skeptical of my story but let it pass, choosing instead to impart cheery news. "Your receivables are down over twenty percent. That is not a sustainable trend."

I shuffled my feet and averted her steady gaze. A semi-retired forensic accountant, Gertie did my books more out of pity than any need for income. Her hair was dark with streaks of pewter, and her eyes were robin egg blue, their brightness undiminished with age. She wore that no-nonsense look that I was sure she saved just for me. "Kavanaugh's going to pay me on a monthly basis," I offered up. "That should help."

She pursed her lips and nodded. "Well, you better tally up his hours and round up when you do." Then she added, "You know, Cal, you could make that twenty percent up if you stopped your pro bono work for a while. Losing that day plus the rent on the building's killing you."

"Aw, come on, Gertie, you know I'm not going to do that. I'll get back on track."

She drew a corner of her mouth up into a half-smile and nodded. "Sure you will. By the way, I just read in *The Oregonian* the other day that Portland has the hottest rental market in the U.S. Mendoza could probably quadruple his income at Caffeine Central. He's not going to jack up your rent, is he?" A fifth-generation Oregonian, Gertie was skeptical of foreigners, particularly individuals coming from a communist country whose collusion with the Russians almost triggered World War III.

I laughed, hoping it didn't sound forced. "Of course not. Nando wouldn't do that." But to myself I said, he wouldn't, would he? I quelled that disquieting thought and changed the subject. "Speaking of money, I just heard about a screaming deal." Her forehead wrinkled up at me. I had no standing with her when it came to money. "Uh, there's an investment firm in Lake Oswego that's offering six and half percent returns."

Her look turned full-blown skeptical. "That's a high return for this environment. Must be for the one percent."

I nodded. "They buy debt cheap and collect on it."

She scowled and shook her head. "You're not think—"

"No. I wouldn't touch it, even if I had the two hundred and fifty thousand minimum, which I don't."

"Good," she said. "Those gains are tainted." We finished up, and I watched as she strode up her south pasture with long, purposeful strides, her boots leaving heavy prints in the still green grass. Before she left, she promised me a blueberry pie from fruit she froze last summer. Gertie made her pies from scratch, and there simply wasn't anything better. She must have felt sorry for me.

I walked back down through the vegetable garden, a fallow, weed-choked field now, and into the garage, gathered up a coil of heavy galvanized wire and a stout pair of wire cutters, and headed down to the south fence line. My arm wasn't feeling much better, but I wanted to repair the hole cut in the fence by the intruder who poisoned Archie and attacked Winona. The fence was installed by the mining company that had extracted and crushed basalt from a deep seam running east to west below my property line. The seam was depleted years before I moved in, but the six-foot chain-link fence was still standing virtually good as new. The intruder had cut a three-foot vertical slice in the links and forced the two sides apart, creating just enough space for him to squeeze through. I imagined him doing that while Arch lay dying on the other side, and a fresh wave of anger washed over me.

When I tried to bend the two stiff sides back in place I nicked my hand. "*Ouch*. Should have worn gloves," I said to Archie, who lay on the damp grass next to me with his ears down and his big, watchful eyes tracking my every move. I ran a finger lightly along the jagged tips of the severed wire. They were sharp as razors, their cut edges like shark's teeth in a leering, vertical mouth. Archie got up, wagged his backside, and whimpered in sympathy. I wondered how much of his ordeal he remembered. By the look in his eyes, a lot, I decided.

I'd just finished bandaging my hand when my cell buzzed in my pocket. "Two hundred is not enough," Nando said, as if we had never ended our previous conversation.

He was referring to the recalcitrant tattoo artist. "Okay. Double it. Anything beyond that, I'll have to get the client to sign off."

"I hope this tattooed lady is worth it," he responded.

"You and me both."

I had no sooner signed off with Nando than Archie announced a visitor. I went out the kitchen door and rounded the porch just as Candice was getting out of her Fiat. She looked none the worse for wear having spent an evening with Blake Daniels. Archie greeted her like a long-lost friend and, dropping to one knee, she reciprocated. I smiled at my dog's behavior and knew instinctively that the two of them would get on.

After explaining my appearance once again, I invited her in and we sat down at the kitchen table. She wore a maroon visor, maroon and gold sweats with ASU emblazoned across the top and down the pant legs, and white tennis shoes. She smiled a bit sheepishly. "Pardon the outfit. I've been playing tennis in

McMinnville. I play a guy every Saturday who played at the U of O. We make it a kind of Pac 12 rivalry thing."

"Who won?"

She beamed a smile. "I did."

I wasn't surprised. She was tall and trim and moved with the fluid grace of a true athlete. "So, how did it go with Blake last night?"

The smile faded. "Oh, God. To think I was actually interested in him. He can't pass a mirror without stopping to admire himself, and he may own a winery, but he doesn't particularly like wine. He drinks Scotch, lots of it." The smile reappeared. "But he's into me. He's taking me to dinner tomorrow night at the Joel Palmer House."

"Did you pick anything up?"

"Not yet, but I did learn he gets really talkative after he's had two or three drinks. I brought up Lori early on, probably too early." She laughed. "I told him you had the nerve to ask me where I was the night she was killed. Then I said, 'Better watch out, he might ask you next,' you know, as a joke. He laughed at that, but let it drop right there without another word."

"Interesting, but, uh, that's skating pretty close to the edge, don't you think?"

She shook her head. "Nah, he bought it. What was even more interesting—after a couple of belts he started asking me questions about Truc."

"What kind of questions?"

"Oh, he started out real general, you know, how's it going over there? But he kept getting more and more specific about customers and sales, that sort of thing. I didn't tell him anything that's not already public information, but I have a feeling more questions are coming." She laughed. "I finally had to start making out with him to shut him up."

I groaned and fought back the image forming in my head. We talked some more, and when we finished up I shook my head and exhaled. "I still don't like this, Candice. It's too damn risky. You should stop right now."

Her face hardened the way I imagined it looked when she was about to blow a ninety mile-an-hour serve by an opponent. "No way, Cal. I can handle this guy."

To be honest, I went through the motions knowing she wouldn't change her mind. Candice knew no fear, but that just meant she knew no fear within the universe she inhabited. I'd seen much, much more than her and knew there was plenty out there to be afraid of.

In the best case, Blake Daniels was an alcoholic creep. In the worst case…well, I didn't want to think about that.

Chapter Twenty-nine

Jim's second arraignment came and went the following Monday without incident. On Tuesday morning of that week, I took Arch out for a walk and then crossed the 99W for a coffee at Bake My Day, determined to resist having a *pain au chocolat*. The sun had made a surprise appearance, and the fall air sparkled like a jewel. To my surprise, Blake Daniels sat at a small table in the back, absorbed in the *Wall Street Journal* and sipping a coffee. He was an occasional customer at the bakery, but I hadn't seen him there since the murder.

When my double cappuccino came up, I took it and pulled up a chair at the table next to him. His facial skin was taut and surprisingly tanned, his hair swept straight back in a dark, undulating wave. I found myself wondering how I'd look with dyed hair. His eyes registered something between surprise and enmity when he looked up at me. "Well, if it isn't Dundee's answer to Perry Mason, or is it Robert Kardashian?" he said, grinning at what he obviously considered a clever remark.

I sipped my coffee and forced a smile to hide a ripple of anger. "I've been called worse."

He returned the smile. It was edged with delight. "Did you get those bruises in court the other day? Looks like you got a steep hill to climb, counselor."

I shrugged. "Indictments are a dime a dozen. Jim Kavanaugh's out on bail, and that only happens in murder arrests when the prosecution's case is weak."

Blake smiled again, but it was his turn to force it. "You're his lawyer. What else are you going to say?"

"Mind if I ask you something?"

He leaned back a little, wary. "Be my guest."

"Have you received an offer to buy your place from a real estate firm called Hanson?"

His eyebrows rose. "Yeah, I did. So what? Offers like that come in all the time."

"Just wondering how widespread it was." Managing a more relaxed smile, I added, "Did you enjoy Amis' bash?"

His face clouded over faster than an Oregon day. "The man has no taste in wine. I offered him five cases of my best stuff, and he told me he couldn't fit me in." He lifted his hawk eyes, and their color intensified as if a fire had ignited behind them. "But he was pouring plenty of Kavanaugh's swill."

I nodded and gave him what I hoped was a sympathetic look. "I don't blame you for leaving the party early."

He blinked a couple of times, as if he were turning the comment over. His cold-burning eyes stayed on me. "What's it to you when I leave a party?"

I waved a hand dismissively. "Nothing. Just wondered why you left early and now I know. Amis wasn't pouring the right wines."

He got up, folded the paper, put it under his arm, and faced me. His eyes narrowed down, and his face grew rigid. "It's a damn shame what Kavanaugh did to that beautiful woman. If you get him off, you better be thinking about a new place to live because you're not going to be welcome in Dundee." With that he turned and left.

I drained my coffee and went outside to fetch Arch. He popped up and began wagging his backside. "Which is it, Big Boy," I asked him, "Perry Mason or Robert Kardashian?"

• • ● •• •

"Found her," Nando said when I answered his mid-morning call. "The extra two-hundred dollars tipped the balance. Her name is Maura Conisson." He spelled it for me. "She's thirty-eight years old, single mother of a seven-year-old son named Joshua. Works as a pharmaceutical sales rep for an outfit called Fizon. They distribute for Pfizer and other big drug companies. They're downtown in the Fox Tower. She lives in North Portland, off Mississippi." He gave me her address and cell number. Nando was a thorough investigator.

"Nice work. What else have you got?"

"We watched her movements yesterday. "She left for work at seven fifteen, parked in the SmartPark at Tenth and Yamhill, and stopped in at Elephant's Deli for a coffee and roll, which she took up to her office. She was back down at Elephant's around noon for lunch and left the Fox at around five fifteen. Drove straight home. We did not see her son coming or going. She is in sales, so she probably travels, but we do not know her schedule."

"Anything else?"

"I have run a complete background check on her. She is from Seattle and went to Seattle University, a biology major. No priors. Her husband died six years ago. Brain aneurism. I will send the complete report in a PDF file. Do you want us to track her tomorrow?"

"No. This is great, Nando. "I'll take it from here. Uh, anything on Isabel Rufino?

"Not yet. No one answers at the number you gave me. But I can now put the man who found Maura on this job. He is my best investigator."

I cleared my calendar for the next two days and then called Sean McKnight. After I gave him the news and we discussed what I planned to do next, he sighed into the phone, the sound of a defeated man. "I suppose it's still worth all this to get the photos back."

"Listen Sean, we can take another tack. We probably have enough now to go to the police and have her and whoever's behind this busted. Of course, that means the photos could possibly see the light of day along with a lot of publicity."

There was a long pause before he sighed again. "No. Let's stay the course. I owe it to my family and the church, and Amanda...I mean, Maura. My heart tells me she's a victim here, too. I'll be praying for you, Cal."

I punched off and smiled grimly at the Reverend's promise of divine communication. The last time someone told me they were going to pray for me, I got the crap beaten out of me.

I called Winona next and told her what was up and that I was coming into town for at least one night. "I want to talk to you about strategy. I'll have one shot at this and I don't want to blow it again."

She laughed. "Okay. My consultation fee for how to approach a shady female is that you cook dinner tonight."

"It's a deal, provided you do the grocery shopping." She agreed and I gave her a list of ingredients I would need.

• • ● • •

"Oh, you brought the good stuff," Winona said as she removed the two bottles of wine from a bag I'd placed on the counter, one bottle of Jim's 2012 reserve pinot and a younger wine from a neighboring vineyard. I opened the younger bottle first and poured us each a glass. She'd already changed the bandage covering the gash on my temple and examined my bruised left arm, which was less sore and swollen each day. She'd had the stitches removed from her forehead that week, and although the whitish scar stood out against her burnished copper skin, it looked like it would fade with time.

We were in her kitchen area with Archie lying off to one side, watching our every move. Brown rice cooked on the stove, and I busied myself chopping shallots, ginger, and garlic while we discussed Jim's case. "So, nothing's lining up," I was saying. "Isabel's my only potential direct link to the killer, but I'll be lucky to find her and even luckier if she agrees to cooperate. I still think she ran because she knows something."

I scraped the ingredients into a sauce pan and added a cup of the young wine, a bag of dried cherries, some butter, and a dash of pepper and put the pan on a burner. Winona said, "Eddie's a good-looking man. I could see him becoming Lori's lover. After all, Lori was more attractive than his wife."

I drank some wine, shook my head, and told her about his alibi and the fact that he and Sylvia were the owners of a highly successful investment business. "They don't need Le Petit Truc. Besides, they both seem to revere Jim."

"What about that creep of a stepbrother?"

I unwrapped a pork tenderloin and seasoned it with curry powder and salt and pepper. "Yeah, Abernathy's got anger issues. As you know, Jim wouldn't set him up in the cannabis business, and he's still livid about it."

Winona sipped some wine. "So he killed Lori just to get back at Jim?"

I shrugged. "He was probably as mad at her as he was at Jim, but a motive for murder?"

"Does he have an alibi?"

The cherry sauce was reducing nicely, filling the loft with a rich aroma. "The police report said he was with Lori's mom, and that's what he told me when I asked him. But, you know, the mom's dying of cancer. She could have been sedated or something. I put the meat under the broiler, started building a salad, and handed Winona a small dish. "Make us a dressing, two thirds olive oil, one third red wine vinegar, salt and pepper, a little lemon juice, then take the rice off. It should be done."

Winona laughed. "I love it when you go into your bossy chef mode." She made the dressing and transferred the steaming brown rice into a bowl. "Then there's Candice and lover boy Blake Daniels," she went on. "What about them?" I explained what Candice was up to, and she shot me a skeptical look. "You trust her?"

I shrugged again. "Jim does, and I have no reason not to. Blake's a different story. He's my best candidate for Lori's lover, and he left Amis' party in time to have been the intruder. Candice said he's showing a lot of interest in Jim's business, too."

Winona laughed. "That and four bucks will get you a latte in Portland."

I nodded as I stirred the cherry reduction sauce and tasted it. "Umm, not bad. I think we're there." I took it off the stove, puréed it in a blender, then checked the meat. Pink in the center. Perfect. Every so often things clicked in the kitchen, and this was one of those times. I opened the bottle of Jim's reserve pinot and we toasted each other by candlelight before we began to eat.

Halfway through the meal Winona brought us back to the problem facing me the next day. "So, how are you going to approach this Conisson woman?" We kicked it around, and by the time we finished some Ben and Jerry's mango sorbet I had a plan of sorts. I called Sean McKnight to fill him in.

Later that night, she held my arm as we took Arch for a walk. The streets were silent, the rain had held off, and a light breeze from the east carried a faint scent of the river. Back in the apartment, Winona stretched and said, "Great food, great wine. There's only one thing missing."

"What might that be?"

She took my hand. "Come on. I'll show you."

Chapter Thirty

At four-thirty the next afternoon I bought a twelve-ounce cup of black coffee at Elephant's Deli and crossed the street to Director Park, a paved plaza that sat atop six stories of underground parking. A sharp departure from the verdant parks in Portland, it featured an expansive glass canopy for protection against the weather, a large, semi-circular fountain, and plants sprouting from concrete pots. A low cloud cover urgent with rain threatened that day but never materialized, so I sat out on the lip of the fountain with my eye on the building across the street. I took a couple of photos of Maura Conisson out of my pocket and studied them again, although I was pretty sure I'd be able to spot my quarry with no problem.

Winona had persuaded me to approach Maura out in the open. "Catch her out on the plaza," she'd said. "She'll feel more vulnerable there, and you'll have the element of surprise. If you confront her at home, on her turf, she's likely to slam the door in your face."

A steady trickle of people began exiting the tower around 4:50 with the glut at 5:10. I didn't see her and worried I'd somehow missed her. After all, she could be travelling or working late or God knows what. But at 5:16 a lone woman came out and strode across the street and into the park, a thin briefcase in one hand. I didn't have to move, because she was heading right toward me. She wore a corporate uniform—a white blouse beneath a dark blazer with slacks and ankle boots. Even in the low light,

I could see red highlights in her auburn hair, but my eyes, and I suspect, the eyes of many people, were drawn to her face. It wasn't anything in particular about her features—large, wide-set eyes, a sloping, delicate nose, and full lips. Maybe it was how they were arranged in a perfectly oval face perched on a slender neck. I really can't say, but there was no question Maura Conisson was a beautiful woman.

I stood up, stepped in front of her, and smiled. "Hello Maura. My name's Cal Claxton. I'd like to talk to you about Sean McKnight."

She hesitated for a moment, then sidestepped me and kept walking with her eyes focused straight ahead. "I don't know what you're talking about," she said over her shoulder. "You've got the wrong person."

I fell into step with her. "No I don't. You were involved in an effort to shake him down. I'm an attorney, not a cop, but unless you talk to me, I'm afraid there could be dire consequences for you."

She lengthened her stride. "You're crazy. Leave me alone."

I kept pace with her. "You're involved in the commission of a felony, Maura. You're flirting with a prison sentence if you don't cooperate. Think of your son, Joshua." She slowed down and snapped me a startled look. "If you help Sean McKnight we might be able to work something out."

She stopped, faced me, and tried to marshal a look of righteous indignation, but instead her face went slack and her eyes grew wide as the shock of my words sunk in. Her chin trembled when she finally spoke. "I'm listening."

"We can talk down the street, at the Virginia Café. I've got a booth reserved in the back."

We walked in silence down Park Avenue to the café. I'd been in earlier and given the bartender twenty bucks to reserve the last two booths in the back, one for us to talk and an empty booth for a buffer. The light was dim, and when she hesitated I said, "Go ahead. Sit down. I just want to talk." She finally slid across from me into the booth, all the while averting her eyes from mine. "We can't change what happened," I began, "but we have a chance to make some things right here. Sean just wants the pictures back. Not for his sake, but for the sake of his family and his church."

Maura furrowed her smooth brow. "Pictures? What are you talking about? I had an affair with Sean. That's all I know about."

"Cut the crap, Maura. There's video footage of the two of you in a motel bed. You had to have known about that."

She looked stunned for a moment, and what color was left in her face drained away. "I knew pictures of us going in and out of motels were being taken. That was the deal." She looked directly at me. "I did not know about any bedroom shots. I swear." She wrung her hands. "Oh, Christ."

"I don't care whether you knew or not. We want the name of the person who paid you for this so we can get the pictures back." I locked onto her eyes. "If this happens, Mr. McKnight has told me he won't go to the police to press charges, and you can go about your life. But if he doesn't get the pictures back he's going to the police and tell them everything. He will not be blackmailed." She looked at me, unblinking. "That could mean hard prison time for you, Maura."

She sat there for a long time clasping and unclasping her hands, her eyes focused on the surface of the stained, rough-hewn table. "What if the blackmailer doesn't cooperate?"

"Then you're both screwed," I answered. "We're coming after you."

She went silent again, her hands moving restlessly. The noise level in the café was building as a happy hour crowd began to filter in. Then her hands stopped, and she closed her eyes. When she opened them again they were flooded with tears. She looked at me and said in a barely audible voice, "Do you think Sean could ever forgive me?"

"If you cooperate, perhaps. He's been deeply hurt and has already paid a heavy price."

She sighed. It sounded like the weight of the world had just come off her shoulders. "I'm so sorry I did this to him. My son.

He's sick. Cancer. I needed the money. I did it for the money. I never wanted to hurt Sean."

I nodded and let the conversation go for a while, as Maura told me about her son, Josh. He had leukemia and needed a lot of expensive home care after his initial treatment at Doernbecher Children's Hospital. "Home care wasn't covered by my insurance. I couldn't take off work, so the bills piled up, and I was going to lose my house." She dabbed her eyes with a napkin. "I did it for my son. And I hated myself every single day for it. I only got half the money, twenty thousand dollars. I'm supposed to get the rest when the deal—whatever that is—goes through. I'd give the money back, but most of it's gone."

I shrugged. "I'm not concerned about that." I met her eyes and held them. "Who was it, Maura? Who talked you into this?"

She let out a long breath. "He's an ex-client of mine, a psychiatrist out your way named Richard Amis."

Richard Amis? I leaned back in the booth. Well, I'll be damned, I said to myself. Life is, indeed, full of surprises.

Chapter Thirty-one

By this time, I'm sure the Virginia Café was buzzing with after-work revelers, but all my attention was riveted on Sean McKnight's seductress, Maura Conisson. I leaned forward in the booth. "How long was Amis your client?"

"About two years. He was always interested in my personal life, always asking me how things were going, that sort of thing. He was very easy to talk to, and after Josh got sick I started pouring out my heart to him." She shook her head and swung her eyes to mine. "It was like free therapy sessions, you know? God knows I needed it."

I nodded. "How did he recruit you?"

She dropped her eyes and studied the table for a few moments. "I got a new territory, but one day he called out of the blue and invited me for coffee. I didn't think much of it. I mean I didn't think he was hitting on me or anything. Anyway, he kind of broke down and told me this story about a man who'd seduced his wife. It was threatening to break up his marriage."

"That was a lie," I said.

She nodded. "I didn't know that then. Anyway, he asked me to get involved with the man." She shook her head with a bewildered look. "I just laughed at him, but then he offered me twenty thousand dollars up front and another twenty if I pulled it off. That got my attention. He said it would help him save his marriage and teach the man a lesson." She brought her eyes back up, and they were filled with remorse. "I was desperate, he knew it, and he gave me just enough reasons to rationalize it. Of course, as I got involved with Sean, I began to doubt what Amis had told me, but it was too late. It's been self-loathing ever since."

I asked a series of questions that helped me fill in the rest of the details, how she was vague about where she lived and where she worked, how she used the cash to pay off debts and extend Josh's home care when she was meeting Sean. It was a juggling act, but she told herself she was doing it for her son.

"How did the videotaping work?"

"Richard always rented the rooms and gave me the key. He told me to tell Sean that I'd taken care of it so his name wouldn't be involved. That means Richard had access to the rooms." She looked at me, her eyes filled with an earnestness that was hard to discount. "Tell Sean. *Please.* I didn't know about the videos."

I said I would and then asked another question. "You sold Amis a lot of anti-anxiety drugs, right?"

"Yeah, he was one of my best customers, four stars on our corporate rating system. He got all kinds of freebies. People think the AMA cracked down on this sort of thing, but there's still plenty going on under the table."

"So you bent the rules to keep him happy?"

Her brows went up in surprise. "Uh, what do you—"

"I'm just curious. He's got a reputation as a pill pusher."

She sighed. "My boss told me to keep the Xanax and Klonopin flowing to him. He liked the sample packs. Gave them out like candy to get people started. I don't think it was a money thing with him. I think he just liked having people dependent on him."

When I had most of the disgusting picture, I said, "Look, Maura, this is how it's going to work—we're going to confront Amis. I'm going to tell him that if he doesn't return the photos and video clips, we're going to the police where you will fully cooperate. He might threaten you or try to buy you off. It's your job to convince him that you're not going to waver. If you don't convince him, and we don't get everything back, Sean will take the whole thing to the police and both you and Amis are going down. And I can't guarantee who will see those shots of you and Sean in bed."

She swallowed and closed her eyes for a few moments. I thought she might be getting sick. Then she straightened up and looked at me, her jaw set, her eyes blazing. "That can't happen. I'll do whatever it takes."

"Good. I'll be in touch. And if you tell *anyone* about this, the deal's off. Understood?"

She nodded and got up to leave, then hesitated for a moment and turned back to me. "How did you find me?"

"Trade secret."

She shook her head and managed a wisp of a smile. "Believe it or not, I'm glad you did."

I ordered a Mirror Pond and called Sean McKnight. "Richard Amis? Are you kidding me?" he said when I broke the news. "He came in to talk to me, maybe three or four times at the church. I didn't know him, and he wasn't a member of our church."

"How did he approach you?"

"He said he was having a crisis of faith, but now that I think about it he kept turning the conversation back on me, asking me about my sense of integrity, my commitment to my church, saying how much he admired me. At one point he told me about his marital problems, and I responded by admitting to him that my marriage was weak, something I never admitted to anyone before." McKnight sighed. "I remember thinking afterwards that the whole thing was a little strange, and I had this vague feeling of being manipulated. But I'd never counseled a psychiatrist before."

"He was sizing you up, seeing if your character would dictate giving up your money and your property to protect your family and the church. He sized up Maura just as cynically."

"Will she cooperate?"

"I think so." I told him about her sick child and how desperate she was for money.

"I knew there had to be a reason she did this. She's a good person, Cal. Amis took advantage of her."

"Yeah, well, we'll see how this plays out. I'll be in touch. Meanwhile, not a word about it to anyone. We've got a good shot here."

After McKnight left I sat back in the booth and mulled the situation over while I finished my beer. It looked like Maura was in, and the revelation that Amis was distributing drugs like candy might give me added leverage. I shook my head thinking about McKnight's reaction. His feelings for Maura surfaced again, the woman who had literally destroyed life as he knew it. And now, after talking to her, it seemed she had feelings for Sean as well. It was crazy, but at the same time somehow touching.

Shakespeare said love was merely madness. The man had a point.

Chapter Thirty-two

The next morning I had Nando on the phone. "That's right, his name's Dr. Richard D. Amis. He's a psychiatrist practicing out of McMinnville. Search all your databases, do a full background check, the works. I want to know exactly who I'm dealing with."

I called Jim next and told him I wanted to check in with him and Candice. She'd left me a voice mail following her latest date with Daniels, and I wanted a firsthand account. We settled on lunch at Le Petit Truc, and Jim said to come early if I wanted to catch some of the barreling operation. When I set out that day, the bright autumn sky made me squint, and a bank of clouds along the Coast Range looked like a whitewashed, if somewhat fluffy, Great Wall of China. Seemingly overnight, the vineyards were flecked with reds, yellows, and gold, and soon there would be nothing but row upon row of stark, leafless vines on the hillsides, like orderly boneyards.

I parked and went into the warehouse, figuring I would find Jim there. Archie plopped down at the entry without even bothering to sniff the air inside. Fermenting grapes were definitely not his thing. I saw Jim and Juan at the end of a long canyon of wine barrel racks. Jim was placing a stainless steel nozzle into the bung hole of a barrel. The attached hose led up to a fermenter tank hoisted on the tines of a forklift operated by Juan Cruz. Jim wore the lab coat that was more purple than white, and wine spatters dotted his forehead. When he saw me he broke into a broad smile. "History in the making," he said. It was a smile like the Jim Kavanaugh of old, and I was glad to see it back.

As I got closer, his smile faded. "Whoa, you're more beat up than you admitted."

I shrugged, managing to smile. "Bloodied but unbowed." I'd told him about the meeting with Isabel Rufino but hadn't dwelled on the beating I'd taken. It was embarrassing, after all.

He shook his head. "You're going to rue the day you took me on as a client."

I shrugged again. "So how's the barreling going?"

"Great," he said as he twisted a valve on the nozzle, and looking over at Juan, added, "She's on. That should empty this fermenter." He looked back at me and wrapped on the barrel with wine-stained knuckles. The staves were smooth and gracefully curved, the bare wood reminding me of the oak rounds I split the other day. "In France, it takes a seven-year apprenticeship before you can even begin to make these beauties. The technique hasn't changed in three thousand years." He wrapped the barrel again. "This wood's over a hundred years old, and the staves are air-dried for at least four years before they're used."

A sucking sound signaled that the fermenter had drained. Jim shut off the valve and disconnected the hose as Juan trundled off in the forklift to dispose of the empty fermenter and hoist up another full one. "Wine storage in oak began with the Romans," he went on, and then launched into the chemistry of aging pinot noir in oak that was cut short when Candice hollered from the other end of the aisle that he had a phone call. He hadn't finished, but I heard enough to convince me that aging wine in one thousand dollar oak barrels wasn't just a marketing gimmick.

Juan shut off the forklift and declined a lunch invitation so he could run some errands. I followed Jim into the wine tasting room, where Candice sat scowling at her computer screen. "I picked up some sandwiches," she said without looking up. "They're on the bar."

When Jim closed the door to the adjoining office to take the call, I unwrapped a sandwich and took a seat across from her. She looked up and gasped. I suffered through another explanation of my bruises, then said, "Got your message. At least the food was good at the Joel Palmer House, huh?"

She laughed. "Yeah, no breakthroughs, but the sturgeon with lobster mushrooms was scrumptious. But don't be discouraged. I'm still laying the groundwork." She glanced at the office door as if to confirm it was shut and said in a lowered tone, "I hope Jim doesn't take this the wrong way, you know, like I've lost my virtue or something. Men can be so judgmental."

"Has he said anything?" She shook her head. "You don't have to do this, you know. You can stop right now. We haven't learned anythi—"

Her eyes flashed daggers. "*No*, Cal. I didn't tell you everything on the phone. I'm convinced something weird's going on. He had more questions about the business, really bored in on that and what I knew about the case against Jim. I didn't tell him anything, of course. We went back to his place, and I got a look at his study when I went to the bathroom. He keeps his computer in there and lots of papers and files. I'm going to check it out one of these nights after he lapses into a drunken stupor."

I stopped chewing. "Jesus, Candice. I don't think that's—"

"Don't worry. I'll be careful." She smiled slyly. "Post-coital slumber's deep, especially after a bottle of Scotch."

I suppressed a laugh this time. "So, what's weird about him?"

She leaned forward and fixed me with her gaze. "He seems obsessed with Lori's death. Back at his place, he threw back a couple more Scotches, and when I was leaving he grabbed me by the shoulders, his eyes all fierce and crazy looking. 'How can you work for that man?' he said. 'He's a murderer, Candice. He killed Lori because he was afraid he'd lose his winery when she divorced him. He's a monster.'"

"How did you respond to that?"

"Well, I didn't buy it, of course, but I didn't show it. I just looked at him, you know, kind of in disbelief, as if that was the first time I'd heard anything like that. I want him to think he's winning me over." She shrugged. "This is probably just an act to get me to open up about Truc and the case."

I shook my head. "I still don't like it."

She drew her mouth into a resolute line and set her jaw. "Cal, I'm not afraid of him. I'm taking him to the airport tomorrow night and picking him up on Sunday. The romance is blooming. Trust me."

I nodded reluctantly. There was no use arguing with this woman.

At that point, Jim came back into the room. He sat down next to me and massaged his forehead with the fingers of both hands. "That was our liability insurance agent," he said, looking up at Candice. "He's a nervous wreck, asked me a bunch of questions. The jerk acts like he's never had a client indicted for murder before."

"He can't cancel our liquor control bond, can he?" Candice asked, an alarmed look spreading across her face. "That would shut us down."

Jim looked at me. I shrugged. "I don't think so, but he might refuse to renew it, force you to go elsewhere."

Jim waved a hand in disgust. "He was vague, told me he'd get back to me." He pulled his pant leg up, rolled his sock down, and began scratching the skin above his ankle bracelet. "This bloody thing's driving me crazy. Itches all the time. Which reminds me, I had to cancel my east coast marketing trip and a couple of key winemaker dinners since I can't leave the goddamn state now."

"And our distributors are pissed about that," Candice chimed in.

Jim took a sandwich and began eating. The room fell silent for a long time. I felt obliged to say something lawyerly and encouraging, but I just didn't have much to offer. And my battered appearance seemed to be a metaphor for how the case was going. I finally broke the silence by mentioning that Nando Mendoza was still looking for Isabel and that I'd managed to hire one of the best blood spatter experts in the country. They weren't confidence builders, but it's all I had. What I didn't say, and what I'm sure occurred to both of them, was that costs were rising, adding to the money hemorrhage.

After we finished the sandwiches, I told Arch it was time to go. Candice stood up next to Jim, propped a forearm on his shoulder, and cocked her head toward him in a show of support. Jim looked at her, then me, and cracked the faintest of smiles. "Bloodied but unbowed. I like that. Pretty much sums up the situation."

Candice's face grew serious. "We believe in you, Cal," she said. Jim nodded to underscore the expression of confidence.

Great. Just what I needed.

I left without answering as a wave of self-doubt and dejection washed over me. I kept telling myself it's not your fault Jim's life is in free fall. You're doing everything you can. But I couldn't shake the feeling that I was letting him down, and Candice and Juan, for that matter. You've got to do more, a nagging voice kept insisting. But what?

Back in law school we were warned not to become emotionally involved with our clients. That, I can tell you, is easier said than done, at least for me.

Chapter Thirty-three

"Dr. Amis practiced in the wine town of Healdsburg, California, before coming to Oregon," Nando said. It was the next morning, and he was giving me a preliminary rundown on Amis as we ate breakfast at the Bijou Café in downtown Portland. "His record there was not unblemished," he went on. "He was censored twice by the California Medical Board, once in 2002, and then again, six years later. He moved to Lafayette in 2009, to start anew, I assume."

"Censored for what?"

Nando shrugged. "The records are sealed, which means the board did not see fit to pull his license. However, I did find a newspaper article stating he was being sued by a family in Santa Rosa after the suicide of their daughter. The family claimed Amis was too liberal in his distribution of anti-anxiety drugs to the young woman, but Amis' lawyer denied any wrong-doing."

I nodded. "Sounds about right. Did the suit go forward?"

Another shrug. "That was the only reference I found. Perhaps the matter was settled out of court. The background search is not complete. Something else may surface."

"How about Maura Conisson?" I said next. "How is the surveillance going?" I had asked Nando to have one of his investigators watch her apartment, not because I mistrusted her, but more because I felt responsible for her safety and didn't trust Richard Amis in this regard.

"She is safe and sound," he reported.

He filled me in on the search for Isabel Rufino next. "We found a young man who knows this woman and the two men she is associated with," he began. "They are trying to break into the Portland heroin trade, we were told. Small time stuff along the Springwater Corridor."

"Good work," I said enthusiastically.

He raised a cautionary hand. "We were told they were living in a large campsite a mile or so from where you had you unfortunate encounter, but when we arrived there, we discovered it had just been dismantled by the police. The mayor is playing musical chairs with the homeless people."

I shook my head in frustration. "*Damn*. So close. Any hope of still finding her?"

He nodded. "Yes, if they continue to sell drugs in Portland, we will find her."

"How many hours do you have in this?"

He paused for a moment. "Ten, give or take. Do you wish me to continue?"

The meter was spinning, but I felt I had no choice. "Yeah. Keep going. I need to talk to her. And remember, Nando, no revenge-taking."

I left the Bijou that morning feeling better than I should have. I hadn't learned anything new about Amis, and the search for Isabel would continue. But I believed Nando when he said he'd find her. As for Amis, at least I had something concrete to focus on—taking the bastard down. And maybe, just maybe, that would open a new path into Jim Kavanaugh's case.

• • ● • •

There was only one person in the queue that morning at Caffeine Central, a young woman, maybe twenty-five, who had been given a one-month eviction notice at her apartment in the southeast neighborhood of Brooklyn. The city had put new rules in place requiring at least ninety days' notice, but a lot of landlords hadn't gotten the memo or hoped the tenant would move out without a fight. "I can't find a place that fast," she told me. The inked-in tail of what must have been a fierce dragon slithered from her left shirt sleeve, but her eyes were fringed with concern bordering on fear. "There's *nothing* close in, I don't have a car, and I just lost my job."

I wrote a letter while she waited that put the landlord on notice that if he followed through with his threat, she would be entitled to three month's rent plus damages if she decided to sue. I printed it out on letterhead, signed it, and gave it to her in a stamped envelope to mail. "This should slow him down. If it doesn't, let me know," I told her. "Good luck finding a new place and a new job."

She left smiling, but we both knew this only postponed the inevitable—that she would probably wind up with a long commute from out near Gresham. Why, I wondered, must one person's good fortune come at the expense of another's? I had no answer, only a resolve to keep trying to make a difference in the small space around me.

At 12:05, the bell on the door at the entry jingled. I went into the deserted waiting room and ushered Maura Conisson into my office. Her chestnut hair was up in a careless bun, a strand looping down across her forehead, and although her eyes looked tired, there was an element of resoluteness in them.

"I'm glad you showed up," I told her as I shut the door and motioned for her to sit. "Have you had any contact with Amis?"

A hurt look spread across her face. "Of course not," she answered, her chin trembling slightly.

"Good. You get one chance to square this," I reminded her. I didn't like playing the asshole, but I felt it was necessary. She might eventually feel the heat from Amis, and I wanted to scare her into being ready.

Her expression morphed into annoyance. "You made that abundantly clear. Look, Mr. Claxton, I'm here to make this as right as I can. Can we move on?"

I nodded. "Okay, let's go over what's going to happen next."

I took her through my plan, such as it was, and answered a string of questions. When we finished, she leaned back in her chair and sighed. Her eyes softened, and as she relaxed her extraordinary beauty seemed to bloom in front of me, a beauty she wore without vanity or self-consciousness. "How's Sean?"

"Shattered. He didn't deserve this."

Her eyes welled up, and tears began streaming down her cheeks. "I'm...I'm so sorry. Will he ever forgive me?"

I handed her a tissue. "Maybe you would know better than me?" Looking at my watch, I added, "You better leave now. And remember, Maura, you get one chance. Don't blow it." She dabbed her eyes, got up, and found her way out, her shoulders stooped, her steps a little hesitant. I watched her go, feeling like she got the message, but not feeling very proud of the messenger.

I called Sean McKnight next and filled him in. The first thing he said when I finished was, "She's not in any danger is she? I mean, Amis wouldn't threaten her or harm her, would he?" I assured him she would be safe, and when I clicked off, shook my head again. He seemed more worried about her than getting the damn pictures back.

I was beginning to feel more like a couple's counselor than a lawyer.

Around three thirty that afternoon, I took Archie out for a walk and then put him in the back of the BMW. At my request, Jim had found out where Lori's mother, Irene Halstead, was staying. Northwest Hospice and Palliative Care was out on Powell Boulevard. "You going to question her?" he asked, a little surprised.

"I'm not sure, but I'd like to know if she's up to it. Aaron Abernathy told me to stay away from her, but she's his alibi. Maybe she'll talk to me."

The hospice was set back from the street, a two-story brick Georgian affair with two white columns propping up a flat-roofed, drive-through entry. I parked in the adjoining lot and cracked a back window for Arch, who was snoozing in the backseat, and zipped my coat up against a brisk, moisture-laden wind that swirled in from the east. It was 3:50 and visiting hours began at four. My plan was to get in and out fast to avoid running into Aaron Abernathy.

The lobby was empty. So far, so good.

"I'm here to visit Irene Halstead," I told the young woman at the desk.

She glanced at her watch and gave me a sympathetic, if practiced, look. "You're family or a close friend?"

I responded with my best smile, the one that says trust me. "Yes."

She looked mildly puzzled, started to say something, but let it pass, and after tapping something into her computer, said, "You're a bit early, but just a moment, I'll have Logan show you to Mrs. Halstead's room." Logan, a twenty-something with heavy ink on both forearms, materialized and led me down a narrow corridor with an antiseptic smell and a worn carpet. I felt sleazy about my deception, but it faded in a hurry when I reminded myself that Jim Kavanaugh's life was on the line.

Logan knocked softly at number 135, waited for a moment, and entered. "It's Cal Claxton, Mrs. Halstead. He's come to visit you."

Irene Halstead had lost an appalling amount of ground since I saw her at Lori's funeral. Her face was drawn, the pale skin seemingly stretched over bone, her eyes deep in discolored sockets, her forearms thin as sticks. But as I drew nearer I saw that her eyes burned with a kind of primal fierceness I'd seen in the eyes of the dying before. I suddenly had second thoughts about being there, but it was too late to turn back. I cleared my throat after Logan quietly let himself out. "Hello, Mrs. Halstead. I met you at the funeral. I'm Jim Kavanaugh's attorney." Better to be up front, I decided.

Propped at a forty-five-degree angle in her bed, she looked blank for a moment. "Oh, I remember you. What do you want? I already gave a statement to the police."

There were two chairs next to her bed, but I remained standing. "I'm sorry to disturb you, and I know you talked to the police, but I wondered if you would be willing to answer a couple more questions. I won't take up much of your time."

She pointed a bony finger at one of the chairs. "Sit." When I did she wheezed a sigh. "I'm not sure I care anymore who killed Lori. She's gone." She swung her eyes to me and smiled thinly. The fierceness had turned to profound resignation. "Justice. Revenge. They lose their meaning when you're dying, Mr. Claxton."

I nodded, holding her gaze. "I can understand how you feel, but an innocent man's life is in the balance, a man who loved your daughter very much."

Her look turned bitter, and I wished I could have had the last phrase back. "The only thing Jim Kavanaugh ever loved was grapes and winemaking."

"He's grieving now, Mrs. Halstead, believe me."

The fierceness returned to her eyes. "What are your questions?"

I leaned in a little. "After Lori and Jim split up, when she was living in Portland, did she start seeing someone else, you know, a boyfriend?"

She looked away from me. "Oh, I think so, yes, Mr. Claxton. Lori was a dear. She told me everything."

"Did she mention a name to you?"

She closed her eyes for a moment, wheezed another sigh, and coughed. "I can't remember anymore."

"That's okay, Mrs. Halstead. You're doing great. Uh, that horrible night Lori was killed, do you remember if Aaron was with—"

The door clicked open, and we both looked up. I should have known. Never base a plan on luck, because it will invariably be of the bad variety. She said, "Hello, Aaron, I was—"

"What the hell are you doing here, Claxton?" Aaron Abernathy stood in the doorway, his face a study in disbelief, his fists clenched at his sides.

"I'm doing my job. I'm a lawyer."

His stepmother said, "It's okay, dear, I—"

His glare swung to her. "Shut up, Irene. I'll handle this." Then to me he said, "Get out of here *now*, you ambulance-chasing bastard."

I nodded, thanked his mother-in-law, and eased by him, half-expecting to get hit. At the same time, I marveled at how ridiculously ugly his sagging earlobes were. As I moved down the hall he fell in behind me, and when I got to the lobby he went up to the young woman at the desk and pointed at me. "He's not family or a friend. He's a fucking lawyer. Did you let him in here? If you did, I'll have your job, you bitch."

Everyone in the lobby froze as he whirled around and started back down the hallway. I went back to the woman, who had tears in her eyes. "It wasn't your fault. I'm sorry I misled you." I handed her a card. "If your job's threatened or he harasses you in any way, call me. I'll represent you without any charge."

When I got to the car I just sat for a while, decompressing. Archie, sensing I was upset, came up between the seats and licked my face. Abernathy's timing was impeccable, so I still didn't know if he had an alibi for that night or not. His sensitivity to my talking to Irene was suspicious, but, on the other hand, he had every right to be angry with me. More interesting, I thought, was that she seemed lucid enough to be interviewed as a witness. Maybe under questioning she would recall the boyfriend's name. It was worth a shot.

I was going to take Archie out for a stretch, but the sky opened up. He put his ears down and made it clear he wasn't getting out of the car. My dog didn't like rain one bit unless it was clear we were going for a jog. I laughed and pulled out, cranking the wipers to full tilt to see where I was going. It was murky ahead and difficult to see, not unlike the situation I faced.

Chapter Thirty-four

Saturday morning broke with more than the usual fanfare for early November. Half-hearted wisps of fog gave way to rich sunlight that flooded my bedroom like warm honey. The radiator dutifully clunked on, and Archie was out of his bed in the corner the moment I sat up. He placed his front legs out and lowered his head and shoulders in a luxurious stretch. I got dressed and padded down the backstairs to brew coffee. Out my kitchen window I could see clouds building to the south. Not the dark, threatening kind but things of beauty, thick and luminous in the early light. As I sipped my coffee, a pileated woodpecker swooped in, clamped himself on the trunk of a Doug fir down on the fence line, and began to forage, his red-fringe bobbing like a tiny jackhammer.

Arch and I took advantage of the window of good weather by taking a jog up to the pioneer cemetery and back. The bruises on my left arm had changed from deep purple to a Rorschach of grayish yellow, and I even managed twenty pushups at the end of the run. I'd be ready for the rest of those oak rounds in no time. After a shower, I was out on the side porch talking to Jim on my cell. "I need you to invite Richard Amis to Truc this afternoon, say around three. Just tell him you want him to taste the vintage you'll be bottling soon, you know, because you want his opinion. Wild horses won't keep him away."

"I sure as hell don't need his opinion, but I'll do it. What's this all about, anyway?" Jim answered. All I told him was that I needed Amis to be there and that Sean McKnight and another woman would be coming with me. He must have picked up on something in my voice, because he added, "Sounds ominous. Does this have anything to do with my situation?"

"I don't know yet. It's possible that it could. Are you okay with that?"

"Ah, yeah, sure. I'm trusting you on this, Cal."

"Okay. Tell Amis to go to the wine tasting room, and let me know as soon as it's set. And, Jim, don't tell anyone about this."

Next, I called Sean McKnight and asked him to come over and was waiting for him when Winona called. She was out on the Snake River again. "We're trying to correlate fish counts at Lower Granite Dam with water temperature and flows," she explained. "Damn, it's cold up here. Why some steelhead pick the winter to migrate is a mystery to me." I brought her up to date, including the latest on the party I was planning for Amis, and after wishing me luck she said, "Did you see the digital edition of *The Oregonian* today?

"No, did you?"

"Yes. I read it on my phone this morning while I was still in my sleeping bag. There's an article in the business section on Eddie and Sylvia's company, Tilikum Capital Management. Some attorney named Arnold Bivens from Seattle is going after them in federal court, a major lawsuit."

"What's his beef?"

"He's claiming they cheated him out of commissions for some accounts he brought to them."

"Any response from Tilikum?"

"Just a quote from Eddie Manning saying he wouldn't comment on pending litigation. Anyway, I just thought I'd pass that little tidbit on."

After we said our goodbyes I went online, pulled up the article, and just finished reading it when Archie announced McKnight's arrival. His silver hair was pulled into a tight ponytail that hung down past the collar of his Pendleton shirt. He was clean-shaven and looked more rested than last time I saw him, although his eyes still had vestiges of sadness and resignation. He dropped to a knee to greet Arch, then looked up at me. "He called this morning. He wants the fifty thousand in cash tomorrow, said he'd give me instructions for the drop in the morning."

"What did you tell him?"

"What you told me to say—that I would have the cash and that I decided to take the offer for Stone Gate so that I can get this behind me."

"Good. Come on in. Let's talk about what we're going to do today."

After McKnight got his instructions and left, I made myself a double cappuccino, and because the day remained clear, took it out on the porch. The woodpecker was still at work, although he had moved up the tree a good thirty feet. I sipped my coffee and thought about Richard Amis, a man who used his medical training and experience to seek out two vulnerable people and manipulate them into committing acts they would have never done on their own. Equal parts disgust and anger welled up in me like steam in a hot boiler. Amis would walk away this afternoon, free to continue practicing medicine and doling out pills, but I made a promise to myself—if he stayed in Oregon I would find a way to strip his license and send him to jail if it was the last thing I ever did.

I wasn't going to get mad, just even.

Chapter Thirty-five

"Oh, so you're in on the tasting as well," Richard Amis said to me when I opened the door to the wine tasting room at Le Petit Truc at 3:05 p.m.. His thick-lidded eyes betrayed disappointment, because, let's face it, he didn't consider me a worthy judge of a truly fine wine. I didn't have command of the jargon, and I sure as hell didn't have a wine cellar with five thousand bottles in it. He wore a light blue cashmere sweater and a pair of Sperry topsiders below sharply creased khakis, his version of dressing down, no doubt. After all, he might have to root around amongst those messy wine casks.

I gave him a Chamber of Commerce smile and invited him in. He followed me, took the seat at the tasting bar, and looked around. "Where's Jim?"

"He's tied up right now." I sat down across from him, dropped the smile, and looked him square in the eye. "Actually, I'm the one who wants to talk to you." His eyes widened a bit, and his look became instantly wary. "I know that you're blackmailing Sean McKnight, and I want it to stop immediately." There's nothing like getting right to the point.

He didn't flinch as a half-smile, half incredulous look spread across his face. "This is a joke, right? What in the world are you talking about, Claxton?" The man was calm under fire. I'll give him that.

"You know exactly what I'm talking about, and if you don't give back every copy of the pictures and videos my client is going to the police to file charges. You'll face felony extortion, loss of your license, and hard jail time. That's a certainty."

The color left his face like someone pulled a plug, but he managed a look of righteous indignation as he stood up. "You have no evi—"

"Yes, I do." I stood to face him. "We know about your whole, disgusting scheme. Sean, come out."

Sean McKnight came out from the adjoining office, all six-four of him. "He's right, Richard. If you give me the pictures and videos this is as far as it will go. I give you my word."

"What pictures? What videos?" He started for the door. "Excuse me, gentlemen, but this is absurd."

McKnight stepped in front of the door, and I said, "We have proof, Richard. Maura, come out."

Maura Conisson stepped out of the office. Amis stopped in mid-step and faced her. "Hello, Richard. If you don't do what they ask, I will testify against you."

He forced down a look of astonishment and managed a laugh. "And, and incriminate yourself?"

She glanced at Sean before looking back at him. "I don't care what the costs are to me personally. I'll tell the police everything. I'm sorry I ever got mixed up in this."

"If she cooperates, she won't be charged," I chimed in. "They'll cut her a deal. It's over, Richard."

Standing in the center of us, Richard Amis put his hands on his hips and looked around, trying hard to maintain his composure. The only sound was the distant whine of a forklift out in the warehouse. Finally, he sighed and dropped his hands and his head simultaneously. Checkmate.

I motioned with a nod for Sean and Maura to leave. As they let themselves out, I said in a softer tone, "Sit back down, Richard. Let's talk about this." When we were facing each other again, I went on. "We want *everything*, hard copies, digital copies, negatives, and we want them by eight o'clock tonight." It was short notice, but I wanted to keep the heat on him. "If you hold back *anything*, or if any of the images or videos surface publicly, we will go directly to the police. If you speak to Maura Conisson or Sean McKnight or have any contact whatsoever with either of them, we will go directly to the police. Am I clear?"

His head was down, his shoulders slumped, and one hand fidgeted with the other on the bar. He nodded without looking up.

"There's one other thing. I want you to tell me what you know about Lori Kavanaugh, who she was seeing after she left Jim and before she was killed, and anything else that might be relevant to the murder case."

His head came up, his eyes flared, and for a brief instant I thought I saw fear in them. "I know *nothing* about her love life or anything else that could help you defend Jim Kavanaugh. I was just, ah, supplying her with anti-anxiety medication. She shared very little with me."

I held his gaze, and again he didn't flinch. I wasn't sure whether he really didn't know anything or just wasn't going to tell me. In any event, my bluff fizzled. Amis was smart. He knew the only leverage I had was to threaten to expose his blackmail plot to the police, and that was counter to Sean McKnight's interests. We sat there for a long time just looking at each other. Finally, I said, "I'll be at my office tonight. Bring the images there. I'll expect to see you by eight o'clock." He nodded and got up to leave. I asked, "Tell me, Richard, why the hell did you try this?"

He turned to me, his eyes suddenly filling with passion. "Sean McKnight's parcel is one of the largest and finest pieces of acreage in the Dundee Hills. There are only a few small, tucked away corners in the entire world where one can grow pinot noir grapes optimally, and the Dundee Hills is one of them. So, what is he doing with his acreage? Hazelnuts? Kiwis? What a travesty. What a monumental waste. One could be making world-class pinot noir on that land." He lifted his chin and looked at me with contempt, his patrician bearing seemingly materializing out of nowhere. "Would he sell it? Of course not. God knows I've tried to buy it. He's just like all the other stubborn landowners in the Hills."

"So, you decided to just take it from him?"

He looked at me as if I'd asked a stupid question. "He's desecrating that land, Claxton." He shook his head, a gesture of pity. "You're just a small man with ordinary passions. You'll never understand someone like me, someone who deplores mediocrity and strives for true greatness."

"Is your pill pushing part of your striving for greatness?"

He glared back at me, raising his chin even higher. "I won't dignify that with a response."

I crossed my arms and held his eyes. "Get out of here before my ordinary passions get the better of me."

I followed Amis outside and watched him drive off in his black Land Rover. I found McKnight out behind Jim's house, leaning against the fender of his truck. I'd instructed him and Maura to park back there so Amis wouldn't see their vehicles when he came in. He was smiling, but his eyes looked troubled. "Thank God that's over," he said, pumping my hand. "I can't begin to thank you enough, Cal."

"Well, it won't be over until eight tonight. He's agreed to bring the images to my office. I don't want anything to do with them. They'll be yours to burn or whatever."

"He won't back out, will he?"

I shook my head. "No. I don't think so. You were both very convincing." I glanced back to where her car had been parked. "She's gone, I see."

His face went dark, like when the sun suddenly ducks behind a cloud. "Yeah, she, ah, left. Said how sorry she was again. I asked her if she wanted to get some coffee, you know, to talk about what we've been through." He blew a breath out and blinked his eyes rapidly for a moment. "She said no, that she thought it best if we didn't see each other again." I said, 'Okay, yeah, that made sense.'" He forced a wan smile. "After all, we made quite a hash of it, she and I."

I nodded. "Give yourself some time to decide what's best for you, Sean."

He looked at me, his eyes suddenly brimming. "I got my farm back, but my life's a shambles. And all I can think about is *her*. What is wrong with me?"

I'm not a touchy-feely kind of guy, but I stepped forward and gave the good Reverend Sean McKnight a hug. "Go home now," I told him. "You've been through it. Take some time to sort things out."

I stood there as he pulled out from behind Jim's house and onto the drive leading through the vineyards, his truck swirling grape leaves in its wake. The fine weather was starting to break, and although I couldn't see the clouds from where I was standing, I could smell rain in the stiffening breeze. I could only shake my head at the irony—imagine me giving advice to a man of the cloth. And what did I tell him? Time's a healer alright, but it'll hurt along the way. I'd left that last part out. I wondered what he was going to do. The Reverend had a good heart, but it looked like it had staked a claim that flew in the face of everything he stood for.

There was something else on my mind, something that stirred a ripple of excitement in my gut. Now there was no question in my mind. Richard Amis knew more than he was telling me, and I needed to find out what it was.

Chapter Thirty-six

After breakfast the next morning, I attacked the woodpile out behind the garage again, splitting the oak rounds with renewed energy. My left arm radiated some pain but held up well enough. The squall that had blown through left a mottled, uncertain sky behind, and each time the wind gusted I got rewarded with a sprinkling from the branches of a nearby Douglas fir. That was okay because I loved the sound of the wind in that tree, the kind of sifting murmur a receding wave makes on a sandy beach.

The hand-off meeting with Richard Amis the night before went without a hitch. After we made the exchange, I gave him another chance to level with me about Lori Kavanaugh, but he continued to stonewall. His denials were even more adamant this time around, suggesting he rehearsed his response a bit. I called Sean McKnight and told him I had the images. He dropped by to pick them up, and after he left I called Maura Conisson to give her the news. I'll admit to a bit of meddling here—before I signed off I said, "Why don't you have coffee with Sean, give him some closure." She said she would think about it.

At around ten that morning, I hauled my phone out of my jeans, sat down on one of the rounds, and called Nando. "You're up early," I said when he answered, his voice a shade on the testy side.

"Yes. Ordinarily, Sunday is my day to rest, but I am in my office right now writing a sales contract for the property on SE 16th I told you about."

When he finished rhapsodizing about the great deal he was about to strike, I said, "How old is the house you're going to tear down?"

"It was built in 1914, I believe."

"You better hurry," I chided. "I just read that the city's considering requiring developers to dismantle houses built in 1916 or earlier."

"*Dismantle*? What does this mean?"

"It means you can't just tear it down. You've got to take it apart piece by piece and recycle as much of the material as you can."

Nando muttered something in Spanish I didn't understand, and then we got into it, him arguing for a *laissez faire* approach to development and me arguing for some kind of restraint before the character of Portland's lost forever. At a lull, I said, "Can you do me a favor?"

"Of course."

"There's a lawyer in Seattle named Arnold Bivens. I want to talk to him today, if possible. I tried the online white pages but struck out. Can you use one of your databases to get me his home phone or his cell phone number?"

"Yes, Calvin. I will call you back."

I went back to my wood chopping. Archie lay off to the side, next to a grimy tennis ball. He paid rapt attention to my every move, because I promised him a game of fetch when I finished. When I finally rested the ax against the side of the garage, he sprang to his feet with the ball in his mouth, his eyes blazing with excitement. We finished our game, which featured a somersaulting catch that could have made a good ESPN highlight reel, and retreated into the house just as the sky opened up. I gave him his weekly bone, and after finishing a lunch of Gruyere cheese, walnuts, and sliced apple, all washed down with a glass of Sancerre, Nando called back with Bivens' home and cell numbers and his private e-mail address.

Privacy in the digital age? Forget about it.

Arnold Bivens picked up on the third ring of his cell phone. I introduced myself, apologized for calling on a Sunday, and told him I was thinking about investing in Tilikum Capital Management. "I saw the item about your lawsuit in *The Oregonian*. Doing a little due diligence," I explained.

The line went quiet, and I thought I lost him. "How did you get my cell phone number?"

"From a friend who made me promise I wouldn't tell on him." That was the truth.

More silence. "I can't talk about the lawsuit, so I don't see how I can help you."

I breathed a mental sigh of relief. He's buying it. "I know that," I said hastily. "I'm just wondering if your lawsuit represents a threat to the health of the company."

He paused for a couple of beats. "Oh, I hope they feel it, but it won't put them out of business. I just want what's owed to me."

"I see. What about the Cornerstone bankruptcy? Know anything about that?"

"Tilikum lost a nice income-generator. Collecting on student loans is lucrative."

"So what will the loss do to them?"

"Oh, it's a bump in the road. They've good cash reserves and one of the sharpest owners in the business—Eddie Manning. That son of a bitch is a financial whiz kid."

"So, even though you're suing them, sounds like you're recommending them to me."

He chuckled. "Yeah, I guess I am. If private investment firms blow your skirt up, I'd say you couldn't do much better than Tilikum."

That was all I got from Arnold Bivens. I thanked him, and when I punched off, leaned back in my old roller chair and looked at Arch, who was gnawing his bone in the corner. "So, Big Boy, looks like Tilikum hasn't taken any shots below the waterline." My dog stopped chewing and looked up at me for a moment and then went back to his bone as if to say high finance didn't interest him.

It was still raining, and the house had taken on a chill. I went into the kitchen, brewed up a double cap, and brought it back to the study along with a couple of squares of dark chocolate to nibble on. The events and personalities I encountered over the last month were clunking around in my head like cars with flat tires. I did what I usually do when this happens—I took a single sheet of paper and wrote out a list to focus my thinking. This is what I came up with—

1. The killer—Known by Lori Kavanaugh (her lover?) and seen by Isabel Ruffino. Cold blooded—bludgeoned Lori to death and executed Luis Delgado. Nearly killed Archie?

2. Blake Daniels—dislikes Jim intensely, would love his acreage. Lori's lover? Left Amis' party early, so could have been Arch's poisoner. Whereabouts night of murder unknown.

3. Eddie and Sylvia Manning—holding note on Le Petit Truc. They could foreclose if Jim defaults. Have solid alibis for night of murder and are financially well off.

4. Aaron Abernathy—angry at Jim and Lori for not bankrolling his pot biz. Won't let me talk to his stepmother to confirm his alibi night of murder. (asked Eddie and Sylvia for money, too)

5. Richard Amis—psychiatrist, pill-pusher, and blackmailer who covets land in Dundee Hills. He's not telling me everything he knows.

6. Candice Roberts—caught with Blake Daniels at Amis' party. Is trying to play Daniels, but no results yet (Could she be playing me??)

7. Isabel Rufino—where the hell is she?

I sat staring at the list for a long time. I put Eddie and Sylvia together, because I had no reason to separate them at that point and no motive to ascribe to either of them. Candice was getting close to Blake Daniels. Would she find something linking him to Lori or where he was the night of the murder? Could I trust her? I felt I could, but I reminded myself to be cautious.

I finished one of the chocolate squares, dropped the other in my coffee and stirred it in, deep in thought. Aaron Abernathy was an angry man, but what motive—other than hatred of Jim—would he have to kill Lori?

Then there was Richard Amis. Was he involved in Lori's murder, or was he just a run-of-the-mill blackmailer? My gut said the former because I was damn sure his lust for Dundee Hills acreage didn't stop at Sean McKnight's property line. He'd recruited Maura Conisson to blackmail McKnight. Was he using someone to frame Jim?

My mind had calmed, but nothing really jumped out at me except a sense that I wasn't looking for one person, that there were interconnections at work here. But what interconnections? I had no idea, but I kept coming back to Richard Amis. Was he the key to this?

I picked the pen back up and scrawled "Interconnections??" across the bottom of the sheet and tacked it to the wall in front of my desk, then downed my homemade mocha and got on with the rest of my Sunday.

That night around eleven I walked Archie and said goodnight to the great horned owl who called to us like a lone sentry from his roost high in the Doug fir up near the gate. I was tired, and my left arm was sore from the wood chopping, but I managed twelve more pages of *Winter's Bone* before I dozed off with the lamp still burning on the table next to my bed.

I incorporated the first ping from my cell phone into a dream I was having. The second ping woke me up. I fumbled for my phone, tapped the text bubble, and this came up: Hey, he's out cold and I'm snooping around. This is cool!

It was a text from Candice Roberts from inside Blake Daniels' house. My mind cleared in a hurry.

Chapter Thirty-seven

I swung my feet out of bed and sat there squinting at the little screen. Just like Candice to make light of this, I thought. Should I text her back and warn her again to be careful? I wasn't sure that was wise. The incoming message would make the same ping that woke me up. She must have read my mind because another text came in that read:

> Don't worry. He drank a lot of Scotch and took some pills.

Pills? I decided a text was worth the chance.

> What kind of pills?

> Don't know. I'll look.

A long pause ensued, maybe ten minutes. I sat there listening to Archie's steady breathing, hoping she was okay. I got up and was pacing around the room when two photographs pinged in. I sat back down on the bed and put my phone under the light. Candice had photographed what looked like two sides of a small white pill. I looked carefully at the first image and could just make out a G inscribed on it. The other side of the pill was divided by a horizontal line with CN inscribed in the top half and 0.5 inscribed on the bottom half. I typed "What pill has CN and 0.5 on it?" in my browser and quickly learned that Blake Daniels was using Klonopin, a benzodiazepine used to treat anxiety and a notoriously addictive and destructive drug when abused. I looked up Xanax, the drug Lori had been abusing with the help of Dr. Feelgood. Another benzodiazepine. Not the same as Blake's, but the same family. Did this connect Amis and Daniels and Lori? Not directly, but it did make me wonder where Daniels was getting his pills.

I texted Candice back:

> Thx. We'll talk tomorrow. Be careful!

I went back to bed, but sleep evaded me. I finally sat up and started reading again and had nearly finished *Winter's Bone* when I finally drifted off. I dreamed I was slogging along on snowshoes somewhere in the Cascades, but when I looked down, discovered it wasn't snow I was moving through but small white pills. Crazy.

I got to the office early the next morning, and after filing a motion on the divorce case I'd taken on, I called the hospice and asked for an appointment to interview Irene Halstead that evening. As expected, I was told they'd been given strict orders to keep me out by her next of kin, Aaron Abernathy. Next, I called the prosecutor handling the Lori Kavanaugh murder, Helen Berkowitz. We were never that friendly, and I was sure the bail hearing widened the breach. It was no secret that Helen didn't like men all that much, but I didn't take it personally. In fact, I admired her for forging a career in a male-dominated field like prosecutorial law.

I got right to the point. "Helen, I'm planning to talk to Lori Kavanaugh's mother, Irene Halstead. She has pancreatic cancer and is in hospice care. I went to visit her last Friday. Her stepson interrupted me, but I was able to verify that she's still coherent."

"She was thoroughly questioned, Cal. You have her statement."

"I know, but I'm interested in some details of Lori's life while she was living apart from Jim Kavanaugh. I think she might have had a lover." I also wanted to hear Halstead verify Abernathy's alibi but didn't share that. In the police interview, Halstead stated they were together that night, but I wanted to reopen the question. Being close to death can change a person's perspective, as she herself admitted.

Berkowitz laughed. "I know you like to fish, Cal, but this is over the top."

"This is potentially exculpatory evidence, Helen," I snapped back. "I'm going for a court order. Aaron Abernathy's blocking my access to Halstead. He's going to have to explain to Judge Whitcomb why I shouldn't be allowed to talk to his stepmother. If you want someone present, let me know."

She laughed again. "The woman's dying, for Christ's sake. Good luck with that."

That afternoon I closed up shop and headed out to get a firsthand account of Candice's latest espionage work. The sun had broken through, but the clouds building in the south hinted it was to be a short appearance. As Arch and I approached Le Petit Truc, I found the undulating sweep of the vineyards oddly comforting. Maybe it was the orderliness of the rows that stood in stark contrast to my life at that juncture, or maybe it was the fact that winemaking hadn't changed much at all in the last two thousand years. At least some things in this world weren't moving at warp speed.

Archie and I found Jim, Juan, and a crew of six working a section of the vineyard that sloped off to the southwest. "No rest for the wicked," I said to them as we approached.

Juan paused with a shovel balanced in his hands and smiled. "This compost does not spread itself."

Jim rested on his shovel and squinted at me. He looked good, but he always did when I caught him working. "Soon as we finish spreading this compost, we're going to plant the section with native grasses and wild flowers.

"What's that going to do for you?"

"It'll help keep the weeds down, but more importantly we hope it'll bring in beneficial insects and organisms indigenous to this soil. It's an experiment. We'll see what happens."

I looked around. "Leaves are almost gone. When do you start pruning?"

Juan groaned. Jim chuckled. "February. Everybody hates pruning, but it's absolutely critical."

Juan nodded. "Wine may be sophisticated, but growing grapes is simple farming. No shortcuts."

We riffed on that for a while, and then I left them to their work and set off to find Candice. "How's business?" I asked when I found her in the wine tasting room. Her slate blues looked tired, and her hair was piled carelessly on her head, making her look even taller than her six feet.

She hugged Arch and frowned up at me theatrically. "You don't want to know. One of our main distributors is dropping us. Just got the word this morning. Haven't broken it to the boss yet."

I sat down across from her, and she closed the lid to her laptop and looked directly at me. "What kind of pills is that asshole using?"

"Klonopin. It's an anti-anxiety—"

She nodded. "Benzos. That figures. They're popular in the valley these days."

"Did you see him taking them?"

"I saw him take some with his Scotch, but he didn't think I noticed. They were lying loose in a drawer next to his bed." She blushed a pale shade of red and looked away. "Jesus, Cal. I'm doing this for Jim, but he's going to think I'm some sort of harlot."

"No, he won't. He thinks the world of you."

"Sure he does," she said, and then her look turned hopeful. "At least he's made it a point not to ask me anything about the dates."

"Good. I'll keep him updated," I said and brought her back to the night before. "So, you took a pill from the drawer. Did you put it back after you photographed it?"

She pursed her lips momentarily. "No. When I went to put it back, Blake began stirring, so I held on to it."

"Hmm. Will he miss it?"

"I doubt it, but if he does, I'll just tell him I wanted to try one." She fixed me with her eyes. "Blake's popping pills like Lori. Have I found a connection?"

I shrugged. "It's certainly a possibility. Klonopin and Xanax are first cousins. Did you learn anything else?"

A thin smile spread across her face. "Besides the fact that he's a lousy lover? Well, he did pump me about the case some more. I told him you were lining up witnesses and experts, but that you seemed really worried about Jim's chances. That seemed to please him, and he warned me again about how evil Jim is, that he murdered an innocent woman. It was weird."

I nodded and took her through some more details about the case that she could casually drop, points that weren't strategic but sounded like inside information.

"Another thing. He asked me if I ever took my work home. He's hinting around about Jim's books."

"What did you tell him?"

"Oh, I laughed and said I bring stuff home all the time, like I didn't catch his drift. I figure he'll come back to me on that, Cal. He's grooming me."

I turned that over for a few moments. "Let's do this—tell him I'm asking you all kinds of questions about the business, that you're summarizing a lot of information for me. Meanwhile, why don't you and Jim cook something up to show him, like bogus sales volumes, costs, that sort of thing? Make the numbers better than they actually are."

She smiled, nodding slowly. "Oh, I like the way you think. We can do that."

"Did you get a look in his study?"

"Couldn't chance it. Like I said, he was starting to stir."

"When will you see him next?"

She frowned. "Wednesday night. He has tickets to a play in Portland."

"Good. Try to find out where he's getting his pills. If they're prescribed there might be a pill bottle around."

At that point, Jim came in. The three of us kicked around how best to cook the books for Blake Daniels, and when we finished Jim turned to me. "Sylvia and Eddie are having a big bash this Friday night to celebrate Tilikum's twelfth anniversary."

"You should go."

He laughed and waved a hand. "Not this time. They're pulling in all their big investors. You think they want me there?"

I shook my head. "You're—"

"I'm not going," he cut in. "It's going to be at some posh hotel downtown. I was thinking you and Winona should go. You know, consider it a perk for having me as a client." That made all three of us laugh. "Seriously, it'll be nice. I want you to go and enjoy yourselves."

I nodded. "Okay, I'll see if Winona's up for it and let you know."

I left that day wondering if I could talk Winona into going to the Tilikum party. I had to smile, thinking about what her reaction would be, and I could hear her groaning already. But the smile was short-lived when I thought about Candice's continued involvement with Blake Daniels. Her work was starting to pay off, and this time I'd encouraged her to stay involved. What if something happened to her?

I was all too familiar with slippery slopes, and this had all the earmarks of one.

Chapter Thirty-eight

"What's this hospice thing all about, Claxton?" It was the next morning, and Judge Clarence Whitcomb was on the line with Helen Berkowitz conferenced in.

I explained the situation, and Berkowitz and I reargued our positions. When we finished, I added, "Time is of the essence, your honor. It's pancreatic cancer."

A long pause ensued. I hoped he was looking at his docket. Whitcomb sighed into the phone. "Okay, I'll issue a show cause for Abernathy and the hospice. We'll try to hear this sucker on Thursday at three if we can round the parties up." Whitcomb put his clerk on, and I gave her Abernathy's home and work addresses and the name and address of the hospice. I smiled to myself at the thought of hipster boy being slapped with a subpoena. Oh, to be a fly on the wall.

The temperature took a dive that day, and by the time Arch and I headed for The Aerie, a cold rain was trying its damnedest to morph into sleet. I was toweling off Arch at the front door when Sean McKnight pulled up. I invited him in, but he stopped at the foot of the front porch steps and looked up at me, seemingly oblivious to the slush pattering around him. "No, thanks, Cal. I was, ah, just passing by and wondered if you would happen to have Maura Conisson's phone number or address. She's unlisted. I'd like to get in touch with her."

I thought of the suggestion I gave Maura to call him. Apparently, she hadn't gotten around to it. I grimaced. "Can't do that, Sean. I'm bound by confidentiality not to disclose her personal information." She wasn't really my client, so that wasn't completely true. But I was uncomfortable sharing the information. "She knows how to contact you. Give her some time."

He nodded and absently wiped a dollop of slush from the bridge of his nose. "Well, okay. I understand. I—"

"You sure you don't want to come in?"

He told me no and drove off as I stood there shaking my head. I understood how he felt; the kind of utter desolation that ensues when your moorings are suddenly cut. Should I have given him Maura's number? No. You've meddled enough, I reminded myself. Still, I worried about the good Reverend.

• • ● • •

Wednesday night came and went with no surreptitious texts from Candice Roberts. She called me Thursday morning. "It was an early night," she said. "Blake got a little drunk, and I didn't see any pill bottles lying around. Like we discussed, I told him I was busy going over Le Petit Truc's books because of a bunch of questions you asked me. He practically salivated, Cal. He's going to ask if he can look over my shoulder. I'm sure of it."

She told me they were seeing each other again on Saturday night. After she punched off I sat there deep in thought. Was Daniels just a ruthless competitor who wanted an inside track in case Le Petit Truc came on the market? Or was he a stone cold killer? I sighed and looked over at Arch, who tilted his ears forward in a gesture of attentiveness. "One thing's for sure, Big Boy," I told him. "I'm going to find a way to make Candice's next meeting with Blake her last." The risk was just too great.

The show cause hearing on Thursday afternoon was a slam dunk. Aaron Abernathy didn't bother to show, and the hospice's attorney agreed to the interview, provided it didn't last more than thirty minutes and a doctor was present to supervise. I argued for a Friday interview but settled for Saturday at noon.

After a busy Friday at Caffeine Central, Archie and I sped through a shopping spree at Whole Foods before finally finding a parking space three blocks from Winona's loft in the Pearl District. It was the same story everywhere in town—cars were starting to outnumber parking spaces in significant numbers, one of the prices of Portland becoming a cultural phenomenon and the darling of millennials with means. She greeted Archie, then hugged me and the bag full of groceries I carried. "Come right in. I'm starving."

"You only love me because of my vegetarian chili," I said.

She laughed. "Not true. I love you for your pork tenderloin with cherry reduction sauce, and anything you do with salmon, too."

The plan was to have a quick meal and then drop by the Tilikum party at the Sentinel Hotel. Winona had agreed to go, but, as I expected, only grudgingly. "It'll be fun and besides, I'm curious to see what the vibe is," I explained. "When liquor flows, tongues get loose."

She made a face. "Okay, but you owe me, Cal Claxton. I find social gatherings of well-to-do white people a little on the soul-sucking side."

While we sipped one of Winona's Sancerres, I cooked and she brought me up-to-date on the precarious plight of the steelhead runs on the Snake River and why the four dams on the river needed to go if the runs were to survive. We kicked that around, and by the time I added spices to a simmering skillet of diced tomatoes, peppers, black beans, and Kalamata olives, our conversation had turned to Jim's case.

"I'm on overload at the moment, but I feel like I'm close to something, a breakthrough, maybe," I said, and went on to tell her Nando had confirmed that Isabel Ruffino was still in Portland, that Blake Daniels had a benzo habit like Lori Kavanaugh, and that I had an appointment the next day to interview Lori's mother, Irene Halstead, who might know who Lori's lover was.

"Even if Halstead can't remember a name," I went on, "I'll have a shot at establishing reasonable doubt in court if she confirms there was a lover."

"What about that scumbag, Richard Amis? He could be Daniels' supplier, and who knows what mischief they might've cooked up together?"

I shrugged and smiled sheepishly. "I said I was close to something. Trouble is, I'm not sure what." I tasted the chili. "This is ready. Let's eat."

Chapter Thirty-nine

It was still cold, but the sky had cleared so we walked to the Sentinel Hotel, which was over on SW Eleventh in a turn-of-the-last-century, art nouveau building on the Historic Register. We entered through a set of imposing white marble columns into a lobby with a vaulted, coffered ceiling, intricately patterned marble floors, priceless-looking Oriental rugs, and massive leather furniture. "Figures," Winona said, looking around at the understated opulence.

We were directed to the Governor Ballroom, where an attractive young woman at the entry checked off our names. Jim Kavanaugh may have been a *persona non grata*, but his best pinot noir and pinot gris were flowing freely along with copious amounts of a sparkling wine made by another Dundee winery, Argyle. Sylvia Manning waved from across the room and worked her way through the crowd to greet us. She wore a conservative black dress accented with a silver necklace and, except for a trace of pale pink lipstick, was without makeup. Her smile was genuine, but I caught something in her eyes—worry, maybe, or just nervous tension. "Cal and Winona, so nice of you to come."

"We just stopped by to extend our congratulations on year twelve," I said. "Consider us Jim's surrogates."

Her face clouded over. "Oh, God, I feel terrible about not including Uncle Jim. I wanted to, but Eddie felt it wasn't a good idea." She glanced around. "Our biggest investors are here tonight."

I nodded. "He understands. You have a business to run. Is Eddie going to speak?"

She glanced at her watch. "In about five minutes. He has a great message tonight."

Eddie Manning took the stage, casually carrying a glass of wine. He wore a finely tailored blue suit, red power tie, and a single stud in his left ear that winked in the overhead lights. After thanking everyone for coming he said, "I'd like to propose a toast tonight to the two groups of people who've made Tilikum Capital Management such a success over the past twelve years. First, to our investors. We've always said your money is our sacred trust." He paused, smiled, and opened his hands. "Well, you believed in us, and look what's happened." A patter of laughter and applause ensued, and for a moment I thought he was going to tear up. "Thank you from the bottom of my heart." He raised his glass, took a sip, and went on to toast his employees, whom he praised as "the smartest, hardest working investment professionals in the business."

He touched on the business next, which he described at one point as "robust with the prospect of significant upside" and then went on to give a pitch for a new investment fund—The Tilikum Private Client Fund—that was reserved especially for the well-heeled investors in attendance. I glanced over at Winona, who rolled her eyes, and I figured that, like me, she was wondering who would be in Tilikum's debt collection crosshairs this time.

Whoever said it takes money to make money got it right.

Eddie finished to rousing applause, and after a huge cake was cut and shared along with more wine, toasts, and gift giveaways—a bevy of MacBook Pros, iPads, Bose headphones, and the like—he announced that Tilikum had reserved the Jackknife Bar in the hotel for the rest of the night, drinks on the house. I looked at Winona with raised eyebrows, she shrugged a yes, and as we drifted into the bar with the crowd, I bent close her. "Just for a while. Let's split up, see what's being said."

Winona peeled off with a group of Tilikum employees, I guessed salespersons by their buttoned-down, non-tattooed appearances, and I headed for the bar where a row of silver-haired investors were ordering a first round. Eddie stopped by, greeted them all by their first names and pumped my hand. "Welcome, Cal. Glad someone from Dundee's showing the flag," he said, flashing a brilliant smile. He went on to explain to the assembled group that the new investment fund would be based on purchasing medical debt. "We'll buy it pennies on the dollar with an opportunity to collect the full amount," he explained. "Exceptional opportunity." Eddie left to mingle elsewhere, and I listened to the group discuss Tilikum's prospects. They were all bullish on Tilikum's prospects, to be sure.

Since I wasn't driving, I ordered another drink—a Rémy Martin VSOP—and worked my way down the bar. By this time the crowd was moving off the topic of high finance as voices and laughter filled the room. I was talking to a couple of mid-level managers when I noticed Sylvia enter the bar. She stopped, her hands found her hips, and her look directed me to Eddie, who stood at a small, round table in a corner of the room. His smile flashed as he gestured to two young and very attractive female employees, who seemed enthralled with his every word. Sylvia watched for a few moments, then spun around and left without Eddie even noticing. I set my drink down, excused myself, and followed her.

She didn't stop until she was out on Eleventh Street. "I didn't know you smoked," I said as I joined her.

She blew out a plume of bluish smoke and tried unsuccessfully to smile. "Yeah, well I quit but just started up again." She took another long drag on her cigarette.

"You seem upset. Is something wrong?"

She exhaled very slowly as if considering my question, then swung her gaze to me. Her eyes filled but didn't spill over. "All I ask is that he not be so obvious about it." She inhaled again before going on, the smoke tumbling from her mouth as she spoke. "I don't care about a fling or two as long as he's discreet, you know what I mean?" I nodded. She laughed bitterly. "Like John Kennedy or Bill Clinton, he just can't seem to help it."

I nodded, not quite knowing what to say.

"Then there's Uncle Jim's situation." She inhaled and blew out another cloud of smoke that drifted down 11th Street. "God, what a mess."

"Don't worry about Jim. We'll get that sorted out."

She swung her gaze back to me, her look making it clear she knew I was speaking more out of desire than conviction. "I hope so," she said, forcing a wan smile before dropping the cigarette and grinding it out on the pavement with a toe of her high heels. "Better get back to the party." She gritted out another smile. "Appearances, you know."

When I re-entered the Jackknife Bar I found Winona laughing uproariously with a group of female Tilikum employees. I waved at her, and after hugs all around she broke free from the group and joined me. I wasn't surprised that she quickly bonded with those women. Winona's frank demeanor had a way of disarming people and inviting trust and friendship. I wished she had been out there with Sylvia rather than me.

Sylvia had joined the high rollers at the bar, and I didn't see Eddie, so we slipped out of the Jackknife without saying goodbye. The night air held a damp chill, and Winona leaned into me and grasped my arm as we walked down 11th toward Burnside. "So, what do you think?" I asked.

"Interesting. I want in on that private fund."

I laughed. "You can't afford it. It's going to be medical debt this time. Lots of that out there these days."

"Ugh. How utterly disgusting."

"Did you hear anything interesting?" I asked.

"Not much except that Eddie is going to be the next Warren Buffet. Oh, and he's quite the womanizer. Did you see him in the corner with those two young women?" I nodded. "And he's not just a flirt from what I heard."

"That's for sure." I told her what Sylvia let slip. We walked along in silence for a while.

Winona said, "Like I said before, Eddie would have been a nice catch for Lori, and now we know the guy's a serious player."

"True, but if he was her lover then I'm wrong about the lover being the killer, because Eddie was at a Mozart concert the night Lori was killed."

Winona shrugged. "So? Maybe he was her lover and had someone else kill her."

"Maybe, but he has no motive, either. Tilikum's thriving, and it's clear he'd rather make money than wine."

We fell silent again and continued to walk. Sure, Eddie was a player, and I detested that kind of behavior as well as his way of making a living, but that didn't make him a killer. Nothing implicated him, or for that matter Sylvia, and given Jim's affection for them both, I was glad of that.

Chapter Forty

"Good luck, Cal." Winona stood at the front door to her loft with Archie beside her. It hadn't been hard to convince my dog he needed to stay behind. After all, he and Winona were great buddies, and there was the promise of a long walk in Tom McCall Park, which I'm sure he understood.

Against heavy odds, the clear sky from the night before still held sway, although a moisture-laden breeze from the south signaled change. I took the Ross Island Bridge across the river and parked in front of the Northwest Hospice and Palliative Care Center at eleven-fifty. I took a couple of minutes to review my notes before going in. Helen Berkowitz told me she would send a lawyer from her office to sit in on the interview, but except for an elderly couple and their miniature poodle there was no one in the lobby. I was relieved to see that the woman whose job I'd almost cost was still behind the main desk. She was scowling at a computer screen as I approached.

"Good to see you again," I said in a bright tone. "I'm here to see Irene Halstead."

Her eyes swung from the screen to me, then her mouth drooped at the corners, and her forehead sprang a set of deep wrinkles. "Oh, Mr. Claxton, I left a message at your office. Mrs. Halstead has passed away. I'm so sorry."

I stood there for a moment as her words sunk in. Damn, damn, damn. "I'm sorry to hear that. What happened?"

"I don't have any details. Would you like to speak to my manager?"

The manager, it turned out, was in an office behind the reception desk, a middle-aged woman with a sympathetic, if somewhat dour demeanor. After the receptionist introduced me, she said, "We tried to reach you, Mr. Claxton."

"I know, and I appreciate that. I just have a few questions." She nodded and leaned back in her chair. I said, "What time did Mrs. Halstead die?"

"Last night around nine o'clock. It was a peaceful transition, and she wasn't alone."

"Oh? Who was with her?"

"Her stepson, Mr. Abernathy. He's been a blessing. So faithful."

"No one else?"

Her brows lowered a fraction, but her expression didn't change. "That's correct."

I nodded. "I suppose Mrs. Halstead had taken a turn for the worse."

She leaned forward. "Actually, she seemed to have rallied, but that's sometimes the case toward the end, I'm afraid."

"Really? I didn't realize that happened."

She nodded knowingly. "It's a kind of a last hurrah, you know, when the body senses death is eminent."

I smiled. "A last hurrah unless it's a genuine rally, I suppose."

"Yes, although genuine rallies against pancreatic cancer are quite rare." She sighed quietly. "We'll miss Irene. She was a sweet soul."

I thanked her and turned to go but then thought of one more question. "Forgot to ask—what funeral home has she been taken to?"

"Van Scoy Memorial. They're over in Northeast."

When I got to my car I Googled the mortuary, a family-owned business on NE Broadway, whose website promised "Cremations at a price you can afford." I called them. No, they had no information yet on the funeral arrangements and whether or not there would be a viewing, I was told. "We'll post that information just as soon as it becomes available."

Rain began pelting the windshield, making my view of the parking lot blurry. It was an apt metaphor for my state of mind. How hard would it have been to smother Irene Halstead with a pillow? I wondered. She was, after all, weak as a kitten. The thought of that sent a chill down my back. Or, maybe Abernathy killed her some other way, something an autopsy might pick up. I laughed at that. No way I could force an autopsy unless there was something suspicious about her death, and a "peaceful transition" didn't conjure up much suspicion. Sure, she had apparently rallied, but that could be explained away, too.

I started the car, flipped on the wipers, and watched their back and forth sweep. On the other hand, Abernathy had been good about visiting his stepmom, the faithful stepson. So it was no surprise that he happened to be with her when she died. And his denying me access could have been motivated by a desire to protect his loved one, as he claimed more than once. True, it looked like he'd placed her body on a fast track to cremation, but, then again, it wasn't that unusual these days, was it?

Chapter Forty-one

Sparks arced from the grinding wheel, painting my garage in a flickering, eerie light. It was the next morning, early, and I was putting an edge on my ax before attacking what was left of the oak rounds. I went back to Winona's after the hospice fiasco, but I wasn't particularly good company. She knew my moods and finally said, "You aren't in a bad mood very often, Cal Claxton, but when you are, you're insufferable. Why don't you go back to The Aerie and regroup? I've got things to do today."

That was Winona—straight to the point and invariably on target when it came to me.

I worked out behind the garage until there wasn't another log to split, and then set about re-splitting some of the pieces, until I had a nice stack of kindling as well. It was bitterly cold but clear, and I was sweating by the time I ferried a wheelbarrow load to the porch and finished stacking the logs. I stood back and admired my work—a woodpile that would see me through the winter with the bonus of a psyche eased of some acute frustration.

I retreated into the house, took a hot shower, and it wasn't until I stepped into the kitchen to make some lunch that I noticed the blinking light on my answering machine. I punched "play" and listened to the recorded message: "Hello Cal, this is Richard Amis. I need to talk to you as soon as possible." There was a long pause before he resumed speaking. "I need help, and under the circumstances you're the only person I feel I can turn to. Eleanor's out of town so we can talk here. Call me, please, or just come by." I jotted down the number he left, dialed it, and got a recording. I stood there tapping a pen on the countertop while I tried to fathom what he would be calling me about. I always needed business, but not from a sleazy, pill-pushing psychiatrist.

I had things to do that Sunday, so I decided to wait for him to call back.

I finally fixed a faucet that had leaked for the past two months, got caught up on my e-mail, and had just lain down for a nap when someone rapped on the front door. It was Gertie Johnson, bearing the blueberry pie she promised. "Sorry this took so long, Cal, but I've been chockablock this week. She thrust a plastic pie caddy into my hands. "It's not my best, you know," she said. "Those frozen berries just don't cook up right. Too soft."

I laughed. "From spectacular to just amazing. I'll suffer through." When she left I went immediately to the kitchen and made a double cappuccino. Coffee and home-baked pie. I couldn't resist, even if it was four in the afternoon. While I sipped and ate I replayed Amis' message. The voice was strained, for sure, maybe even a little fearful. I called him again, and again he didn't answer. I drained my coffee and looked at Arch. "Up for a ride, Big Boy?"

As I drove down through the Hills that day, the sky was streaked with red as though the sun had bled to death somewhere behind the cloud cover. I turned south on Pacific Highway and fell in behind a stretch limo with tinted windows and a sign on the back that read Willamette Valley Wine Tours. Wine tasting was big business in Dundee, even in November. When I finally crested the long drive into Amis' place, I was relieved to see several lights on inside, suggesting he was home. I parked on the drive, well back from the house, cut my lights and watched. The thought occurred to me that this might be some kind of trap set by the man whose blackmail scheme I'd thwarted, but that seemed silly. After all, he'd left a readily traceable call on my answering machine, hardly the act of someone plotting revenge.

Nothing stirred around or in the house. I told Arch to relax, made my way to the front porch, and rang the bell next to a set of massive front doors inset with vertical glass panels. No one appeared in the entry hall, but I could hear strains of classical music coming from inside the house.

I followed a manicured path tracing the circular contour of the house to the patio on the west side of the structure. Wisps of steam rose from the spa built into the corner of the swimming pool and the music, Mahler's Fifth, I think, was also playing on a set of outdoor speakers. The French doors leading into the house were ajar. I leaned in and announced myself a couple of times. No answer, which was not surprising because the house was huge, and Mahler was probably piped into every room.

As I turned to go around to the back of the house, something on the floor caught my eye—a trail of faint marks that stood out against the polished marble surface like a dotted line. Spaced like footprints, the marks faded before they reached the French doors where I stood. As if on cue, Mahler moved to hushed violins, so I called out again. Nothing.

I entered the room and dropped to one knee for a closer look at the marks. Footprints, for sure, the faint contours of a shoe sole outlined by something that had dried dark red. Wine, or was it blood? I moved along the marks and just below the arched entry into the room, one of the prints showed a hint of a waffle pattern like the one I saw the night Archie was poisoned. I stood up, and a cold chill slithered down my back. The print was roughly my size, just like the earlier one. I took my phone out and quickly photographed the print from a couple of different angles.

The light was low in the hallway, but I could see that the footprints came from the direction of an open doorway to my left, the entry to Amis' wine cellar, I recalled. The smell of wine hung heavily in the air, and I relaxed a little. Maybe the footprints were from wine after all. A spill, perhaps?

I moved down the hall and stopped at the foot of the stairs. The cellar lights were on and the smell of wine even stronger. I called out again and waited through a few more bars of Mahler before taking the stairs. I found Richard Amis in his beloved wine cellar. He lay face up in a pool of wine and blood next to the shattered statue of Bacchus. The wine came from several bottles smashed on the floor, and the blood from a series of blows he'd taken to the head. I checked for a pulse. There was none. His half-moon eyes stared back at me, as blank as those of Bacchus, the God of wine, whose head lay next to his outstretched hand.

I stood up in shocked disbelief, pushed down a wave of nausea, and forced myself to focus. Was the killer still in the house? Not likely, since the dryness of the blood indicated the attack happened earlier, maybe an hour before. Judging from the broken bottles and sodden cloth caddy lying next to him, Amis must have been carrying a load of wine when he was attacked. I imagined him backing up as the killer came down the stairs and then trying to deflect the blows with the bottles as he backed into the corner occupied by Bauccus. I shuddered as I pictured the violent attack.

I didn't see anything resembling the murder weapon, a blunt instrument of some kind that crushed his skull in two places, at least. The blows were vicious, judging from the vertical spray of blood that stained his pride and joy, the landscape painting of Le Petit Truc hanging in the alcove above him.

I got the hell out of the cellar and called 911. That's when I noticed more tracks leading to a room further down the hall toward the back of the house. The intruder must have gone there after killing Amis. I glanced at my watch. I had five, maybe ten minutes before the police arrived. The room was Amis' study, and it had been ransacked. The contents of a wooden filing cabinet were strewn across the floor, the records of Amis' patients, consultation summaries, and prescription logs. Using my handkerchief, I sifted through the tangled mess as best I could. I didn't find Lori Kavanaugh's file. On a whim, I looked for a file on Blake Daniels but saw none.

A stack of opened mail sat next to a phone on the desk. I went through the envelopes and was surprised to find two with Tilikum Capital Management return addresses. The first envelope contained a statement for the third quarter, showing earnings on an investment of four hundred fifty thousand dollars. I whistled when I read it. A letter from the second envelope informed Amis that as a "top tier client," he was eligible for the new "Tilikum Private Client Fund," the fund Eddie Manning described at the party.

Books from the bookcase and the contents of the desk drawers were also scattered on the floor. There was no sign of a computer anywhere in the room. A tear-off calendar on the desk had the day's date and a jotted message:

Pick up Eleanor. United Flt. 4223. 8:35.

I felt a sharp pang of sorrow for the couple. Amis was a vile human being, but he didn't deserve to die like that. Nobody did. And his wife? My heart went out to her. Thank God it wasn't my job to break the news.

I was tempted to check out the rest of the house, but five minutes had passed and I'd seen enough to know it wasn't a burglary gone bad. It looked like the killer was after Lori Kavanaugh's psychiatric file and any digital records stored on Amis' computer. Amis' murder could have been collateral damage, but that seemed unlikely.

I followed the bloody footprints back outside and joined Archie in the Beemer to wait for the police. My dog put his head up next to mine and licked me a couple of times on the ear. I patted his head and then called Jim Kavanaugh and was told that he, Juan, and his crew had worked all day in the southwest vineyard, eight until five. Next, Candice told me she played tennis from twelve to two thirty and then went to Le Petit Truc to work on inventory.

I scrolled down my contact list and punched in Sean McKnight next. "Where were you between noon and four today?" I asked after we exchanged greetings.

"I was here at Stone Gate. Why do you ask?"

Is there anyone who can verify that?"

A long pause followed. "Uh, yes. I had a guest this afternoon."

"Who was it?"

Another pause. "Maura Conisson. She called yesterday, and I invited her out so we could talk. Why? What's this all about, Cal?"

"I'm at Richard Amis' place. I just found him beaten to death in his wine cellar."

McKnight sucked a breath. "Oh, my God, that's terrible."

"Anyone else see you and Maura together?"

"Uh, no, I don't think so. We were alone here at the farm all afternoon."

"Okay. Let me think about how to handle this. Meanwhile, don't discuss this with anyone, even Maura. I'll get back to you."

I punched off and sat there for a few moments, my mind flashing back to the crime scene photos of Lori Kavanaugh. Amis had received a similar beating. There was the bloody footprint, too. Would it match the one I found at my place? My gut said yes. Of course, if the abortive blackmail scheme comes to light, McKnight and Conisson would become immediate suspects, given what Amis inflicted on them. Sure, they could alibi each other, but that would be viewed with a high degree of skepticism.

As McKnight's attorney, I had an obligation to protect him and wasn't about to divulge any more information than I had to. At the same time, I could not withhold evidence in a murder investigation under any circumstances. So it would depend a lot on the kinds of questions I was going to get. To top it off, it looked even more likely that the two murders were related somehow, which meant I had two cases with clients whose interests might conflict. That was never a good thing for a lawyer.

I exhaled a long breath, which got me another slobbery kiss from Arch. "Now I know what the Flying Wallendas feel like," I told him.

Chapter Forty-two

"So you got this phone call from Mr. Amis asking you to come see him, right?" Detective Hal Ballard said. The crime scene was sealed off, and we were talking in the large, marble-floored room containing the footprints. I'd taken him and his partner, Sonia Rodriquez, through the gist of what I'd found. Now they were circling back for more details.

"That's right. He said he needed help."

"For what? Rodriquez asked.

I shrugged. "I don't know, and he didn't say."

"You saved the recording, right?"

"Yes." I explained how I called back several times and finally drove over and went around to the side of the house when no one answered the front door bell. "Classical music was blaring inside the house," I told them. "I figured he hadn't heard the bell."

"Why would you go into someone's house just because you saw some footprints on the floor?" Rodriquez again.

I shrugged. "I knew they were footprints, and they looked odd, you know, with a dark reddish cast. It was a hunch, I guess. They just sort of drew me in."

"You thought blood?"

"Actually, my first thought was wine, but I wasn't sure. The print of the shoe sole was the clearest. Like I told you, that print is going to match the one found inside my fence line, I'm sure of it. You should have a photograph of it in your files." I wasn't really *that* sure, but I didn't want them to blow the fact off. I saw Ballard underline something in his notes.

"Why did you go clear into the cellar?" Ballard continued.

"I smelled the wine. Thought there might have been some kind of accident." I saw my opening and went for it. "Listen, that footprint's key. The person who broke into my house was looking for information on the Lori Kavanaugh murder. The person who broke in here and killed Amis was wearing the same shoes and killed him in a manner very similar to Kavanaugh. Richard Amis was Lori's psychiatrist, so he would know an awful lot about her personal life. That's why he was killed. I'll bet the murderer has gone through Amis' files, too."

Rodriquez rested her hands on her hips and looked me in the eye. "That's a lot of guesswork, counselor." She paused and then added, "Did you go into his study?"

"Nope," I lied, hoping I hadn't left any prints.

Ballard shot me a skeptical look but didn't pursue it. "Do you know where James Kavanaugh was today?"

I nodded. "He was working out in his vineyard with a half-dozen other workers from eight until five. You can check his ankle bracelet."

Rodriquez looked at Ballard, then swung her eyes back to mine. Her face had tightened. "You talked to him already?"

"I called him while I was waiting for you. Thought you might ask that question."

Ballard put a hand on his forehead and ran it back until it found his receding hairline. A two-day growth bristled on cheeks that were on a fast track to jowls. His eyes narrowed down. "Do you know any reason why Amis would call you?"

There it was—a broad question that could force my hand about the blackmail case. I needed to keep this about Jim and Lori. "About the Kavanaugh case?"

"Yeah, of course."

"I don't know for sure. I think he had some information he wanted to pass on to me. He told me in an earlier conversation he didn't believe Jim Kavanaugh killed his wife."

"Why did he wait so long to contact you?"

I shrugged again. "I don't know."

At that point Rodriquez looked at her watch and frowned. "I need to go if I'm going to catch Mrs. Amis at the airport." I guess she drew the short straw on that one.

Ballard took me through another round of questions before releasing me. "I'll want you tomorrow in McMinnville for a formal statement and follow-up. We'll let you know the timing."

I told him I'd be there and left him wearing a troubled look, his shoulders slumped, his hands buried in his pockets. He knew this development could give me a toehold for an alternate theory of the case—that the killer wearing the waffle-soled jogging shoes was still out there while my client was wearing an ankle bracelet.

But I wasn't kidding myself. I was walking a very thin line here between answering the questions and withholding evidence in a murder case. I could argue that we were only talking about the Kavanaugh murder, that I didn't feel the blackmail case was germane, and that I was bound by confidentiality, in any case. It was a weak argument but bolstered by the fact that Sean McKnight, who stood six-foot four, could not fit into a size nine or ten jogging shoe. And Maura Conisson, who stood maybe five-five or five-six, would swim in them. And I couldn't picture either one of them extracting revenge for their ordeal by committing such a violent act. That made no sense at all.

The pictures were gone, the blackmail case closed.

I stopped off at Le Petit Truc on my way back to The Aerie. Archie was grateful for a little freedom and wandered off into the darkness. "Behave yourself, Big Boy," I told him.

I found Jim and Candice in the wine tasting room with half a bottle of wine between them. "Join us, Candice said, "we're getting drunk for no reason whatsoever."

Jim laughed and slid a chair in my direction with his foot. I filled them in on what I'd learned, leaving out the blackmail side of the story and stressing that this might be a path to creating reasonable doubt in some jurors' minds. Candice poured me a generous portion of wine in a tulip glass. I swirled, sniffed, and took a long pull, probably more than was proper wine drinking etiquette. I let it rest there for a moment on my tongue and couldn't think of when I'd tasted anything better. "Just what I needed," I said, breaking into the first genuine smile of the day.

We kicked the Amis situation around for a while before I turned to Jim and changed the subject. "Sylvia apologized profusely for not inviting you to their party."

Jim smiled. "Hell, they did me a favor. No way I was going to plunge into another goddamn social event with the jewelry I'm wearing around my ankle."

I said, "You were right. That was some bash. They gave away a boatload of tech gear as part of the celebration, and after serving your pinot and some bubbly, Eddie bought the Sentinel bar for the evening, drinks on the house."

"The Jackknife?" Candice said, her eyes registering surprise.

I nodded. "It must have cost a fortune. That has to be the most expensive bar in Portland."

I nodded. "I, uh, noticed that Eddie's quite the ladies' man." Jim's eyes swung to mine. "He was giving a couple of young saleswomen some intense training over in the corner of the bar after his speech. I think Sylvia got upset with him."

Jim waved off my comment. "He's a flirt, for Christ's sake, always has been. So fucking what?"

"Have you heard from them this weekend?"

He caught my drift immediately, and his face went hard like ceramic. "Oh, so now Eddie needs an alibi for today?"

"Damn it, Jim. This isn't personal. I'm trying to eliminate people here."

"He and Sylvia flew to Phoenix Saturday morning. Some kind of business foray. They'll be back Tuesday. Satisfied?"

"Sure. Thanks. Uh, one other thing—what about the relationship between Amis and Eddie? Did you know Amis is an investor at Tilikum?"

Jim tugged on his beard for a moment. "No, but it wouldn't surprise me. Eddie asked me to introduce him to Amis at one of our tastings. They seemed to hit it off."

I turned to Candice. "What about Blake Daniels? Do you know where he was today?"

She shook her head. "We had a date for tonight, but he cancelled yesterday. Said something came up. I'm seeing him Wednesday night. I'll dig into it." She hesitated a moment, glancing at Jim, then back to me. "Of course, we already know Blake's hooked on benzos, which could connect him to Amis." It was something we hadn't shared with Jim, just to keep the lid on.

Jim's eyebrows dipped, and the vertical folds of flesh appeared on his forehead, announcing his anger. "So, Daniels is a junkie, too, huh? Maybe that bastard got Lori hooked." By this time, rising blood had reddened his neck.

I jumped in before Candice could say anything else. "He uses pills when he drinks. We don't know if that's significant or not. Keep your cool, Jim."

I turned to Candice. "Keep an eye out for a pair of jogging shoes, too. Like I said, they have a typical waffle-pattern sole." I showed her the pictures on my phone, then e-mailed them to her.

We polished off the bottle, opened another, and the conversation slipped away from murder and mayhem. Her thick blond hair down, her face unadorned with makeup, Candice sipped some wine and leaned back. "You know, a lot of people bitch about the rainy season in the Northwest, but I like it."

Jim raised his glass to her. "Agreed." And the vineyard likes it, too. The roots are growing like crazy out there right now."

Candice sighed. "Then in March the vines wake up again, the buds break, and the cycle starts all over." She placed her hand over Jim's for a moment and squeezed. "No wonder I love this business so much."

We talked about wine, the Dundee Hills, and the joys of living in the Northwest until the second bottle was gone. I collected Archie and left Jim and Candice there, basking in that mellow mood. In all honesty, I felt a little envious. Their work was so connected to the land, and the product they produced so tangible.

What was I doing with my life? I mused. What was my product? Application of the law, I supposed, or an outcome favorable to my client in the best of cases. Compared to making wine, sterile, you could say, and, aside from a bit of paper and ink, ephemeral. But my product could have profound and lasting consequences. There was something else, too. I didn't always like the people who practiced my trade, but I loved the law and believed in the institution.

I looked back at Arch as I pulled out of Le Petit Truc. "I guess it takes all kinds, Big Boy."

Chapter Forty-three

At 9:02 a.m. the next morning, I called Van Scoy Memorial and was told that the service for Irene Halstead was going to be a private affair, by invitation only. "Will there be a viewing?" I asked.

"No. I'm afraid not. Mrs. Halstead's remains were cremated yesterday at the request of Mr. Abernathy."

"Wow," I said after I punched off. "Dead Friday night, cremated Sunday. It doesn't go any faster than that." If there was any evidence of foul play in her death, it had gone up in flames.

I tapped in Aaron Abernathy's number next and he picked up. "What do you want, Claxton?" he greeted me.

"I, uh, just wanted to say that I'm sorry for your loss and apologize for that incident at the hospice. My fault for not checking with you first."

The line went silent. "So you slap me with a subpoena? What the fuck. I just wanted Irene to die in peace."

"I completely understand. But if I don't do my job thoroughly, my ass is on the line, you know what I'm saying? I'm sure you can understand that." More silence at his end. "I was wondering if there will be a viewing or a service. I'd like to send some flowers."

"Spare us, please. It's strictly private. She's ashes now, and we're going to scatter them in the Pacific. That's what she wanted."

"Oh, the cremation must have been yesterday. Did you attend?"

Another silence. "You got anything else, man?"

Keeping my obsequious tone, I signed off and then called the woman at Van Scoy back and asked if anyone from the family attended the cremation. "Why no," she told me. "It was done with great dignity by our staff. People tend to shy away from the actual cremation, I'm afraid."

Well, Abernathy could still have an alibi for yesterday, but at least I knew he wasn't at Van Scoy Memorial, witnessing his stepmother's cremation.

I got a call from Detective Ballard asking me to come by his office at eleven that morning. I didn't know how long that interview would take, and I had some other matters at the courthouse to attend to, so I dropped Archie off at Gertie's. I didn't want him hanging around the property alone. I doubted he'd ever trust food from a stranger again, but I sure as hell didn't want to chance it. "I'll take him for a walk to the cemetery after I finish your billing," she told me.

Ballard and Rodriquez hauled me back over everything, dotting a few i's and crossing a few t's. Very few. I did get them to admit Lori Kavanaugh's file hadn't turned up. I didn't bother asking about Blake Daniels. Apparently, the upstairs bedrooms had been tossed, and some cash and jewelry were missing, according to Eleanor Amis. A preliminary examination of the footprints photographed at my place compared to those found in Amis' house revealed similarities but not necessarily a match. This would be something for experts to argue about if and when Jim's case came to court. "We're not through with the crime scene yet," Ballard told me, "but it's looking more and more like a burglary gone very bad."

That's about what I expected from an overworked investigative unit. They already had an arrest in the Kavanaugh murder and clearly didn't want any complications from this crime. "What about Lori Kavanaugh's missing file and the computer records?" I asked. "Why would a burglar take those?"

Ballard shrugged. Rodriquez said, "Who knows? Things get lost in the shuffle."

"Lost in the shuffle, my ass," I let slip before I had a chance to corral the comment. I left without saying another word, and if it had been colder outside I'm sure steam would have been condensing around my ears. Mission accomplished by the killer, I decided.

I went back to my office and slogged my way through a couple of afternoon meetings and a call to my blood spatter expert witness. He was confident, he told me, that the high resolution photographic evidence submitted by the Sheriff's Department, as well as the clothing, showed definitively that my client, James Kavanaugh, had no traces of high velocity blood spatter on his person.

That was a morale booster, although I knew that Helen Berkowitz was most assuredly lining up her bevy of experts, who would dispute my guy's findings, point by point. Dueling experts are a way of life in the modern courtroom. Facts, it turns out, are not always robust, stand-alone entities but slippery little critters that are hard to pin down.

I was just closing the backdoor to my office that afternoon when my cell phone chirped. "Cal, it's Sean McKnight. I'm at the Sheriffs' Office in McMinnville. I've been hauled in for questioning regarding the Amis murder. I told them you were my attorney, that I wanted to talk to you before the interview. Do you know what's going on?"

"No, I don't know a thing. Listen, Sean, just stay quiet until I get there." As I weaved my way down to the Pacific Highway I had a strong sense of déjà vu—another murder and another Dundee Hills neighbor in potential trouble. At the same time, I felt like a noose was tightening around my own neck.

Now what?

Chapter Forty-four

There wasn't a fresh molecule of air in the Yamhill County Sheriff's interview room, and the garish fluorescent lighting lent a kind of inquisition vibe to the space. Sean McKnight was calm and centered, as if there weren't anything else that could rattle him after what Amis had put him through. I asked for some one-on-one time, but as expected Detective Ballad turned me down. "We'd like to interview him first, and since you've opted to join us, follow up with another chat with you." That made sense, of course. We were both potential suspects in Amis' murder, and Ballard wasn't going to provide an opportunity for us to coordinate our stories.

I nodded and looked at McKnight. "I don't know what this is all about, Sean, but I wouldn't talk to them without an attorney present. I can help you find one."

He looked puzzled. "You can't sit in?"

"I could, but it's not a good idea. I'm a witness in this thing, I'm afraid."

McKnight paused, seeming to turn this over in his mind. "Well, I'm sure that's the prudent thing to do, but, you know, I really have nothing to hide here. Maybe the best thing is to just get it over with."

I shook my head. "I don't advise that. You don't know where this is going yet."

"I know, Cal, and I respect your opinion, but I'm through

holding things in." He exhaled a breath and turned to Ballard. "Let's get on with it, Detective."

I exited the interview room as Detective Rodriquez passed me going in, nodding curtly. I took a seat in the empty, poorly lit hallway, my mind churning over the situation. Had I made the right call in shielding McKnight and Conisson? I went back over my initial exchange with Ballard, when he asked me if I knew any reason why Amis would have called me. Was that question open-ended enough that I was obligated to reveal the blackmail case? No, I decided once again. The question was asked within the narrower context of the Lori Kavanaugh case, and my answer was an honest one.

This provided little solace, however. I was on a legal knife edge, and I knew it.

My thoughts turned to why Ballard was suddenly interested in McKnight. I could only guess at this point, but I was pretty sure I knew the answer, and it wasn't a good one for either him or me.

Ten minutes into McKnight's interview, Rodriquez left the room and hurried down the hall toward the back of the building. I had a hunch where she was headed. An hour later, McKnight came out, looking none the worse for wear, and I was invited in to join Ballard.

"Coffee?" he said when I sat down.

"Yes. I thought you'd never ask. Black."

He left the room and came back with two steaming cups— mine paper and his a chipped mug that had *Sarcasm. It's What I Do* inscribed on it. His perpetual three-day growth looked like it could sand iron, and his pinkish pate showed through thinning hair in the overhead lights. He blew on his coffee, took a sip, and pulled a thumb drive from his shirt pocket and held it up. "We found this digital storage device in a desk drawer in Richard Amis' study. The killer missed it. It contains a series of photographs and video clips involving Sean McKnight and a woman. Someone in our department recognized McKnight, and now, thanks to him, we know the woman's name is Maura Conisson, a Portland resident. The material on this drive is sexually explicit." He laid the drive on the table in front of him and swung his eyes up to mine. "Care to comment, counselor?"

Yep, I said to myself. Should have known Amis would hold back a copy of the pictures. After all, he'd gone to great lengths to make them, and who knows, he might've been a voyeur as well. I had no choice but to lay out the blackmail scheme, which I assumed would match what McKnight had told them. Ballard peppered me with questions, and by way of summary I said, "So McKnight came to me and asked for help. He wanted to keep this under the radar for obvious reasons. I was able to locate Conisson and convinced her to cooperate with us in getting the materials back. In exchange, we offered not to press charges against either her or Amis. The terms were accepted, materials were transferred to McKnight, but apparently Amis saw fit to keep a copy. We had no knowledge of that."

Ballard leaned back and steepled his fingers. "So, as a result of Amis' actions, McKnight's wife leaves him and he loses his church. Even a man of God would be pissed at that."

"You'd think so, but that's not the case. His anger's directed at himself and nobody else, believe me. I've never seen a man take a hit like that with so much grace and forgiveness. He, uh, practices what he preaches. Literally."

Ballard kept his fingers joined and puckered a cheek in a one-sided smile. "So, the afternoon that Amis is killed, McKnight's with his lover, the woman who helped wreck his life. Man, this is weird."

I shrugged. "Not really. Once I confronted her, Maura Conisson was genuinely sorry for the role she played in this. I'm sure McKnight told you about her little boy. Now they're both trying to get their lives back on track."

Ballard puffed a breath, then leaned forward and locked in on me. "Why did you withhold this information from us?"

"I was compelled by client confidentiality. Yesterday the conversation turned on the footprints and the possible connection of Amis' death with Lori Kavanaugh's. Check your notes, Hal. The blackmail deal was finished, case closed. It wasn't relevant, and I knew that McKnight and Conisson both had solid alibis."

Ballard laughed. "Yeah, they're each other's alibi. How convenient. Looks to me like either one or both of them had a pretty good motive to beat Amis to death."

I shook my head emphatically. "You're not going to find anything, Hal. McKnight didn't do it. Hell, he must wear a size twelve or thirteen shoe. And, do you think he would have left that thumb drive lying around? Come on, give them a break. Both he and Conisson are innocent bystanders in this murder."

If those blows landed, Ballard didn't show it. "I'm no lawyer," he said, "but I do know that attorney-client privilege is no excuse for suppressing evidence. I'm afraid Helen Berkowitz is going to take a dim view of your actions."

"I'm not worried," I said with more conviction that I felt. "Last time I checked, I have an overarching responsibility to my clients."

After Ballard cut me loose, I waited out in the hall with McKnight. I figured Rodriquez was dispatched to pick up Maura Conisson, and sure enough, forty minutes later we saw them both come in and watched as Rodriquez hustled her into a side door. McKnight turned to me, concern clouding his eyes. "Will she be all right?"

I shrugged. "Murder charges aside, she has another potential vulnerability—she participated in the blackmail scheme, although she also helped make it right. I'm not sure how they'll look at that. In any case, she shouldn't talk to them without a lawyer."

McKnight leaned into me. "Can we get word to her? I'll pay for the attorney."

"No, she'll have to make that call when they ask her whether she wants a lawyer present."

McKnight allowed himself a chuckle. "Good luck with that. I know her. She'll want to get the truth out just like me."

We waited on a hard bench in that echoing, godforsaken hallway for Conisson to re-emerge. McKnight seemed reluctant to talk about his personal life, but I did learn that the break with his wife was final and that his church had appointed a search team to find his replacement. "What are you going to do now?" I asked.

He shrugged and swept back his silver mane with both hands. "I'm not sure yet. God hasn't revealed his plans for me."

Maura Conisson appeared an hour later looking shaken but resolute and decidedly beautiful. She nodded to me and took both of McKnight's outstretched hands in hers as their eyes locked together. They didn't hug. There were no surprises in her recap of the interview, which she prefaced by saying, "It was humiliating to have to replay all the disgusting things I did. My God, Sean, I can't believe you're still here." McKnight, of course, reassured her.

I drove them both to Stone Gate Farm so that he could take Conisson back to Portland. "It's a good sign none of us are being held," I told them in parting. "They might show up at your places with search warrants, although I don't think they have enough to get a judge to sign them. If they do, call me right away and tell them to wait until I get there. I'm not your attorney on this matter, but I can advise you. If they can't connect you to the crime scene with physical evidence, that'll be the end of it." For you, at least, I said to myself.

"What about the thumb drive? What will become of it?" McKnight asked.

"As long as you two are suspects, it'll remain in the Sheriff's custody. After that, well, it's sort of in no man's land." They flinched in unison. I raised both hands in reassurance. "I promise I'll try to get it back so that you can destroy it."

I left them silhouetted against the porch light at McKnight's farmhouse. As I pulled away, I thought of McKnight's comment that he was waiting to find out what God had in store for him. I laughed and shook my head. I was no prophet, but I was pretty sure that whatever God cooked up for the good Reverend was going to involve Maura Conisson.

Chapter Forty-five

That night at The Aerie I fed Arch, warmed up some leftovers for me, and then we both settled in front of the fire for a little quiet time. Like the echo from the Big Bang, the Amis murder resonated in my head. I suppose I should have been more concerned about the fates of McKnight and Conisson, but I just didn't see that going anywhere. A more likely and immediate threat was me getting some sort of censure from the Oregon State Bar, but I couldn't do anything about that at the moment, so I set it aside.

What really got me wondering was how the brutal crime fit into the greater scheme of Lori Kavanaugh's murder and the attempt to frame Jim Kavanaugh for the deed. There were two smoking guns. First, the fact that Lori Kavanaugh's patient file was apparently missing. Had Amis been murdered for that file? Second, there was the bloody footprint potentially linking his death with the break-in at my place. I went into my study and pulled out the photos taken inside my fence line and compared them to the shots on my phone taken at Amis' place. Pretty damn close, but a lot of shoe soles looked alike, I admitted.

As for suspects, Blake Daniels' whereabouts during the time of the murder was unaccounted for, and Aaron Abernathy's alibi was shaky at best. Eddie and Sylvia Manning appeared to have solid alibis. All three men were of medium build, suggesting I couldn't rule any of them out based on shoe size.

I leaned back to the groaning chorus of my old roller chair and exhaled a long, slow breath. There was some kind of web holding this all together, but the tendrils were too fine to see. Fresh anger and frustration washed over me. It wasn't just the lives of innocent people that were under attack here. It was as if my very home, the Dundee Hills, with its gently rolling slopes, breathtaking views, and miraculous soil, was under siege as well. Someone driven by greed and envy was loose on the land, and it looked like it was falling to me to put a stop to it.

• • ● • •

On Tuesday, around mid-morning, Ballard called to inform me that Helen Berkowitz had asked for a preliminary report regarding the initial Amis murder interview. "Go easy on me, Hal," I told him, half-jokingly. "The attempted blackmail's peripheral to Amis' murder, you'll see soon enough."

"I'll give her the facts, Cal. It is what it is."

"Come on, Hal, it hardly ever *is what it is*, and you know it."

"Yeah, well, I just want you to know there's nothing personal here."

I told him I knew that and hung up. At least Ballard was a straight shooter, I told myself. Helen Berkowitz, on the other hand, might be a different story.

After taking Archie out for a stretch, we drove to the Brasserie where I left him sulking in the backseat. The sun had burst through after a brief shower. Clad in forest green shiplap siding and spewing a wisp of smoke from a brick chimney, my favorite eatery looked exceptionally inviting. I entered through the bar, and the first person I saw was Blake Daniels nursing a glass of Scotch and reading his ever-present *Wall Street Journal*. I sat down next to him, and when he looked up, I said, "We've got to stop meeting like this, Blake."

Sunlight from a side window illuminated a few flecks of gray along his part line, a flaw in the dye job. A corner of his mouth turned up slightly, but his eyes narrowed down. "Seems like you're always finding *me*, Claxton."

I flashed a smile I hoped would pass for amiable. "How was the crush?"

"Not bad. Maybe our best." He seemed to catch himself, and his face stiffened. "When's Kavanaugh's big day in court?"

"A trial date hasn't been set."

He shot me a look and started to respond just as Bettie James appeared from out of the kitchen. Daniels had her top up his Scotch, and I ordered the plat du jour, a *salade Niçoise* with ahi tuna and a glass of Sancerre. As Bettie poured my wine she said to both of us, "Did you hear about that shrink Amis over in Lafayette who was beaten to death in his own wine cellar? My God, what's goin' on in this world?"

We both nodded, and I said, "Uh, it turns out I discovered the body."

Bettie said, "What?" I was watching Daniels, who had brought his glass of Scotch to his lips, causing me to miss the critical first read in his eyes. Also, he wore a long sleeve shirt buttoned at the wrists so I couldn't see whether he had any defensive wounds to suggest he'd been involved in a life and death struggle. Damn.

"Yeah," I went on, "I was dropping by to pick up some wine he'd put aside for me. Found him in his cellar alright." I shook my head. "It was terrible"

I stayed vague on the details while they both pumped me for information. Finally, Bettie said, "Don't mean to speak ill of the dead, but I heard that man supplied a lot of benzos for the glitterati around these parts."

I nodded. "He's the valley's Dr. Feelgood."

She shook her head as a look of disgust spread across her face. "Right. But not the one in the Aretha Franklin song. She was singin' about sex, not drugs." That quip made both Daniels and me chuckle. Bettie looked at me. "You think that drug business got him killed?"

I shrugged and felt Daniels' eyes on the side of my face. I turned to him. "You ever hear anything about Amis pushing pills?"

He averted my gaze, and a muscle rippled along his jawline. "Can't say that I have, but there's a lot of that going around, I hear." He drained his drink, nodded to Bettie, and said, "Put it on my tab. Gotta run." He turned his hawk eyes back on me, and they went predator cold. "I hope your client gets the death penalty."

When he cleared the back door, Bettie said, "Whoa, that was harsh. What's up with him?"

"He thinks Jim Kavanaugh killed Lori, or that's what he wants me to think. I'm not sure which."

Bettie considered that for a moment. "How's the case looking?"

I groaned and massaged my forehead with my right hand. "We're developing some good alternate theories of what happened, but, you know, it seems to be one step forward and two back."

"So, you found Amis' body. I'm thinking there's some tie-in here with Lori's murder, right?"

I nodded. No reason to hold back on Bettie, one of the sharpest knives in the drawer and a person I knew I could trust. "Yeah, I think so."

She wrung her hands on her apron and grimaced. This is the Hills, Calvin. Peaceful grape-growing country. Two murders?"

I held up three fingers. Her brows shot up. "Three," I said. "That guy they pulled out of Chehalem Creek with a bullet in his head—he's involved, too."

Bettie put her hands on her hips and sucked a breath. "Good God almighty. You'd think this was Chicago or somethin'."

I finished lunch, and when I rejoined Arch in the car, I said, "Well, whataya know, Big Boy, we caught a break today. If I don't miss my guess, Blake Daniels knows plenty about Dr. Feelgood."

Just like that, I had a tendril connecting the two.

• • ● • •

On Wednesday morning, I checked in with Nando by phone. "I have the good news and the not-so-good news. Which would you like to hear first, my friend?" It wasn't the greeting I was hoping for.

I sighed into the phone. "The good news."

"We have the name of one of the men associated with Isabel Rufino. His name is Vicente Arias. He has a long rap sheet and is wanted on distribution charges at the moment."

"Good." I waited for the bad news.

"We thought he, Isabel and the other man would just relocate on the Springwater Corridor, which would make finding them not too difficult. However, it was announced today that the city will sweep the entire corridor of all homeless people and homeless camps. The sweep will begin tomorrow, and people are already scattering throughout the city to find new places to live. It is like Isabel just got put into a blender with hundreds of others."

I blew a breath out in frustration. "Surely having another name will help you."

"Perhaps. Do you wish us to continue?"

"Yes, dammit. You've got to find her, Nando."

That afternoon, the mother of the young girl who had boosted the designer jeans showed up at my office unannounced. She carried a plastic bag in one hand and a worried look on her face. She took a seat and slid the bag across the desk to me. "I found this in Tiffany's bedroom this morning." She dropped her eyes and shook her head. "I never thought I'd be sneaking around in her room, but I just don't trust her anymore."

I opened the bag and removed the contents, a handful of multi-colored pills. She looked at me anxiously as I examined them. They were pastel pink and blue with little hearts, stars, and butterflies on them. "These are probably Ecstasy, you know, the pills that are popular at raves. They can cause all kinds of mental and physiological responses, some of them bad. Of course, they could be something brand new I've never heard of."

She flinched and nodded. "I'm a single mom. She's already in trouble. What should I do?"

"Look, I'm no drug counselor. What I can tell you is that kids at this age can get way out ahead of where you think they are. Social media and the net have pretty much destroyed innocence."

I met her eyes. "Confront her without being accusatory. Try to find out how far this has gone." I worked in what I hoped was a comforting smile. "Chances are she's just acting out, and you can nip this in the bud. But if you sense she's got a problem, get professional help right away."

She left my office standing a little straighter, perhaps. I shook my head at the irony. Me, the drug counselor. But I'd seen a lot in my one-man practice over the years, as the drugs got more and more destructive and began—as in the Jim Kavanaugh case—to spill over into the realm of prescribed, highly addictive medicines.

The sun lingered that afternoon, so Arch and I closed up shop early, raced back to The Aerie, and took a fast jog up to the Pioneer Cemetery. The wind had quieted down, and as we stood there among the tombstones, gulping in the sweet Oregon air, my phone chirped. It was Candice returning my call. "Are you still on with Daniels tonight?" I asked after she greeted me.

"Yes, a play in Portland, like I told you. Knowing the horny bastard, we'll probably go to his place afterwards."

"Listen, Candice. I have reason to believe that Amis was Daniels' drug supplier."

"Oh."

"I think you should have a headache tonight until I sort this out."

A long pause ensued. "We're so close, Cal, and it's more important than ever that I get something on him."

"No, Candice. This guy could be a brutal murderer."

"I'll be okay, Cal. I know how to handle him. I'm not afraid."

"Candice, I—"

"Tell you what, if I don't find anything tonight, I'll hang it up, okay?"

It wasn't okay, but I agreed because I knew it was the best deal I was going to get. "Keep me in the text loop," I said as we signed off.

Archie led me home, and he must have sensed my second wind, because he ran me hard. That night, after everything quieted down, and we had paid our respects to the great horned owl out by the gate, I lay in bed reading. After finishing *Winter's Bone*, I'd been reading *Silence* by Shusaku Endo as a change of pace.

As usual, I drifted off, and the ping of an incoming text caused me to jerk upright, catapulting the book off my bed. I rubbed my eyes hard and read the text with blurry eyes. It was two in the morning, and Candice Roberts, my intrepid undercover agent, was at it again.

Chapter Forty-six

> More open with his drug use this time. Ground
> some Klonopin, snorted it, washed it down with
> Scotch. He's in bed now, out. Stay tuned.

I sat up on the edge of my bed and cleared my head. Watch
your step, I texted back.

Five agonizing minutes later this came back:

> Double checked med cabinets, kitchen drawers,
> nosed around bedroom. No prescription bottles.
> No sign of jogging shoes. Study next!

It must have been between ten and fifteen minutes later that
this came in:

> No drug bottles in study. Lots of notes and papers.
> Hold on.

I waited, sitting on the edge of my bed, hardly allowing myself
a breath. Archie picked up on the tension in the room and came
over and laid his big muzzle on my thigh to comfort me.

Ping.

> Hey! Found something. Holy shi

I waited for the rest of the text to come through. Maybe her
finger slipped, or she dropped her phone, or her battery crapped
out. I rejected the last possibility. I couldn't imagine a cool head

like Candice letting her battery get low on a night like this. That made no sense. No, she had hit the send button without completing the sentence and now the line was stone cold dead. If she had dropped the phone, she would've picked it up and kept sending to reassure me. I was sure of that.

No, goddammit, this felt like a worst-case scenario, like she was interrupted.

I got dressed as fast as I could, stopped to grab a small flashlight and my coat, and dashed for the garage with Archie right beside me. I stopped at the pegboard that held most of my tools and threw a stout crowbar onto the front seat of the Beemer. I could have gone for the Glock up in my bedroom, but that would have taken longer, and I felt I didn't have a second to lose.

A wet, heavy fog had oozed its way up from the valley and lay like a cold blanket across the Hills. I switched on my fog lights and cut my speed in half as I made my way down Worden Hill toward Blake Daniels' Rolling Hills Estate, home of mediocre pinot noir offered at a value price.

I nearly missed the sharp left that bore off to the east and took me first past the Le Petit Truc acreage, then Sean McKnight's massive holdings, and finally along the southern edge of the Rolling Hills Estate. But that night there was nothing to see but milk white fog that condensed on my windshield and sloshed off my wipers.

No coherent plan formed in my head as I worked my way along that dirt road. My objective was simple—make sure that Candice Roberts was in no danger. I didn't give a good goddamn what kind of scene I made. The subterfuge with Blake Daniels was over.

I was maybe a half-mile from the turnoff to Rolling Hills when I caught the movement of something off to my left, just inside the tree line. I slowed down and craned my neck. There it was again. Something dashed between two trees! Archie let out a single, sharp bark. I slammed on my brakes, grabbed the crowbar and the flashlight, and hopped out of the car with Archie right behind me.

A form materialized out of the woods, and there, illuminated by my flashlight, was Candice Roberts. "Cal, oh my God, is that you?" She stood in front of me in nothing but a pair of bikini panties, her hands clamped over her bare breasts. Her hair was soaked and stringy, she was shivering almost uncontrollably, and her eyes blazed with a kind of crazed excitement. Her knees were raw and bloody, and blood was dripping down from a gash on her left shoulder. Archie whimpered and sidled up next to her.

"Yes, it's me." I ripped my coat off, covered her with it, and helped her into the car. I got a blanket from the trunk and spread it over her once she was in the front seat. "Are you okay?"

"Hell yes," she said between shivers. "I'm okay. Just cold and a little scratched up."

Anger boiled up in me like hot oil. "Did Daniels do this?"

"No. Not directly." She managed a laugh. "I was in his study. His computer wasn't passworded, so I pulled up his calendar. I looked on the night of the murder, October third, and several days on either side. He had lots of entries, but the night of Lori's murder, his agenda was blank. So, no alibi for that day that I could see."

"What about the Sunday Amis was killed, November thirteenth?"

She smiled. "Same thing. Nothing entered for that date. He cancelled our date for that day, said something came up, but nothing was penciled in." She went on, "There was a stack of memos, personal mail, bills, all kinds of shit, on his desk. I was working my way through that when I looked up, and there he stands in the doorway staring at me with the scariest look I've ever seen in my life."

"What did you do?"

She laughed again, more a release of nervous tension than anything. "I panicked, that's what. There's a door in the study that leads out to the side yard. I blew out that door like I had a rocket tied to my butt. No way he was ever going to catch me."

"Did he chase you?"

She shrugged. "I never looked back, and I didn't hear anything. I fell a couple of times and scratched myself up." She looked down at the gash on her shoulder. "Nothing serious."

I breathed an audible sigh of relief and put the car in gear. "Let's get the hell out of here. He might be out there somewhere."

"Coming after us?"

"I don't know. He might have a gun or he might call the cops, accuse you of burglary. Who the hell knows?"

"Burglary? I was his guest. And I'm practically naked."

"Oh, I hadn't noticed."

She laughed, despite herself. "Well, I don't think that little shit's going to be rushing off to the police." She looked me full in the face, and allowed the faintest smile to crease her still-blue lips. "I found something in there, Cal." She reached into her panties along her hip and pulled something out. "You've got to see this."

I didn't see any headlights in my mirror, so I pulled over onto the narrow shoulder and switched on the dome light. She handed me what looked like a slightly mangled birthday card. The outside read simply:

Happy Birthday, Stud Muffin.

I opened it up. The inside read:

A hard man is good to find
I'm glad I found you!
L

Below the initial L, the sender had left the lip print of a kiss in blood red lipstick. Candice pointed at the L. That's Lori's handwriting, I'm almost positive. And that's her favorite lipstick color, for sure."

"There's no date on this," I said.

"I know, but it was in with a stack of other cards and letters wishing him a happy birthday. Most were dated August 16. I'll bet anything that's his birth date. The timing fits, Cal. That would have given him plenty of time to cozy up to her and set up the murder."

My pulse ticked up a notch. "You're sure about the initial? I mean it's only one letter."

She exhaled a long breath. "Looks like it to me. She always signed her stuff with just the initial L. Jim would know for sure."

I nodded. "Right. We need to show this to him right now."

She barked a laugh. "Not until you take me home to change. This is going to be humiliating enough. I want some clothes on when I face him."

On the way to Candice's place, she said, "If Jim recognizes the signature, do we have enough to go to the cops?"

"No. Afraid not. I'm glad you grabbed it, but it's not valuable as evidence in court. We could establish a chain of possession, but we'd have a huge credibility problem. How could we show the card wasn't altered somewhere along the line?"

"Shit. I never said I was Sherlock Holmes, you know."

I laughed. "Taking it was the smart thing to do, Candice. Who knows what would have become of it? If Jim can confirm this, we'll know Daniels is the lover. That's huge. Did he see you take the card?"

"No. I'd already stashed it in my panties when he found me."

"Good. That should give us an advantage, although he's going to know you were looking for something."

"There's one glitch, Cal. I, uh, dropped my phone on his desk when he surprised me. He's going to read all our texts, everything. Stupid, stupid me."

I shook my head. "No, don't beat yourself up. It couldn't be helped. I'm just glad you got the hell out of there."

She took a couple of nibbles on the cuticle of her thumb then laughed. "Yeah, well, it's not the way I drew it up, but at least I found something. I wanted to do my part, you know? For Jim."

We should all command such loyalty, I thought. It occurred to me that Lori Kavanaugh was a fool to have ever left Jim. It also occurred to me that perhaps Jim ought to consider what's right in front of him.

I was now pretty sure I knew the identity of Lori's lover. But the next steps were about as clear as the fog we were driving through. The trouble was, after Daniels finished reading all those texts he'd know I was curious about his whereabouts on key dates, interested in his drug use and source, and very, very suspicious.

So much for the element of surprise.

Chapter Forty-seven

It must have been four a.m. before we got to Le Petit Truc. The fog was breaking up, but there was no hint of light yet. I rang Jim's doorbell, then pounded on the door when there was no response. Candice stood next to me in boots, jeans, and a maroon and gold ASU sweatshirt, with Archie at her side like a mascot. Her hair was washed, towel dried, and twisted into a loose bun, and her wounds, she assured me, were cleaned and bandaged. Jim opened the door in a pair of boxers, the coppery hair on his thick chest like a living sweater, and his beard swirled into divots and snarls like an angry sea.

He looked at me, then Candice, then back to me. "Jesus, what's happened?" he asked through eyes struggling to focus.

"Can we come in?" I said. "We need to talk."

He shuffled off ahead of us into the kitchen, offered us seats, excused himself, and came back wearing a thick terry robe and a pair of worn slippers. "So, what is it?"

I turned to Candice, who handed Jim the card. "I, uh, found this in Blake Daniels' study last night. We're wondering if you recognize the handwriting on the inside?"

He took the card, and as he read it his face seemed to grow hard, like marble. He stared at the contents for several seconds, then nodded. "That's her initial. That's how she signed things, with a curly L. He put the card up to his nose and smelled the lip print, closing his eyes. "That's her lipstick, too," he said, his voice falling to a near whisper. "I swear I can still smell it." He handed the card back to Candice, his eyes wet. She took it and looked away.

"That's Blake Daniels' birthday card," I said. "Looks like Lori started seeing him after she left you."

Jim stared off into the middle distance between us, shaking his head slowly as color rose in his face like an incoming red tide. He reached to the center of the table, picked up an ornate sugar bowl that probably belonged to his grandmother, and threw it against the cut glass mirror hanging on the opposite wall. The mirror and the bowl exploded, spewing sugar and shards of glass and porcelain across the kitchen.

The act was sudden, the noise deafening. Candice and I sprang to our feet and stood there, stunned. Archie began barking ferociously, came across the room, and stood between Jim and I with his fangs bared. I calmed Arch down and Jim dropped his head into his arms while Candice ran down the hall to the bathroom, sobbing all the way.

I did the only thing I could think to do. I made a pot of coffee. By the time the coffee was brewed, and I'd swept up the kitchen, Jim had gotten hold of himself, Candice had come back with dry but puffy eyes, and Arch was back in the corner with a watchful eye on Jim. I looked at the two of them and decided they didn't need some kind of emotional intervention for which I was singularly ill-equipped. I poured us each a steaming cup of black coffee and said, "Okay, if we're through with the histrionics, let's figure out where we are. You can both help me think this through. First, we have compelling evidence now that Blake Daniels was seeing Lori after she moved out of Le Petit Truc. We know that Lori probably knew her murderer, that he probably drove to the scene with her. My theory all along has been that she thought they were going to kill you, Jim."

Jim winced at this but remained silent. The cold, menacing look that had formed in his eyes made me nervous.

"But the killer turned the tables on her," Candice said.

"Right. When they got to the turnout that night, Lori called Jim to set the frame in motion, but she gets killed instead of Jim."

"The killer needs a ride from the crime scene," Jim piped in, "so he hires a driver to pick him up."

"That's right," I added, "A guy named Luis Delgado. And his payment's a bullet in the head. But his girlfriend, a woman named Isabel Rufino, somehow gets a look at the killer and manages to get away after she learns of Delgado's death."

Jim shakes his head. "And Isabel's MIA in Portland."

"Yeah, but I haven't given up on finding her."

Candice blew on her coffee and took a tentative sip. "Blake Daniels fits perfectly here, and he doesn't appear to have an alibi for the night of the murder."

"At least you didn't see anything marked on his calendar," I add. "That's no guarantee."

Jim sipped his coffee and scowled into the cup. "Yes, but what's in it for him? With me and Lori both out of the way, I guess he figured he could come in and swoop Truc off the market." He looked at me and chuckled. "Wouldn't he be surprised?" Candice looked puzzled, and Jim continued. "If both Lori and I are out of the picture, Truc reverts to Sylvia and Eddie, who probably wouldn't put it up for sale."

Candice nodded and smiled. "Your silent partners."

"Right. Now you know."

I said, "But that doesn't take Daniels off the hook. He had no way of knowing about your deal with the Mannings, so gaining Truc could have been a motive."

Jim nodded. "That's right. Only Sylvia, Eddie, and I knew about the loan and the note, as far as I know."

"And he hated Jim's guts," Candice added. "Don't forget about that." Jim grunted and she swung her eyes to me. "You told me earlier that Richard Amis might have been Blake's drug supplier. Are you suggesting he killed Amis, too?" She wrinkled her brow. "How would that fit into this?"

I hesitated for a moment. "I'm a witness in the Amis murder, so this is sensitive territory. I can tell you that Amis was trying to acquire Stone Gate Farm, Sean McKnight's place, but he failed."

Candice's hand flew to her mouth. "Oh, my God. That would consolidate Le Petit Truc, Stone Gate, and Rolling Hills. That's the trifecta—the primo acreages for growing pinot noir grapes in Oregon and maybe the world consolidated into *one* vineyard. What a coup that would be."

"So Daniels kills Amis, too, so that he can have it all," Jim said, his look turning even more deadly. He closed his eyes, and we both looked at him. "I'm fantasizing about the best way to kill the bastard."

"Damn it, Jim," I said, "we can't prove any of this yet, but we're close. Don't do anything stupid to screw it up."

He opened his eyes and looked at me as if coming out of a trance. "I said *fantasizing*, okay?"

We sat in silence for a while processing the implications of what we just hammered out. Candice topped up our coffees all around, then looked at me. "So, what do we do now?"

"First, we find a safe house for you. Daniels has your phone, and he knows we've been looking hard at him. If he's the killer, he has to believe you're a major threat to him." Of course, I was a major threat, too, but I let that one lay.

"She's staying here," Jim said with finality. "My guest room." He stood up, excused himself, and came back a couple of minutes later carrying a double-barreled shotgun and a box of shells. He broke both barrels open, slid a cartridge into each chamber, and snapped the breach shut. "I'll take care of her."

Out of the corner of my eye I thought I saw Candice flinch momentarily. The protective gesture was welcome, I'm sure, but it wasn't in her psyche to be protected by anyone. I looked at her for a moment and she nodded. To Jim, I said, "Okay, so you need to run her over to her place and let her pack a bag." To Candice I added, "Don't wander off on your own, you know, to go into Dundee or something, until this gets sorted out. I'm going to need time to put some things in place." I looked at them both. "Meanwhile, everything we discussed stays in this room."

"Are you going to the police?" Jim asked, as they walked me to the front door.

"No. Not yet. We'll need much, much more to nail him." I turned to Candice and hugged her. "Thanks, again. We owe all this to you. That was a gutsy thing you did." I glanced over at Jim, who stood there with a look of pride and something else, something softer and deeper but hard for me to read.

I left the two of them standing on Jim's porch that morning, Jim cradling his twelve gauge shotgun like a mountain man and Candice standing tall next him with a look of stubborn defiance. Whatever concerns I had about Blake Daniels mounting some sort of retaliation receded from my mind.

Chapter Forty-eight

As Archie and I headed back to The Aerie that morning, the leafless vineyards to the west were silhouetted in a layer of vivid gold below a sky still dark with purple cloud. The sun breaking through seemed an apt metaphor, but I knew that, just like the Oregon weather, this case had a habit of changing in a hurry. The scenario we arrived at that morning was good as far as it went, but like I warned Jim, we had no solid evidence implicating Blake Daniels in anything. More work was needed.

I was more hungry than tired, so after feeding my dog and brewing a double cappuccino, I fixed breakfast—a three-egg mushroom and spinach omelet to which I added red pepper flakes, green onion, and a topping of grated Gruyere cheese. That, along with a couple of slices of Dave's Killer Bread slathered with Scottish marmalade, restored my energy.

We got to the office around seven and after reading my e-mail and the news of the day, I called Nando's cell. "Yes, Calvin, what can I do for you this morning?" he answered. I was surprised he even picked up at such an early hour, and the fact that he sounded cheerful was even more surprising. It turned out he closed on the property in southeast Portland the afternoon before, an event he was obviously still savoring. "I am doing the catch-up," he explained. "I have been neglecting my janitorial business for too long." In an unguarded moment some time ago, Nando admitted to me that he started the business to provide entry-level employment for immigrants like himself. Like Jim, he didn't want to draw attention to his good deeds. Maybe that's why I like them both so much.

I steered the conversation back to my situation, gave him a quick sketch of what happened the night before, and said, "I need a tail on Daniels, Nando, but he might be looking for it. Can you handle something like that?"

The line went quiet for a few moments. "This can be done using two cars. It is what I believe you call a tag team. The car directly behind the suspect is alternated to minimize suspicion." He paused again. "It works well in the city. I cannot guarantee it will work in Dundee. Once off the Pacific Highway, the traffic is light, the cars more noticeable."

"Of course, no guarantees. I need to watch him for a while. It's all I can think to do." I exhaled. "Let's give it a try."

"Okay, my friend, we can do this, and I am coming myself. I will need a suitable car, a used pickup truck would be best. My Lexus will stand out."

I told him I'd take care of the truck and got Hiram Pritchard's agreement that Nando could use his old Ford 150 that he drove to work and back. An hour later Nando sat across from me with one of his investigators, a small, wiry man named Miguel Fuentes. I pulled a map of the Dundee Hills up on Google Earth and showed them where Rolling Hills Estate was located. "It's still early," I said. "If we're lucky, he hasn't left to go anywhere yet."

"We will station ourselves well down the road on either side of his drive, here and here" Nando said, pointing to two spots where the road curved sharply. "We will not miss him."

"Good. I want to know where he goes today, how long he stays there, and anything he does that looks out of the ordinary." I showed them where Candice's condo was next. "If I'm right about this guy," I went on, "he might head there after dark to case the place. She's not there, so there's no danger."

Nando fixed me with his gaze. "What about you? Are you a target?

"Possibly." I smiled. "I've got your Glock to keep me company. I'll be fine."

He huffed a laugh. "Be sure to load it, Calvin." I got no respect when it came to gun knowhow.

"Can you do this around the clock?" I asked.

Nando looked insulted. "Of course. Tonight, one of us will watch for his headlights and one will sleep. If he slips out, we will know."

After they left, I sat there drumming my fingers on my desk. I knew it was a weak plan and with two people on the clock, expensive. My only hope was that Daniels' movements would reveal something, a man who was panicked at what Candice and I knew, or a man who urgently needed to talk to someone, a co-conspirator, perhaps. The spring of hope bubbled on.

I worked through lunch that day, stopping only to take Archie out for a short walk. It was dry, and the only evidence of the sun was a diffuse silver glow backlighting the mottled cloud cover. Archie sniffed the southerly breeze, catching, I imagined, notes from the river that were not accessible to my nose. We were on our way back when Nando called to tell me Daniels was on the move. "Good," I said. "Stay in touch."

Early that afternoon Helen Berkowitz called. After an icy greeting she said, "I've spoken to Detective Ballard about the Amis' murder and your conduct in the investigation." She paused for effect. "I'm a little disturbed by what I heard and would like to talk to you about that."

I closed my eyes and counted to three. "Ballard has both of my statements, Helen. The blackmail case was ancient history when he interviewed me."

She laughed. "Ancient history? Sure it was. Shall we set a date?"

I pushed the date off a week and couldn't resist leaving her with a parting shot. "You know, Helen," I said, "in the midst of all these distractions I've got a solid alternate theory of the Lori Kavanaugh murder. I'm looking forward to the trial." Okay, it wasn't solid, but I felt like things were finally moving. And, damn it, it felt good to say that.

An hour later I got a call from Nando. Daniels had driven to McMinnville and gone into a building on NE 6th Street. He gave me the address, and I immediately recognized it as the law office of Comey and Burns, a couple of well-known attorneys. Hmm, I thought, the actions of someone worried about being arrested? Could be. There was another possibility. Daniels was exploring how to haul Candice and me into civil court for invasion of privacy. After all, we'd provided him with a pretty explicit text trail. I judged that a long shot, although some people have an insatiable appetite for litigation.

Nando called again, a little more than two hours later. "He's at Candice Roberts' condo," he reported, his voice elevated noticeably. "I'm watching him with my binoculars. He just put something in her mailbox, and now he's leaving. I can have Miguel follow him while I retrieve whatever it is."

"Okay, but be careful it's not a bomb or a snake."

Nando called back five minutes later. "It's an envelope with a badly smashed cell phone in it."

"Bring it with you." I chuckled. "I assume he removed the SIM card before he smashed it."

Nando called again twenty minutes later. By this time the sun had set behind a thickening cloud cover, and the skies had opened up. "It looked like he was headed back to Dundee, but we lost him. A truck jackknifed on 99W and all traffic is blocked. As soon as this clears, I'll send Miguel to Rolling Hills to see if he can pick him up again, and I'll check in at your office."

It wasn't long after that call that I heard a sharp rap on my backdoor. Archie grumbled a bark, stretched, and got up from his corner perch. I stood and removed the Glock from a desk drawer, tucked it into my belt at the small of my back, and pulled my sweater back down to conceal it. Butterflies took flight in my stomach as I switched on the back light and opened the door.

"Evening, counselor." Blake Daniels stood in the rain in front of me, his hands plunged into the deep pockets of his Gore-Tex rain gear, his eyes narrowed and his face taut as a drumskin.

"Hello, Blake," I said, without stepping back to grant him entry. "What can I do for you?"

He glared at me for a moment. "Aren't you going to invite me in? It's wet out here."

"Sure," I said, and stepped aside, watching with relief as his hands came out of his coat empty. I gestured to Archie, who went back to his corner, then pointed at the coatrack. "You can hang your gear there." He doffed his raincoat, and I didn't see the telltale sag of a weapon. He took a seat, and I returned to my desk, the Glock uncomfortable but reassuring at my back and my dog watching with interest from his perch.

He squared his shoulders and met my gaze with his hawk eyes. "So, you decided to run a little scam on me, and you recruited that bitch Roberts to help you." He laughed bitterly. "Too bad she wasn't a better lay."

"Funny, that's what she said about you."

He laughed. It was laced with bitterness, and his eyes flashed anger.

"What do you want, Blake?"

He pushed the sleeves of his shirt up on either arm unconsciously and leaned forward. A vein had popped out on his neck that was almost as prominent as the ones on his thick forearms. "I want to know what the hell's going on. I've already talked to my lawyers, and if I don't get some answers I'm going to sue your ass into oblivion."

I nodded and held his gaze. "I see. You're anxious to have your drug addiction and alcoholism come to light?"

His eyes flashed again. "Is that a threat?"

"No, Blake. It's just a fact. You need to get some help."

"Fuck you, Claxton. I take Klonopin for anxiety, and I drink like most people in this world. I own a winery, for Christ sake."

I nodded. "Okay, but you still haven't told me why you're here."

He leaned back, and his eyes narrowed down to dark slits. "I know you'll do anything to get your buddy Kavanaugh off, but you're not going to mix me up in this thing."

"You were having an affair with Lori after she left Kavanaugh. I'd say you mixed yourself up."

His eyes registered no surprise. He'd obviously discovered that his birthday card was missing. He hesitated for a couple of beats. "So what if I was. That doesn't mean I killed her."

"If you've got nothing to hide, why didn't you come forward with this?"

He glared at me, the anger back in his eyes. "I didn't want to get involved, that's why. It looked unseemly, particularly for Lori. And I didn't know anything that would help, anyway."

"You don't know that," I said. "Where were you the night she was killed?"

His eyes fixed me again, and he allowed the slightest smile. "I was with another woman. It meant nothing, just habit." His eyes softened. "Lori was different."

"You can prove you were with someone on the night of October third?"

"Sure. I was with a woman named Gloria Bertolli, at her place. Check it out. She lives in Newberg."

I jotted the name down and took another tack. "You were getting your Klonopin from Richard Amis, right?"

He averted my gaze. "I told you, I suffer from anxiety. Richard was, uh, treating me informally. You know, we met on the wine circuit, and I didn't have time for any of that psycho babble"

"Informally? You mean he was supplying you with drugs without really treating you?"

He shifted in his seat. "I'm not saying anything more about that."

"Where were you last Sunday when he was killed?"

"I was with Gloria."

"Of course you were."

We sat there looking at each, the space between us crackling with tension. Suddenly the back door burst open, and Nando came in with his right hand poised on his left side, ready to draw. Archie sprang to his feet in full alert. "Nando," I said, putting up a hand to calm him and my dog, "it's okay. Mr. Daniels was just leaving."

Daniels had swung around, and when he got up Nando shot him a look that dripped with malevolence. He glanced at me, then back at Daniels. "You are sure?"

"Yes, it's okay. We're done for now."

"For now?" Daniels said. "Bullshit. You've got nothing on me. We're done unless you're craving a lawsuit."

I turned to Nando. "Did you bring the cell phone?"

"Yes." He stepped forward, retrieved the envelope from his coat pocket, and placed it on my desk. I opened it and spread out the contents.

Daniels looked at the mangled parts, then raised his eyes to mine. I said, "That's the end of it between you and Candice Roberts. She was trying to help an innocent man who's being framed for murder." I glanced at Nando and then looked back at Daniels. "If you even look at her cross-eyed you are going to have a world of hurt. Are we clear?"

He laughed with a bravado that sounded forced. "Don't worry. I'm through with that bitch." He started for the door but turned back, his face a mix of anger and something else, maybe sadness. "You're defending a killer, Claxton. Kavanaugh killed Lori because he was afraid she'd force him to sell his precious Le Petit Truc. How can you live with yourself?"

"Don't forget your coat on the way out," I replied.

When the back door shut, I looked up at Nando. He said, "So, he walks away?"

I shrugged. "I got nothing on him except proof that he was Lori's lover, proof I can't use in court. My cover was blown to hell when he found that phone, and now yours is, too."

Nando shook his head. "This is the two pounds of shit in a one pound bag I have heard about."

"Yep. That about sums it up."

Chapter Forty-nine

I laid Nando's Glock on the desk and retrieved a half full bottle of Rémy Martin and two glasses from the bottom drawer of my filing cabinet. "I need a drink, and so do you," I said, as I poured us each three fingers. By this time, the rain was drumming on my flat roof with an intensity I knew would have consequences. I got up and put a bucket in the washroom, directly below a discolored spot on the ceiling that I knew from experience would leak. "Can't find the source of that damn leak," I said as I sat back down.

"I have a good roof man," Nando replied. "I will send him to fix it. A leaky roof in Oregon is not a good thing."

We raised our glasses out of friendship and drank. I welcomed the soft burn of the amber liquid as it found its way into my stomach. "I thought you were going to shoot him right on the spot."

Nando laughed. "Yes. When I saw his car parked in your lot, I became worried for your safety." He opened his coat to display his shoulder holster and smiled in that wily way of his. "I am packing the heat," he said. "What about Miguel? Shall I call him off?"

"Yeah. Surveillance is out of the question now." After Nando made the call, I took him through my encounter with Daniels and answered some questions. When I finished, he drained his Rémy, wiped his bottom lip with a fingertip, and said, "You still believe this man is the murderer?"

I nodded. "He's the best lead I've got. Why else would he lie about being Lori's lover?"

My friend shrugged. "People lie about affairs all the time, Calvin. Perhaps he was trying to protect her honor like he suggested to you."

"Fat chance. This guy's no knight in shining armor."

Nando nodded. "Okay. What is it you want to do next?"

I drained my glass, set it down, and chuckled. "I seem to be in perpetual search of women. I need a line on Gloria Bertolli now. She lives in Newberg." I paused for a moment and met his eyes. "And I don't want you to give up on Isabel Rufino. Add Miguel to the effort if it'll help. This case's riding on it."

We had another glass of Rémy, and our conversation drifted off to other, less immediate subjects, like soccer for Nando and for me the fact that winter steelhead were arriving, and I didn't have time to get my line wet. After he left, I sat there thinking about my friend and his improbable journey from Cuba to Florida to Portland and his wholehearted embrace of everything American—the good, the bad, the ugly. Nando's character was complex, but I knew there was always one thing I could depend on—his loyal friendship.

I was tired and Archie needed to be fed, so instead of stopping by Le Petit Truc, I called Jim and Candice to bring them up to date. "This thing's still in flux," I told them, "so stay on your toes. Let me check his alibi out before we do anything."

Jim stayed silent at this, but Candice said, "I don't care what that woman says, Cal. He did it. I know he did."

The next morning my divorce-case client arrived for his scheduled meeting right on time. I listened patiently and jotted a few notes while he droned on about how his wife wanted everything, the wine and cheese shop, the house, the dog. He looked at me at one point and said, "I used to love that woman, and now I could kill her." That's a human enough response, I thought, but one normal people don't act on. I thought of what Blake Daniels had said about Jim, and I admit it gave me the slightest pause. Was Jim in the normal category? Yes, I told myself, he is. How could I believe otherwise at this juncture?

Nando called later that morning and gave me Gloria Bertolli's address, cell phone number, and place of employment. An hour later I was standing at the counter of the Radiant Glow tanning salon in Wilsonville. I rang a bell, and a young woman came through a beaded curtain. She was blond, but her skin was a deep brown, almost mahogany, a combination that did not occur in nature. I wanted to scream "haven't you heard of melanoma?" but, instead, introduced myself and asked for Gloria Bertolli.

She smiled, flashing teeth so white they were bluish. "I'm Gloria."

"I was wondering if we might chat for a few minutes, or later if that works better."

"What's this about?"

I explained the situation, and she agreed to talk, suggesting the Starbucks down the street. It didn't surprise me that she seemed to expect my visit, since Daniels would have given her a heads-up. No surprise either that she confirmed being with him the night of October third and the afternoon of November thirteenth. After all, Daniels had told me she would. "Where were you two during these, uh, dates?" I asked.

She blushed through her tan. "At my apartment in Newberg both times."

"Anyone see you there?"

She paused for a moment. "No. I don't think so."

Her responses seemed perfunctory, like they were rehearsed. When we finished, I thanked her, then said, "You know, Gloria, you might get subpoenaed to be a witness in a murder trial. If you are and you testify, you'll be under oath and subject to cross-examination. If you lie, it's a felony, and you'll do jail time. Think about it."

I left her sitting with her coffee, an unsettled look on her face. When I got to the car, I said to Arch, "It's still early, Big Boy. Time for one more stop." I took the I-5 north and thirty minutes later was maneuvering into a parking space a block down from the Smiling Leaf pot shop. I figured my best bet to engage Aaron Abernathy would be at the coffee shop across the street. I glanced at my watch. It was 2:05. He liked his coffee breaks. I just might get lucky. I had no agenda, but it seemed every time I talked to my hipster friend I learned something, and God knows I could use some new information.

I was starving, so I ordered a double cap and a scrambled egg served up on a croissant. I just finished my sandwich when Abernathy strolled in. He hesitated at the door when he saw me, then averted his gaze and entered, as if by not looking at me I would go away. He was in full uniform—the ever-present retro shades, plaid shirt, skinny jeans, and two-tone suede shoes. His ear lobes seemed to sag even more, as if he'd gone up a size in the silver gauges adorning them. Bigger is better, right?

He sat with his coffee three tables down from me. "Jesus, Claxton, what do you want now?" he said as I joined him.

"I was just in the neighborhood. Thought I might catch you. How's the pot business?"

He scoffed at me and motioned in the direction of the Smiling Leaf across the street. "Those losers don't know the first thing about running a weed business. I've got a hundred better ideas."

"Still want your own shop, huh?"

He shot me an incredulous look. "Who doesn't?"

I nodded. In his world, I guessed, everyone aspired to owning a weed shop. I took out a notepad for effect. "I'm filling in some details here. Wondering where you were the afternoon your stepmother was cremated?"

His look slid from annoyed to angry. "I don't have to tell you shit."

I smiled. "Well, you can take that position, but I can make you testify under oath. Doing it over coffee is a lot less stressful, trust me."

He took a sip of his drink and frowned. "I was bummed out. Stayed at my apartment and played video games." I made a note. It was something I might be able to check if it came to that. "Anyone join you or see you there?"

"Nah. What's with that day, anyway? So what if I didn't want to watch Irene go up in smoke?"

I nodded again. "Uh, have you ever heard of a psychiatrist named Richard Amis?" I watched his face, wondering what was going on behind those damn dark glasses.

"Who the fuck is he?"

That pretty much ended the conversation. Abernathy didn't appear to have an alibi for Amis' murder, and even if a forensic examination of his computer or Xbox showed activity during the time Amis was murdered, he'd be hard pressed to prove it was him. It wasn't much, but it was more than I had coming in.

On the way home I exited at Wilsonville and was well down Newberg Road when my hands-free chirped. "Cal, it's Winona. How are you?"

The sound of her voice lifted my spirits, and I pictured her dimples drilling down on either side of her mouth. "Still at the Center?" I was referring to the Hatfield Marine Science Center in Newport on the coast. I knew she was attending a meeting there.

"Boring conference on toxic algae. Back tomorrow. What's up with you?"

I puffed a breath out in frustration. "A lot and nothing." I told her about Candice's harrowing escape and my weird confrontation with Blake Daniels.

"What about his alibi?"

"I just spoke with Gloria Bertolli. She backed him up." I laughed. It came out bitter. "In other words, I don't have shit."

"Did you believe her?"

"No. She seemed well-rehearsed. I think I could break her down if I ever got her on the stand." I exhaled a sigh. "Blake was my best bet. Now it feels like I'm back to square one."

"You can't rule him out, Cal, and there are other suspects, too."

"True. I also talked to Aaron Abernathy today. Thanks to his stepmother's death, I'll never know if he was really with her the night Lori was killed, but I just learned he has no alibi for the afternoon Amis was killed." I exhaled again. "But so what? He has no ties to Amis that I know of. And why would he kill Lori in the first place? It makes no sense."

"There's the power couple, Eddie and Sylvia," Winona offered.

"Nothing new there. Sure, they could secretly covet Le Petit Truc, I guess, but I haven't seen anything like that. They have ties to Amis through their investment firm, but they have solid alibis for both murders." I paused for a moment, shaking my head. "Maybe I'm just chasing my tail. Maybe others are involved here, people I know nothing about who have motives I haven't even thought of. Who the hell knows?"

"That's not it, Cal," she snapped back. "You're close, but you're missing something. Go home and get a good night's sleep. I don't know why, but I have a feeling this is going to break soon." Her voice got thick. "And, Cal, be careful, please."

That got my attention. Words like that from Winona always did. I assured her I'd watch my back and signed off. It started to mist, and in the dying afternoon light the swirling droplets lit up like jewels in my headlights. Sharp curve upon sharp curve loomed up in the road along the Willamette River, reminding me of the case I'd been pulled into. It had been a long, frustrating journey, and now I felt a palpable sense of anticipation.

Chapter Fifty

I let Archie off at the gate, and he galloped into the darkness barking at something. "Archie," I called after him, "Get your butt back here right now." I heard him circle around out in the field and then saw the white blaze of his chest as he approached. "Good boy," I told him as pulled up and sat down in front of me. I patted him on the head. "No more running off chasing things, you understand?" Of course he did.

When I got into the house, I put the Glock on the kitchen table instead of back in my bedroom closet where I normally stored it. I felt a little silly with that cannon sitting there, but I promised Winona I'd be careful, after all. After feeding Arch, I stood with the refrigerator door open, surveying the food desert I'd created by a lack of shopping. My cell buzzed just as I shut the door in disgust. It was Jim. He and Candice were meeting Eddie and Sylvia at the Brasserie for dinner, and he invited me to join them. "Perfect," I told him.

Stunning in an orange caftan, Bettie James looked harried but happy, the way she always did when her restaurant was crowded. I hugged my friend, and she said, "My new sous chef's running the kitchen tonight for the first time. I'm a little nervous."

"He has a good teacher," I told her. "Don't worry."

Jim waved from a corner table, and I joined him and Candice. We exchanged greetings and I said, "Gloria Bertolli told me she was with Daniels at the time of both murders."

"Surprise, surprise," Candice said. "You don't believe her, do you?"

"No. She seemed evasive and rehearsed."

"Can you challenge her story?" Jim asked.

"We'll take a closer look at her. Maybe we can put her someplace else on those two days. She'll make a lousy witness, in any case."

"What about the Rufino woman?" Jim asked.

"We still think she's in Portland, and we've intensified our efforts to find her," I said. Jim winced and Candice shifted in her seat at the less than encouraging news. "It looks promising," I added. That wasn't strictly true, but I felt like I had to give them something.

We sat through an awkward silence. Candice looked at Jim and patted him on the forearm. "Your hospitality's been great, but I'm moving back to my condo. I'm not afraid of that creep, Daniels."

I figured that was coming and wasn't all that adverse to it. I'd put Daniels on notice about Candice, and, besides, she wasn't really a threat to him because he knew what she knew from the text messages on her phone. Jim was adamant that she stay at Truc, but he gave in fairly quickly. There was no arguing with Candice, and he knew it.

The Mannings entered the restaurant a few moments later. Jim waved to them, and as they approached I kicked myself for not warning him and Candice to keep the latest information confidential. Surely they know the drill by now? I told myself. Sylvia's hair was down and her low wattage smile up a few notches, and Eddie's diamond stud winked above a trim, black turtleneck sweater. Sylvia took a seat next to Jim, hugged his arm, then said to the table, "So glad you could join us. We were in the mood for some of Bettie's delicious food." Right on cue, Bettie appeared with the menus, and we ordered—what else?—two bottles of Jim's reserve pinot to get us started.

After the wine was poured and we ordered our meals, the conversation turned to the weather. The remnant of a typhoon that ravaged the south Pacific had been sucked into the jet stream and was moving toward Oregon and Washington. "They're calling it a monster storm," Sylvia said.

Eddie laughed and looked at Jim. "Remember that storm, what, four years ago now?"

Jim grinned and nodded. "I've never seen such big waves."

Eddie said to the rest of us, "We have a place in Pacific City, and every time there's a winter storm we're there." His look turned wistful. "The Pacific's beautiful when it's angry."

Jim leaned in. "There's a spot out on Cape Kiwanda where you can see the wave action up front and personal. The ground shakes under you when they break. It's magnificent."

Sylvia puffed a breath. "Oh, the Cape's magnificent alright, but dangerous. People die out there all the time." The thought of seeing big surf like that thrilled me. It was a part of the Oregon scene I hadn't experienced, and I made a vow to fix that.

Our food arrived, and Eddie began expounding on Tilikum Capital Management's aggressive new growth plans. "We're adding new revenue streams all the time," he explained. "It's an exciting time for us."

"We just opened an office in Manhattan," Sylvia chimed in. "We're going after the European market."

The European market? I thought but didn't say. Should have known. Cheap debt is just another global business. I glanced at Jim. He had a look of pride on his face, pride for the success of his niece and her husband, but as far as I knew he was blissfully unaware of how they actually made their money. I didn't like their business model one bit, but I wasn't about to prick his bubble. Blood is thicker than business practices, right?

Eddie swung his eyes around to Jim. "How's the wine business?"

Jim stroked his beard and frowned into his wineglass. "Not so good. We're, ah, losing a lot of customers as the word gets out about my indictment." He glanced at Candice, who went on to describe the situation, including the loss of three major wholesalers, in more detail. Jim looked at me and forced a smile. "But we're making great progress on my defense."

All eyes at the table turned to me. "Well, we're building an alternate theory for the crime. We—"

Jim cut in. "We just found out that son of a bitch Blake Daniels was having an affair with Lori after she moved out. And he's using some lying woman in Newberg as an alibi for the night she was murdered."

Before I could say a word, Sylvia cut in, her eyes widening in surprise, "My God, Jim. Are you implying that Blake Daniels might have killed Lori? I know there's bad blood between you two, but why—?"

"We don't have a lot of answers yet," I said, shooting Jim the most withering look I could summon. "As a matter of fact, the whole thing's speculative, and none of this can leave the table."

Eddie looked at me. "Bravo, Cal. Sounds like you've made some real progress. You must have some good people working on this."

I glanced at Candice, who lowered her eyes and smiled, and then at Jim. "I use a top-notch PI firm in Portland. They—"

Jim, who had missed my warning look, butted in again. "There's a witness in Portland who can identify—"

I laughed and put a hand up to cut him off. "That's confidential, Jim. I can't go into that."

That ended the shoptalk, and the conversation during the rest of the meal revolved around wine, the monster storm, and the prospects for an early opening of the ski season. As we were leaving the Brasserie, Eddie hung back a little and said to me in a lowered tone, "Look, Cal. Jim's telling Syl and me that he doesn't want any help on his legal fees. You know, the guy's got a mountain of pride. Maybe you could quietly split off the PI invoices and let me handle them. That might help."

I nodded. "That's damn nice of you, Eddie. I'll do that." I stood there and watched while he caught up with Sylvia and took her hand. Yep, I decided, blood is thicker than business practices.

• • • • •

Busting Blake Daniels' alibi for the night of Lori Kavanaugh's murder was ridiculously simple. The next morning I checked the website for the Radiant Glow tanning salon in Wilsonville to confirm they were open for business the night of October third, and they were. It was a small operation, so I figured my gambit was worth a shot. I called the salon, and when a male voice answered, I said, "I was in your salon back in October, on the third, in the evening. I, uh, misplaced my wallet that night, and I'm afraid I was rude to the person on duty."

"I see," the male attendant said, sounding cautious.

"Well, I found my wallet." I laughed. "It had fallen down between the seats in my car. I want to apologize and offer a small reward to the attendant for putting up with me. Can you look up who was on duty that night? That was the third of October," I repeated.

The pause was long enough that I worried he'd hung up. "Uh, just a moment," he finally said, "I'll check." Some really bad, fingernails-on-the-blackboard pop music came on for what seemed an ice age, and then he returned. "Uh, Gloria was working that night. Sorry, but I'm not allowed to give you her last name."

"That's okay," I said brightly. "There's only one Gloria working there, right?"

"Uh, yeah. She'll be in this afternoon if you want to stop by."

I called Nando next. "Blake Daniels is an amateur," I told him. "He must have cobbled that story up with Gloria Bertolli in a big hurry."

"Good investigative work, Calvin," my friend said when I finished explaining what I'd done. "What about the other date, the day the psychiatrist was killed? Chances are, she also lied about that, too."

"True, but that's not as crucial since her credibility as a witness is blown to hell. What we need now is a way to smoke Daniels out, get him to do something stupid, something that will incriminate him."

"Yes," Nando agreed. "This man is not the bright light in the harbor."

We kicked some ideas around but didn't come up with anything that seemed promising. We agreed to think about it and get back together. At that point, Nando said, "We have a lead on where Isabel and her friends may be living."

"You do?"

"Yes. A source has told us they are now squatting in a house on Holman in inner Northeast. We are going to check it out as soon as Miguel and two others arrive."

"That's great, Nando. Listen, if she's there, call me and sit tight. Don't spook her. I'll be there within an hour."

I leaned back in my swivel chair, looked at Arch, and pumped a fist. "Winona was right, Big Boy. Things are moving."

Chapter Fifty-one

A monster storm may have been brewing out in the Pacific, but that afternoon was a perfect late fall day. Hawks patrolled the azure skies above the valley, which stretched out in what was now the muted, tattered coat it would wear until spring. The birds flocked at my feeders. They seemed particularly active, a sign, perhaps, that they sensed the looming change in the weather. I finally got around to raking what was left of the fallen apples in the side yard and ferried another load of oak to the porch, all the while waiting for Nando's call.

He finally called around three. "People are definitely squatting in this house," he told me, "but no one is home. I have left Miguel to watch. Stay tuned, my friend."

Archie lobbied me for a good hour before I finally put on my jogging shoes and took him for a run with my cell phone in tow. The rest of that day dragged by, with Nando calling twice more just to check in. Finally around midnight, just as I fell asleep, he called again to tell me two men and a woman arrived, and that he got a good enough look at the woman to confirm she was Isabel Rufino. "Excellent," I told him. "Let's move in early tomorrow. They'll be more trusting in daylight. I'll be there at eight sharp."

I slept fitfully that night and was up at six. I just finished a double cap when my cell chirped. "We have a complication," Nando said. "Isabel and one of the men left by car this morning, early. We followed and, ah, detained them."

"Detained them?"

"Don't ask, Calvin. They are not in a position to complain to the police, I assure you."

"Where are you?"

"At my office in Lents. She is quite the little spitfire, this woman. She is telling me she won't talk to anyone about anything."

"Tell her I am not the police, that I'm trying to find the man who killed Luis Delgado. Tell her I think she ran from Dundee because she is afraid of this man. If we found her, he can, too."

After an exchange of barely audible, rapid-fire Spanish, Nando said, "She says she does not know this man."

"Did she see him? Ask her if she saw him."

Another blur of Spanish. "She says she was in a car with Delgado when he met a man. The man was furious that she was there." More Spanish. "Delgado became afraid but took the job the man offered. Delgado told her that if anything happened to him, she should run."

"Can she describe this man? Was he tall, skinny, fat, what?"

More Spanish, followed by Isabel's laughter. "She said he is an ugly gringo. He has big silver rings in his ears. That is all she remembers."

I was speechless for a few moments. "My God," I said more to myself than Nando. "Listen, I think I know who this is. I'm going to text you a photograph to show her. Give me a few minutes."

I punched off and called Jim, who answered in a groggy voice. "Aaron? Yeah, I have some pictures of him with Lori. Why?"

"I need a picture of him right away. The best head shot you've got. Make sure his gauges are showing."

The line went quiet for a moment. "*Aaron?* Christ, almighty. Have you found that witness, Cal?"

"Just text the photo as quickly as you can."

Five minutes later I forwarded a fairly good shot of Abernathy to Nando, who called back moments later. "It is him, Calvin. She has no doubts."

"Okay. Get them some coffee, breakfast, make them feel at

home. I'll be there in an hour. I want to talk her into coming forward. We need this on the record."

I wasn't sure how the day would stack up, so I dropped Archie off at Gertie's. An early riser, she was up, of course. Clouds were forming to the south, and the trees began swaying in a stiffening breeze. It was a Sunday, so I made good time into Portland and found a parking spot across the street from Nando's office.

Nando was right. Isabel Rufino was a spitfire, and she looked even further removed from the image of the innocent young woman I'd found in the house in Dundee, an event that seemed an age ago.

She smiled faintly when she saw me, recognition flickering in her eyes. "I am sorry about the beating," she said through Nando's translation. "We mistook you for someone else. Forgive me."

I shrugged off the apology and explained what I wanted. She said, "I have given you the identity of this man, and now you can catch him. You do not need me."

"I may need you to catch him," I explained. "If you come with me to the police, I will protect you from ICE."

She smiled, and I sensed a wisdom beyond her years. "I will not talk to the police. You cannot protect me."

"Deals can be worked out in exchange for information," I countered, but it was clear she wasn't going to cooperate. Finally, I turned to Nando. "We're done here." As she and her male companion were leaving, I said quietly to Nando, "Have Miguel keep tabs on them. I think I can talk the McMinnville Sheriffs into bringing her in as a material witness in the Delgado case. She might finger Abernathy under the threat of deportation."

Nando and I walked across the street and ordered coffee and croissants at a little shop that was holding its own against a Starbucks two blocks away. Like most of southeast Portland, Lents residents were loyal to their indie businesses. "Aaron Abernathy," I said after we sat down. "It fits. His only cover for the night Lori was killed was Irene Halstead, his stepmother, and when I talked to her, she seemed ambivalent." I grimaced. "She died in his presence shortly after that." Nando raised a thick eyebrow. I nodded. "He could have easily smothered her to keep her quiet." I sighed and opened my hands. "But for what end?"

"What about this Blake Daniels fellow? You suspect he lied about his whereabouts the night of the murder. Maybe he was involved."

"Yeah, maybe he put Abernathy up to it and helped him somehow." I nodded and smiled grimly. "Maybe he promised him a pot shop. That's probably the one thing Abernathy would kill for."

Nando shook his head. "If I were Daniels, I would have given myself a better alibi for murder." Then he chuckled. "But we know this man is not the bright light."

I left Portland feeling elated that I now had a good fix on who really killed Lori Kavanaugh and, probably, Richard Amis, as well. But, at the same time, I felt deeply troubled. First of all, I still had no forensic evidence connecting Abernathy to either crime, just a solid theory. Second, his motives were unclear, and other pieces of the puzzle, including whether Blake Daniels was involved or not, didn't seem to fit together very well. More work was needed, which seemed to be my mantra these days.

The monster storm was beginning to live up to its billing. On the return trip the going was slow on the I-5 as gusts of wind and sheets of rain buffeted my old Beemer. When I reached Dundee, I stopped at my office to empty the leak bucket in the washroom, which was a quarter full of rainwater. I made a mental note to remind Nando to send his roof man as promised. I was hungry, so I dashed across the 99W for a sandwich at the bakery and then stopped off at the B & S Grocery to stock up before I headed into the Red Hills. Once on Eagle Nest, I cruised by my gate only to find a large tree branch across the road, blocking the way to Gertie's house. I called her and said I'd walk over to get Archie and clear the branch with my chain saw on the way back.

I pulled into my garage, and when I got out of the car I heard a noise behind me and then a voice. "Put your hands up where I can see them, Dude, or I'll blow a hole in your back."

My stomach dropped, and a chill shot down my spine. I thought of my promise to Winona to watch my back. I hadn't.

Chapter Fifty-two

I didn't have much experience with guns, but I knew the metallic double click I heard was a round being injected into the chamber of a handgun. "This thirty-two's trained on the middle of your back," Aaron Abernathy said. "If you try anything I'll kill you right here. Your timing's sweet, Claxton. I just got here a while back myself. Thought I might have a long wait. And no dog, either. Too bad, I was going to shoot the mutt this time."

"Confirming what a pitiful coward you are."

He slammed the sole of his shoe into the small of my back, and I stumbled forward. "Shut the fuck up. I'm so tired of hearing you drone on. If you'd just left things alone, you probably wouldn't be in this mess. But you had to keep poking your nose into everything. Now, get your ass in the house. This needs to look like another burglary. Move."

He followed me to the front door, and when we entered the hall a strong gust of wind pinned the door open and flooded the entry with a blast of cold air. I moved down the hall and stopped just past the big radiator and the thermostat that rested above it.

"Keep moving, dude. Into your study where your computer is."

"Okay," I said, but turned partway so that I could see him.

He raised the pistol so that it was pointing at my face. "I said—"

CLUNK. The radiator belched right on cue. The sudden noise startled him, and his eyes pivoted involuntarily from me to the direction of the noise. I lunged for the gun, grabbed it with both hands and managed to twist the barrel away from me. Two shots rang out, and hot water spewed from the radiator and ricocheted off the wall, spraying us both. I slammed his hand down hard against the iron fins. He cried out and another shot boomed in the hallway, the bullet drilling into the oak floor. I slammed his hand again and felt something give—a bone, I hoped. He cried out as the gun slipped from his grasp and lodged itself behind the iron behemoth.

I let go of his hand and threw a straight right that caught him flush on the eye and then a roundhouse left that caught him in the ear. Pain shot through my fist as it connected with one of the gauges embedded in his earlobe. He cried out and spun away from me, and when I stepped forward, he kicked me in the knee, a sharp, withering blow. My knee buckled but I managed to keep my balance. He launched another kick, at my groin this time, but I twisted away and the blow smashed into my hip. I grunted and stepped forward, unsure if my knee would hold me, and threw another punch that caught him on the mouth, splitting his lip.

He staggered back, and we stood there for an instant, panting and taking the measure of each other. Without his dark glasses, his eyes were now visible. I read fear in them, and I'm sure he saw what was in mine—a cold determination to end this. This was a fight to the death.

I lunged at him, but my knee buckled, and he spun out of my grasp and was gone out the front door. Fight or flight? He chose the latter.

I hobbled over to the radiator to retrieve his gun, but it was wedged in behind the leaking structure so tight I couldn't budge it. I made it into the kitchen, grabbed the Glock off the table, and started after him. I hadn't gotten far down the drive when I heard a ragged scream just above the sound of the wind. I turned around, wincing in pain. The sound came from the south fence line, I was sure of it. Of course! He'd gone to the hole in the fence, the one I had yet to repair.

I started off around the house, the pain in my knee multiplying with each step. When I finally got to the fence line, I could see he'd squeezed through the opening in a big hurry. A few shreds of clothing were caught on the razor-sharp wire. I looked more closely. There was something else caught there, lower down. "Ugh," I said involuntarily. Two pieces of bloody skin, and below them, blood still visible on the wet ground, much more than I would have expected from the cut lip I gave him. I pictured him catching his leg on the wire and then trying to rip it free in his haste to escape. The trail of blood led off to the east, on the path that would take him around the base of the old quarry, to the gate and his car somewhere on the other side.

As I stood there, the pain in my knee rose to the point where I was feeling nauseous. My best bet was to get my car and try to head him off, but first I called 911 and told the operator I had fought off an armed intruder who had escaped into McCallister Quarry. She told me help was on the way. I hobbled back to the garage, and that's when what was in the back of my mind came to the fore—how did Abernathy know I was on to him? I pulled my phone back out and called Jim, but he didn't answer.

I called Candice. "Where's Jim?" I asked when she picked up.

"He's with Eddie and Sylvia. They've gone over to Pacific City to watch the storm. They're predicting thirty foot waves."

"Did Jim say anything about the case to you or Eddie?"

"Uh, yeah. Eddie was pumping him for news. Jim said you had him text you a picture of Aaron Abernathy. They both got really excited. Did the witness come through, Cal?"

"Oh, shit," I said. "Do you have the address in Pacific City?" She gave it to me, and I punched off without saying another word.

Abernathy was still on the loose, and the cops were on their way to The Aerie. But that could wait. I needed to get to Pacific City as soon as humanly possible.

Chapter Fifty-three

I tossed a heavy rain slicker into my car, and as I got behind the wheel, my knee shot a lightning bolt of pain through me. I thought about retrieving some ibuprofen from the house, but that would take too long and hurt too much. I tried to call Jim, but he didn't answer, which didn't surprise me. I left him a message warning him of my suspicion of Eddie, but despaired of his ever listening to it. His cell phone habits were probably worse than Nando's.

I punched the address Candice gave me into Google maps, and after I was underway, Siri informed me that I was on the best route and would arrive in Pacific City in one hour and sixteen minutes. Probably more like two hours, I figured, considering the weather. I glanced at my watch. It was 1:05 p.m.

I took the 99W south and eventually connected to Route 22, a straight stretch of flat highway through the valley. The road carried so much water that I kept my speed below sixty to avoid hydroplaning. The storm was intensifying. Gusts of wind rocked the Beemer, and sheets of rain periodically overwhelmed my wipers to leave me hurtling forward like a blinded missile.

As I sped toward the Coast Range, I went back over everything, and the conclusion was the same. Somebody tipped Abernathy, and tipped him fast. If it wasn't Jim, and it wasn't Candice, it *had* to be Eddie. I thought about what I knew. If Abernathy was the executioner, then Eddie, the smartest guy in the room, must have been the mastermind behind him. Eddie knew Abernathy, after all, and had flown below my radar because he had a perfect alibi for Lori's murder and Richard Amis', as well. What was missing was why. Why would Abernathy do Eddie's bidding, and what motivated Eddie in the first place?

I was sure it had to do with money, greed, and wine, and I had some ideas about how the pieces fitted together. But they were just that. Ideas.

The slashing rain began to let off some, but the wind built steadily as I began climbing into the Coast Range. The Doug firs bordering the road swayed, and sheared-off branches skittered across my path like wounded birds. At the summit, I took Route 130, which wound a torturous path down to Highway 101 and on to Pacific City. The small coastal town sat on the banks of the Nestucca River in the southerly contour of a scenic area of sand dunes and rock headlands called Cape Kiwanda.

Siri instructed me to take the bridge across the Nestucca and then, after paralleling the shore line for half a mile, a right onto a lane that meandered up a low bluff affording a commanding view of the Pacific. Eddie and Sylvia's place sat at the top of the lane, a tastefully weathered, cedar-shingled affair with two large bay windows facing west. I parked two houses down, got out and put my slicker on, then slid the Glock into a deep pocket. The butterflies took flight again, but at the same time I felt a little less sure. What if I was wrong about this? How would that look?

There was another possibility, too. What if Abernathy had reached Eddie, and I was walking into a trap? I pushed that chilling thought aside. Just get Jim out of harm's way, I told myself.

Lights burned in the house, but I didn't see any movement through the bay windows. My knee hurt like hell, but I forced myself to walk without a limp up the driveway and onto the front porch. Sylvia answered the door, and her face broke into a smile that crinkled the corners of her eyes. "Cal, what a surprise. Come in, please."

I didn't move. "Uh, are Eddie and Jim here?"

The relaxed smile stayed, but her brow crinkled just a little. "Actually, you just missed them. They've gone down to the headlands to watch the waves."

"I, uh, that's what I had in mind." I smiled. "You know, I had some free time, and it's on my bucket list. Maybe I could hook up with them?"

The smile got brighter. "Sure. They're about halfway out on the rocks. There's a great place right on the edge that Eddie loves to watch from. Just drive north and park next to the brew pub. You'll have to climb the dune then work your way out onto the headlands. It's a tough hike, but if you stay on the north side, you can't miss them." I thanked her, and when I turned to go she laughed and said, "They'll be the only fools out there on a day like this. Be careful, Cal. Those rocks are treacherous even when they're dry."

And even when you have two good knees, I said to myself.

I followed the main road to its terminus and parked back from the Pelican Pub and Brewery, because the surge was lapping up close to the front of the building. The pub was closed and sandbagged, but people stood in the parking lot, watching the storm-tossed Pacific. The dune was a hundred and fifty yards or so up the beach. The storm clouds seemed to be breaking up, although shreds of mist blew in periodically to obscure the view. Offshore, intermittent sunlight reflected off lines of huge breakers that swept in from the horizon and detonated like cannon shells. The crowd oohed and aahed at the spectacle.

The dune was higher and steeper than I thought, but I pushed through the grinding pain. At the top, I was breathing hard, sweating, and spitting sand. The entry to the headlands was fenced off and posted with signs warning of danger. I slipped through the fence cables and took to the north side as instructed by Sylvia. The surf thundered as I worked my way along the slick rocks, and every time the mist parted I ducked down to stay out of sight, a move that invariably rewarded me with a jolt of fresh pain.

Maybe ten minutes in, I saw a blur of yellow up ahead. The mist broke, and I glimpsed a big man in a yellow slicker. A moment later he disappeared behind a large rock fronted by a stunted, wind-twisted cypress tree.

It was Jim. He was still alive.

The gates of my adrenal glands opened as I slid the Glock out of my coat, tucked it in my belt, and moved ahead. Where was Eddie?

I worked my way up to the rock and peered around it. Jim stood with his back to me on an exposed, narrow ledge. A thermos stood next to him, and he held a steaming cup of coffee. An incredible view of the raging Pacific stretched out in front of him. I stepped onto the ledge behind him. "Greetings, Jim," I said. "Where's Eddie?"

Jim spun around, his eyes registering surprise, but before he could speak, I heard a voice behind me. "I'm here, taking a leak."

I turned, and Eddie stepped out from an overhang of the rock, zipping his pants with one hand and training a gun on us both with the other. His face was tense, his eyes narrowed down. He glanced down at the gun in his hand. "Didn't think I'd need this, but there you go." He looked at me. "You're supposed to be dead, Claxton. I see something went off course."

"What the fuck are you talking about, Eddie," Jim said, stepping forward. "And what's that gun for?"

I put a hand out to stop Jim. "Wait, this is no joke. He was planning to kill you out here."

"Still am," Eddie said. "Drop that coffee cup, Jim. I don't want to be wearing it." Then to me he added, "And take that cannon out of your belt very slowly with two fingers and drop it."

The Glock clattered onto the rocks in front of me. Jim shook his head. "Why, Eddie? What is this madness?"

"It is madness," I said. "Killing us will only compound your problems, Eddie." I raised my voice over the crash of a line of breakers. "Abernathy's in custody."

Eddie studied me for a moment, then smiled knowingly. "No, he isn't. If he was, the cops would be here, not you."

Jim said, "Aaron Abernathy?"

"Yes," I said. "Eddie hired him to kill Lori and frame you."

Jim groaned, his eyes got huge, and he took a step forward. Eddie raised his weapon, and I grabbed Jim's arm to stop him. "Why?" Jim repeated.

Eddie shrugged. "I need the money. I can't let Tilikum go under." Then he wagged his pistol at us. "Let's get this over with. Out on the ledge. You two are going to have a tragic accident. Happens all the time out here."

Jim and I looked behind us. The cliff edge was maybe three feet away, and, as if on cue, the impact of a huge wave sent reverberations through the rocks and a geyser of spray into the air. Eddie waved his gun again, impatiently. "Go on. Move."

A sense of unreality washed over me, but there was no way I was going to make this easy for him. I swallowed hard and looked at him dead on. "No, Eddie. You'll have to shoot me, and that'll be impossible for you to explain."

Taking my cue, Jim said, "You'll have to shoot me, too, Eddie."

Frustration bordering on panic clouded his face. He raised the weapon and swung it from me to Jim and back to me. "A bullet kills you, for sure. I'm giving you a chance—"

Jim and I both saw her before she spoke. "Eddie," Sylvia Manning said, "what in the world is going on here?"

Chapter Fifty-four

Eddie Manning turned partway in response to his wife's voice. Jim, who was standing closest to him, saw his chance. He lunged forward and struck the hand holding the gun a powerful, downward blow with a clenched fist. The gun discharged into the rocky shelf we were standing on. Sylvia grunted, clutched her stomach, and slumped to the ground.

We all froze for a moment, trying to comprehend what happened. Eddie cried, "Syl. Oh, my God!" and dropped the gun. I went for it, and Jim and Eddie both knelt next to Sylvia.

"Jesus. She's hit," Jim said. He stood, grabbed Eddie by the hair with one hand and by a wrist with the other, and dragged him across the rocks to the edge of the cliff. Eddie kicked and screamed all the way, but he was helpless in the face of Jim's anguished fury and almost inhuman strength.

"No, Jim!" I screamed. "Don't make things worse. Put him down."

Jim looked back at me, his eyes filled with rage and grief.

"Don't do it. We have to get Sylvia out of here."

Jim's head swiveled back to the raging Pacific. He thrust Eddie even closer to the edge, and his captive's screams went up an octave. A wave smashed into the rocks, driving up a geyser of spray that rained down on them, and for a moment, I feared they'd both gone over the edge. An eternity passed before they reappeared.

Jim spun around and dropped Eddie like a bag of dirt. I scooped up my Glock and raced to Sylvia's side. She was conscious but bleeding from a wound in her stomach. I removed my slicker and sweater, then peeled off my tee shirt and placed it against the wound. "Can you hold this?" I asked Sylvia. She nodded with closed eyes and clutched her hands around the wadded shirt.

"Jim," I said, "pick her up and carry her out of here. I'll take care of Eddie. Go. As fast as you can. I'll call 911."

Jim picked his niece up effortlessly and started back toward the sand dune. I held the Glock on Eddie while I put my slicker back on and then summoned an ambulance to meet us in the pub's parking lot. I didn't reveal that there had been a shooting. I knew that would draw the cops and immediately complicate matters. I wanted answers from Eddie first. I figured I deserved them.

My turn to wag the gun. "Go," I said. "I'll be right behind you." I really didn't need the weapon. Eddie's shoulders were slumped, and his head was down. A beaten man. He turned to me, his eyes streaming tears down a face. "She's the only thing I ever loved. Will she make it?"

"You better hope so. Get going." Once underway, I said, "Why did you have Amis killed?"

He grunted and turned to me, his eyes blank discs, his voice barely audible. "This whole mess was his fault. When we became friends, we understood each other almost immediately. We both take what we want. We were drinking one night after he invested a chunk of money with Tilikum. He drank too much and told me he was going to take Stone Gate Farm. He didn't tell me how, but said I'd be impressed if I knew. That same night he also told me Lori was going to leave Jim, and that she hated him. That planted a seed in my mind about Le Petit Truc. Cornerstone was teetering on the brink of bankruptcy, and when they finally folded it dawned on me what I might have to do."

"So Tilikum's going under?"

He stumbled then caught his balance. "Yes. Fucking Cornerstone was a much bigger account than anyone knew.

When they went belly up, we started hemorrhaging money. We're private, so I was able to keep the lid on."

"What about the auditors?"

"Manipulating auditors to buy time was the least of my worries. I've been trying to bring in new revenue, but I ran out of time." His eyes met mine, pleading for understanding. "I couldn't let Tilikum fail. My reputation, everything I built, would have been destroyed. And Sylvia? God, if she knew I was running a Ponzi scheme what would she think of me?" He shook his head. "Now I know how Bernie Madoff felt. You don't want to run a Ponzi scheme, it's *forced* on you." He looked at me again, his hands open in supplication. "I had no choice. Truc was my only chance to make Tilikum whole again, with nobody the wiser."

I nodded to keep him talking and waved him up the trail. "Why go from framing Jim to killing him out here?"

"I didn't want to kill him," he said over his shoulder. "I just wanted his land. But I underestimated how much my wife loves her uncle. Even if he was convicted, I realized Syl would never agree to take his goddamn vineyard."

"How did you recruit Abernathy?"

"That was easy. I offered him money so he could buy into a marijuana business, what else? I told him to go to Lori and offer to kill Jim. I figured that bitch would jump at the chance, and I was right. They weren't blood, those two, but they were cut from the same cloth." He looked at me and a wisp of a smile spread across his face. "You should have seen the look on Aaron's face when I told him it wasn't Jim he was going to kill. I made his day."

My stomach turned, and I regretted having talked Jim out of tossing Eddie over the edge. "But why kill Amis?" I asked again.

"He figured out my little scheme and told me he'd keep quiet about Lori's murder if I cut him in on Truc. I told him to fuck off, but then I got worried that he might run his mouth, so I sent angry man in to take care of him." Eddie stopped and looked back at me, his expression incredulous. "Can you believe Amis? What a scumbag."

I shook my head and wagged my gun again. "You two were a match made in heaven, for sure."

Eddie and I reached the parking lot just as the ambulance was pulling away, with Jim riding next to Sylvia. I called 911 again and told them there had been a shooting on the headlands.

I'd just punched off when my cell chirped. "Claxton? This is Detective Ballard. Where the hell are you? You called in an armed assault and then you bugger off? And we found Aaron Abernathy out in the quarry behind your place bleeding to death. You better have one goddamn good story for all this."

I laughed. "I do, Hal. I can explain everything now."

Chapter Fifty-five

Early That Next Spring

Before the wisteria vine leafs out in early spring, it pushes out clusters of purple petals that drape and fall, not unlike bunches of grapes. The arbor at the rear of the tasting room at Le Petit Truc was ablaze with the blooming plant and below it, in the dappled sunlight, a small group of friends had gathered in celebration. Word had just arrived that one of Truc's pinot noir wines won a top medal at the prestigious Decanter World Wine Awards held annually in London.

Jim Kavanaugh was as proud as a man could be. "There were more than 16,000 wines in the contest. My 2012 Reserve was one of the thirty Best-in-Show, Platinum medals given out."

After some bravos and clapping, Sylvia Manning hugged her uncle's arm the way she always did and said, "I'm so pleased for you." She was thin and pale but on her way to a full recovery. A fragment of the bullet from Eddie Manning's gun had lodged in her stomach, requiring two major surgeries to repair the damage.

"What did they say about the wine?" I asked.

Jim shrugged and smiled mischievously. "They said it was better than all the grand cru Burgundies in the competition. That's all I heard."

Candice rolled her eyes, then glanced down at the award letter in front of her. "They said more than that, Jim. They said it was elegant, with oak spices, and a complex tannic structure combined with a soft, refreshing finish."

Jim looked at Juan Cruz, his foreman. "Just what we were going for, right?"

Juan laughed. "Yes, our grapes always do exactly as they are told."

Jim grinned, and a look of unabashed joy spread across his face. "Seriously, I want you all to know that I couldn't do this job without Juan and Candice." He raised his glass. "You two are the best."

The banter stayed light and jovial, and when Sylvia excused herself to take a nap, the group thinned out until it was just Jim, Candice, Winona, and I, with Archie snoozing in the corner. "How's she doing?" I asked Jim, referring to his niece.

He stroked his beard with a big hand and frowned. "Okay, considering. She never had a clue about Eddie. She knew he was playing around, but the rest was a total shock." He sighed and managed a smile. "I'm not worried, though. She's a survivor."

Jim, of course, was a survivor, too, and was working hard to put the murder of his beloved wife behind him. The knowledge that Lori thought she was luring Jim into a death trap was a bitter pill, but at the same time, it helped him see her death with considerably less despair.

I said, "The case is buttoned up. Hal Ballard called me the other day to tell me Eddie agreed to plead guilty to two counts of aggravated murder to avoid the death penalty. Aaron Abernathy has been indicted on three murder counts—Lori, Amis, and Luis Delgado—and one count of attempted murder on me. There's no promise of mercy for him."

"What about Lori's mom?" Jim asked. "Did he kill her, too?"

I shrugged. "He hasn't admitted it. We'll probably never know for sure."

Candice said, "Is there more than just Eddie's word that he killed Lori and Amis?"

I chuckled. "Oh, yeah. Abernathy's shoes were like the Rosetta Stone. The crime lab found traces of blood and DNA on them from both victims."

Jim said, "How did they get him for Delgado's murder?"

"Ballistics," I said. "The gun he came after me with was used to kill Delgado. As you know, it got stuck behind my radiator."

We all laughed at that and clinked glasses. They knew the story of how my belching radiator saved my life.

Jim shifted in his seat, and his look grew somber. "I know Eddie's cooperating and all, but this thing's upside down. Abernathy was just a tool. None of this would have happened without Eddie. He's the one who deserves the needle." He shook his head. "The bastard's all contrite now. Keeps asking for Sylvia to visit him, but she's having none of it."

"Good," Winona and I said, almost in unison. I couldn't disagree with Jim, although from a personal standpoint, the thought of Abernathy bearing the full brunt of the law was a welcome one. He tried to poison my dog, after all, and I was still walking with a slight limp.

"What's the latest with Tilikum Capital Management?" Winona asked.

Jim huffed a breath. "It's toast. Eddie was sending out false earnings statements and using invested monies to pay withdrawals, which were accelerating. There isn't nearly enough money left to make anyone whole. A lot of well-to-do people are suddenly pitchfork angry, and lawsuits are sprouting like weeds."

Winona made a face. "Will Sylvia get dragged into that?"

"Not too much. Eddie was such a manipulator that everything having to do with the business is in his name, so she's not a big target." He laughed. "But the reputation of the firm that audited Tilikum is shot to hell, and they're going down as well. Eddie had them completely snowed about what he was up to."

I shook my head but didn't comment. I hated to see people lose their investments, but there was a certain poetic justice in the fall of Tilikum, a company that made rich people richer by preying on college graduates and sick people saddled with debt.

Candice topped up our wineglasses and said, "I was at the Brasserie on Monday, and Bettie James told me Blake Daniels has gone into rehab at Hazelden in Newberg."

"Glad to hear that," I said, looking at Candice. "One of the twelve steps is making amends. You might be hearing from him."

Candice nodded. "I hope I do. I'd like to tell him I'm sorry, too, for spying on him." She looked at Jim and smiled. "I was just trying to help my boss clear his name."

Jim laughed. "That wasn't in your job description, you know."

Candice looked at me. "Why do you think he didn't come forward and then tried to fake an alibi?"

I shrugged. "He didn't want to get involved in a murder case, I guess." What I didn't say was that I was pretty sure Blake Daniels had strong feelings for Lori Kavanaugh and was actually trying to protect her honor. Such are the workings of the human heart.

Jim turned to me and raised his glass. "Thanks again for arranging the deal with Sean McKnight."

"I didn't do much," I said. "Sean scrapped his kiwi project, so I just suggested he talk to you about growing grapes on that swath of land. He's going to Syria, you know, as a volunteer with Doctors Without Borders. He's leaving in a couple of weeks.

"That's hazardous duty," Jim said.

I nodded. "For sure. It's penance, I think."

"What about the woman he had the affair with?" Candice asked.

"Maura Conisson? I had lunch with her last week. She told me she's going to wait for Sean, that they both believe they have a future." I didn't mention that Hal Ballard had given me Amis' thumb drive as a personal favor, and that I had pressed it into Maura's hand as she was leaving.

It was getting late, and looking southwest from the terrace the vineyards of Le Petit Truc seemed to stretch to the horizon and fade into the soft, reddish glow of the setting sun. The leaves on the vines had unfurled, and soon clusters of flowers would appear, marking another round of an ancient cycle that called out the best in some and the worst in others.

We said our goodbyes and watched as Jim and Candice walked back toward the house. Halfway there, Jim took her hand.

"Well, well," I said, "looks like Jim finally sees what's right in front of him."

It was spring, and salmon and steelhead were leaving the Pacific to end another ancient cycle in the upper reaches of Oregon's rivers. Winona and I figured to tie into a couple of those beautiful fish in the coming weeks. Life was good again in the Dundee Hills.

To see more Poisoned Pen Press titles:

Visit our website: poisonedpenpress.com/
Request a digital catalog: info@poisonedpenpress.com